The White Cockade

A NOVEL OF THE AMERICAN REVOLUTION

MARK JAMES MILLER

Black Rose Writing | Texas

ISBN: 978-1-68433-779-8
PUBLISHED BY BLACK ROSE WRITING
www.blackrosewriting.com

Printed in the United States of America
Suggested Retail Price (SRP) $20.95

The White Cockade is printed in Chaparral Pro

*As a planet-friendly publisher, Black Rose Writing does its best to eliminate unnecessary waste to reduce paper usage and energy costs, while never compromising the reading experience. As a result, the final word count vs. page count may not meet common expectations.

Praise for

The White Cockade

"The opening salvos of the American Revolution come to life via this historical novel that follows the impact of the war on one Boston family caught in the maelstrom... Readers witness the brutal battles of Lexington and Concord and later Bunker Hill. Miller's narrative alternates between page-turning action and sections filled with personal and family drama...The author's meticulous attention to atmospheric cultural details and descriptions of period weaponry add up to a narrative win."

–Kirkus Reviews

"What I loved most about this book is the cohesion brought about by intextuality. In exploring his themes of love, kinship, marriage and betrayal, Miller used a story within a story and dialogue to advance the storyline."

–Online Book Club

"The characters are very well-developed, and the settings are vivid and realistic as we follow Josiah for a year of his life. I felt a wrenching disappointment when it ended, and I sincerely hope it is the first in a series. I want to live the next step in Josiah's story."

–Sublime Book Review

"Riveting! Mark James Miller has done it again! This tale desperately needed to be told, and Mr. Miller nailed it. From the very first page, the very first word, I was captivated... A unique cast of characters makes it difficult to pick a favorite, as they all feel real... The build-up and the action made it impossible to put this page-turner down. I thought about the events long after I closed the book. It was a wonderful reading experience and time well spent."

–Tracy Ball, author of Civil Warriors

"Set against the backdrop of the Revolutionary War, The White Cockade is timeless in its treatment of human emotion and human foibles. While we all know the outcome of the war that is described in vivid detail, Miller's wonderful and engaging cast of characters keeps us turning the page to find out what they will do and how their lives will be affected by the war...A great read!"

–Sara Fraser, author of Just River

To My Wife Carol Burmeister Miller

The White Cockade

*"My true love he is listed
He wears a white cockade."*
–Traditional song

CHAPTER 1
THE HAPPY HARTFORDS

Boston, March 1775

"You can't sit on the fence forever," Walter Hartford was saying to his older brother Josiah. "Sooner or later everyone is going to have to take a side. You are going to be with us Patriots or with the British and the Tories. There won't be any other way."

"It will never come to that," Josiah declared. He walked over to the big window that overlooked the harbor below and looked down at the flickering lights of the wharves and the ships at anchor, for night had fallen and the moon was already out. Hugo is down there somewhere, he thought, Hugo Chamberlain, the best friend I ever had. "Wars always begin with the noblest of motives and by the time they end those noble motives are long forgotten. This war you envision against the British will be no different."

Josiah, Walter, and their sister Jessica were gathered near the fireplace, talking about the ever-growing conflict between the British who ruled the American colonies and the Patriots who opposed them. It was the main topic of conversation in Boston these days, and Josiah found it wearisome. If there was a war he had no intention of taking part in it.

His brother Walter felt differently. He was a member of the Sons of Liberty, the most radical faction of the Patriot movement, and he spent his days spying on the British for Paul Revere or else engaging in brawls and rock fights with the Tories, as those Americans who were loyal to England were called. He was so dedicated that Revere had chosen him to be one of

"The Thirty," nimble, quick-footed young men who watched everything the British did and then dutifully reported it to the husky silversmith.

"Did you tar and feather any Tories today?" Jessica asked Walter in a tone that was half-teasing and half-serious. Like all the Hartfords, Jessica was not one to be quiet for long. She knew the Sons of Liberty saved their special wrath for the Tories, breaking their windows and painting big red "T's" on their doors to mark them as traitors to the cause of American liberty. More outspoken Tories were tarred and feathered, a hideous process that both Josiah and Jessica found revolting. Walter admitted it was a horrible thing to do, but it was only what a traitor had coming to him.

Jessica was nineteen, the second eldest of the Hartford sisters, and she had the same dark hair and oval face that her mother, Martha, had passed on to her three daughters. Her countenance was always cheerful and happy, radiating the inner joy that the Hartford family was known for. Even Walter, the most serious of the Hartford children, could never remain angry for long, and when his episodes of anger passed he was as happy as the rest of his brothers and sisters.

There were six of them: Josiah was the oldest. He had been followed by Mary- Louise a year later, then Jessica, Walter, Anne, and Patrick had all come in quick succession. They were not a large family by New England standards, where ten and even twelve children were not uncommon, but they were an exceedingly happy one.

"Nothing like that," Walter maintained. "All I did today was watch the harbor, and report to Mr. Revere the names of the ships that came in."

"Did the *Achilles* come in?" Josiah asked, trying to conceal his eagerness. The *Achilles* was the ship Hugo Chamberlain was on.

Walter's expression plainly said yes, making Josiah's heart beat faster. Four years I've been waiting for this, he thought.

"When will we get to see Hugo?" Jessica asked.

"I'm not sure I want to see him at all," said Walter. "He's a British officer now."

"British officer or not, he is still your brother," came another voice, that of their mother, Martha, who had come out of the kitchen where she had been overseeing the preparation of the evening meal. She too had been anxiously awaiting news of Hugo Chamberlain's return. "He's one of us and he's come home. That is all that matters," she said.

"In other words," Jessica said to Walter, "leave your politics somewhere else when we see him."

Now Alice, the maid, came out of the kitchen where she had been helping Maureen, the cook, getting dinner ready. "Mrs. Hartford," she said in her distinctive Irish accent, "Maureen needs to ask you something about the party we're planning for Saturday night." Even though she was speaking to Martha she kept her eyes on Josiah all the while. Jessica caught the look and smiled to herself.

"Tell her I'll be right there, Alice," said Martha.

"Yes ma'am." Alice curtsied, looked at Josiah again, and then made her way back to the kitchen.

"So it's true that Hugo's ship is in the harbor?" Martha asked.

"So it seems," said Josiah, looking to Walter for confirmation.

"Yes, I saw it come in," Walter admitted. "Bristling with cannons, sailors and more soldiers. Just what we don't need in Boston right now."

"Let us pray we can put all that aside when we see Hugo," said Martha, and then went back to the kitchen.

"You'd best remember that," Josiah cautioned. "Forget your politics when Hugo comes over, unless you want to upset Mother and Father."

"That will to be hard to do," Walter said sharply. "Considering what old Gage and the bloody-backs have been doing, holding my tongue is asking a lot."

Boston had been placed under martial law after King George learned of the events of December 17, 1773. That was the night a group of Sons of Liberty, Walter Hartford among them, had disguised themselves as Mohawk Indians and gone aboard three British ships anchored off Long Wharf: the *Dartmouth,* the *Eleanor,* and the *Beaver,* and dumped more than 400 chests of East India Company tea into the cold water of Boston harbor. This had enraged His Majesty to the point where he said, "The Americans will either be loyal subjects to our rule or they will no longer be part of the British Empire! Force is needed now, force is what the Americans have been asking for, and by God force is what they are going to get!"

Walter found this terribly amusing. Josiah did not. Antagonizing the British to the point where war could begin did not seem wise. He did his best to see both sides of an issue and while he agreed that the Patriots had many legitimate grievances against the British none of them were worth shedding blood over. In the past the English had always rescinded their more oppressive laws, and even though he had no use for kings and thought monarchy a form of government whose time had passed, as kings went George III was not as bad as most.

•　　•　　•

At Harvard he had belonged to a debating society called the Pandorians, named after the Greek myth of Pandora's box. The Pandorians weren't afraid to open any box and see what was inside, and they debated anything and everything from the existence of God to the struggle of good versus evil. British rule in the American colonies and the Divine Right of kings were favorite topics, and while the Pandorians rarely reached any definitive conclusions their debates were always lively and interesting.

Josiah loved the academic life at Harvard. Having recently graduated he had wanted to stay and pursue his master's degree. Only the news of his father's ill health had brought him home in January. It was expected he would, much against his will, take over the business Benjamin Hartford had founded more than thirty years ago, Hartford Ships.

The shipbuilding business had made the family wealthy. Their home, Hartford Manor, sat on Beacon Hill looking down at the harbor and was one of the largest and finest in all of New England. Josiah, who loved his father and admired his accomplishments, did not want to run the shipyard and did not think he would be any good at it. He was a man of ideas, not a man of business. He loved the teachings of the great philosophers—Plato, Aristotle, Voltaire, Hume, Rousseau, Kant, Locke—and he enjoyed thinking of how to apply their ideas to the world and to life. He wanted to talk about the thoughts of the Enlightenment, not what kind of wood was needed to build the hull of a sloop. Is this my destiny, he wondered, to set my books aside and build ships?

Josiah was twenty-one. He had a handsome triangular-shaped face, with high cheekbones sitting above a narrow chin, a trait shared by his father and Walter. He wore his chestnut colored hair long and tied in the back in a fashionable queue. In his white knee breeches and silver buckled shoes he was every bit the young Boston gentleman, at six feet one taller than average, with a lean, wiry build that gave him a cat- like quickness that he employed when practicing his favorite sport of fencing, and Josiah Hartford was one of the best fencers in New England.

Martha reappeared from the kitchen. "Will one of you go upstairs and tell your father and Patrick to come to dinner?" she asked. "And I need someone to go find Anne as well."

"I'll go tell Father," said Josiah.

"I'll go with you," said Walter.

"I'll go find Anne," Jessica volunteered.

Followed by Walter, Josiah started up the broad staircase. Hartford Manor had four stories and years ago Benjamin had converted half of the fourth floor into an observatory for studying the planets and the stars. He had the finest opticians in New England build him the biggest and best telescope in the colonies so he could look up at the night sky. Night after night he studied the heavens and carefully recorded the way the stars changed their positions relative to the earth. He took note of Saturn's rings and how the moon didn't revolve but had a side that was always dark. He tracked the passages of comets and saw meteors rocketing across the sky. He read Ptolemy, Copernicus, Tycho Brahe, and Galileo.

When Josiah and Walter entered Benjamin was sitting in a large chair, reading a treatise by Johannes Kepler. Patrick, the youngest of the Hartford children, sat nearby. He had been intently studying a book—Josiah assumed it to be about mathematics, for mathematics were Patrick's passion.

"Father," he said as Josiah and Walter entered, "what is on the other side of infinity?"

"Perhaps that's where God is," Benjamin answered.

"How do you know there is a God?" asked Josiah. "Has anybody ever seen Him?"

"Older brothers One and Two," said Patrick joyfully, closing his book. "I'm so happy to see you again."

Patrick Hartford had little realization of time. He might have seen someone only an hour ago and yet he would greet them as if they had been apart for weeks. By the same token, a person he hadn't laid eyes on for months might be received with a casual, "Oh hello, how are you?" as he continued reading whatever book he had in front of him. He hugged his two brothers now, as if they had just returned from a long trip.

"What are you reading, Patrick?" asked Josiah, when Patrick released him from the tight squeeze he had just delivered, for even though he was only sixteen Patrick was nearly as tall as Josiah and much heavier, and when he hugged someone he did it with a great deal of enthusiasm, sometimes more than the person could bear.

"A book," Patrick said enthusiastically, holding up *La Géométrie* by Rene Descartes. "It's about algebra. He has the most interesting things to say about it. But I'm disappointed he doesn't go into calculus."

"You'll have to get through geometry first," said Benjamin, unfolding his long form from his easy chair and smiling.

"How are you feeling, Father?" Josiah asked.

"I've never felt better," said Benjamin. "How could a man not feel good, when his three boys are with him?"

Benjamin Hartford was in his late fifties and his hair was a vivid white. He was clean-shaven, tall and erect, and had, until recently, been an exceptionally vigorous and active man, capable of running the largest shipyard in New England, take a prominent role in civic affairs, and study the stars at night. People often compared him to an oak tree, for his steadiness and endurance. But last December, while bounding up the stairs on his way to his observatory a sudden pain in his chest caused him to gasp for air and lose his balance. Grasping the ornate wooden bannister, he hung for several minutes before he was able to sit down and there he remained until his daughter Anne found him, his head covered in perspiration and panting for breath.

"Father!" Anne exclaimed. "Father, for God's sake what's the matter?"

"Nothing, nothing, I'm all right," Benjamin managed, but it was obvious to Anne that her father was far from all right, just as it was to her mother, who arrived a moment later and was just as nonplussed as her daughter when she saw the state her husband was in.

"Go get Walter and Elias—quickly," she told Anne.

Martha Hartford was a sensible woman, down to earth and not inclined to lose her head no matter what the situation. She wasted no time in hand wringing, and when Walter and Elias (the family's butler and Benjamin's personal servant) arrived she ordered them to carefully pick up the protesting Benjamin and carry him to his bed, in spite of his repeated declarations that he would recover any moment. She then directed Elias to go and fetch Dr. Warren as quickly as he could.

Dr. Joseph Warren, in addition to being one of the leaders of Boston's Patriot movement, was also the city's best known and most trusted physician, and his diagnosis was as simple as it was direct: Benjamin's heart was weak. He must rest, avoid over- exerting himself, and not get too excited. He must, in other words, take life much easier, advice that Benjamin at first chose not to heed.

After spending a week in bed Benjamin rose like a phoenix, determined to resume his former vigorous life, but another collapse on the stairs and another visit from Dr. Warren convinced him this wasn't possible. Much against his will, he acceded to the doctor's orders.

"I imagine your mother sent you up here to tell me dinner is ready," said Benjamin. When Josiah and Walter both answered in the affirmative Benjamin rose from his chair and putting one arm around Walter's shoulders and the other around Josiah's, and send, "Let's all go downstairs and not forget for a moment how blessed we all are."

"Blessed by whom, Father?" Josiah asked.

"Call it Fortune, call it Heaven or call it God Almighty, we are extremely fortunate people," Benjamin said.

They trooped downstairs, Walter, Benjamin and Josiah walking three abreast on the broad staircase and Patrick closely following, a smile on his big broad face and looking about in wonder at the paintings on the walls and the chandeliers that hung from the ceiling, as if he was seeing them for the first time.

As they approached the dining room Josiah noticed Alice, standing excitedly near the entranceway of the servants' stairs and gesturing to him.

"Go on, everyone, I'll join you in a moment," he said.

"Is something the matter, Oldest Brother?" asked Patrick.

"No, not at all, Alice wants to tell me something."

Walter gave him a strange look before going into the dining room. Did he suspect what was going on between him and Alice?

"What is it?" he asked quietly.

"This came for you while you were upstairs, Josiah," she said breathlessly, handing him a letter.

Josiah's heart skipped a beat, for on the outside was written, "Josiah Hartford, Esquire," with a circle contained within a square drawn below it, and when he saw that, Josiah knew who this note was from.

He could barely contain himself from letting out a cry of joy, and forgetting about Alice he turned and went toward the dining room as fast as he could. Alice reached for him, hesitantly, as he turned his back to her, then dropped her arms in disappointment before returning to the kitchen.

Josiah sat between Jessica and Patrick, and as soon as he was seated Benjamin said grace. "Our Father in heaven," he said, "thank You for what we are about to receive. Thank You for the many blessings you have shown us, Your children of the family Hartford, and help us to show our thanks to you for what you have done."

Everyone said "Amen," (even Josiah, who said it just to be polite) and as the food began to be passed around Josiah opened the envelope and then rattled a glass with a spoon to get everyone's attention. "I just received this note," he announced. "My dear friend," he read, "my long voyage across the Atlantic is over and I have returned to Boston at last. Please give me a day to recover and then come to Castle Island in the evening day after tomorrow for our long-awaited reunion. My love to you and all the wonderful Hartfords, my second family. Your friend, Lieutenant Hugo Chamberlain, King's Own Regiment."

There were cheers and applause around the table. Even Walter clapped, albeit less than enthusiastically. "Oh, how wonderful," said Benjamin. "Our family will be complete again. I feel as if someone has been missing these four years."

"I still can't conceive of Hugo as an officer," said Jessica. "He was so against all that before he went away."

"It's his father, Lord Roger," said Josiah. "He made him join the army."

"He seems awfully proud of it," said Walter, examining the note Hugo had sent. "Notice how he underlines 'King's Own Regiment,' as if that makes him something special."

"I hope when he comes to see us you'll drop all your political talk," said Benjamin.

"Yes, Walter," Martha reiterated. "Let's have none of that when he's here."

•   •   •

Alice, Maureen, and Elias came in and out of the dining room, collecting dishes as they were emptied and bringing new ones in on the dumbwaiters. Maureen, small and thin with light blond hair, made a marked contrast to Elias, who was large and whose dark skin reflected his Indian and African forebears. Alice kept stealing glances at Josiah, who carefully avoided looking back at her.

"She's doing it again," Jessica said to Josiah in a low voice.

"Who?"

"Alice. Making sheep's eyes at you."

"I don't think so, Jessi."

"Along with Mercy Willingham, that makes two of them," said Jessica. "Who knows how many others there might be. You're becoming a regular ladies' man."

"Go on," said Josiah.

"Deny it all you want," said Jessica. "I can tell when a girl's in love."

How do I tell Alice to stop that? Josiah wondered.

He felt a twinge of nervousness. Alice's longing glances toward him were becoming more and more obvious. He had started something with her and he didn't know how it was going to end.

"Enjoying your meal, Patrick?" he asked.

"Oh yes," said Patrick. "We always have such good food." For one so large Patrick was the slowest eater anyone in the family had ever seen. He seemed to have just gotten started by the time everyone else was finished. He ate dreamily, just as he did everything else, as if only part of him was present and the rest was off in some other world, a world only Patrick knew about. "I think Alexander is enjoying it too."

"Does Alexander eat?" Josiah asked in surprise.

"Sometimes," Patrick smiled.

Alexander was Patrick's invisible friend. Ingrid, the German governess who had taken care of the Hartford children when they were small, said Alexander was a fylgia, a spirit that would guide Patrick through his life. Having one was a great blessing, she said, reserved for only a few special people, and Patrick was going to be very special.

Ingrid had taught them German, and the older children—Josiah, Mary Louise, Jessica and Walter had become fluent in the language, Josiah speaking it best of all.

Of all his brothers and sisters, Josiah felt a special fondness for Patrick. His otherworldliness, his innocence, the fact that he would never be able to function in the world the way other people did made Josiah, and the rest of the family, feel protective of him. What would become of him, Josiah wondered, if anything happened to the rest of us?

When dinner was over and Alice and Maureen were clearing away the last of the dishes Jessica made an announcement. "When everyone has finished I'd like you all to come into the drawing room with me," she said. "I just learned a new song and I'd like to play it for you on the piano and sing it too."

"Oh, what joy," said Patrick. "I love it when you sing us a new song, Jessica. Can you sing some of the old songs too?"

"Maybe, but this is the one I want to sing the most, since I only finished practicing it today."

"Sister Anne," Patrick asked, "why can't you sing the way Jessica sister does?"

"Because not many people can sing as well as Jessica," Anne replied.

"Let's all go into the parlor," Benjamin suggested, "and hear this new song Jessica has learned."

The family went into the drawing room. The Hartford fortune rested on shipbuilding and Hartford Manor reflected that, with the walls covered with paintings of ships and scenes of the sea. There was also a large portrait of Martha shortly after her marriage to Benjamin, and another of Mary-Louise and her husband, Daniel van der Molen, who lived in New Jersey.

As soon as they were all in the drawing room and settled in on the chairs and sofas, Jessica went to the piano that sat nearby. "This song is called 'The White Cockade,'" she said.

"One day when I was walking," she sang,
Out on yon fields of moss
I had no thoughts of enlisting till
Some soldiers did me cross
They kindly did invite me
To a flowing ball and down
They advanced, they advanced
Me some money
A shilling from the crown."

Jessica sang beautifully, slowly and with complete control over her voice, Josiah thought.

"My true love he is listed
And wears a white cockade
He is a handsome young man
Likewise a roving blade
He is a handsome young man
He's gone to serve the king
Oh my very, oh my very
Heart is aching
All for the love of him..."

"What a beautiful, sad song," said Martha when Jessica finished, amidst the general applause and smiles.

"What does the "white cockade" mean?" Anne wanted to know.

"It's a kind of cloth flower," said Josiah. "A white cockade, worn on a hat, is a symbol of revolt and resistance in some parts of Europe."

"Older brother knows everything," said Patrick.

"Not by a long shot," said Josiah, although it was nice that Patrick thought so. Later that evening Josiah went up to his room on the fourth floor of Hartford Manor, lit his lamp and got into his bed, then opened a volume of Rousseau. But he couldn't concentrate and so he got up and looked out the window. His room faced west and was down a long corridor from his father's observatory, and from here he could see the Charles River shimmering in the moonlight, the lights of Charlestown on the peninsula known as the Charlestown Neck and the darkness of Breed's Hill and Bunker Hill beyond, where he and Hugo had loved to play when they were boys. With Benjamin's health in the state it was in his father no longer spent as much time at night in the observatory so he had the top floor of Hartford Manor to himself. He loved the quiet it offered, a chance to think and reflect. He couldn't stop thinking of Hugo, and his return, and most of all he thought of the last times he had seen his friend, as he was getting ready to leave for England.

There was a soft rapping on his door—three quick knocks, followed by two more—and he unlatched it, knowing already that it was Alice, knowing already what would happen once she came inside, and he was barely able to close the door before she had thrust herself into his arms, holding him with a tight desperation, as if she now had hold of something she never wanted to let go of.

"Josiah," she whispered, "oh at last I have my arms around you. I've been wanting you all day."

"No one saw you, did they?" he asked.

"No," she said, "no, I was careful. I'm always careful. No one saw me."

Alice had fiery red hair which was covered with a white bonnet during her working hours, so it was all the more striking when she took off her scarf and revealed it. Her eyes were a vivid green, like the green hills around County Cork that she had left behind when she came to Boston.

When Josiah came home from Harvard after learning of his father's heart attack, he had seen the new maid his mother had hired and immediately felt an enormous attraction for her, a feeling she returned with equal fervor. Her fiery red hair and flashing green eyes, as well as her strange accent, caught him as surely as a net and before he knew it she was in his bed night after night. She would leave her room on the second floor where the servants slept and tip-toe up the side stairs to offer him pleasures and delights neither of them had ever known before. He had plunged into this headlong, surprising himself, for Josiah saw himself as a careful man who never did anything without thinking about it first. But now his feelings for Alice were fading and he realized what he had felt was merely an infatuation. But Alice's feelings for him were growing stronger every day, and he knew he had started something that could end badly for them both.

"Love me, Josiah, I want you to love me," she said, pulling him toward the bed.

This has to stop, he said to himself. It has to. It's not right for me to be using her this way, because that's all I'm doing. I don't love her, badly as she wants me to, and I certainly can't marry her. And what would Mother and Father say if they found out about this? Some of his friends at Harvard had visited prostitutes and invited him to go along with them, but he never did, and when others bragged about their sexual conquests he always took it with a grain of salt and never seriously questioned the general feeling that sex was something that didn't happen until you were married.

Besides, everyone expected him to marry Mercy Willingham, the daughter of the Hartford's best friends, with whom he had practically grown up and who was as much a part of the family as Hugo Chamberlain. It seemed a good match, the intertwining of two wealthy Massachusetts families. But like the expectation that he would take over the shipyard, Josiah felt he was being pushed into something he wasn't sure he wanted. Mercy was beautiful, intelligent, pleasant to be with, but he was as unsure about spending the rest of his life with her as he was about taking over the shipyard.

He was suddenly aware of Alice lying beneath him, feeling her strong maid's hands on his back and pulling hard.

"I just feel so funny inside, sometimes," she said.

"I've never been in love before. I'm terribly afraid of losing you, Josiah."

"You better go," he said. "You better get back to your room. Maureen might notice you're gone."

"Oh, she sleeps soundly," Alice protested, but in a few moments she got out of bed and put her nightgown and robe back on. "I love you," she said, going toward the door.

"Good night, good night," he said, in the most gentle tone he could manage, the one he thought lovers used so he wouldn't have to say what she wanted to hear. But it didn't work.

"Won't you say you love me, Josiah?" she said.

He got up, kissed her on the forehead. "Out you go," he said, "and have pleasant dreams."

"I'll dream of you," she said, going out the door. "I always dream of you, Josiah."

I have to put a stop to this, he thought, as he heard Alice's footfalls fading as she went down the long corridor toward the side stairs. I've got to end this. But I don't know how.

CHAPTER 2
THE REUNION

Two days later Josiah stood at Long Wharf, showing the sentries the special pass that Hugo had sent to Hartford Manor by courier earlier in the day. *This is where we stood four years ago*, he thought, *the day Hugo left for London*.

It was not a day he could forget. He and Hugo Chamberlain had become friends almost the moment they met.

The Chamberlains had just arrived in Boston. Hugo's father, Lord Roger Chamberlain, purchased a house on Beacon Hill only a few blocks away from Hartford Manor. Soon Hugo, to escape the unhappiness there—for Lord Roger was an abusive, violent man—spent as much time with the Hartfords as he could. By the time he had departed for England he was virtually one of them. Martha often spoke of him as her "fourth son and seventh child," and Hugo, whose mother had died years ago, beamed with joy whenever he heard this.

The Chamberlains had come to Boston from London. Lord Roger had displeased King George III in a way no one would speak of and had been banished at His Majesty's personal command. Lord Roger Chamberlain, known as "Roger the Terrible" for his fierce temper and his skill with a sword, had once been a hair's breadth of becoming Prime Minister under King George II. But he had been exiled to the American colonies by the late monarch's grandson for abusing his wife, a cousin of the king's, to the point where she had taken her own life, unable to bear her husband's beatings any longer.

Few people knew of this. The King wanted it kept secret, and Lord Roger did not want what he did in his drunken rages to get about. Hugo had never been told the truth about what happened to his mother. He had been told that she had suddenly taken ill and died. Soon after, the family had to leave for America.

It was in the hope that he might be able to win back the King's favor that Lord Roger insisted on Hugo returning to London and make his career in the army. Lord Roger had purchased a Lieutenant's commission for Hugo in the King's Own Regiment, the same one he had served in, and ordered him to go to London and report for duty.

This was done very much against Hugo's will. He did not want to leave Boston, he did not want to be in the army, and he especially did not want to leave Josiah and the Hartfords. But Lord Roger was not a man to be denied. The Chamberlains were one of the "Two Hundred," the 200 wealthy and aristocratic families that had ruled England for centuries. He was going to regain his family's place at court, and his son was going to play his part, like it or not.

For nine years Hugo and Josiah had been inseparable. Night after night they sat up late in Josiah's room, talking about metaphysics and philosophy, wondering why things were the way they were and what could be done about them. They read the Enlightenment philosophers like John Locke and Baruch Spinoza, and loved talking about their ideas and how to apply them to the troubled world they lived in.

"I barely remember England," Hugo said the day he and Josiah said goodbye. "Boston is home to me now. You are my family. You, all the Hartfords. I'll be back," he promised. "We'll see each other again, I swear." There were tears in his eyes. Josiah wept too.

"You're the best friend I've ever had," he said. "I can't bear to think of life without you. Here," he went on, reaching into his pocket. "I know you said you didn't want a farewell gift. But when I saw this I knew I had to get it for you." He showed Hugo the medallion. "See? It's the lemniscate, the infinity symbol."

"*Absolutus infinitus*." Hugo read the inscription out loud. "No gift could be better, Josiah. I'll think of you every time I see it."

"All those times we talked about where we fit within infinity, where does infinity begin and where does it end—this will make you remember them," Josiah said.

"I'll never forget," Hugo vowed.

They had embraced and said goodbye and then Hugo had gone up the gangplank at Long Wharf and boarded the *Cerberus*. He had waved goodbye from the railing, and had stood there all the while as the ship weighed anchor, raised its sails, then eased its way out of the dock and headed through the harbor toward the open sea. Josiah had remained on the wharf until the ship was out of sight. He didn't cry anymore but had simply gone home and once alone in his room had taken out his sword and gone through some fencing motions, as if Hugo was there and they were practicing together as they always had, all the while vowing silently to never forget his friend.

•   •   •

But now, as he prepared to see Hugo for this first time in four years, Josiah's heart was racing. Some words he had spoken the last time he and Hugo had fenced were echoing in his mind, words that he wished he could take back.

Hugo's father, Lord Roger, was a hard man and a harsh taskmaster. Tall and wasp-waisted, he had cruel black eyes and the face and manner of a man used to being obeyed without question. He was one of the best fencers in Europe and had insisted on his son learning "the art of the fence." Seeing Josiah's eyes light up as he watched Hugo being instructed Lord Roger began teaching Josiah too, and he had immediately seen Josiah's natural talent. As he taught the two boys he was as severe with his son as he was lavish with his praise for Josiah. This was done partly in the hope that excessively praising Josiah would spur Hugo into trying harder, but also because he saw Josiah's innate ability with a sword: Josiah learned effortlessly, whereas Hugo learned with more difficulty, not possessing Josiah's inborn gifts.

"Come on Hugo, be a man! Fight like you mean it!" Lord Roger would say if he felt Hugo's efforts were not up to par. Josiah had seen how badly these words hurt Hugo. He yearned for his father's approval, and his efforts to get it always came to naught.

For all of that Hugo became an excellent swordsman, able to defeat nearly anyone. But he was never able to equal Josiah, and a few days before Hugo left for London Lord Roger had insisted on the two of them having one final match. It was this match that haunted Josiah.

Under Lord Roger's stern eye they fought, and it seemed for once Hugo might win. He had been practicing night and day for this moment and Josiah, so used to winning, was not at his best. But when Hugo tied him in points and the momentum clearly shifted his way, Josiah, not wanting to lose, called out "Come on Hugo, be a man! Fight like you mean it!"

The hurtful words had their effect. Hugo hesitated just enough for Josiah score the winning point. But Josiah was ashamed of what he had done, and wished he could have found the words to say he was sorry. But he hadn't been able to, and all he could do was hope Hugo didn't hold it against him.

•　　•　　•

Neither of the British sailors who rowed Josiah to Castle Island at dusk said anything; one worked the oars and the other the rudder, and both stared stoically ahead, intimidated by the well-dressed young Boston gentleman who had come to Long Wharf in what was obviously a very expensive carriage, drawn by four spirited white horses and driven by a finely dressed, dark skinned man who jumped down from the driver's seat to open the door for his charge. The sailors, wearing their striped shirts and round black hats that identified them as British tars, were as quiet as the sentry on duty at Long Wharf, who said nothing when Josiah showed him the pass Hugo had sent. The pass, marked with an official stamp of the British Army, seemed to carry its own weight, for the sentries had moved expeditiously after seeing it, as had the sailors, as if the pass frightened them, because it was signed by someone high in the military hierarchy.

Josiah showed his pass again after he got out of the boat, threw a glance at the lights of nearby Dorchester Heights, and found himself in the midst of one of the strongholds of the British Empire in the American colonies. The stone fortress dominated the skyline, with the Union Jack flying high above the turrets. Soldiers and sailors were everywhere. The island was surrounded by British warships, the ubiquitous flag fluttering from the masts amidst all the ropes and rigging of the sails. British warships were no rarity in the waters around Boston, but there were more of them lately, their cannons prominently displayed, as if the British sought to remind the rebellious people of the colossal firepower they could call on if they thought it necessary.

"Where is the Officer's Club?" he asked the sentry.

The soldier pointed toward the main entrance to the fortress and Josiah made his way up the pathway, his heart pounding in anticipation. More sentries stood at the oversized wooden door amidst the castle's stone walls. He showed his pass one more time and was admitted into a cold, grim looking set of rooms and corridors, then through another door into an enormous room filled with the scarlet and white uniforms of British officers, and as he looked anxiously about for Hugo he saw a huge Union Jack hanging from one wall and an equally large portrait of King George III on the wall opposite. Beneath the portrait of the King a string quartet played chamber music, a big fire burned in a huge fireplace, and Josiah now caught his first glimpse of Hugo Chamberlain.

•　　•　　•

Four years had added at least three inches to his friend's stature, so one of the first things Josiah noticed that whereas when Hugo had departed Boston Josiah was two inches the taller of the two, now they were exactly the same height. Hugo, resplendent in his scarlet Lieutenant's uniform, stood talking with a group of young officers like himself. He was gesturing excitedly, waving his hands about, a habit of his Josiah remembered well.

The atmosphere in the room was festive. A great deal of drinking was going on, accompanied by loud, aggressive laughter. The British officers had the arrogant self- assurance of men who are ready for anything.

"Hugo! Hugo!" Josiah called.

"Josiah! Josiah Hartford!" Hugo's face lit up and he fairly sprang out of the circle of officers, several of whom turned to look at what he was such a rush to see.

Hugo seized Josiah in a powerful embrace, nearly lifting him from the floor. They shook hands and thumped each other on the back, both laughing and beaming with delight.

"Praise God and King George," said Hugo. "I've waited for this day for so long, I never thought it would come. Just look at you, Josiah Hartford! Just look at you!"

"Just look at you, Hugo," said Josiah. "Look at how big you've gotten."

"How's your fencing?" Hugo asked. "Still at it? Remember our last match? I almost had you. But you won in the end, you dog."

"Four years," said Josiah. "I wondered if you would ever come back to Boston."

"Well, here I am," said Hugo, stepping back a bit and holding both hands in the air. "What do you think?"

Hugo did look the same as Josiah remembered, still possessing the same black hair and thin lips that marked the Chamberlain family, although the cruel set to the mouth seemed more pronounced than before. Hugo's skin was still fair, a sharp contrast to his dark hair, and his eyes—black like those of his father—seemed harder than Josiah remembered, as if the youthful innocence Hugo had when he left was long gone. Much more than Josiah remembered, Hugo resembled his father, "Roger the Terrible."

"You look splendid, Hugo. You're still the circle in the square, the Vitruvian Man," he said, referring to one of their favorite subjects, the argument about whether a circle could be formed from a series of squares. They had spent many nights discussing this, as well as other subjects like what would happen if an irresistible force encountered an immoveable object. But the circle in the square was Hugo's favorite, and he had talked about it so often that it had become his nickname.

"I mean, what do you think of my uniform?"

"I can hardly believe it," said Josiah. "An officer. You're an officer."

"One of the King's Own," said Hugo. "In the finest army in the world. I'm on General Gage's staff, his adjutant, in fact." When Josiah didn't respond to this Hugo went on. "Being on the commanding officer's staff is considered a great honor. I forget you aren't a military man."

"Nor will I ever be," declared Josiah. "And I'm surprised at you, choosing the army. You used to scoff at that."

"I was young, and so, so foolish," Hugo replied. "I didn't know any better. Josiah, there is so much I want to tell you, so many things I've learned since I went away. But first tell me, how is your family? Are they all well?"

"Yes, and so excited that you're back they can hardly sleep.

"I can't wait to see them," Hugo began, but his remarks were cut short when one of the officers he had been speaking with when Josiah arrived now left that small circle and came walking over to stand beside him. He looked Josiah in the eye, then turned to Hugo.

"This is your friend?" he said coldly.

"Indeed it is Ban. Josiah, allow me to introduce you to Lieutenant Banastre Tarleton. Ban, say hello to my dearest friend in the colonies, Josiah Thomas Hartford."

Josiah smiled and put out his hand. "Nice to meet you, Lieutenant," he said.

Tarleton hesitated. Then with notable reluctance in his manner he took Josiah's hand in a strong grip, gave it two brief jerks and let go. He did not smile but kept on looking Josiah challengingly in the eye.

"Josiah here is one of the smartest men you'll ever meet," said Hugo.

"An intelligent American? Are you sure that isn't a contradiction in terms?"

"He's also one of the best men with a sword you'll find on either side of the Atlantic," Hugo went on. "He can beat you, Ban."

"Really?" Tarleton said scornfully. "I thought the colonials' favorite weapons were rocks and snowballs thrown from an alley or behind a wall when a man's back is turned." He looked Josiah over, taking in his height and measuring his reach, the disdainful expression unchanged. "Perhaps we can have a match sometime. I'll find out if you're any good."

"I'm out of practice," said Josiah. "I don't think I'd be able to give you much of a challenge."

"So I would have thought," Tarleton said.

"Don't let him fool you, Ban," said Hugo. "He always says that before he beats the pants off some unsuspecting soul."

Tarleton, like Hugo, was dressed in the scarlet and white uniform of the British officer. Josiah's first impression was that he had never seen a man quite so handsome or as cold and haughty in manner. If it wasn't for the powerful shoulders and the tight bulge of muscle that showed beneath the scarlet coat Tarleton could have been thought femininely beautiful, like a debutante in full blush of womanhood. But there was nothing effeminate about him. He moved lithely, with an athletic grace, much like Josiah and Hugo did. His large, icy eyes were disconcerting. There was a ruthlessness in them that Josiah found disturbing. His face, with its sharp upper lip that resembled a beak, was like that of a great bird of prey—a falcon, Josiah thought, and from this day forward, whenever he encountered Banastre Tarleton, the image of a falcon came to his mind. Tarleton's hands increased that impression, for they contained long fingers, like talons made to rend and tear whatever they caught hold of.

"I met Ban in London," Hugo explained. "We got our orders to come to Boston at the same time, and we were on the same ship coming over."

"How do you like Boston, Lieutenant?" asked Josiah.

"A wretched place. It should be given back to the Indians," Tarleton replied. "Hopefully we'll have this business settled soon and we can go to somewhere civilized."

"I'm rather hoping for some action," said Hugo.

"Action?" said Tarleton. "Here? Perhaps we'll get the chance to teach these colonials a lesson. Nice to meet you, Mr.—Um—Mr. Hartford."

Tarleton turned abruptly away and Hugo took Josiah by the arm. "Don't mind him, Josiah," he said, indicating a table near the string quartet. "You must understand that we hear nothing but terrible things in London about Boston. Mobs spitting on British soldiers, good-for-nothing scallies challenging British rule, radicals dressed like Indians throwing fine English tea into the harbor. Colonial bumpkins drilling in the countryside as if preparing to take on the British army. It makes people angry, and Ban, I'm sorry to say, takes it all to heart."

"Not everyone feels that way," said Josiah.

"Of course not. I told them in London they should not judge an entire city by the actions of a few rabble rousers. I lived there for nine years, I told them, and I know the real people of Boston—in fact, all of America—are good people, loyal, obedient to His Majesty. But you know how people are. Unreasonable, always ready to assume the worst about something they know little about. It's a shame. But why speak of that? Have some wine. Let's have some good talk like we did in the old days. How are your mother and father? I've missed them ever so much."

"Well enough," said Josiah. "Father's heart is weak, and he tires easily—"

"Oh bother that! The curse of age. Death will come to us all one day."

"Dr. Warren says he must be very careful. He can't over-exert himself or it could be fatal."

"Ha!" Hugo scoffed. "Your father is one of those people who will live on and on. The Happy Hartfords! I always envied you for having such a happy family."

"You were a part of it."

"I know. I hope I still am."

"Of course! Nothing could change that. Mother always referred to you—"

"As her fourth son and her seventh child," Hugo interrupted. "That made me so happy."

"We're like brothers," Josiah declared.

"Maybe even more than that," Hugo agreed. "When can I see everybody?"

"Mother is planning a dinner party in your honor on Saturday night. Can you come?"

"I'd hate to be the man who tries to stop me!" said Hugo. "I'll bring Tarleton along."

"Tarleton?" Josiah said doubtfully.

"Yes. I'll see that he behaves himself. He isn't so bad once you get to know him. Best man on a horse you ever saw. Good with a sword too. And what a fellow for the ladies! Killed a man in a duel over a woman."

"Killed? You're not serious."

"Yes, in London. Seems a fellow there took exception to Tarleton bedding his wife. An old story: Rich, middle-aged man with a much-younger wife he couldn't control. Caught Tarleton and his wife together, then was silly enough to challenge Ban to a duel. I don't believe Ban really intended to kill the old fool. But he thrust higher and harder than he meant to and got him right through the heart. Quite the scandal for a while. That's one of the reasons he was sent here, exile, but it will also give him a chance to redeem himself. Now tell me about the family. You said in one of your letters that Mary-Louise married a Dutchman?"

"Daniel Van Der Molen is his name. Has a farm in New Jersey."

"How is dear Patrick? Can he still add and multiply the way he used to?"

"Yes, he's even better at it now than he was."

"How about Anne? How old is she now?"

"Anne just turned seventeen, quite the little beauty, and something of a flirt too," said Josiah.

"She was so small when I left," said Hugo. "Goodness, it seems so long ago. Tell me something, Josiah. You haven't gotten caught up in any of this nonsense, have you? This foolishness about 'rights' and 'freedom'? You aren't part of that, are you?"

"The colonists have some legitimate grievances," said Josiah.

"Of course they do, of course they do," Hugo agreed patronizingly. "We know that. Parliament has passed some stupid laws. But it has been wise enough and generous enough to retract them. And the colonists' concerns, some of them, are valid and should be heard. And the King will hear them and I know he will act accordingly.

"He is the wisest of men! But this foolish defiance, this Continental Congress meeting," he said scornfully, "this drilling in the countryside, it has to stop, Josiah. A King put on his throne by Almighty God does not take kindly to backwater colonials challenging his power. And this insanity of acting as if they want to fight the British army—that is just plain madness! We have the mightiest military machine ever created on this earth. Not even Imperial Rome at the height of its power had the kind of might we have. We have defeated the best armies and the best navies in the world. If these hotheads like Adams and Hancock don't stop this, they are going to find themselves ground up like so much horse fodder, and a lot of innocent colonials along with them."

This kind of talk made Josiah uneasy. "You've changed," he said. "You were never so militant before."

"I've grown up," said Hugo. "I've learned a great deal. And I've stood in the King's presence. It was the most incredible feeling, Josiah."

"You speak of him as if he were God."

"I suppose I do."

"He isn't God. No man is."

"He is the man selected by God to rule over the greatest empire in history. You can't deny the significance of that, Josiah."

"Empires fall. None of them last forever."

"Not this one," Hugo declared confidently. "This is the one empire that will never fall."

"Rome fell. Carthage fell. Alexander's empire fell. Empires don't last forever."

"This one will," Hugo maintained. "But let's get back to you, Josiah."

"My feelings about war haven't changed," said Josiah. "They accomplish nothing except get a lot of people killed for no purpose."

"You don't know how glad I am to hear you say that," said Hugo. "I'm so relieved. Old friends can't let politics come between them." He raised his wine glass. "To old friends."

"Some talk of Alexander
And some of Hercules
Of Hector and Lysander
And such great names as these
But of all the world's great heroes
There's none that can compare
With the toe-row-row-row-row-row
Of the British grenadiers."

Led by Tarleton, a group of officers were lustily singing "The British Grenadiers" on the other side of the room. Tarleton was like a man conducting an orchestra, leading the others with broad, sweeping motions and singing in an excellent tenor voice.

"Your friend is a good singer," Josiah observed. "You seem very certain of things, Hugo. I ask myself too many questions."

"You give me too much credit, Josiah. I ask myself questions too. But some things I'm sure of. The British Empire was created to bring civilization to the world. When I met the King, Josiah—I wish I could tell you what that was like. What a moment! That is a feeling worth dying for."

"Would you give up your life so readily?" said Josiah. "For a man whom some people say is not all that intelligent, not enlightened, but an autocrat?"

"You're wrong!" Hugo exclaimed. "You've been listening to that rebel foolishness, reading those rebel newspapers. You shouldn't delve into that, it's dangerous. The people who spread that are going to pay dearly for it."

"People should have the right to examine all sides of an issue," said Josiah. "We are living in troubled times. Remember the talks we used to have? People need knowledge so they can decide which way to go."

"There is a place where rights end and treason begins," said Hugo sternly. "Don't let any of my fellow officers hear you talk like that. But I think we are agreed at least that we do not want to see any blood shed here, either British or American."

"I do not want to see any killing," said Josiah.

"I'm so glad to hear that," Hugo said.

"It's getting late," Josiah said. "I'd best be getting on."

"Wait," said Hugo. "Tarleton is making a toast."

Tarleton had leaped upon a table, the falcon's face florid with drink and excitement. Kicking the cups and saucers out of his way, he stood with his glass raised high. "Gentlemen, a toast," he proclaimed. "I give you His Majesty, King George III!"

"To the King!" came the resounding reply from all throats except Josiah's, who wasn't sure how he should be reacting to all this.

"To the Empire!" said Tarleton.

"To the Empire!"

"To Great Britain, the greatest country on earth!"

"To Great Britain!"

Hugo zealously joined in all this, but Josiah, unsure of what he should do, remained silent. Hugo looked at him disapprovingly.

Tarleton, still the center of attention and obviously enjoying it, threw his glass shatteringly to the floor. All the others followed suit, and when the sound of the breaking glass died away Tarleton, in his high voice, sang:

> *"When Britain first, at heaven's command*
> *Arose from out the azure main*
> *Arose, arose from out the azure main*
> *This was the charter, the charter of the land*
> *And guardian angels sang this strain*
> *Rule Britannia, Britannia rule the waves!"*

By now every man in the room was standing and singing as loudly as he could. Every man except Josiah, who stayed where he was.

"Sing!" said Hugo. "Stand up and sing! People are going to get the wrong impression of you."

Josiah remained seated, however, and saw the angry glances being thrown his way. He had heard *Rule Britannia* sung many times before but never like this. It was not so much a song as a battle cry, sung by men eager for war.

Mercifully the song came to an end. Hugo gestured for Josiah to stand. "We'd best get you out of here," he said. "You've offended everyone in the room and made me look bad too."

•   •   •

At the dock the same rowboat that had ferried Josiah from Long Wharf was waiting, with the same two tired-looking sailors standing by. Hugo looked at them reproachfully.

"Stand at attention, sailors," he barked, and both men stiffened. "Take my friend back over to the wharf and be quick about it, or I'll see you get a good hiding." To Josiah's quizzical glance Hugo said, "You have to treat them that way or they won't respect you. Say, I almost forgot." He unbuttoned the top of his tunic, reached inside, and brought out the medallion.

"You still have it!" Josiah said.

"Of course. You gave it to me, and it brought me luck, made me what I am today."

"That wasn't why I gave it to you," Josiah reminded.

"What difference does it make?" said Hugo. "I think of you every time I see it."

They shook hands, and Hugo then embraced Josiah again and held him tightly for a moment. "How are you getting home?" he asked.

"The carriage is waiting."

"Is Elias driving?"

"Of course."

"I can't wait to see him either. Goodbye for now, Josiah, and I will see you on Saturday."

The carriage was waiting at Long Wharf. Elias opened the door for Josiah. "How is young master Hugo?" Elias asked.

"He seems well enough," said Josiah, although when he got into the carriage he realized he did not feel the joy he had expected to feel after this first meeting with Hugo. Hugo had changed, he was certainly not the young man he had tearfully said goodbye to four years ago, when he had sailed, at his father's orders, for London.

CHAPTER 3
DINNER AT HARTFORD MANOR

At last there came the knock on the door everyone had been waiting for. Elias opened it and there stood the two young British officers, splendorous in dress uniforms that were so bright they seemed to glow. The carriage that had brought them to the Hartford home rolled away across the cobblestones and into the darkness.

"Elias!" cried Hugo with delight. "How good to see you again!"

"Master Hugo!" said Elias, bowing. "How wonderful you look."

"You can call me Lieutenant Hugo now, Elias. This is Lieutenant Tarleton."

"I'm honored, sir."

"A Negro," Tarleton observed. "We don't see many of those in London." He handed his coat and tri-cornered hat to Elias, as did Hugo. "Are there many Negroes in Boston?"

"Elias and I are old friends, aren't we, Elias?" Hugo went on. "Elias taught me how to shoot a bow and arrow."

"I thought only the Indian savages used a bow and arrow."

"His mother was an Indian."

"Really? A half-Negro and a half-Indian." Tarleton looked as if he couldn't imagine such a thing.

"Elias also plays one mean fiddle," Hugo said. "So you remember, Master Hugo?" said Elias.

"Who could forget? You're the best fiddle player in Boston. I learned to dance with you playing the fiddle. Wait until you hear him play 'The Lillibulero,' Ban."

They were interrupted by the appearance of Benjamin, followed closely by Josiah and Walter.

"Mr. Hartford!" Hugo cried, coming forward to wring Benjamin's hand. "You are looking so well."

"As well as can be expected for an old fellow with a weak heart."

"Oh, I can't stand that sort of talk. You're like an oak, Mr. Hartford, planted in the firm soil that will last forever, like God and the British Empire. I've looked forward to seeing you for so long. May I present Lieutenant Tarleton? Ban, this is Mr. Benjamin Hartford, one of Boston's true gentlemen, and the builder of the finest ships in all the American colonies."

"Welcome, sir," said Benjamin. "Welcome to my home."

"I didn't know there were any great gentlemen in Boston, or in any of the colonies," said Tarleton, extending his hand. "I'm glad to find out there are. I'm truly honored to meet you, Mr. Hartford," said Tarleton, politely bowing his head. Yet Josiah thought he detected just a touch of mockery in Tarleton's voice, and once again he was struck by the man's aloofness and arrogant manner, as well as by his physical beauty and falcon's face.

"Good to see you again, Mr. Tarleton," said Josiah, after greeting Hugo. He shook hands with Tarleton, who smiled courteously enough but shook hands in a squeezing fashion, as if trying to test Josiah's strength, making good use of his long, talon-like fingers, and looked him in the eye in a way that made him realize the man was taking his measure. "This is my younger brother Walter."

"I never thought I would shake hands with a British officer," said Walter. "They are not very popular in Boston these days."

"You aren't one of these radicals, are you?" asked Tarleton. "One of these Sons of Liberty we hear so much about?"

"Walter, please," said Benjamin. "Let's not have politics ruin the evening. We are gathered here to celebrate Hugo's return. Politics are tearing the city apart."

Josiah noticed Tarleton staring at him. For a moment their eyes locked. Tarleton's eyes were cold, just as his manner was cold, but there was more to it than that. They were cruel, the eyes of a killer, and he remembered Hugo saying Tarleton had killed a man in London.

"I understand that your slave, the one who let us in, is half-Negro, half savage Indian," Tarleton said to Benjamin. "Isn't that an unusual combination? Or is that kind of misogyny common here in America?"

"Elias is no slave, Mr. Tarleton. We have no slaves. He is a free man, in my employ."

"A free Negro," mused Tarleton. "I've heard of them. But he must have been a slave at some point. Did you buy him and set him free?"

"Elias' father was a runaway slave who took refuge with the Huron. He eventually was adopted into the tribe and became one of them, marrying an Indian woman. During the war the militia attacked their village, killing nearly everyone, including Elias' parents. Elias was about ten years old. A pastor serving with the militia brought Elias back to Boston with him, saw to it that he went to school, and placed him with us."

"Imagine mating with a savage Indian woman," said Tarleton. "I suppose you served in the Seven Year's War, Mr. Hartford."

"I hoped then, just as I hope now, that one day mankind will reach a place in its development wherein war will no longer be necessary."

"What an idea!" said Tarleton. "How disappointing that would be for us, eh Chamberlain? What would you and I do if there were no more wars?"

"Something useful, I would hope," said Walter. "Something that would benefit people, rather than harming them."

"Then how do you propose to solve problems between nations?" Tarleton parried. "Diplomacy may have its place, but without the threat of war behind it, you might as well just sing hymns. War is what builds empires, creates great nations, and separates the hero from the coward."

"War is responsible for most of the misery of mankind," said Josiah.

"But from that misery rises greatness, like the Phoenix rising from the ashes," Hugo said. "When I stood in the King's presence before we left London I felt an incredible surge of power and strength inside me, as if some great hand had taken hold of me and was going to guide me from now on. Then the King said to us, 'Yours is a high duty, my brave boys, and a noble one.' That was the moment of a lifetime, wasn't it, Ban?"

"Oh, indubitably," said Tarleton, not appearing to be so enthusiastic over this as "At that moment I knew what my life's mission would be," Hugo went on. "To live—and if necessary to die—fighting for the Empire."

"You want to die for old King George?" Walter asked, incredulously.

"Can you think of anything better to die for?"

"Yes—freedom, liberty, a republic of free and equal citizens. Not some fat old German with a crown on his head."

"Take care, Walter," said Hugo. "You speak of our King."

"He is not my king."

"He was put on his throne by God Almighty."

"I don't believe in God," Walter declared, and once again he was silenced by a stern look from Benjamin.

By now they had all moved into the drawing room, where Anne, Charles Waite and Patrick were gathered about the piano, where Jessica sat, playing a soft tune. Hugo's eyes fell upon Martha, who had just emerged from the kitchen. "Mrs. Hartford! Oh my gosh, now I am going to cry," said Hugo, the words leaving his mouth before he had a chance to consider them.

"Hugo, my seventh child," said Martha, holding him tightly. "How wonderful you look."

"*I* look wonderful! You are the one who deserves that title," said Hugo joyfully.

"Welcome home, Hugo," said Martha.

"This does feel like home to me," Hugo admitted. "It always has."

"And it always will be," said Martha. "You've never been out of my thoughts these past four years."

"Nothing could make me happier than hearing you say that," said Hugo. Then he saw Patrick standing nearby and smiling shyly.

"Patrick, is that really you?"

"Hello Brother Hugo," said Patrick. "I've missed you. Where have you been?" Patrick put out an oversized hand, his tone implying that not four years but only a few days had passed since he and Hugo last saw each other.

"I can't believe it's you!" said Hugo. "You've gotten as big as a house!"

"Yes, that's true," Patrick agreed. "I am a big person. I am strong too."

"You're as tall as I am and two times as wide!"

Tarleton whispered to Hugo, "Is this the one you told me about?"

"Yes, he is the strange one," Hugo whispered back, *sotto voce*.

Tarleton, to Josiah's surprise, stepped up to Patrick and said gently, "You must be Patrick. I've heard so much about you," and shook hands in a courteous manner.

"What have you heard about me?" Patrick asked shyly.

"That you are a good chess player, that you can do mathematical calculations faster than anyone else in the world, and that if someone tells you their birthday you can tell them exactly what day of the week it was."

Patrick smiled delightedly. "My oldest brother taught me to play chess," he said, looking at Josiah. "He tried to teach me to fence, too, but I'm not so good. I'm too slow."

"You are a special young man," said Tarleton. "I hope I can get to know you better."

"Yes, that would be nice," said Patrick. "I would like that."

"I made Ban a number of promises when I asked him to come with me tonight," said Hugo, gesturing excitedly with both hands. "I promised him that the food would be unforgettable, the women beautiful, the company stimulating, that he could hear Jessica play the piano and sing, that he could get a tour of Hartford Manor, and that he could see Josiah fence." When he saw the look in Josiah's face he said quickly, "And don't give me any of that 'I'm out of practice' routine,' I know you too well. Do you still have your foils?"

"Yes, in my room," said Josiah reluctantly, for he had no interest in a fencing match with Hugo tonight.

"Then we must fence later," Hugo declared. "I intend to beat you this time." To Tarleton he said, "Just imagine, Ban. We learned how to fence together. My father was our instructor."

"Being instructed by Lord Roger Chamberlain himself," said Tarleton, genuinely impressed.

"My father used to say that Josiah Hartford could be one of the premier fencers of the world if he kept at it," said Hugo.

"He said the same of you," Josiah pointed out.

"Yes, but not in the same way. I was never quite as good as you. You were the one in a thousand, he said, who could be better than anyone else."

"I'm looking forward to see you two go at it," Tarleton said, eyeing Josiah. Then he said, "Which is the one with the angel's voice?"

"That would be this one, Jessica, who has also grown a great deal since I saw her last," said Hugo. "She has a voice of gold."

"Mr. Tarleton is quite the singer himself," said Josiah. "I heard him the other night, at Castle Island."

"I'm sure I'll enjoy hearing you," Tarleton said to Jessica.

"Do you play, Mr. Tarleton?" Jessica asked, indicating the piano.

"Poorly. My mother arranged lessons for me before I left home, but I'm afraid my talents don't lie in that direction."

"In what direction do they lie, then?" asked Jessica.

"Soldiering, fencing, and singing," said Tarleton. "My passions, however, are card-playing and horseback riding."

"Those seem strange combinations," Jessica observed.

"Not at all. We soldiers love to sing as we go into battle."

"Do you intend to sing as you go into battle here in Massachusetts?" asked Walter sharply, again drawing a rebuking look from Benjamin.

"Let us all hope it never comes to that," Hugo interjected. "Mr. Hartford, may we have that tour of Hartford Manor now?"

Benjamin, Josiah, Walter, Patrick, Hugo, Tarleton, all began making their way up the broad, ornate staircase. They were trailed by Charles Waite and Anne, who were talking animatedly to one another, Josiah noticed.

This Tarleton was certainly a strange fellow, Josiah thought. One moment he acts as if he wants to kill someone and the next he is as genteel as any gentleman could be. But it was Hugo that bothered Josiah the most. He kept waiting for that feeling of joy he had expected when reuniting with Hugo to come to him, and it hadn't, nor had he felt that old feeling of friendship that they'd had when growing up. He kept waiting for it, but it just wasn't there.

They were on the second floor now and Benjamin was showing Hugo and Tarleton some of the paintings that graced the walls.

"You've traveled a great deal, Mr. Hartford," said Tarleton.

"It's my ships that have done the traveling," said Benjamin. "I went to sea as a cabin boy at thirteen. I did see a great deal of the world but soon I realized I would be better at building ships than sailing them."

Tarleton's attention was drawn to a series of shelves containing the commemorative silver bowls that had been bestowed upon Hartford Ships when a new vessel was launched.

"These are lovely," he said. "We do this in Liverpool too."

"What is that, Ban?" asked Hugo.

"When a new ship is completed and ready to be launched, the owner comes to inspect it. If he's pleased, he presents the builder with a porcelain or silver bowl, like these, with a drawing of the ship etched inside and a few words of appreciation for the quality of the work. These are exquisite, Mr. Hartford, just exquisite."

"Thank you, Lieutenant," Benjamin replied.

"Do you still go to visit the Willinghams at their country home every spring, Patrick?" asked Hugo.

"Oh yes," said Patrick. "I'll be going in a few days. Josiah and I will ride there together. It is twenty-two miles from here to Concord," he declared. "Alexander will go with me."

"So, you still see Alexander. How is he?"

"He is well. He's here, right now."

"Who is Alexander?" asked Tarleton. "And where is he?"

"Oh, you can't see him. I've never seen him either. I will someday, when I go to heaven. That's what Ingrid always said. But he is here."

"Is he a ghost?" Tarleton asked.

"No, he isn't a ghost," said Hugo. "He's a spirit that goes everywhere with him."

"An angel, then."

"That's closer," said Hugo. To Josiah he said, "So Ingrid went home? Back to Germany?"

"Yes, she said she missed her Fatherland."

"Ban, they had the most amazing governess. She taught us German and told us these fairytales that would make your hair stand on end. Little girls menaced by wolves, a girl in a tower, a boy and girl lost in a haunted forest..."

"Enough," said Tarleton. "Anymore and you'll give me nightmares."

"Change of subject," said Hugo. "Ban, tell Patrick your birthday."

"I was born on August 21, 1754," said Tarleton.

"That was a Wednesday," said Patrick unhesitatingly.

"Amazing!" said Tarleton.

"Ask him something else," said Hugo. "What is 125 times 51?"

"Six thousand three hundred and seventy-five," Patrick said instantly.

"Patrick, what is the square root of 87?"

"9.33."

"What is the reciprocal of 10?"

"One-tenth."

"What is 1,166 times 2,276?"

"2,644,712," said Patrick.

Tarleton stared in amazement, but Josiah was becoming disturbed. He had seen people, astounded at Patrick's abilities, treat him as if he were some kind of freak, and he feared this could be where Hugo and Tarleton would take this. "Patrick isn't a circus act," he said. "Why don't we go see the third floor?" From below, in the drawing room, came the sound of Jessica playing the piano and singing "The White Cockade."

"My true love he is handsome
And comely for to see
And by a sad misfortune
A soldier now is he..."

"What a lovely voice," Tarleton observed.

"You should sing with her, Ban," said Hugo. "You'll sound good together."

"Perhaps we can."

•   •   •

When they arrived on the third floor Josiah noticed that Charles and Anne were no longer with them. Where had they gotten off to? He went back downstairs, and encountering Alice, who was busily lighting the lamps, asked, "Have you seen Anne?"

"Yes, they went toward the library when everyone else went upstairs."

"They?"

"Yes, Mr. Waite was with her. Josiah, can I see you later?" she pleaded.

"Not tonight," he said.

There was no one in the library. But Josiah thought he heard something in the dark corridor that ran alongside it, and lighting a hand lamp and thrusting it ahead of him, heard a feminine voice calling out in surprise, and he saw Charles and Anne in the darkness. A moment ago they had been locked in a passionate embrace but now they broke off (but did not let go of each other), their faces showing surprise and guilty fear as they looked at Josiah.

"Josiah, this isn't what you think," Charles stammered.

"Why, you two!" Josiah burst out. "What is this?"

"Josiah, please," said Anne. "Don't tell anyone."

"You deserve a good thrashing," Josiah said, stepping toward Charles with a clenched fist.

Charles held out a hand defensively.

"Josiah, I swear this is nothing dishonorable. We love each other."

"Is this true?" Josiah asked Anne.

"I love him. He loves me," said Anne.

"How long has this been going on? Have you spoken to my father?"

"Not yet, but I will when the time is right, I promise."

"Josiah, please don't tell Mother or Father," Anne pleaded.

"You need to get downstairs and help Mother in the kitchen," Josiah said. "And you need to get back upstairs before anyone notices anything. Leave separately. Anne, go first."

Anne kissed first Josiah, then Charles, then scampered happily away, out of the corridor and then toward the stairs. "I ought to punch you right in the nose," Josiah said to Charles.

"You can if it would make you feel better. But I swear I love her, Josiah."

As they reached the stairs Josiah paused, then said, "I'll be honored to have you as a brother-in-law, Charles."

"Then you're as big a fool as I am!" said Charles, grabbing him playfully by the shoulders and shaking him.

The tour had reached the fourth floor by the time Josiah and Charles rejoined the others. Benjamin was showing everyone his observatory and his telescope, as well as his books on astronomy.

"What are you reading these days, Mr. Hartford?" asked Hugo.

"I just began this," said Benjamin, holding up Sir Isaac Newton's *Mathematical Principles of Natural Philosophy*.

"Some of my fondest memories are right here, and down the hallway in Josiah's room," Hugo went on. "How many nights did we sit in here, talking about books and philosophy and history, and wondering what is out there?"

he gestured toward the sky. "We looked at Venus and Mars and the rings of Saturn. Walter, you remember?'

"Do I?" Walter said enthusiastically. "We sat up till the early morning hours, talking and reading and looking at the stars. Hugo, you liked Venus the best."

"Now I prefer Mars," said Hugo, winking at Tarleton. "The God of War suits a soldier much better than a planet named after Aphrodite."

"There are times when Aphrodite has to come before Mars, though," said Tarleton, "if you know what I mean."

There was general laughter all around. Hugo, looking delighted, said, "These days I prefer Machiavelli for my serious reading. Are you familiar with him, Walter?"

"Of course. 'Divide et imperium.' Divide and conquer. It won't work here."

"We'll see. You say your foils are in your room?" Hugo said to Josiah. "Perhaps now would be a good time to get them."

"I'll do that," said Walter. "I want to see this." When he returned Hugo eagerly took one, tested it, asked for another, and, liking it better, saluted Josiah with it and then stepped away from everyone, slashed it through the air in a practiced, professional manner. Josiah could tell by the way Hugo manipulated the foil that he would have a battle on his hands when they fenced. Tarleton took one and did the same, and Josiah, with his practiced eye, could tell that Tarleton was no amateur with a sword either.

Now Alice appeared, breathless after running up four flights of stairs. "Mr. Hartford," she panted, "Mrs. Hartford sent me to tell you that it is time for everyone to come downstairs to dinner. And, Dr. Warren is here."

"Oh, he made it after all," said Benjamin in a tone of pleasant surprise and heedless of the dismayed glances Hugo and Tarleton exchanged. "He's so busy, he wasn't sure if he could be here."

Walter was delighted. He gave Patrick a friendly push on the shoulder and said, "Dr. Warren is here, Patrick. Now we'll have some great conversation."

"We could hang for this, Chamberlain," Tarleton said to Hugo as they began the journey downstairs.

"Hang?"

"Having dinner with Dr. Joseph Warren. We might as well be dining with Samuel Adams himself. Wait till old Gage hears about this. He'll have us both locked up."

"Not likely," said Hugo. "Mrs. Gage and Dr. Warren are good friends."

"Good friends?"

"Very good friends, so the rumors go."

"Ah," said Tarleton. "Perhaps Boston isn't so boring after all."

CHAPTER 4

THE FENCING MATCH

In spite of his relative youth—he was thirty-four—Dr. Joseph Warren was Boston's leading physician and one of its best-known citizens. His charm, wit, and lively conversation made him one of the most sought-after dinner guests in the city. He was of average height, broad shouldered and considered extremely handsome. Like nearly all the men in Boston he kept his light colored hair tied back in a queue, and while he could be serious his blue eyes had a merry twinkle to them that was rarely absent. His wife's death two years ago had made him a widower with four small children, and while he had not even thought of remarrying yet he was rumored to be linked romantically with several Boston ladies, married as well as unmarried.

But Joseph Warren was more than a doctor and a young man about town. He was one of the most prominent leaders of the Patriot movement: President of the Massachusetts Provincial Congress and Chairman of the Committee of Safety, the bodies that had determined to raise an army with which to oppose British rule and which were responsible for recruiting men and gathering supplies to be used in the forthcoming conflict. He was considered by the British as belonging with Samuel Adams and John Hancock at the very top tier of the rebel leadership. Fewer men were more hated by the British officers of Boston, but whereas Adams and Hancock had left the city for the safety of the countryside, Dr. Warren remained in Boston, openly continuing both his medical practice and his Patriot activities, to the consternation of the British and the Tories, who could not understand why General Gage had not had him locked him up long ago.

"You're just in time, Joseph," Martha was saying as everyone began arriving in the dining room. "Dinner is only now ready to put on the table."

"I would never miss an opportunity to have dinner at the Hartfords," said Dr. Warren, still in the process of removing his overcoat and his hat and giving them to Elias. As he shook hands with everyone he saw Hugo and Tarleton, and his eyes widened in surprise. "Am I to be arrested before dinner, or can I dine first?" he asked facetiously. Then, recognizing Hugo, he said, "Is this who I think it is? A prodigal son returned?"

"Yes, Doctor Warren, Hugo Chamberlain. *Lieutenant* Hugo Chamberlain, of the King's Own," said Hugo. "And this is Lieutenant Banastre Tarleton, also newly arrived from London."

Josiah wondered how Tarleton would react to being introduced to Dr. Warren. Tarleton looked disconcerted, an expression Josiah would not have expected from such a self-confident man, and he shook hands with the doctor after giving him a brief nod but saying nothing.

"Let's all sit down, shall we?" said Benjamin, and the entire company went into the dining room to sit at the huge table, the women and younger children at the far end, the one closest to the kitchen, and the men at the other. Josiah sat across the table from Hugo and Tarleton, with Dr. Warren on his left and Walter on his right.

"Joseph, will you say grace for us?" asked Benjamin.

Dr. Warren smiled, and then putting his hands together in front of him, began, "Our Father in heaven, we thank you for what we are about to receive. We thank you for allowing us to gather here in friendship. We ask you to bless this gathering and to bless our troubled land, and we ask that peace continue to prevail over war. This we ask in Jesus' name, amen."

There was a chorus of "Amens," from everyone at the table, even from Josiah and Walter, whose agnosticism was just as pronounced as his brothers'. Then Martha arose and signaled Maureen, Elias and Alice, who began bringing out the food.

"Didn't I tell you?" Hugo said to Tarleton as they both gazed at the sumptuous dishes that were soon spanning the table from one end to the other. "The Hartfords set one of the finest tables in the colonies."

"You weren't exaggerating," Tarleton agreed. "The King himself would feel satisfied here—except for some of the views of the company present."

"If you are referring, Lieutenant, to my speech last week at the Old South Meeting House, commemorating the fifth anniversary of the Boston Massacre, the King would only be disturbed if he finds the truth offensive, for I spoke no words that were false," said Dr. Warren.

Hugo bristled at the words "Boston Massacre." Among the British the incident of March 5, 1770, in which a squad of British soldiers had opened fire on a group of angry Boston civilians, killing five of them, was no massacre but self-defense. The soldiers, provoked beyond human endurance by the taunts, insults, snowballs and rocks hurled at them by the mob, had discharged their weapons because they had no other choice. But to Bostonians the dead were sainted martyrs in the cause of "American liberty,"— and every year they held a gathering at the Old South Meeting House on Salem Street to commemorate the event. This year Dr. Warren had been the keynote speaker. He was an accomplished orator and, dressed in a toga like a Roman Senator, he had denounced the British and their rule in the colonies in especially harsh terms. Dozens of British officers had attended the speech in an effort to intimidate him, and when he refused to be silenced they had held up handfuls of bullets and nooses while he spoke, to show the Doctor that they thought he deserved to either face the firing squad or be hanged, sentiments Hugo heartily agreed with. But before he could say anything Hugo felt Tarleton's strong hand restrainingly on his knee.

"I must say, Doctor," said Tarleton, "that I give you my grudging respect for your speech." Hugo gave Tarleton an amazed looked, as did Walter. "To give such a speech with all those British officers present—that took courage, more than most people have, and I do admire you for that."

"Thank you," Dr. Warren bowed his head in appreciation. "I would not have expected those words from you."

"Mind," said Tarleton, "had I been there, I would have held up a rope too. But you are a brave man, sir."

"Brave, perhaps, but misguided," commented Hugo.

"Misguided?" Walter said.

"Yes. Challenging the King's rule and his authority."

"He's a tyrant," Walter declared. "All you have to do is look at the Intolerable Acts if you want proof."

"If you mean the Boston Port Act, the Massachusetts Government Act, and the Administration of Justice Act," said Hugo, the thin lips getting red, "those laws were passed by Parliament at His Majesty's urging to restore order here and deal with the Sons of Violence." He concluded by using the derogatory term the British had for the Sons of Liberty, and it had the intended effect, for Walter became visibly angry.

"No, I mean the Intolerable Acts," Walter maintained, "the tyrannical dictates that have closed our port and replaced the government we elected with toadies appointed by the King."

"Those measures were passed because of the outrageous actions of some of the radical hotheads of Boston," said Hugo, "like tarring and feathering royal officials, harassing people loyal to His Majesty, and throwing perfectly good tea into the water. The King has been very patient, but patience has its limits. If these outrages don't stop, some very bad things are going to happen here."

"You may close our ports," said Doctor Warren calmly. "You may try to impose laws on us. You can appoint officials we didn't elect to attempt to govern us. You may attempt to tax us without allowing us any representation in Parliament. But we won't obey your laws. We won't obey your officials. We won't pay your taxes. For more than 150 years we have governed ourselves, elected our own representatives, and obeyed the laws we make ourselves. We will never bow down to tyranny, and there aren't enough soldiers in England to ever make us do so."

"Hear hear," said Walter. "We'll have our freedom, or we'll die fighting for it." Josiah wanted to put an end to the argument, so now he stood up and interjected, "Let's have a toast: To Hugo's return!"

"To Hugo's return!" everyone said, and Hugo's face took on a more pleasant expression and he settle down to eat his food, as did everyone else.

Maureen, Alice, and Elias went in and out, clearing some dishes away and bringing new ones in. Alice kept looking over at Josiah, trying to get him to look her way, but he took no notice of her. He kept trying to steer the conversation away from the troubles in Boston and onto more philosophical subjects, which he had always loved discussing with Hugo, but he couldn't get anything started.

"Maureen is just as pretty as she was when I left," Hugo said to Josiah as the cook brought out a dish of roast beef. "Maureen, are you married yet?"

"No, Master Hugo."

"Well, you haven't lost any of your talents. The man who marries you will eat well!"

"Thank you, Master Hugo," she said shyly.

"And who is this?" Hugo said when Alice appeared, carrying plates of fruit. "I don't remember seeing you before."

"I'm Alice, sir, the maid," she said, curtsying.

"You sound Irish," said Tarleton.

"I am, sir. From County Cork."

"I'm surprised, Mr. Hartford, that you don't have a larger household staff. In England, in a house this size, there would be four times as many servants as I see here."

"We prefer doing our work ourselves, rather than be waited on," Benjamin explained.

"Something I am struck by since I've come here is the overall abundance of everything," said Tarleton. "You Americans live so well. I've never seen anything like it."

"Where are you from, Lieutenant?" asked Jessica.

"I'm from Liverpool. Like Boston, a big trading port. My grandfather was in the shipping business, Mr. Hartford, as was my father."

"Oh, so you're related to *those* Tarletons," said Benjamin.

"You know of them, Father?" asked Josiah.

"I know of them. A very large and prosperous company." From the look on his father's face and his tone Josiah got the idea there was something more to be told about this, something Benjamin did not want to say in public. "Their ships traverse the world," he went on, "just like ours do."

"Ban's father was the Lord Mayor of Liverpool," said Hugo.

"Are you planning on going into politics too, Mr. Tarleton?" asked Jessica.

"Perhaps someday I will," Tarleton said.

"If your father is the Lord Mayor of Liverpool, that should make it easier for you."

"My father *was* the Lord Mayor," said Tarleton.

"Did he get voted out?"

"No, Miss Hartford, he did not get voted out. He died, two years ago."

Jessica threw both hands together in front of her, as if in prayer, and said, "Oh, I'm sorry! Forgive me for bringing it up."

"Please don't be distressed, Miss Hartford. You didn't know. Besides, we were discussing me, and I am my own favorite subject."

"Well," said Jessica, recovering herself, "so we were saying you have chosen a military career."

"My father and mother both wanted me to study law, but I was rebellious," said Tarleton.

"You're not telling us the truth," said Jessica knowingly.

"Don't let Ban's rough edges fool you," said Hugo. "He has a good mind when he chooses. He attended Oxford and was accepted at Middle Temple Law."

"Middle Temple Law?" said Doctor Warren, visibly impressed.

"What is it?" asked Walter.

"Only the most prestigious law school in England," said Josiah. "I heard people speak of it at Harvard."

"I attended for a time," said Tarleton, "but I decided I wanted to see the world, so I joined the army."

"Ban is like me," said Hugo. "He wants to paint the world British Red."

"You mean spread the empire," said Walter.

"The British Empire is a force for good, Walter, whether you want to admit it or not. We are on a mission to civilize the world, to make it a better place, to spread Christianity to the heathens."

"What makes you think you have the right to do that?" Walter asked.

"It is ordained by God. The British Empire will last forever because we have been chosen by God to do His work. Am I right, Ban?"

"Oh, absolutely," said Tarleton, who did not, it seemed to Josiah, to be as zealous about this as Hugo was.

"The British Empire will not last forever," declared Doctor Warren. "No empire does."

"You and Josiah appear to agree on that," said Hugo, recalling his conversation with Josiah at Castle Island the other night. "But you're wrong. Our empire is exceptional. The laws of history don't apply in our case."

"And you really believe that?"

"Don't misunderstand me, Doctor," said Hugo, gesturing with his hands in the quick motions that Josiah always associated with Hugo, his long fingers reaching out as if he wanted to grasp the words he was formulating and shake them for added emphasis.

"I love Boston, and I love the people here. I don't want to see them slaughtered by the most powerful army in the world."

"You overestimate what military might by itself can accomplish," said the doctor. "There are limits to what you can do by force alone. Yes, you can kill a man, you can throw him into prison, but you cannot control what he's thinking! We all know that from the British point of view the colonies were founded to be a market for English goods, and the colonies in return have supplied England with the raw materials she needs. It has worked out well for both of us. But what will the colonies be worth to the King if you kill us all?"

"Come now, Doctor Warren," Hugo was saying, "you can't truly believe in the colonists making war against the British Empire. No good can come of that."

"Nobody in his right mind wants war. But I won't tamely submit to tyranny," the doctor declared. "We prize our liberties here, more than anything else."

"One of the things I find most curious about America," said Tarleton, "is that you have the governor of New Jersey who is devoted to the King and the Empire, and yet his father is one of the most outspoken of the rebel leaders. A very puzzling place, America."

"You are referring to Benjamin Franklin," said Doctor Warren, "and to his son, William, who is the Royal Governor of New Jersey."

"And he is despised by the patriots there," said Walter. "I saw that when I visited our sister Mary Louise last year."

"I see a lot of pain and sorrow coming soon," said Patrick, who was sitting nearby. "Is your brother a prophet?" Tarleton asked Jessica, who sat across from him and to his left.

"He does have second sight sometimes," Jessica admitted. "What else do you see, Patrick?"

"I'll have to ask Alexander later. He isn't saying right now."

When dinner was over everyone went into the drawing room. Jessica went to the piano and played a few chords. She was barely getting started when Hugo said, "What about our fencing match, Josiah?"

"Let's postpone it," said Josiah.

"The British against the Americans," said Tarleton eagerly. "Hugo, you have to win for the honor of the Empire."

"Josiah, you have to win for the cause of freedom," said Doctor Warren. "You've got to do it, Josiah," said Walter. "You've got to beat him."

Josiah felt he was being pushed into this, but he could see no honorable way out. Hugo had already taken hold of one of the foils and was slashing it about in the air. This was followed by stretching himself into a forward lunge position, first on one leg, then on the other, for, just as Lord Roger had told them both over and over, quickness and flexibility were the essentials of "the art of the fence."

"Quickness of mind, quickness of hand, quickness of foot," Lord Roger had said. "Never forget that."

The furniture was pushed back to provide enough room for Josiah and Hugo to fence. Elias rolled the carpets back as Hugo and Josiah prepared. Hugo's confident manner made Josiah uneasy. Every motion he made suggested a certainty of purpose and a surety of victory. Josiah had not done any real fencing since he left Harvard and he knew that against an opponent like Hugo even with the most razor-sharp reflexes the slightest hesitation could make the difference between defeat and victory. Everyone stood watching and waiting.

"Tarleton will be the judge," said Hugo. "Agreed?"

"Agreed."

"The first to score twelve hits is the winner. Agreed, Josiah?"

"Agreed. I need a few minutes to get prepared."

Josiah went through a few warm-up exercises of his own, stretching and bending the way Lord Roger had shown them. He slashed the air with his foil, twisted and turned, feeling his muscles becoming malleable, and saw that Hugo was doing the same. "Fencers ready?" called Tarleton, and Josiah noticed the beak-like upper lip had become, it appeared, sharper.

Hugo and Josiah stood facing each other, six feet between them. "Cross your swords!" said Tarleton. They crossed their foils in the approved manner. "I've waited four years for this," said Hugo, smiling, but there was a deadly earnestness behind the smile. "You won the last time, Josiah. My father always said I could never beat you. Tonight I'll prove him wrong."

"Fencers at the ready," said Tarleton. "Do you swear to fight according to the laws of chivalry and the code of the duel? Then, fencers salute!"

Hugo and Josiah saluted one another, raising their foils to eye level and then lowering them. "*En guarde!*" said Tarleton.

Josiah raised his left arm behind him, bending his elbow at shoulder level, left foot at a 90 degree angle to his front right foot, his knees bent over his toes, his foil "splitting the square" as Lord Roger had instructed, that is, held at forty-five degrees.

"Fence!" cried Tarleton.

"Ha!" Hugo cried, and advanced faster than Josiah had anticipated. He parried Hugo's attack but before he had time to riposte, Hugo had scored a hit. Josiah felt the blunted point strike his arm.

"Point, Hugo," said Tarleton, and when Hugo attacked again, Josiah once more parried.

"Hit!" shouted Hugo.

"No," said Josiah, for the cut had come close but missed. "Judgement," said Hugo.

"Denied," said Tarleton.

He's going to be fair at least, thought Josiah.

Hugo attacked again and again. His forward lunge had improved dramatically, and Josiah at first could do little more than fend him off. No doubt of it, Hugo had gotten better by leaps and bounds, and before he knew it, Josiah was down by five points.

Tarleton called a break while both men caught their breaths. "You better get to work, brother," said Walter. "He's beating the pants off you. You'd best go on the offensive."

"I would, if I could get off the defensive first," said Josiah.

"I've got him," Hugo said to Tarleton. "Five to zero! I swear to God I've got him."

"Don't be so sure," said Tarleton.

"Why?"

"Because you're at your best already, but he's just getting started," said Tarleton.

"He's good, isn't he?" said Hugo.

"He's damn good," Tarleton agreed.

They began again and Hugo quickly scored two more points. It was now seven to nothing, and Hugo only needed five more points to win the match. But when Hugo came at him again Josiah felt his old razor-like focus returning. "You. Your sword. Your opponent," Josiah said to himself, and the words rang in his mind, for Lord Roger had instructed him this way. "Nothing exists," Lord Roger had always said, "nothing exists outside what's taking place here: You, your sword, and your opponent. Nothing else. Nothing else!" Early on Lord Roger had taken note of Josiah's ability to focus his attention this way—far better, his Lordship had always said, than Hugo ever could, and it was this along with Josiah's quickness of hand and foot that had inspired Lord Roger to take a real interest in Josiah's abilities and start training him on a daily basis.

Josiah had always been exceptionally quick on his feet, able to move backward and forward with astonishing speed. While at the Harvard Fencing Club someone had once commented that Josiah Hartford was the only person he had ever seen who could move forward and backward at the same time. When Hugo advanced Josiah moved back, darting just out of range of Hugo's foil. He parried downward and scored a hit on Hugo's shoulder.

"Point, Josiah," said Tarleton.

Josiah thrust downward again, then up toward Hugo's chest, moving back and then forward.

"Point, Josiah," Tarleton cried.

Josiah quickly scored three more points. Tarleton called a break.

"The momentum has swung his way," Tarleton said to Hugo. "He's getting better every second. If you don't finish him off soon, you're going to lose."

"Never!" vowed Hugo.

"Come on, Older Brother," said Patrick. "You can do it!"

"Fence!" said Tarleton. Hugo faked to his left, and scored another point. But when they began again he tried the same trick, and Josiah, seeing it coming, used the opening it created to score a point of his own.

The score was now eight to six and Hugo's confident expression was fading.

Josiah, scored one, two, three more points and was now in the lead for the first time.

Josiah felt his focus getting even stronger. Now he knew he would win. In the next exchange he scored two more times, and another break was called.

"You've got him. One point to go," said Walter.

"I'd better do it quickly," said Josiah. "I'm getting tired, and he's desperate."

"This is it," said Tarleton. "*En guarde!* Fence!"

Hugo was purely on defense now, and nothing Josiah tried was working to score that last and final point. "Come on Josiah, be a man!" said Hugo. "Fight like you mean it!"

So he hasn't forgotten, Josiah thought.

Josiah's inner voice told him now would be the right time to use a move Lord Roger had taught him. It was a move to be used cautiously, for it would only work once. He faked right, then spun about, bringing the foil all the way around his body and behind him, scoring to Hugo's arm.

"Damn!" shouted Hugo, and then realizing there were ladies present, said, "Sorry!"

"Well done, Josiah, well done," said Dr. Warren, shaking Josiah's hand. "What a comeback you made. I thought he had you."

"So did I," Josiah admitted.

Hugo, standing a few feet away, heard this. But he had acquired some measure of self- control, and coming over to Josiah he offered his hand. "Josiah, you are just too good." To Tarleton he said, "What do you think now?"

"Like I said, he's damn good," said Tarleton.

They shook hands and then embraced, to the applause of everyone present.

Dr. Warren went out of his way to shake Hugo's hand. "You fought well and you are a good sport," he said. "A true gentleman."

"Thank you," said Hugo reluctantly.

"And you did an excellent job," he said to Tarleton.

Jessica had left the piano to come and congratulate Josiah as well. Now she took Tarleton by the arm and said, "The Lieutenant and I are going to sing a duet."

"Oh, we are?" said Tarleton, surprised. "Do you know 'Barbara Allen?'"

"Yes, it's one of my favorites," Tarleton admitted.

"Then that is what we are going to sing," Jessica declared.

"I heard you sing the other night," said Josiah, still wiping the perspiration from his brow. "You have to sing tonight."

Tarleton's protests were drowned out as Jessica led him over to the piano. She said down while Tarleton leaned an elbow on the top. "I'll sing a verse, then the Lieutenant will sing a verse," said Jessica.

"In Scarlet Town, where I was born
There was a fair maid dwellin,'
Made every boy cry well-a-day
Her name was Barbara Allen."

Now it was Tarleton's turn.

"Twas in the merry month of May
When green buds all were swelling
Sweet William on his death bed lay
For love of Barbara Allen
"He sent his servant to the town
To the place where she was dwelling
Saying you must come, to my master dear
If your name be Barbara Allen
"So slowly, slowly she got up
And slowly she drew nigh him
And the only words to him did say
Young man I think you're dying
He turned his face unto the wall
And death was in him welling,
Good-bye, good-bye, to my friends all
Be good to Barbara Allen
When he was dead and laid in grave
She heard the death bells knelling
And every stroke to her did say
Hard hearted Barbara Allen
"Oh mother, oh mother go dig my grave
Make it both long and narrow

Sweet William died of love for me
And I will die of sorrow
And father, oh father, go dig my grave
Make it both long and narrow
Sweet William died on yesterday
And I will die tomorrow
Barbara Allen was buried in the old churchyard
Sweet William was buried beside her
Out of sweet William's heart, there grew a rose
Out of Barbara Allen's a briar"

They sang the last verse together:

"They grew and grew in the old churchyard
Till they could grow no higher
At the end they formed, a true lover's knot
And the rose grew round the briar."

They finished to a huge round of applause. "Lieutenant, you have an amazing voice," said Benjamin, just Elias came into the room, carrying his fiddle with him.

"I sent for Elias," Benjamin went on. I thought it might be time to have some dancing."

"If we're going to dance, let it be the Lillibulero, please," said Hugo.

"Yes, the Lillibulero," Martha agreed.

"That was always your favorite, Master Hugo," said Elias. He looked at Benjamin, who nodded his approval.

"If we're going to dance the Lillibulero, we need more women here," Benjamin observed. "Anne, go and get Alice and Maureen. Perhaps they would like to dance too."

Everyone lined up, the men on one side, the women on the other. The Lillibulero was a lively tune, and Elias played it with an especial zest that infected everyone. When Dr. Warren noticed Patrick standing off to one side near Elias, he said, "Patrick, I'll sit this out, you join the dance."

"Oh no, doctor, I really don't dance," said Patrick. "It is balanced now, seven men on one side and the seven women on the other. I never want to unbalance things."

The two sides moved toward one another and bowed, then moved back and turned a complete circle. The Lillibulero was a popular dance and everyone knew how to do it. As the pairs moved through the line, hopping and skipping, then moving sideways, Josiah noted the happy expression on Hugo's face. He looked especially handsome as he danced, the scarlet coat contrasting sharply with the bright white breeches he wore, and Josiah found himself once again wishing times could be like they were before Hugo left and at the same time fearing that wasn't going to happen. Tarleton, as he would have expected, was a very good dancer, moving with the grace of a bird gliding through the air, and once more that impression of Tarleton as a falcon made its way into his mind.

Josiah loved dancing. At Harvard the men had said he might have made a good dancing master, a title he didn't want any more than he wanted to take over his father's shipyard. Like Tarleton, he moved gracefully and easily through the steps of the Lillibulero, and as he came toward Alice, who, he noticed, did not dance nearly as well as she had said she could, he saw once again her pleading glance. Once again heard a voice saying "You need to put a stop to this."

His mother and father, he saw, were enjoying themselves in the dance, although he hoped Benjamin would not over-exert himself. His mother was smiling radiantly as she danced.

Jessica was obviously having fun, and Josiah saw that she and Tarleton were exchanging glances. What would Walter think, if Tarleton tried to court one of the Hartford girls? That would be amusing—no, not amusing at all, it could lead to all kinds of problems. He saw Charles and Anne exchanging similar, albeit much deeper, looks, and wondered what his father would say when Charles asked for Anne's hand in marriage.

Benjamin abruptly stopped dancing and waved to Charles to come and take his place. "Are you all right, Father?" Josiah asked.

"I'm fine, I'm fine, I just have to rest," Benjamin said, and went over to stand beside Patrick.

"Is he all right, Dr. Warren?" Josiah asked anxiously.

"Yes, I'm sure he is," said Dr. Warren. "He has good sense enough to know when he could be over-exerting himself."

• • •

The dance came to an end, and as the hour was getting late, the guests began to leave, first Charles, then Dr. Warren, and then Hugo and Tarleton. At the door Tarleton said, "Thank you for a most rewarding evening, Mr. Hartford. If everyone in Boston could spend a little time together like this there would be much less tension in the city."

Hugo thanked everyone, and then, as their carriage had returned, the two officers made their way outside into the cold night air. "Hugo certainly has changed, hasn't he, Father?" said Josiah.

"He has, and not for the better, either," said Benjamin.

"Father, when Tarleton mentioned that his family was in the shipping business, I got the feeling there was something wrong," said Walter.

"The Tarletons are very heavily involved in the slave trade," said Benjamin. "Their ships take human beings from Africa to Virginia, all the way to Brazil. An unholy business."

"Does he know, do you think?" asked Josiah. "How could he not?"

"Father, when can I go to the Willinghams'?" asked Patrick, looking up at the stars. "It's that time of year."

"In a few days," said Benjamin. "Josiah, will you take him?"

"We'll ride to Concord together, Oldest Brother," said Patrick happily."We'll have so much fun, visiting the Willinghams. And you can see Mercy."

"Don't you mean, Mercy can see him?" said Walter.

"Yes, definitely," said Patrick. "Mercy's in love with him. Everyone knows it. When are you going to marry her, Josiah?"

"Let's go back in the house. It's cold out here," Josiah said.

They returned to the house. Josiah stood by the big fireplace to warm himself. He was glad the evening had gone well, but he was concerned that his winning the fencing match might drive Hugo further from him. Could it be they had outgrown each other? He paused, fearing that it could be true no matter what he thought or did.

I may be about to lose something very valuable, he thought. Something I will never be able to get back again.

CHAPTER 5
JOURNEY TO CONCORD

As Patrick had said, it was the time of year when he went to visit the Willinghams in Concord. Even though he was sixteen now and big for his age, his going on his own was out of the question. If he ever got so far away from home as to lose sight of it, there was a good chance he wouldn't be able to find his way back. So one evening a few nights after the dinner party the family sat in the drawing room discussing how best to get him from Boston to Concord. While the family talked and Jessica played "Nobody's Jig" on the piano, Patrick sat near the front window, holding a book and looking intently at its pages, his face solemn.

"When would you like to leave, Patrick?" Martha asked.

"Why, anytime," Patrick said, not looking up from his reading. "I go there every year since I was ten. The sun has already passed the equinox so it is time for me to go. But I don't know if I'll ever come back again."

"Why would you say that, Patrick?" Martha's face took on a worried expression. Like everyone else, she knew that what Patrick said about the future often came true. But Patrick only smiled and kept on reading.

"Is that something Alexander told you?" Anne asked.

"Alexander doesn't always tell me things directly, Youngest Sister," Patrick replied. "Sometimes he just hints at them. I suppose I could leave now, Mother," he said to Martha. "I can go and pack my clothes if you want."

"It's almost dark now," Martha said, still looking worried. "It would be best to wait until tomorrow. Josiah will go with you."

"You'll take him, won't you, Josiah?" Benjamin asked.

"There is so much to do at the yard, Father," Josiah said. "We're behind on that three-master. Maybe it would be better if Elias takes him in the carriage."

"Oh no, please," Patrick interjected. "I don't want to go in the carriage. I want to ride on Cleopatra, and have Josiah go along with me."

"I don't see what the difference is, as long as you get there," Josiah pointed out.

"It's Mercy, I'll wager," Jessica said knowingly.

"It isn't that, not at all," Josiah protested, but both Jessica and Anne knew better.

"Mercy has a crush on you," Anne declared.

"Crush? She's head over heels in love with him," said Jessica. "Remember how she behaved when she was here? She wants to marry him, and she is one girl who always gets her way."

She had stopped playing "Nobody's Jig" and changed over to "Greensleeves."

"Alas my love
You do me wrong
To cast me off discourteously..."

"It's time you started thinking about getting married," said Martha. "Mercy would be a good match for you."

"What are you reading, Patrick?" Josiah asked, wanting to steer the conversation in another direction.

"I'm reading about pi. And also about Pythagoras. I'm taking this book with me when I go to the Willingham's. I can't wait to tell Scotty about it. The square of the hypotenuse is equal to the sum of the squares of the other two sides."

"Yes, that is the Pythagorean theorem," Josiah said.

"Pythagoras lived more than 2,500 years ago," said Patrick. "That's a long time. Scotty will be amazed to learn that pi is an irrational number. You can go on calculating it forever. Do you know what the first twelve decimal points are? 3.141592653585."

Later that evening Benjamin asked, "So you'll take Patrick?"

"If you insist, Father."

They were in the observatory on the fourth floor. Together they looked down on the city below.

"I'll have Elias get the horses ready. You can leave after breakfast tomorrow. Where is Walter?"

Josiah shook his head, but his denial wasn't altogether true. He didn't like lying, especially not to his father, and he knew Walter was with his friends in the Sons of Liberty, plotting more of their antics.

"The yard can get along without you for a few days. Go to Concord, take the time off, and think about Mercy." He smiled. "Just don't do anything you could regret later on."

"What do you mean, Father?"

"You're young, Mercy's young, it's spring and the sap's rising. Your mother and I want grandchildren, but we don't want them to arrive before their time."

"I'll be careful, Father," he promised, but it was Alice he was thinking of, not Mercy.

•   •   •

He and Patrick rode out of Boston the next morning, Josiah on his favorite horse, Caesar, and Patrick on his, a filly named Cleopatra. They rode toward the Neck, where hundreds of soldiers were encamped on either side, row after row of tents laid out neatly and precisely, the soldiers going through their morning duties. Some had their shirts off and many showed scars of the whip on their backs. Josiah knew next to nothing about military life, but he did know that British soldiers and sailors were subject to ferocious discipline. The slightest infraction of a rule, the smallest button not polished to perfection, could result in a brutal flogging that left scars that would never heal. The damage to a man's mind was beyond calculation. The frequency with which British soldiers were whipped resulted in their being taunted as "bloody backs" by the Sons of Liberty, much to the soldiers' resentment.

The seriousness of the soldiers in shining their boots and scrubbing their white breeches caught Patrick's attention.

"Hello," he called to one of the redcoats. "You sure do want those crystal clean, don't you?"

The soldier, a small, black haired man with a face scarred by smallpox, looked up as if he expected mockery. But the hostile look faded when he saw Patrick's innocent expression and welkin eyes. "'Course I do," he replied. "They'll give me a hiding like you never seen if all this don't shine like the sun, they will."

"Oh, that isn't good," Patrick said. "Are you happy to be a soldier?"

"Happy as a he-goat in a pen with ten she-goats in heat."

"That would be nice," said Patrick. "I like goats. What's your name?"

"Me name's Tommy Jones," the soldier replied. All the while they were talking he continued polishing the buttons of his tunic.

"Where are you from, Mr. Jones?"

"I grew up right beside the Mersey River."

"Liverpool," said Patrick. "I know where that is. I shouldn't like to be so far from home."

Patrick waved as he and Josiah continued on their way. Jones hesitated a moment, then waved back.

"What a nice man," Patrick said. "Will they really paddle him if he doesn't shine his boots until they sparkle, Older Brother?"

"No, that isn't what he means, Patrick," Josiah said. "These men are punished with flogging."

"Flogging?" asked Patrick.

"If a button isn't polished right, if their boots aren't shined properly, they can get fifty lashes. They can get hundreds for more serious offenses."

"Oh, but that's terrible!" Patrick cried. "Why are they in that army at all, when they get treated that way?"

"They're poor. They don't have many choices in life." British soldiers came from the slums of the cities like London or Birmingham, or else from farms in the Midlands where there were too many mouths to feed. Others joined because they had been accused of committing a crime and innocent or not, were given the choice of prison or the army.

"Why don't they run away?" asked Patrick.

"Sometimes they do. They call it 'Dutch Leave.' But if they get caught, they get shot."

"Shot?" Patrick was astounded.

"It's not an easy life for them. Sometimes they are even kidnapped into joining."

"Kidnapped?" Patrick repeated in horror.

"Hugo told me. A recruiter will go into a tavern and if he sees a man he thinks would make a good soldier, he puts a silver shilling in his hand. If the poor fellow closes his hand over it, that means that's he's accepted the offer and has volunteered to become a soldier."

"That's horrible," cried Patrick. "Wicked and horrible."

"I understand it's even worse in the navy," Josiah went on. "Discipline is so severe, and life on a ship is so hard, that no one wants to join no matter how poor they are. So the British Navy sends out men in what they call 'Press Gangs,' and they prowl the waterfronts of English ports and when they see a fellow they want for a sailor, they put irons on him and force him onto a ship. Once he's there, he can't leave."

"That's terrible, terrible," said Patrick, and he spent the next several minutes talking that over with himself, saying again and again how awful it was for those poor men in the British Army and Navy.

●　　●　　●

They rode into the pastoral countryside, which was blooming with all the signs of an early spring. The sun shone through a cloudless sky. They rode past Back Bay toward Roxbury, then onto the Lexington Road. The Massachusetts landscape, with its farms and silos and barns, looked so peaceful to Josiah that he wondered if it could have been like this when the world was first created. He imagined soldiers marching over these roads and laying waste this beautiful land, like Europe in the Thirty Years' War, and the thought froze him and he hoped, fervently, that it would not happen.

"Can we stop at the Golden Ball, and eat lunch there?" asked Patrick.

"Why there?"

"They make the best hasty pudding in the world there. They put extra sugar and molasses in it."

The Golden Ball Tavern was known to have some of the best food in Massachusetts. It was neat and tidy and clean, with pictures of King George on the walls and other pictures showing victories over the French and the Indians. There were few other patrons at this time of day, but as Patrick and Josiah sat down at a table near the stairs that led to the rooms on the second floor Josiah was astonished to see Hugo Chamberlain and another young man appear. Both were dressed in civilian clothes, the clothes of a pair of young Boston dandies, knee breeches and silver buckled shoes, vests and long-sleeved shirts, and both carried expensive looking tri-cornered hats.

"Look, Josiah, there's Hugo!" Patrick cried happily. "Hugo! Hugo!" he called.

Hugo turned about, looking surprised, then nonplussed. An unpleasant expression came to the face of the other man, a small blonde-headed fellow. Hugo gave no sign of recognition when he saw Josiah and Patrick, and when they continued to call to him he approached their table.

"Well, Hugo, I never expected to see you here," said Josiah. "Won't you and your friend join us? We're on our way to Concord."

"I'm afraid you've mistaken me for someone else, sir," said Hugo gravely. "My name is Charles Townsend. I'm a surveyor, and that's my assistant, Mr. Lightfoot." He bent his head down and winked. "I hope you enjoy yourselves," he said, bowing politely. He then turned and went to join his companion at a table on the other side of the room.

A dark haired, dark-complexioned serving girl with a white bonnet on her head came to ask what they wanted to eat, and said in a low voice, "Surveyors my ass. They're a couple of British spies."

"Spies?" asked Josiah.

"You aren't Tories are you?" the girl asked. When Josiah assured her they weren't, she went on. "We're sure they're British officers, sent out here from Boston on some secret mission. They've been here the past two days, riding out all day and then coming back at night. They're going to get their heads blown off. Want some wine?"

"Yes," Patrick said eagerly.

"No," Josiah said firmly.

"Oh, please Josiah, just a little?"

"No wine, we have a long trip ahead."

The girl brought them chicken, potatoes, and some cooked vegetables. Patrick ate with his usual slowness, and while they ate Josiah noticed that Hugo and the blonde-headed fellow finished their meal very quickly, never looking toward Josiah and Patrick and speaking in whispers. They left hurriedly and then rode off toward Lexington.

When they were gone the serving girl said, "You know what else? They're a couple of poofs."

"No, that can't be," said Josiah, horrified at the thought.

"I heard them in their room last night," the girl declared.

"What were you doing, listening to something like that?" asked Josiah.

"I heard what I heard," said the girl. "They're mollies, both of them."

"I'll have some hasty pudding for dessert," Patrick said eagerly.

The girl brought the hasty pudding, which Patrick ate happily. "What did she mean," he asked, "when she says Hugo is a 'molly'? That's a girl's name."

"Never mind," said Josiah. When Patrick asked a question that he wasn't prepared to answer Josiah said "Never mind" in a firm tone that by now Patrick had learned to recognize and he never pressed the matter when he heard this. He could tell that Josiah was troubled by what the tavern girl had said.

"Why was Hugo pretending to be somebody else?" Patrick asked when they resumed their ride.

"I don't know. I don't know what to make of it."

"That girl said somebody might blow Hugo's head off," Patrick went on. "Maybe we should warn him."

They rode on, and when they came near Menotomy Village, Patrick, whose eyes were unusually sharp, suddenly pointed and said, "There they are!"

He gestured toward a bridge ahead of them. Hugo and his companion were standing in a nearby clump of trees, looking intently across the open field to the town square, where the local militiamen were drilling. Hugo would peer intently through a spyglass and say something to the other man, who wrote it down in a sketchbook.

They looked up at Josiah and Patrick's approach. Hugo's companion, a small blonde fellow, made a few quick entries in the sketchbook and then carefully put it away in this saddlebags, but before he closed it Josiah had seen an accurate drawing of the bridge and the village square where the men were marching.

"Brother Hugo, we knew you were telling us a fib," said Patrick. "Your name isn't Charles. But I don't know who you are," he said to the other man.

"This is Jeremy," Hugo said uneasily. "We aren't really here, you understand."

"Then what are you doing?" Patrick asked.

"We're on a holiday together," Hugo said.

"Oh, I see," said Patrick. "You're traveling incognito."

"Yes, Patrick, that's right," said Hugo. "We're traveling incognito."

"That's very nice," said Patrick. "Taking a holiday. Holidays are so much fun. What were you drawing in that notebook?"

"Jeremy is an artist," Hugo explained.

"Like Michelangelo or Leonardo?" asked Patrick.

"Yes, like them, Patrick," said Hugo. "He draws sketches of whatever interests him."

"I like to draw what I see," said Jeremy. He spoke with the same upper-class English accent and possessed the same hauteur of the young British officers Josiah had seen.

Hugo was taken aback. He had never expected to see Josiah and Patrick here. He had been happy to take on this mission for General Gage—in fact, Gage had specifically chosen him for this job, since he knew the terrain and he didn't have much of an accent, so the Americans in the countryside outside Boston would not suspect him of being a British officer. He had been delighted that he could take Jeremy Light along, for he had noticed him as soon as he arrived in Boston. The slight build, the baby face, the fair skin— all of that was enormously attractive to Hugo, and with Jeremy having the same feelings toward him, they had consummated their desires last night in their room at the Golden Ball.

Gage's instructions were specific: Scout out the countryside from Boston to Concord. Take notes and make sketches of bridges, stone walls, barns, hills—any place that might serve as a cover for colonial militias to challenge marching British soldiers. They had also taken note of the militias going through their drills. Hugo, like all the other British officers, held the colonial militias in contempt and was certain they posed no risk to a British column. But Gage was cautious. A year in Boston had beaten him down. He was a far cry from the man who had left London a year ago, brimming with confidence that he could put down the rebellion in Massachusetts.

"You must be an officer too, like Hugo," Patrick declared. "Why do you whip your men? That's so mean. Just because they didn't shine their boots right. You really shouldn't do that anymore."

"I've never whipped anybody," said Jeremy, puzzled, not knowing what to make of Patrick.

"Jeremy, tell Patrick when you were born," Hugo prompted.

"Why, I was born February 21, 1756," Jeremy said, looking perplexed.

Patrick did not even have to think about it. "That was a Saturday," he declared.

Jeremy looked first at Patrick, then at Hugo, his face clouded with amazement. "He can tell you anything like that," said Hugo. "Patrick, what is seven to the fourth power?"

"2,401," Patrick said, again, without any apparent effort.

"Patrick, you're amazing," said Hugo. "Now, it's rather important you don't tell anyone you've seen us."

"Why? Is it a secret?" Patrick asked eagerly.

"Yes. An important secret."

"A big secret?"

"Very big, Patrick." To Josiah Hugo said, "Can I count on you?"

"All right," said Josiah, still not sure what to think of all this. Jeremy had gone back to studying the militiamen. They marched, wheeled, presented arms, knelt as if preparing to fire, rose and stood at attention.

"They're doing it just like the redcoats," said Patrick, "marching back and forth."

"They're going to be sorry for it one day," said Jeremy grimly.

"Why will they be sorry?"

"They might get killed, if they start a war."

"Jeremy," Hugo cautioned. "No need to say anything more about that."

"Why would anybody start a war? Wars are no good. The girl at the tavern said the people around here know who you are and are going to blow your heads off," said Patrick.

Hugo and Jeremy both looked up in alarm at this. "We better get back to Boston," said Jeremy.

"Yes," Hugo agreed. "Remember, you haven't seen us." They quickly mounted their horses and rode off down the road. Patrick and Josiah continued on their way.

"What were they doing?" Patrick asked.

Josiah shook his head. The whole episode made no sense—Hugo pretending not to know them, being in civilian clothes, giving a false name, the careful drawing that Jeremy fellow was doing and the way he hid the sketchbook, the keen interest they had taken in the men marching on the Menotomy green—it didn't feel right, any of it, not to mention what that serving girl had said about them. Josiah's knowledge of sexual matters was limited to what he had been doing with Alice late at night in his bedroom and exchanging a few kisses with Mercy Willingham during her family's visit. He knew that sometimes men had relations with other men, but it was so forbidden a subject that it was never spoken of directly but only with hints and innuendos. There had been two men in his class who had been expelled and it was whispered that they had been caught together in bed with their clothes off. The whole matter had been glossed over as quickly as possible by the President of Harvard himself, the Reverend Langdon, who had seen to it that the two offenders were unceremoniously taken off campus and told to never return. After that it was rarely mentioned by anyone. The idea that Hugo could be doing something like that—no, thought Josiah, that serving girl didn't know what she was talking about.

Josiah's feeling of something not being right increased when they neared Lexington. Three men on horses came riding up to them, then halted, blocking the road. Their faces were grim, and they wore the rough clothes of workingmen. Their manner made it clear they were not going to let Josiah and Patrick go past without talking to them first.

The leader, a burly man of around forty, said, "Where are you two bound for?"

"Who are you and why do you want to know?" Josiah countered. He put his hand on the hilt of his sword, unobtrusively but ready to draw it if need be.

"What's your business here?" the man persisted. "What are you doing on this road?"

"Our business is our own," Josiah said, "and this is a public highway."

An awkward moment followed, with the leader trying to stare Josiah down and Josiah looking back at him eye-for-eye.

"We aren't in business," said Patrick, breaking the silence. "We're on our way to visit some friends, the Willinghams. They live in Concord. Our father is in business. The shipbuilding business. But not us."

The three men relaxed and the leader smiled slightly. "You know the Willinghams?" he asked.

"We've known the Willinghams all our lives," said Patrick. "Mercy Willingham is in love with my brother Josiah here."

All three men laughed at this and at Josiah's obvious embarrassment. "Lucky fellow," one of them said. "Mercy is one good-looking girl. But how do you know she's in love with your brother?"

"She said so," Patrick affirmed, bringing about more laughter. "She wants to marry him."

"Paul, these can't be the ones we're looking for."

"You want to tell us what this is about?" asked Josiah. He noticed a medallion with a Liberty Tree on it around the neck of the leader, the one called Paul.

"Have you seen anybody who could be British spies?" asked the leader. "We heard there were a couple of them hereabouts, going around making drawings of the roads and bridges."

Josiah wondered how he should answer. This explained the incident with Hugo: He was spying on the local militia, mapping out the countryside for General Gage as he got ready to send his men out and start the war everyone was expecting. These three men carried pistols in their belts and judging from the hard looks on their faces there was no doubt what they would do if they caught up with Hugo and Jeremy. For a moment he feared Patrick might say something, but he had lost interest in the conversation and sat simply smiling at the three men.

"You must be Sons of Liberty," said Josiah. None of them answered but the looks on their faces clearly indicated he was right. "Then you must know our brother, Walter Hartford."

"We know Walter," said the leader. "He's one of my best boys."

That's Paul Revere, Josiah thought, studying him closely. He had heard the name many times, for all of Boston, Patriot and Tory alike, knew of him. But Josiah had never seen him in the flesh before.

"Paul, if we're going to catch these spies we'd best go look for them," said one of the other men.

"Right you are," Revere agreed. "Say hello to the Willinghams for us, boys," he said, and the three rode off hurriedly, spurring their horses, Revere in the lead.

"Are they after Hugo?" Patrick asked.

"It looks like it."

"Older brother, what is happening?"

"I wish I knew."

"Is the whole world going mad?"

"It seems like it," Josiah admitted.

"Why didn't you tell them when they asked if we'd seen anyone?"

"Hugo's my friend. I don't want him to get hurt."

"So you have a dilemma," Patrick declared. "An ethical dilemma. I know what that is. You don't want to lie, but if you tell the truth something bad could happen."

"That's right."

"Older Brother, if there is a war, what side will you be on?"

"There won't be any war and I won't be on any side," Josiah said firmly.

"Walter says there will be war."

"Walter should be careful what he wishes for. He might not be so happy if it comes true."

"Are you going to marry Mercy?" Patrick asked.

"You are a regular chatterbox today," Josiah said, avoiding the question.

They rode through Lexington without stopping but saw more men drilling on the Lexington Green in front of Buckman's Tavern. Like the men at Menotomy, they drilled vigorously, going left, then right, then left again.

By early afternoon they had reached the outskirts of Concord, and they veered off the highway and rode toward the Willinghams' house. At three stories, it was not as big as Hartford Manor but was still a large and impressive home, with white pillars in front holding up a balcony on the third floor peering down on a broad front entrance. Behind the house was a grove of trees, and two barns sat a short distance away. Chickens roamed the barnyard, clucking excitedly as men came out of the barns carrying long wooden boxes. They carried the boxes into the grove of trees and, placing the boxes in holes they had already dug, proceeded to cover them with dirt and branches, working purposefully with picks and shovels.

"Well! It's about time!" Mercy Willingham stood on the side porch of the house, hands on her hips and a pink bonnet covering her dark hair. "I thought you two would never get here! I've been upstairs watching and waiting and then I finally saw you riding down the back road." She came running down the stairs, carefully holding her dress up so it didn't trail along on the ground, calling to one of the stable boys to come and take their horses. "Come on," she said excitedly. "Come on inside. Mr. Hancock and Mr. Adams are here already."

"John Hancock and Samuel Adams are both here?" asked Josiah in surprise as he dismounted.

"Yes, they've been staying with us. Dolly Quincy, Mr. Hancock's fiancé, is here too. You should see her. She's beautiful. They're getting married this fall." Mercy threw her arms around Josiah, kissed him on the cheek, then whispered, "You know what? "They've 'made' their marriage before they've actually had the ceremony, if you know what I mean."

Mercy loved shocking people with her risqué comments. "You shouldn't talk that way," Josiah reproved, but she only laughed kittenishly.

"I'll tell you about it later," she promised. She then went to Patrick and kissed him as well. Taking Josiah by the hand she led him toward the side porch and up the short stairway into the house.

"What are they doing, Mercy?" asked Patrick, indicating the men who were carrying the boxes from the barn and burying them in the woods. "Are they burying treasure like the pirates do?"

"Mr. Hancock and Mr. Adams sent that stuff here, asked my father to hide it in the barn. Mr. Adams thinks the British might be coming soon, so all of it needs to be hidden away so the redcoats won't find it. I wish people would stop talking about war all the time. All anyone talks about these days is war, war, war."

The Willinghams were a fiercely Patriot family. For many years they had lived on Beacon Hill, not far from the Hartfords, and the Hartford and Willingham children had grown up together. But with the troubles in Boston and the influx of British troops into the city the Willinghams had moved to Concord, to be out of the reach of the British army. Like John Hancock, Mr. Willingham was in the importing and exporting business, with a profitable sideline in smuggling, and as the talk of war increased he had taken it upon himself to smuggle in as many muskets, as much gunpowder, and as many rounds of musket balls as he could, bringing the contraband into the countryside for the militias to make use of as they prepared for a possible armed conflict with the British.

The Willingham House, like Hartford Manor, was always filled with shouts of happy laughter, with the children running about and romping up and down the stairs, often led by the energetic Mercy. She was a tall, willowy girl, with a striking face and dark, deep set eyes. Her uninhibited ways and unrestrained speech caused many a head to wag in amusement and sometimes in disapproval, for she was unusually outspoken for a young woman and never hesitated to say what was on her mind.

The side door led into the kitchen, where several women were busily preparing the upcoming dinner. Still led by Mercy, they went through the kitchen and then into the drawing room, where the guests had all gathered and were clustered into several small groups, some of them standing and some seated on couches and chairs.

The younger members of the family were gathered near the huge stone fireplace, and as soon as Mercy, Patrick and Josiah entered the drawing room, Mercy called out, "Look who's here, Scotty!" and Scotty came scampering over to greet Patrick.

"Scotty," said Patrick excitedly, "see what I have? Geometry!" and he brought out the book and opened it to show Scotty a drawing of the Pythagorean theorem.

"Do you know about pi?" Patrick asked.

"Pie?" said Scotty. "What kind?"

"No, pi, the Greek letter, it's the ratio of the circumference of a circle to the diameter. It's 3.141592653589 when you figure it to the twelfth decimal place. But I know it all the way to the eighteenth place."

"Oh, that pi," said Scotty, and the two of them went off to look at Patrick's book.

Mercy led Josiah over to a group that sat near the front windows that overlooked the Lexington-Concord highway. A man named Isaiah Donaldson stood in front of the other guests, speaking self-importantly. His wife, Cora—Mercy's older sister—sat watching him, as did John Hancock and his fiancé, Dorothy Quincy, although it seemed to Josiah that they were far more interested in each other than on listening to Isaiah Donaldson. Dorothy—known to all as Dolly—greeted him with the same charming smile that had helped make her one of New England's great beauties. John Hancock, so the stories went, was a fortunate man, for Dolly had received dozens of proposals before finally choosing him.

Nearby sat another man whose gray hair, fiery eyes and slightly trembling hands meant he could only be Samuel Adams. Josiah had met John Hancock many times, since Hancock moved in the same social circles as the Hartfords, but he had never been introduced to the famous Samuel Adams. Since the Tea Party of December 1773 Adams had been rarely seen in Boston, and over the past six months he had tended to stay out of the city altogether, knowing that General Gage intended to arrest him and that there were more than a few British officers who had vowed to shoot him on sight. His hands, which shook from palsy, held a handsome, solidly-made black walking stick, and he listened to the lawyer Donaldson speak with a slightly ironical expression on his face.

"There are more and more incidents like this," Donaldson was saying, "between the town authorities and British soldiers who don't think they need to obey our laws. Well, it only stands to reason that the more soldiers there are in the city, the more of these we can expect—"

"Look who's here!" Mercy announced. "Everyone, I present Mr. Josiah Hartford of Boston."

Josiah smiled at Mercy's announcing him this way, and Donaldson's face plainly said he did not appreciate his oratory being interrupted by Mercy's loud voice. He stopped speaking and tried his best to hide his irritation as Josiah greeted Mercy's parents, Jessup and Patricia Willingham. John Hancock rose, reluctantly, from Dolly Quincy's side and came over to shake hands with Josiah, then led him to meet his fiancé and introduce him to Samuel Adams as well.

"I know your brother Walter well enough," said Adams, tapping his walking stick in his palm. "What I want to know is why you haven't joined the Patriot movement?"

"One Hartford is enough for any revolution," Josiah said, half-jokingly. Adams didn't smile.

"You'll have to make up your mind one day," he predicted.

"So my brother keeps telling me."

"Mr. Donaldson was just telling us about an incident that took place in Boston the other night," said Mr. Willingham. "It sounds dreadful."

"As I was saying," Donaldson continued, "there's a section of Boston known as 'Damnation Alley' and while I won't say why it is called that in the presence of ladies, it is very popular with certain British officers.

"Two nights ago a group of them, led by a young lieutenant who has only recently arrived in the city, went to this disreputable part of town after an evening of gambling and drinking at the Plymouth Club. They went to a place called Mrs. Erskine's, and after they had done their dirty business there, and again I won't say what this entailed in polite company—"

"Oh, for God's sake, Isaiah, why don't you just say it?" said Mercy impatiently. "They went to consort with prostitutes, and that part of the city is better known as Mount Whoredom. We all know it."

"Mercy Willingham!" her mother, Patricia, said in a shocked tone. "Don't talk like that."

"I just wish Isaiah would come to the point," said Mercy.

"The point is," said Donaldson, once again plainly irritated, "these officers came out of this house of ill-repute—"

"You mean house of prostitution," said Mercy. To Josiah she whispered, "He is such a windbag."

"Yes, Mercy, if you insist, a house of prostitution, all of them drunk and feeling quite rambunctious. They began harassing some civilians that were going by, telling them to sing 'Yankee Doodle Dandy' and saying that American women are nothing but ladies of the night."

"Whores, you mean," said Mercy, once again eliciting a reprimand from her mother. Dolly Quincy, Josiah noticed, smiled at this as she had at Mercy's other remarks.

"You tell them, Mercy," she said in a voice that was just loud enough for everyone to hear.

"Well," Donaldson continued, adjusting his spectacles, "the civilians went to the Town Watch for help. When the Town Watch arrived they tried to arrest the worst offender, this Lieutenant Tarleton, who drew his sword and wounded one of the Watchmen!"

"Tarleton?" asked Josiah. "Banastre Tarleton?"

"You know him?" asked Donaldson.

"He was a dinner guest at our house a few nights ago."

An uncomfortable silence followed these words. Josiah broke it by saying, "Please go on, Mr. Donaldson. What happened next?"

"There was a general melee afterwards between the officers and the Town Watch, and then a squad of British soldiers came. They rescued the officers, who left, cursing the Town Watch, (whom I gather cursed them back), and no one else, fortunately, was harmed."

"So what does all this mean?" asked Mr. Willingham rhetorically. "It means the British think they are above our laws, and their soldiers can do whatever they want."

The Town Watch was Boston's police force, twelve outsized men who patrolled the city streets armed with billhooks, four-foot long oaken clubs that sported a curved metal hook on the end. Clashes between them and riotous British soldiers were happening more and more. Each time the Town Watch took a soldier into custody word quickly spread among the British and the Tories that the man had been brutally beaten, and each time the hatred between the constables and the British deepened.

Mercy, accompanied by her mother, had left the drawing room and Josiah wondered if Patricia might not be giving Mercy a dressing-down for the way she had been speaking. But they reappeared a moment later, both smiling, and Mercy, in her booming voice, said, "Dinner is on the table, everyone!"

Josiah found himself seated next to Mercy and knew it was no accident that he was placed there. Patrick and Scotty Willingham were still talking excitedly about Pythagoras and how to compute the value of pi. John Hancock and Dolly Quincy sat together, and Samuel Adams was sitting across from Josiah.

"Take the Mandamus Councilors," Adams was saying as everyone began to eat. "The fat German King George suspends our elected leaders and replaces them with these jackanapes who report only to him. They have tyrannical powers and they think they can replace 150 years of freedom with what they dictate to us."

"And they're finding out that it won't work, not here in Massachusetts," said Donaldson. "The only place it's safe for these slavish boors is in the city where the soldiers can protect them. Out here it's a different story. Our patriot boys are making them pay a price for their treachery."

"What do you mean, Isaiah?" asked Hancock.

"Oh, you haven't heard about the Lorings?"

"The Lorings? Who are they?"

"They lived in Roxbury, they were our neighbors, in fact," said Cora Donaldson, speaking up for the first time. She was a quiet person, the opposite of her sister Mercy. "Joshua and Elizabeth. They had a nice house."

"It's not so nice any longer," said Donaldson. "Our Liberty Boys started painting red T's on their doors right after Loring got himself appointed as the Mandamus Councilor for the region. This was a warning he had better either resign or they should leave town. When they didn't take the hint, windows started being broken at night, and eventually the house was set on fire."

"I never could stand that Loring fellow," said Adams. "Unprincipled opportunist from head to toe."

"His wife, Elizabeth, goes around flaunting herself," said Mercy. "Since they've moved to Boston now I shouldn't be surprised if she doesn't go to work at Mrs. Erskine's."

"Please excuse my daughter," said Patricia Willingham, "who doesn't seem to know how a proper young lady should talk in polite society."

"It's just that I never saw anything like that, the way she went around with her nice ones out there for everyone to see. She's a regular wagtail."

"You're becoming a wagtail yourself," Josiah said.

"You flatter me, Josiah Hartford," she said, reaching under the table and touching him on the leg.

"Will there be war, Samuel?" asked Jessup Willingham.

"Oh please, not more talk about war," Mercy said in a low voice.

"The day the first shot is fired will be a glorious one for our country," said Adams.

"You don't really want war, do you?"" said Dolly Quincy.

"The British Empire cannot allow a few pesky colonials to continue defying it the way we have," said Adams. "That might spread to other colonies. So very soon it is going to have to try and beat us down. And once war begins, our liberty is assured."

Josiah thought of Hugo and Tarleton and the other British officers who were eager for war to break out. "How can you be so sure we'll be victorious?" he asked. "War is like an evil genie. Once loosed from its bottle you never know which way it will go."

"We don't have to win," said Adams. "We just have to fight, and keep fighting until the British realize they can't get the kind of victory they want. When that happens, they will go home, and we will be free."

"You make it sound so very easy, Samuel," said Dolly.

"No matter what," said Adams, raising a glass with a shaky hand, "we have some wonderful times ahead. To our liberty!"

"To our liberty!"

· · ·

After dinner Josiah went outside to look up at the full moon. A moment later Mercy was beside him.

"What are you looking at?"

"The moon. And the stars. Do you know that the stars move?"

"How do you know the stars move?" Mercy asked skeptically.

"Father watches them with his telescope. He can see them changing their position from one night to the next."

"Let's go for a walk," Mercy suggested, pulling at his hand.

"Just the two of us? What will people say?"

"We won't go far. No one will mind."

They walked onto the road and toward the town proper. "Can I come to visit?" Mercy asked. "Patrick's come to stay with us, so perhaps I could come to visit you in Boston."

"I'm sure everybody will be glad to see you."

"How is everyone in your family?"

"Father's health isn't good. Dr. Warren says his heart is weak."

"Oh no!" said Mercy, throwing her hands up to cover her mouth. "Is he going to be all right?"

"He has to take things easy. He can't manage the shipyard anymore."

"And that means you have to," Mercy declared.

"I'm afraid so."

"Is that why you have to go back so soon?"

"That's one of the reasons."

Mercy threw both her arms around him in a tight grip and kissed him on the mouth.

"There," she said. "It felt good, didn't it? Let's do it again."

"Mercy, what if somebody sees us?"

"I don't care if they do, and besides Josiah Hartford, it's dark and people don't see so well in the dark, or haven't you noticed?" She laughed, pulling away from him, then came back and tugged at his hand again.

"Our parents think we're going to get married," she said, tugging at the pink bonnet on her head.

"So I've heard."

"Don't you want to marry me, Josiah? Or is there someone else in your life?"

"I'm not sure I want to get married yet."

They were standing on a steep rise in the road now, looking down at the town and the countryside beyond in the moonlight.

"Mr. Hancock and Miss Quincy have consummated their marriage already," Mercy declared. "I hear them at night, in her room. Mr. Hancock sneaks in there when he thinks everybody is asleep. They did it, I'm sure. Have you ever done it?"

"Mercy, you shouldn't go around talking like that!"

Mercy just laughed. "If we were engaged, do you think we would make the marriage before we actually got married? Would you want that?"

"We'd better get back inside," Josiah declared. "You are getting far too carried away."

"I know, I know," she said, "well-brought up young ladies like me aren't supposed to say things like that, or even know about them." She crossed her arms. "Well, I'm different. Is that so bad?"

"No, in fact that is what I like about you."

They walked back toward the Willingham House. "Can I come around April 1? To stay with you, I mean."

"I think that will be all right. April is usually a pretty quiet month, nothing much ever happens in April," he declared, not knowing how wrong he was.

CHAPTER 6
BANASTRE TARLETON

As usual, Lieutenant Banastre Tarleton was winning at cards. Hugo couldn't help but marvel at the man's amazing luck. He always seemed to be dealt a good hand, and he knew how to play his cards perfectly. As the pile of coins and banknotes in front of Tarleton grew and grew, Hugo leaned closer and said in a low voice, "How do you do it, Ban?"

"I'm a born winner," Tarleton replied nonchalantly, using his long fingers to rake in his winnings.

He spoke matter-of-factly, not in a boastful manner but more as a simple declaration of truth. "This is who I am," Tarleton seemed to be saying. Tarleton always won, no matter what he did. Losing never entered his mind.

Hugo did not have the passion for card-playing and gambling that characterized his fellow officers. In London he had gone to fashionable clubs like White's on Chesterfield Street because it was expected of rising young officers, a way to meet the right people and make the kind of connections that would be useful in your career. Hugo was ambitious. He wanted to be a general someday. He wanted to command armies at war. But he did not enjoy gambling, and so he played cautiously, making small bets and folding his cards early rather than take a chance on what seemed a losing hand.

Tonight they were at the Plymouth Club, a popular establishment among the British officers in Boston and the Loyalists with whom they socialized. General Gage seldom gambled or went out anymore, but Lord Hugh Percy, his second in command, could sometimes be seen at the

Plymouth Club, playing cards or having a drink, accompanied by his wife, the beautiful Lady Anne Crichton-Stuart.

During the short time he had been in Boston Tarleton had come to be known as a force to be reckoned with. There was an air of danger about him—one of the reasons Hugo enjoyed his company. You never knew what Tarleton would do next, or why he would do it. He was always ready to take a risk, whether it was in a card game where he bet everything he had on a single hand, or in pursuing a woman he wanted even when it could end in a tragedy, like the affair in London that had climaxed with a man being killed. Banastre Tarleton seemed to court danger.

His recent encounter with the hated Town Watch only added to his growing stature with his fellow officers. As the conversation at the table turned to the situation in the city they all looked at Tarleton with admiration.

"At least we've got one man here who's not afraid to stand up to those Town Watch scallywags," said Major Vickers. "I give you Lieutenant Banastre Tarleton."

Tarleton took the compliment graciously. "Next time one of those swine tries to arrest me he's going to get more than a shoulder wound," he promised, and there was more acclaim for him around the table.

"One of our boys got hit with a rock today," said Captain McKenzie. "Damn near put his eye out."

"Did they catch the wastrel who threw it?" asked Hugo.

"Not a chance, he ran down an alley," said McKenzie. "One of those Watchmen scallies was there, and he didn't do a thing."

"Get this," said Jeremy Light. "A chap got a chamber pot dumped on him. Some damned Boston woman. Pretended it was an accident. Accident my ass."

"There's no end to it, is there?" said Vickers. "Too bad we don't have someone in command who cares about his men."

Among the younger officers it was a given that General Gage was too soft on the Boston civilians. Many placed the blame for this on his American wife, Margaret Kemble.

"I say, Chamberlain, just who is that exquisite creature over there?" Tarleton said sotto voce, looking in the direction of a young woman and her husband who had come into the club.

"Wait—I remember her—that's Mrs. Dinwiddie."

"So she has a husband. So much the better. Is that the joker?"

"Yes, that's him." Hugo gestured toward a pudgy, middle-aged man who stood talking with several other Tories.

"That old puff guts?" Tarleton exclaimed.

"He is Mr. Ebenezer Dinwiddie," Hugo explained. "His wife, Caroline, is one of New England's great beauties."

"Just look at those nice ones."

"Mr. Dinwiddie fought with us in the war with the French," Hugo said.

"I shouldn't care if he rescued the King from the worst pirates in the Caribbean, I would still like to get to know his wife," said Tarleton, winning another hand.

It was past midnight when the game broke up. Tarleton pocketed his winnings, and his face took on an expression Hugo had come to know well: Trouble was looming. When Tarleton combined drinking with winning at cards he became even more dangerous, for he felt there was nothing he couldn't get away with.

They went out into the cold night air. Tarleton threw his arms out expansively and looked up at the bright moon above. "Look at that, Chamberlain," he said. "It's as if heaven itself is smiling down on me, Banastre Tarleton, soldier, sinner, and the happiest creature on earth. What does the future hold for me? Wealth, promotion, more women?" He laughed, then jumped onto a knee-high brick wall, sliding his feet along it, keeping his balance perfectly, stopping only when he came upon a group of officers and civilians who were standing in a circle and talking. When Tarleton saw this group included Mr. and Mrs. Dinwiddie he jumped off and barged into the midst of them. Hugo followed, his sense of foreboding growing.

The Dinwiddies recalled Hugo from his earlier life in Boston. "And who have we here?" said Mr. Dinwiddie, his face in a broad smile as he extended his small plump hand toward Tarleton. "Always happy to meet one of our brave chaps in uniform."

"You have here someone who doesn't believe you are really happy to meet him," said Tarleton. "I'm not sure any colonial is truly happy to meet a British officer these days. But I am willing to be civil for form's sake and so I can meet your lovely wife." He smiled handsomely and bowed to Caroline

Dinwiddie, who, like her husband, did not know how to respond to Tarleton's comments.

"Have you been in Boston long, Lieutenant?" she asked.

"Long enough to learn that there are a great many beautiful women in Boston. That is this benighted town's only saving grace," said Tarleton.

"Perhaps if you remain here long enough you'll see that our city has a great deal to offer," said Mr. Dinwiddie good-humoredly, "and you'll change your opinion."

"Nothing will ever change my opinion of these colonies," said Tarleton. "Only the beauty of its women, like your wife, save them from being the provincial cesspools they are said to be." He smiled again and openly stared at Mrs. Dinwiddie's opulent breasts. "Lovely," he said.

Mrs. Dinwiddie drew away and covered herself. "Really, sir," said Mr. Dinwiddie.

"Lieutenant Tarleton did not mean that the way it came out," said Major Vickers.

With a flicker of his eyes he signaled to Hugo that it was time to get Tarleton out of there; he too could sense trouble coming. But Tarleton continued to leer openly at Mrs. Dinwiddie.

"I wonder what she looks like naked?" he said to Hugo. "No doubt your husband isn't up to the task of taking care of you the way he should. That is a job I would be happy to take on, if you'll let me, as I'm sure you will."

"Sir, you go too far," said Mr. Dinwiddie.

"Sir, I go where I please," said Tarleton mockingly.

Tarleton was so full of himself that it never occurred to him that old Mr. Dinwiddie might take exception to what he said. But Mr. Dinwiddie had fought both the Indians and the French, and he had learned that in order to live among men it was sometimes necessary to draw a line that you didn't allow other men to cross. He carried a heavy hickory walking stick, and he now lashed out with it so that it struck Tarleton on the left side of his face just slightly above his eye. The blow knocked off his hat and opened a large gash above his eye. As Mr. Dinwiddie raised his stick to strike again Hugo and Major Vickers tried to get between him and Tarleton, who had by now drawn his sword and was screaming with outrage. As the scuffle continued four members of the Town Watch appeared, as if by magic, and drove themselves like a human wedge between the combatants. They had seen Mr.

Dinwiddie strike Tarleton and seen Tarleton draw his sword, and now they stood between the Dinwiddie's and the British officers.

Tarleton was a raging fiend. Sword in hand, he was determined to repay blood for blood, and he lunged forward. His intended victim was Mr. Dinwiddie, but he stood safely behind one of the constables, and the sword-thrust merely hit the Watchman's heavy coat and did no damage. The constable struck at Tarleton with his billhook, hitting him in the same place Mr. Dinwiddie's walking stick had landed, deepening the wound and causing Tarleton to cry out in pain. Just at that moment Captain James Gore, on patrol with a squad of soldiers, appeared.

Captain Gore harbored an especial dislike of the Town Watch, having clashed with them many times in the past. He had no use for Americans. Surveying the scene he saw three British officers being menaced by four husky constables. "Forward, men!" he shouted, and eight British regulars forced their way between the officers, the constables, and Mr. and Mrs. Dinwiddie. Gore saw only one way to deal with this. "Order arms!" he shouted, and eight muskets were pointed at the constables and the Dinwiddies.

Captain Gore was known as a man prone to acting hastily, and he was seconds away from giving the command to fire. "Make ready," he ordered, and in the still night air everyone heard the frightening sound of the muskets being cocked. This was more than even Tarleton had counted on, and with one hand to the side of this head and blood running down his face he called out, "Just a moment now Captain," and as Gore ordered "Take aim!" Hugo was already seeing the bodies of the constables and the Dinwiddies lying dead on the cobblestones. But now came another voice, loud and commanding. "Lower your weapons!" Lord Percy stood in the midst of the fracas like an apparition. Tall, reedy, humorless, he spoke with the voice of a man whose words were always obeyed. "I said stand down, soldiers!" he repeated. He and his wife had been about to leave the Plymouth Club when he was told there was an ugly incident in the making outside, and he had hurried out just in time to stop it. "What in God's name is going on here?" he shouted. "Sheath that sword!" he said to Tarleton.

He took the situation in at a glance: He saw the gash on Tarleton's face and the angry looks of the soldiers. He saw the frightened expression of the Dinwiddies and the defiant looks of the constables. "All of you back to quarters, now!" he ordered. "You should all go home," he said to the Dinwiddies and the Town Watch, and in spite of the cold he wiped a bead of perspiration away, knowing that only by seconds he had prevented another Boston Massacre.

•   •   •

"I will send you back to England in irons if you ever do anything like that again!" General Gage roared. "Do you understand me, Lieutenant?"

Tarleton, his head encircled with a bandage, stood rigidly at attention. Hugo, standing nearby, listened as Gage gave Tarleton the worst tongue-lashing he had ever heard. Silently he prayed that Tarleton would take it and not say anything that would get him into more trouble.

"First you wound one of the Town Watch. I was willing to overlook that. Then you try to kill a Boston civilian, as loyal as any man in the colonies," Gage went on.

"General, the man did hit him," Hugo pointed out timorously.

"I'd have hit him myself if he said that to my wife," Gage snapped. "Just so you know I mean what I say, from now on no British officer or enlisted many will carry sidearms when he is off duty. Do you understand?"

"Yes sir," Tarleton said sullenly.

"Get out," Gage said.

Tarleton was dismissed, but the affair left him bitter. It fed his already burgeoning dislike of Americans, whether they were Tories, Patriots, or neutral, and the scar on the side of his face was a daily reminder of what he saw as a terrible injustice done to himself. When the time came, he told Hugo, he would settle the score. Hugo had no doubt he meant what he said.

CHAPTER 7
MERCY WILLINGHAM

It was late in the afternoon when the carriage containing Mercy Willingham arrived in front of Hartford Manor. The Hartfords came outside to greet her and there was a great deal of hugging and kissing and cries of happiness. While Elias, assisted by Alice, carried Mercy's luggage inside—it required several trips—and into one of the guest rooms on the third floor, everyone went to the drawing room and sat down.

"It's so nice to be back here," said Mercy. She had greeted everyone with her usual enthusiasm but had given Josiah an especially long and ardent embrace, and while Mercy was unaware of it, Alice had seen this with dismay. Once Mercy's things had been brought in she returned to her task of dusting the chandeliers in the drawing room, all the while casting furtive glances at Mercy and then at Josiah. "The Hartford men are all so handsome," Mercy said, "but you take the cake, Josiah," and the look on Alice's face grew even deeper when Mercy added, "a regular Adonis, you are.

"And speaking of the Hartford men," Mercy went on, "I don't see Walter."

"He promised to be here later," said Martha. "He said he had something to do in the city."

"Something secret," said Benjamin. "He's very mysterious these days."

"We think he might have a girl he's been seeing," said Jessica, laughing. "But he won't admit it."

"What's this?" Mercy said, getting up and going to a marble statue that sat near the piano and close to the big window that overlooked the harbor. "Is this a statue of Aphrodite?"

"It's new," said Martha. "Benjamin saw it in a shop near Long Wharf."

"The goddess of love," said Mercy. "I always liked her the best."

"A house can always use more love," said Benjamin.

"Love is something the Hartford house never lacks," Mercy declared. "Father and Mother send their regards. Patrick said to say hello to everyone too."

"How is Patrick?" asked Martha. "He isn't homesick?"

"Heavens no!" said Mercy. "He and Scotty spend all day together talking about geometry, the value of pi, and Pythagoras. They also watch the militiamen. They're drilling every day, marching about, left-right left-right. When they aren't drilling they're digging holes and burying boxes of muskets, kegs of gunpowder—why, I even saw them rolling a brass cannon down the street. A cannon! They say they took it out to old Mr. Barrett's farm, two miles out of town. People are putting bags of beans and sacks of flour in their basements, just like they were getting ready for the Siege of Troy. Mr. Hancock and Mr. Adams both think the fighting is going to start soon. I think Mr. Adams wants it more than Mr. Hancock, although Mr. Hancock says if the rebels form a real army he wants to be its commander. But I hope there isn't any war."

"Is there going to be a war?" asked Anne. "What will happen if there is?"

"There won't be any war," Martha said reassuringly. "Don't worry about it, child."

"Why do people have to fight wars anyway?" asked Jessica. "Such a waste."

"I think Elias has brought all your baggage in," Martha said. "Perhaps you'd like to go and rest and freshen up after your trip."

"I would," said Mercy.

"I'll come up with you," said Jessica, and they went up the stairs to the second floor, arm in arm.

"Who's that girl cleaning the chandeliers?" asked Mercy. "I haven't seen her before."

"That is Alice, the new maid," said Jessica.

"She's pretty. Just look at that red hair," Mercy said. Alice wore a maid's uniform that included a white bonnet, but her hair spilled out onto her shoulders and down her back. "Josiah hasn't taken a fancy to any Boston girls, has he?"

"You are so set on getting him, aren't you?" Jessica teased.

"I think he and I could be very happy," Mercy declared.

•   •   •

The Hartfords were delighted to have Mercy visit. Mercy, Jessica, and Anne spent their days talking, laughing, and playing games. Jessica played the piano and they all sang "The White Cockade," "Barbara Allen," and "Over the Fields and Far Away." In the evenings everyone gathered in the drawing room to sing and dance. Jessica played *Aupres de ma Blonde* and everyone sang "Drink To Me Only With Thine Eyes."

Only Alice was not happy about Mercy's stay with the Hartfords. She sensed why Mercy had come, and she resented her from the moment she arrived. But she kept her feelings private, and contented herself with giving Mercy angry, envious glances when she thought Mercy wasn't watching her.

Mercy had come because she enjoyed being with the Hartfords but also because she wanted to be near Josiah. Everyone realized she was intent on getting him to propose to her.

To her disappointment, Josiah did not propose and while they did spend a great deal of time together it was not as much as Mercy had wanted. Having told Benjamin that he would take over the shipyard, Josiah spent his days with his father either in Benjamin's study at Hartford Manor or else at the shipyard itself, "learning the ropes," as the sailors said when a new hand came aboard a ship. He also spent a great deal of time with Charles Waite, who was handling more and more of the company's business and legal matters, and doing it well, according to Benjamin.

Shipbuilding had complexities and nuances he had never thought of, and the fact that his father, a self-educated man, had mastered them all, increased his admiration for Benjamin tenfold. He had always revered his father, but as he began to understand just how difficult it was to build a ship from start to finish, did he for the first time realize how special and talented a man Benjamin Hartford was.

"Your father amazes me," Charles Waite said to him one day as they walked the shipyard. "He can tell you the name of every man who works here, what his job is, and what that job consists of. He can tell you what kind of tools they use, how long it should take them to complete a task, and whether the man should be given more responsibilities, for your father is always watching the men to see what their potential might be."

"That's something he's always believed in," said Josiah, "that people should try to live up to the best of themselves, and that you should help them achieve that, if you can."

They paused beside a ship that was nearing the end of the building process. It faced the water, and was held at an angle by an enormous wooden frame. Men scurried about on the top deck, climbing the masts, and from inside Josiah could hear men working too: hammering, sawing, and drilling with long bits. Men scampered up and down the wooden ladders that lined both sides of the ship. Other men hammered wooden dowels and iron nails into place.

"Your father is a very shrewd man of business," said Charles. "I know, because I've drawn up many of his contracts. He'll build a ship for a trader like John Hancock or Mr. Jessup Willingham, and charge less for it than another builder would, but in return he gets a per centage of the profits the ship makes for the entire life of the ship. And since a ship can last twenty years or more, that comes to a lot of money. That's one of the reasons your family is so wealthy."

"Amazing," Josiah said, with a shake of his head. "I would never have thought of that. I wonder how good a business man I'm going to be."

"Did you know that last year your father built a brig for Hancock, who ordered it painted in the brightest colors possible and named it the *Undutied Tea*?" asked Charles.

"Quite a sense of humor has our Mr. Hancock," Josiah observed. "He also likes to live dangerously. That's the kind of thing that infuriates our British friends. But yes, I knew about it. There was a huge celebration when it was launched."

"You didn't attend?"

"No, I was still away at school."

The launching of a ship was accompanied by a celebration in which the new owner provided free drinks and food for the men who had worked on the ship and their families, and the traditional silver or porcelain bowl was presented. Hancock, however, had to go this one better when the *Undutied Tea* was launched, and he gave Benjamin a golden bowl that now sat prominently in his office. It contained not only a reproduction of the ship but also John Hancock's famously large signature, which he liked to affix to everything he signed.

Charles came to Hartford Manor as often as he could, ostensibly to see either Benjamin or Josiah, but he actually wanted to see Anne as well, and contrived whenever possible to be around in the early evening so he would be invited to stay and have dinner. Soon everyone except Benjamin knew what was going on.

"Josiah," Charles said, "you know how Anne and I feel about each other."

"Of course. I caught you kissing her, didn't I?"

"And you approve?"

"Sure I approve. I told you, remember?"

"But what will your mother and father say?" Charles asked anxiously.

"I'm sure they'll be very happy. You're a fine fellow with a bright future. You'll make Anne an excellent husband."

"But I have no family. I'm an orphan. I have no social standing. Do you think that will matter to them?"

"They won't care about that. You made it on your own, with no help from anyone, just as my father did. They admire that. This isn't England or Europe. All they will care about is what you are, not where you come from. Now, when are you going to speak to my father? You'd best get to it soon."

"I will," he promised. Then he asked, "What about you and Mercy? Maybe we could get married at the same time. A double wedding! Everyone loves those."

"Now it's my turn to procrastinate," said Josiah.

"Aren't you going to marry her?"

"I don't know."

"You've been spending a lot of time together," Charles declared. "You know what everyone is saying."

Charles was right about that. Josiah and Mercy took walks around Beacon Hill and went riding across the Neck and over to Roxbury, then around to Bunker and Breed's Hill, overlooking Charlestown and the harbor.

Everyone assumed they would announce their engagement soon. But Josiah hesitated. Mercy's kiss, when they had been in Concord, felt like a promise of delights to come, delights like those he had known with Alice, but that also made him feel uneasy.

Alice heard the talk of the expected engagement and it made her resentment of Mercy even more pronounced. Although she tried her best to keep her feelings private, it wasn't long before Mercy realized Alice didn't like her.

"I don't like the way that girl looks at me," Mercy said to Jessica and Anne. "She makes me uncomfortable."

"You mean Alice?"

"She looks as if she'd like to step on me," said Mercy.

"She's normally quiet, and pleasant to be around," said Anne, sounding puzzled.

"Where did she come from?"

"Ireland. Her family sent her over here as an indentured servant. I gather they are very poor," said Jessica.

"How did she come to be a maid here?

"Her family 'sold' her for a few pounds—they kept the money—and put her on a ship for Boston. She was supposed to be working as a servant in a tavern called The Crow's Nest, but they really had something else in mind for a young girl like her."

"You mean, they were going to make her into a prostitute?" asked Mercy in a hushed tone.

"Yes, and I'm told some very bad things happened to her. So she ran away, with no place to go, in the midst of a Boston winter. Elias found her half-frozen in the stable one morning. Mother decided to give her a job as a maid.

"She really isn't a very good maid, but she tries hard and Maureen says she's a big help in the kitchen. So here she is."

"What a story," said Mercy. "That poor girl. But what would she have against me?"

"I think I know," said Jessica. "There's a certain someone she admires, the same young man you went riding with today."

Jessica laughed, and so did Anne. But Mercy said, "She'll have to get over that, won't she?" in a determined tone.

•   •   •

Josiah knew perfectly well that everyone in the household was expecting him to propose to Mercy. But her visit was causing him to experience some conflicting feelings he had never felt before.

Josiah kept telling himself that what he was doing with Alice was wrong, and every time she left his room after one of her late-night visits he told himself he would not do this again. But when she came back the next time and pressed her body up against his and he felt his own body responding all of his resolve melted away like snow in the hot sun, and he did what he told himself he would never do again.

He also lived in continual fear that someone else in the house was going to find out what was going on. And Alice seemed to be getting bolder, more brazen, since Mercy came to stay. Josiah did not know why that should be, but it was, and he feared she was going to do something that would give them away.

"Why do you like that girl?" Alice asked.

"Mercy?"

"The one who's visiting."

"I don't like her any better than anyone else," he maintained.

They were lying together in his bed, her head resting on his shoulder.

"She certainly likes you," Alice declared.

"What makes you say that?"

"I've seen how she looks at you. I know what those looks mean. She's in love with you."

Josiah knew he could not deny this, so he didn't say anything, and kept hoping Alice would drop the subject. But Alice was persistent.

"Have you known her a long time?" she asked.

"Our families grew up together. We were together all the time when we were children. Then they left Boston and moved to Concord last year."

"I wish she'd go back to Concord," Alice declared.

"You better go," said Josiah. "Go back to your room."

"Are you mad at me?"

"No, but it's late."

"Josiah. I love you."

"It's still late," he insisted.

Alice dressed quickly, lit a candle, and left Josiah's room. She was able to move about the house quietly in her bare feet and she used the backstairs. But the guest rooms were on the 3rd floor, and Mercy, who had not been able to sleep, was looking out one of the tall windows at the flickering lights of the city and the harbor. When she saw Alice coming down the stairs she was startled, and looked at her keenly, as if to make sure she wasn't a ghost.

"What are you doing?" asked Mercy in a loud whisper. "Why were you up there?"

"I wasn't doing anything," Alice said evasively. "I couldn't sleep."

"So, you just get up and wander about when you can't sleep?" asked Mercy.

"I've got as much right to be up here as you do," Alice said defiantly.

"They tell me you came here from Ireland," said Mercy. "That must have been hard for you."

"What do you care?" asked Alice.

"I shouldn't like to have to do that," said Mercy. "Leaving my home and family behind."

"My family didn't want me, so they sold me and sent me here."

"I'm sorry," said Mercy. "That must be horrible. I can't imagine."

"I'm sure you can't imagine. Now if you don't mind, and if you don't have any more questions for me, I'd like to go to bed."

"Of course," said Mercy. "I couldn't sleep, and it's nice to have someone to talk to."

"Why couldn't you sleep?" asked Alice, pausing. "What's bothering you?"

"I don't know, I guess it's all this talk of war. Doesn't it bother you?"

"The Hartfords are the only people in the world who have ever been kind to me," said Alice. "They took me in when I had no place to go, and they treat me as if they really care for me. So all I'm worried about is what could happen to them if there is a war. Back home I saw what the *Sassenach* can do. I don't want them to do that to the Hartfords."

"The Hartfords are wonderful people," Mercy agreed. "How did it happen that you didn't have anywhere to go? I'm sorry, I'm not trying to be nosy, it's just that—I'd like to be your friend."

"I'll tell you sometime. For now I'll just say I would prefer to have no place to go rather than be raped over and over. You've never had a man force himself on you, have you?"

"Heavens no!" Mercy said in horror. "How awful!"

"You have no idea how awful. Now, good night," Alice said, and Mercy watched as Alice, her red hair a stark contrast to her white nightgown, went along the hallway and disappeared down the stairs.

Josiah had heard every word. He had followed Alice, just to make sure she returned to her room, and he stopped on the stairway above when he heard her start talking to Mercy. Now he turned to return to his own room, but Mercy saw him, and she called out softly, "Doesn't anyone sleep in this house?"

"What are you doing up?" Josiah asked. "Why aren't you sleeping?"

"I was trying to make friends with your maid. She doesn't like me. She was upstairs, but she wouldn't tell me what she was doing."

"She's restless," said Josiah, hoping that Mercy wouldn't put two and two together.

"I feel restless too. I don't know what's going to happen. No one knows, except God. Do you believe in God, Josiah?"

"I'm not sure. I'm either a deist or an agnostic. Sometimes I think I'm one, then I think I'm the other."

"I know what an agnostic is. It's someone who doubts whether God exists or not. But what is a deist?"

"A deist thinks that there is a God or a Supreme Creator but doesn't believe He intervenes in our daily life on earth."

"Perhaps you could tell me more about it, sometime when it isn't the middle of the night," Mercy said playfully. "What was Alice doing? It looked like she was coming down from the fourth floor."

"Why don't you go back to bed," said Josiah.

"We're not even married yet and you're already bossing me around," said Mercy. "I think I will go back to bed, but not because you told me to, Josiah Hartford!"

Josiah went back up the stairs. He felt tired and ready for sleep when he heard footsteps coming his way. He turned and saw that it was Walter, walking softly but fully dressed. Mercy saw him too. "Funny things go on in this house at night," she said, and then went to her room.

"It's late," Josiah observed as Walter entered his room and carefully closed the door. "What have you been doing? Another of your spying missions for Paul Revere?"

"The British are going to strike very soon," said Walter. "Gage just relieved the flanking companies of all duties."

"What does that signify?" said Josiah. Hugo had told him that in the British Army each regiment had what were known as "flanking companies," one of grenadiers, one of light infantry, specially chosen men who guarded the flanks as the regiment advanced into battle. This was a great honor, Hugo had said, and these men were considered elite soldiers.

"It means he has a special assignment in mind for them, and they have to be ready to move out on short notice. Small boats are being collected in the harbor too, the kind that can be used for ferrying troops. The British are saying they are being repaired and repainted but we know better. Mr. Revere is certain they'll be coming across the bay and then through Charlestown Neck. He got that from old Mr. Dinwiddie, who joined our cause after what happened with his wife. If they come by sea, two lanterns are going to be hung in the belfry of the Old North Church. If they come by land, through Boston Neck, one lantern will be hung there. Mr. Revere is certain they'll be going by sea."

"What if they move out during the day?" asked Josiah.

"They won't. They want to keep it secret."

"Once they march, where are they going?"

"That's what we don't know yet. Our contacts inside Gage's headquarters tell us he hasn't decided yet."

"You've got blood on your hands, and your face too," Josiah observed in the candlelight. Anxiously he inspected his brother's face for any sign of damage, like a black eye or a swollen lip, evidence that had to be kept from Benjamin and Martha, but seeing none, he said, "I suppose you've been fighting again."

"I hate these Tories," said Walter, "more than the British. Traitors! We found out some of them were in the city, the same ones who signed up with Ruggles' Loyal Association and told the British where our stores were hidden in Salem. We beat the hell out of them." He rubbed his bruised knuckles with an air of satisfaction. Walter was broad-shouldered and strong, and Josiah imagined he could hit someone and make it hurt.

Even though he tried to stay out of the politics of the city Josiah knew what his brother was referring to. An outspoken Tory leader named Timothy Ruggles had been traveling up and down the coast of Massachusetts, attempting to form "Loyal Associations" as a counter to the Sons of Liberty, and even though their numbers were small, to Walter and the other Patriots even one was intolerable. These people swore an oath that they would be loyal to the King and that they would oppose the Patriots even unto death. In February members of the Salem Loyal Association had informed Gage that the Salem Militia had several brass cannons and some muskets stored in the village. Gage had sent a small detachment of soldiers to seize and destroy those supplies, but the people of Salem had gotten word that the troops were on their way and the Patriots of the town turned out to stop them. As the word spread, militia men from the nearby towns had come, armed with their muskets and ready to fight. But neither side was anxious to fire the first shot, and so after a tense stand-off involving some name calling and rock throwing the British had turned back and returned to Boston. It was a clear- cut victory for the Patriots, but the fact that fellow Americans had revealed where the supplies were hidden left a bitter taste in the mouths of men like Walter. They had vowed vengeance, and the blood on Walter's face and the bruises on his hands attested to that.

"You think fighting is going to solve anything?" said Josiah. "It will only create more enemies, more bitterness."

"There's no other way," insisted Walter.

"I refuse to accept that."

"Oh, here we go," said Walter. "You're going to tell me that in a war, any war, both sides are the same, equally responsible, and so you regard them with equal contempt."

"We are living in the 18th Century," said Josiah. "A time of enlightenment. Do you know how many wars have been fought since this century began? There was the War of the Spanish Succession. There was Queen Anne's War, there was the war between Russia and Sweden, and the French and Indian War. None of them proved a thing. So how is what is going on in Boston today any different from all these others?"

"We have a country to fight for!" Walter said fiercely. "Can't you see what is happening?"

"All I can see is that my younger brother is becoming an accomplished street brawler."

Walter got up to leave, then said, "I thought I saw Alice coming down the stairs when I came in. What was she doing up here?"

"I don't know, perhaps she couldn't sleep."

"I saw Mercy was up also and they were talking. What were they doing?"

"Maybe they're planning a revolution," said Josiah, and with a short laugh Walter went out of his room and closed the door.

CHAPTER 8
THE ALEHOUSE

The soldiers in Boston were becoming more aggressive every day. Josiah felt it each time he encountered a squad of redcoats patrolling the streets: Their provocative swagger, the belligerent way they looked at anyone who crossed their path, the way they handled their muskets—these were men out for trouble.

Stories of British soldiers mistreating Bostonians were heard everywhere. Walter repeated them to Josiah daily: A squad of British soldiers had beaten up some out-of- work young men on suspicion of being Sons of Liberty spies, women were subjected to insulting language, soldiers robbed civilians at gunpoint. Josiah, always the skeptic, inquired as to how many of these incidents Walter had seen for himself, and how many could be verified. Few could, and Walter admitted that what he had seen was not all that serious, just some pushing and name calling, and it wasn't clear who started it. The soldiers were notorious for leering at Boston women and making lewd comments to them, but the American women had no trouble giving it right back.

So while he remained skeptical, Josiah could see the change in the soldiers' attitude. Their faces were grim, and he sensed that it would not take much provocation for them to use their weapons.

He saw little of Hugo. He had, at Hugo's invitation, had a cup of wine with him at a disreputable tavern called "The Crow's Nest," but he had always left after a few moments, not wanting to hear any more about how the British soldiers were going to thrash the rebels of Boston when the time came and how God intended the British Empire to rule the world. He did not like what his friend had become, and he preferred to keep memories of their former friendship alive and not pollute them with the way Hugo had changed.

There was so much to running the shipyard that at times he thought his head would explode. Josiah could not help but see the irony of this. He, who had always looked down on "business" as a refuge for second rate minds, was discovering how wrong he was. As he went about the yard he began to understand that running it, and running it well, was going to be a challenge. Josiah had confidence in his intellectual abilities, and felt certain he could in time master it all. But whether he could ever master it as well as his father—of that he wasn't sure.

He wanted to learn from the ground up, where the process of building a ship started, where it ended, and everything in between. In what had been his father's office, he found plan after plan of the ships Benjamin had built, dating back to when the yard had originally been opened. There was a bust of Hadrian, whom he knew Benjamin admired, near the door, and a sign over the door proclaimed his father's motto: "The higher we are placed, the more humbly we should walk," a quote, he knew, from another Roman his father thought highly of, Cicero. On the walls were more ships' plans, as well as paintings of ships that Benjamin had built.

He watched the men as they worked, wanting to understand what each man did and how he did it. So many different trades were involved: Carpenters, ironworkers, blacksmiths, sailmakers, coopers, wheelwrights, shipwrights, tool makers, mast makers. Then there were all the tools these men used: calipers, mallets, chisels, axes, adzes, saws, hammers, squares. In one of the sheds a man turned wood, shaping it for use in the captain's cabin on one of the ships nearing completion, using a foot powered lathe. Josiah watched, fascinated, as the curls of wood broke off and fell to the floor, to be swept up by a boy of fourteen—an apprentice, he later learned, being taught the trade by a journeyman. The workers, soon understanding who he was, cast curious glances his way, wondering what he would do as the new master of the yard.

He was getting an education, much different from the one he'd gotten at Harvard. Soon he felt comfortable enough to start asking the men questions so he could better comprehend the work they were doing. One day he went aboard one of the ships that was about mid-way to completion. It was a merchantman, and he had memorized its dimensions and size: It had three masts and three decks, it was 141 feet, 8 inches long, 38 feet and 3 inches wide, had a hold 15 feet deep, and would weigh 878 tons when completed. He watched three shipwrights at work, and his attention was caught by what looked like three pieces of highly polished and finely hewn wood put together to form a pyramid. Inside hung a piece of thick cotton string, and at the end of the string was a pointed, cylindrical metal object. This dangled over a small round tin of water.

"Excuse me," said Josiah, "but what is this for?"

"Level," barked the oldest of the three men, the one who appeared to be in charge, for Josiah had seen him giving orders to the other two. He had a bristly gray beard, gnarled hands, and he did not look up from his work when Josiah spoke to him.

"Level?" Josiah parroted.

The gray beard didn't respond, so Josiah continued. "What is that at the end of the string hanging there?"

"Bob," said the man, still not looking up and obviously not happy about being bothered by this young Boston dandy.

"I didn't ask you its name," Josiah said, irritated at the man's uncooperativeness. "I want to know what it is."

"He means it's a plumb bob, that's what we calls it, sir," said another man, younger and friendlier, who quickly introduced himself as Willie. "We use it to keep things straight. A weighted cord or line hanging like that is always perpendicular to level, you see. And free-standing water is always level. Don't mind old Gordon, sir. He's just out of sorts today."

"And every other day too," put in the young man next to him, who said his name was Ruben. "Gordon the Grouch, we calls him."

"Who wouldn't be out of sorts," Gordon said in a raspy growl, "what with lobster backs all over the city and having to put up with lazy good-for-nothings like you all day long."

"Now you know what are his politics," said Willie.

"Don't forget who's master here," Gordon growled.

To Josiah's questioning look, Willie said, "Gordon's the master shipwright. Me and Ruben are just his mere journeymen. We were his apprentices once, though, weren't we Ruben?"

"That was our bad luck," said Ruben, who, like Willie, appeared to be in his twenties. "Gordon's the worst master in this whole yard. Wasps come to him for meanness lessons."

"Fools," said Gordon sullenly. "I taught you everything you know. Thirty year I been here. Now old Mr. Hartford is retired and his whippersnapper son is taking over. What does he know about building ships? They say he's a Harvard man, studied 'phil- os-ophy.' How is going to build ships with 'phil-os-ophy,' that's what I'd like to know. What's he going to do, check his philosophy book when it comes time to put the mizzen mast up?"

Josiah got the impression from the faces of Willie and Ruben that from Gordon a speech like this amounted to an oration. He laughed, just slightly and Willie said, "Gordon, I think that's the whippersnapper right there. Is that it, sir?"

"I'll have to look in my philosophy book to make sure," said Josiah, and with a wink he left to visit another part of the ship.

The next day he watched some of the carpenters who were busily sawing and pounding away on what would be the ships' galley. "What have you got there?" he asked one of them, a young man perhaps a few years older than he was.

"To make this fit right, this corner has got to be square," the carpenter said, and, using a strange-looking tool he called a "jack plane," he trimmed some wood away from the side of the piece he as working on. Once he was satisfied he reached into the pocket of his leather apron and took out a small ornately decorated tube that was attached to a flat piece of iron. He set this on one side, then on another. He looked at it closely, then put it back.

"What is that?" asked Josiah.

"This? Why, this is a spirit level," the man said. "One of my best tools. It's good for a quick check. For something bigger, like the ship's rail, I'd use this," and he removed, from his tool chest nearby a two foot long piece of red colored wood with the similar tubes cut into it and the same kind of bubbles moving around in them. He set it on the deck and pointed. The bubbles moved back and forth and then came to a stop. "See? This deck is perfectly level." He put the level away and then took what looked like two slats of wood joined together to form a 90 degree angle and placed it up against the corner of the wood he'd been working on. He looked at it closely, made some measurements with another wooden tool with marked graduations like a ruler on it, then took a slate and chalk and did some quick adding and multiplying. "Yep," he said, "perfect square."

"What was that you just did?" asked Josiah.

"Just a quick double check," said the carpenter. "We call it the 3-4-5 method. I measure three inches down here, see, and four inches this way. Then I draw a line across here. If this line here is five inches, end to end, then you know your side is as square as can be."

"The Pythagorean Theorem," Josiah smiled, thinking he would have to tell Patrick about this.

"The what?" asked the carpenter.

"Never mind," said Josiah. "What's your name?"

"Johnny Bishop," the man smiled, and put out a large grimy hand. Josiah, not wanting to seem snobbish, took it and tried his best not to show the discomfort he felt. "I'm the new chief carpenter of the yard," he said proudly.

"Congratulations, Mr. New Chief Carpenter," said Josiah. "My name is—"

"Oh, I know who you are," said Bishop. "You'd be young Mr. Hartford, the new yard master."

"Keep on with your good work," said Josiah, and he went about his way.

It was overwhelming, there was so much to learn. Josiah watched as the beams were cut with long saws operated by two men, one on either side, pushing and pulling back and forth until the beam was cut to the right length. Blacksmiths bent hot metal on their anvils, then shaped it by using hammers and long handled tongs. Nearby, coopers made barrels and put copper bands around the stays to hold them tight.

One evening his route home—he was walking—took him past a tavern called The Alehouse, not far from the waterfront. The sun was going down behind Charlestown Neck and from here he could see Breed's Hill and the higher Bunker Hill behind it, and he was thinking about Mercy and Alice and what he was learning at the shipyard when he heard someone call his name. The Alehouse was a favorite gathering place of the Patriots; both John Hancock and Samuel Adams had often been seen there before they left the city, and Dr. Warren, when he had time, was known to stop in and have a Sangaree, his favorite drink.

So Josiah was not surprised when he turned about and saw that it was Walter calling to him.

"What brings you out this way?" Walter asked. "Come inside, have a cup of wine."

"I can't," said Josiah.

"You can't? You have some pressing engagement somewhere with one of your British officer friends? Come on in for a little while."

•   •   •

The Alehouse was large, as taverns went, for it had a 2nd story with several bedrooms that enabled it to also function as an inn. The owner, a bald, roly-poly man known to all as Mr. Phillip, sometimes let these rooms out to people who were in need of a place to stay for the night or simply needed a room to use for what was politely known as a "rendezvous," usually an extra-marital affair or an assignation with a woman from Mount Whoredom.

But The Alehouse was a respectable place. It boasted the best ale in Massachusetts, but it was also well known for some other drinks favored by New Englanders, such as the "Flip," the "Stone Fence," and the "Rattle Skull"—concoctions of beer, wine, rum and whiskey that would test a person's courage as well as their taste for alcohol. The big main room had a high ceiling that reached the 2nd floor, with an interior balcony overlooking it. Enormous chandeliers hung from the ceiling. Below the balcony was a bar, where Mr. Phillip, his wife, and several tavern girls scurried back and forth when the tavern was busy.

There were around 20 people in the tavern. Josiah recognized some of them as men who worked in the shipyard. Gordon, the bad-tempered shipwright, was sitting at a table alone, looking as unhappy in the tavern as he did at his job. He sent one glance Josiah's way, gave no sign of recognition, then resumed his drinking. Josiah also saw Johnny Bishop, the carpenter, who waved in a friendly fashion, as well as others whose names he didn't know. Five men sat playing cards at a round table near the center of the room, including Gordon's co-workers Ruben and Willie; a small pile of banknotes and silver pieces lay in the center of the table. Next to the bar and beside the stairs that led to the 2nd floor three men sat, one playing a fiddle, another a flute, and the other a long- necked, oblonged-bodied guitar, earnestly rendering "Drink to Me Only With Thine Eyes."

"Drink to me only with thine eyes
And I will pledge with mine
Or leave a kiss within the cup
And I'll not ask for wine."

"Who's the gentleman you've got there, Hartford?" called out one of the gamblers, a bearded, scar-faced fellow. From his neck hung a Liberty Tree medallion.

"This is my brother, Josiah," Walter said.

"Bring him some ale," said the scar-faced man.

"My brother is a Harvard man, he'll have wine," said Walter.

"Wine for the gentleman, then," said the gambler.

Soon a blonde tavern girl with a chunky build and bad teeth that marred an otherwise pretty face, appeared with a bottle of wine and a glass on a tray. Johnny Bishop, at Walter's invitation, joined them, and the three of them sat at a small table near the front door and close by the gamblers.

"Who's the big-mouth?" Josiah asked.

"That's Quinlan. A toolmaker by trade. Don't mind him. He's been drinking and he's losing at cards, so he isn't happy."

"What's the main topic of conversation today?" asked Josiah.

"The British are going to march soon," said Walter.

"Everybody knows that," said Josiah.

"What we don't know is where they are going, Mr. Hartford," said Johnny. "Most everybody thinks it will be Lexington, but we aren't sure yet."

"We'll find out," Walter said confidently. "We'll know before the soldiers do."

"I hope you don't mind that some of us are involved with the Patriots movement, Mr. Hartford," said Johnny.

"Your politics are your business," said Josiah.

"We don't need Harvard men," said the scar-faced gambler, Quinlan, in a loud voice. "We need fighting men." He looked at Josiah belligerently.

"That leaves you out, don't it, Quinlan?" said Johnny. "You couldn't fight your way out of a feather bed."

"That would depend on who was in the bed with me," Quinlan said.

"Quinlan, there's ladies here," said Mr. Phillip, who had come out of the kitchen area behind the bar and walked over to the table where Quinlan and the other gamblers sat and stood in front of Quinlan. He held out his hand.

"Bugger all," said Quinlan. "The man thinks I owe him money."

"Pay up, Quinlan," said Mr. Phillip. "Or you won't get another drink, so help me."

"Take off, before I give you one in the gingamobs," said Quinlan sullenly.

"I'll cut yours off if you don't pay up," Mr. Phillip promised.

"All right, you old robber," Quinlan relented. He dug into his pocket and took out a silver piece, then tossed it to Mr. Phillip.

"About time," he said, going back to the kitchen.

"Are you going to play cards, or are you going to talk?" said one of the gamblers.

Quinlan looked at his cards, then, unhappy with what he saw, threw them down disgustedly. "Bollocks," he said, then put four more silver coins into the pile on the table. "You'd think King George himself was dealing my cards." He drained his glass of ale, wiped his mouth with the back of his hand, signaled to the chunky blonde tavern girl that he wanted more.

"I give a Tory a liberty coat last week," he boasted.

"You helped give a Tory a liberty coat," Johnny corrected. "Others were there too. Me, for instance."

Josiah knew what a "liberty coat" meant: It was the Patriots' term for tarring and feathering a Loyalist. Josiah had never seen a person tarred and feathered, nor did he want to. Warm, sometimes scalding, tar was poured onto the victim's body, followed by a bucket of white swan feathers that stuck to the tar. It was the Patriots' favorite way of punishing a Tory, and it was usually reserved for outspoken Loyalist leaders, but now stories were making the rounds that Tories and British soldiers were doing the same to Patriots.

"Well, I did most of the work," Quinlan insisted.

"Have you heard about the new "sheriff" of Boston?" Walter asked Josiah. "Sheriff?" said Josiah. "We've never had a sheriff before."

"He used to be the Mandamus Councilor of Roxbury," said Walter, "before the Liberty Boys there drove him and his wife out. Now he's settled in Boston, and Gage has made him sheriff over us."

Something flashed in Josiah's memory. "Is his name Loring? Joshua Loring?"

"How did you know?"

"I've heard about him. What is he supposed to do, as our sheriff?"

"Nobody knows what his official duties are, but what we keep hearing is that he is using his position to steal anything up to and even including a red-hot stove. He's already thrown several Patriots in jail, and says he won't let them out unless they can pay his price."

"Wouldn't I like to get my hands on him," said Quinlan, who had been eavesdropping on their conversation. "I'd show him a few things." Seeing the chunky tavern girl coming out with more drinks he called out, "Leezy! Sing your song!"

"I can't," Leezy said, smiling apologetically. "Mr. Phillip doesn't want me singing that song anymore."

"Oh, the hell with that old fool. Come on Leezy, sing!"

The other men now began clapping their hands and calling on the girl to sing. The men playing by the stairway stopped their song and they smiled too, and a moment later Mr. Phillip appeared.

"They want to hear me sing 'My Thing Is My Own,'" said Leezy.

"No," said Mr. Phillip, shaking his head. "That song is positively indecent."

"Oh, come on," said a woman sitting near the windows. "Let her sing it. I like the song."

Finally, Mr. Phillip relented. Leezy went and stood near the musicians.

"What is this song?" Josiah asked Walter, who, like the others, was smiling in anticipation.

"Wait till you hear it," he said.

The three musicians began playing a tune that was very similar to the Lillibulero.

After a few chords, Leezy began to sing:

"I, a tender young maid, have been courted by many
Of all sorts and trades as every was any
A spruce haberdasher first spoke to me fair
But I would have nothing to do with small ware.
My thing is my own, and I'll keep it so still
All other young lasses may do as they will
A sweet-scented courtier did give me a kiss
And promised me mountains if I would be his
But I'll not believe him, for it is too true
Some courtiers do promise much more than they do
A master of music came with intent
To give me a lesson on my instrument
I thanked him for nothing, but bid him be gone
A blunt Lieutenant surprised my packet
And fiercely began to rifle and sack it
I mustered my spirits up and became bold
And forced my Lieutenant to quit his strong hold
A fine dapper tailor, with a yard in his hand
Did proffer his service to be at command
He talked of a slit I had above knee
But I'll have no tailors to stitch it for me
Now here I could reckon a hundred and more
Besides all the gamesters recited before
That made their addresses in hopes of a snap
But as young as I was I understood trap
My thing is my own, I'll keep it so still
Until I be married, say men what they will."

The song came to an end with much applause and pounding on the wooden tables.

"Did you like that?" asked Walter.

"It is very risqué," said Josiah.

"The word around the tavern is that Leezy is not as hard to get as the girl in the song," said Walter.

"Are you speaking from experience?" Josiah asked.

"No, only what I've heard."

"Be careful with women like that," Josiah cautioned.

"I think you're the one who needs to be careful," said Walter. Does he know? Josiah wondered.

Now a man sitting near the door shouted, "Soldiers!" The music stopped playing and a moment later the front door bounced open as if kicked and a tall, gaunt British sergeant appeared, his ugly, pock-marked face drawn up in a sneer. He swaggered in, followed by six soldiers with muskets and fixed bayonets. After them came two more men, both in civilian clothes. One was around thirty, handsome and dark haired, and dressed as finely as Josiah and Walter. He wore an expensive-looking black coat and carried a black walking stick with a round gold knob in his hand. The other civilian Josiah estimated to be about ten years older, large and overweight, with an unpleasant, stubble-covered face that bore a scar that started on his cheek and ran all the way to his nose. He was dressed in the same kind of rough clothing worn by the men who worked in the shipyard. While the other civilian's face was bland and businesslike, his face had an eager expression to it, the porcine lips drawn into an expectant smile.

"What's this?" asked Josiah.

"Just some lobster backs. They come in every now and then to harass us. They won't stay long," Walter explained.

"Who are the other two?"

"Never saw them before." Walter sounded puzzled, as if this was not standard procedure.

"Tories, I'll wager," said Quinlan, scowling.

"Fan out," the sergeant said to the soldiers, and the soldiers began to slowly and deliberately walk through the tavern, giving everyone a belligerent stare. Some looked them back, eye for eye; others looked away.

"Why don't you just sit still, Quinlan?" Johnny Bishop advised. "Don't do anything foolish and get somebody killed."

"That's good advice, Quinlan," said Willie, the shipwright. Next to him Ruben, as well as the other gamblers, nodded in agreement. Quinlan was rubbing his big toolmaker's hands together as if trying to squeeze something flat.

While the soldiers stalked around the tavern, the sergeant with the pock-marked face and the civilian in the dark clothes stood near the front, talking and looking about. The other civilian, the scar-faced one, stood off to one side, as if awaiting orders.

Now a man who had been sitting at the bar, quietly drinking ale, got up and made as if to leave, but one of the soldiers stood in front of him, bayonet pointed at his throat.

"Where do you think you're going, Yankee?" asked the sergeant.

"My wife and children are waiting," the man said plaintively.

"Your whore and your brats can go on waiting," said the sergeant. "Get back over there where you were and stay there. Now, where's the owner of this dung-heap?"

Mr. Phillip came out of the kitchen, engaged in what seemed to be his unending wiping of his hands on his dirty-white apron.

"Here I am, sergeant," he said. "What is it this time?"

The sergeant and the two civilians came across the room and stood in front of Mr. Phillip. "You engaging in any illegal activities here, Mr. Phillip?" said the sergeant mockingly. "Any contraband here? Hiding any smugglers upstairs? In your basement? Hmm?"

"Answer is the same as last time, no," said Mr. Phillip wearily.

"You better be telling me the truth," said the sergeant.

Now the sergeant noticed the pile of coins and banknotes on the table where the card game had been going on. His eyes widened greedily.

"What's all this?" he asked.

"We're playing cards," said Quinlan.

"Where would a lazy jackanapes like you get this kind of money?"

"They work for it," said old Gordon, glaring at the sergeant over his glass of ale.

"How do I know you didn't steal it?"

"We're not thieves. We're honest men," said Quinlan.

"Unlike your common bloody back," Walter said loudly.

"Shut up," said Josiah, as the sergeant and another soldier shot him a murderous look. "You want to get yourself killed?"

There were hoots of derisive laughter following Walter's words. Among the patriots it was universally believed that British soldiers were all thieves or other criminals who had been forced to join the army rather than go to prison for their crimes. This was bitterly resented by the soldiers, and

Bostonians had long since discovered that a sure way to get under a British soldier's skin was to call him a thief or a jail bird.

"Easy does it sergeant," said the younger of the two civilians, placing a restraining hand on the sergeant's arm. Josiah now realized that he, rather than the sergeant, was directing this raid, and as the man stepped over to where Josiah and Walter sat and looked at them with piercing black eyes Josiah felt something akin to fear. He noticed that the coat the man wore not only cost a lot but was also brand new, as if he had gotten it from the tailor within the past day or so. The man's deep black eyes seemed unfathomable, and his face made Josiah think of a wolf. He then realized that what he felt was not fear as much as it was an instinctive revulsion. There was something evil about this man.

He looked first at Josiah, then at Walter. "What's your name, young dandy?" he asked Walter.

"Tell me yours, I'll tell you mine," said Walter defiantly.

"My name is Joshua Loring," the man said. "I'm the sheriff of Boston town."

"Talk about speak of the devil," said Walter, as Loring moved along.

"Who's the other, the big one?" asked Quinlan.

"That would be Cunningham, his deputy. He does the dirty work. Watch out for him."

"Everyone will line up over there, in front of the bar," said Loring, in a louder voice. "Right now."

"What is this?" asked Josiah.

"It's an order from your sheriff," the big, stubble faced man named Cunningham said. "Move it, you."

"Are we being arrested?"

"You will be if you give us any trouble," said Cunningham.

Josiah, Walter, Johnny Bishop, Willie, Ruben, even Quinlan rose reluctantly and began moving toward the bar, as did the other men and women in the tavern, as the soldiers menaced them with their bayonets. Only Gordon refused to move.

"Get over there," ordered Cunningham.

"Go to hell," said Gordon.

A soldier prodded him with his bayonet and Gordon sullenly rose to his feet.

Cunningham now produced a burlap bag and gave it to the sergeant. The sergeant eagerly scooped up the money that had been on the table where Quinlan and the others had been gambling and put it all into the bag.

"Hey," said Quinlan. "That's our money." The sergeant just smiled insolently at him.

"This is impounded as contraband until it can be determined who it legally belongs to," said Loring loudly. "Until then, it is the property of His Majesty's Government."

"Thieves," Quinlan spat.

The people were now lined up in a single row in front of the bar, the soldiers holding them at bay with their muskets. Loring, flanked by the pock-faced sergeant and Cunningham, spoke to the group.

"As the duly appointed Sheriff of Boston, I am conducting a search for stolen property and contraband," he said. "Each of you will show me whatever belongings you have with you. If they are yours legally you have nothing to fear. If not, they are going to be impounded until it can be determined who the rightful owner is."

There were angry shouts of protest from the people lined up. "This is robbery," said Josiah, unable, now, to contain himself. "You're nothing but common thieves. Is this what your king wants you to do?"

"Anyone who fails to cooperate will be placed under arrest and taken to jail," said Loring.

Loring, the pock-marked sergeant, and Cunningham started at one end of the line. Cunningham did little except stand and look menacing. The men emptied their pockets, the women their handbags. Loring looked at each item and if it appeared to have any value he would say, "Contraband," and it went into the burlap bag. If it was something worthless he would say, "Keep it," and it was returned. The soldiers kept their muskets leveled at the people all the while, their faces alert for any signs of trouble. They stopped in front of a nicely-dressed young woman and her husband. The sergeant looked at her closely. "You're very pretty," he said. "What are you doing here?"

"I'm here with my husband."

"Is that so? What's your name?"

"Charlotte."

"Charlotte what?"

"Charlotte of Mecklenburg."

The mention of the name of King George's wife brought laughter from the people lined up, but the soldiers frowned angrily and the sergeant's face took on a snakelike look. "You dare to mock our Queen," he snarled, moving closer to her. "Nice earrings. Where did you get them?"

"I gave them to her, sergeant, when we were married," said the man beside her.

"My girl had a pair just like them. Yes, I could swear they were identical. Then someone stole them."

"You mean there's a woman in Boston willing to be seen with you?" said Walter from further down the line.

"Stop it," said Josiah. "You'll get someone hurt this way."

The sergeant simply laughed unpleasantly, and kept his attention on the woman and her earrings.

"I bought those right here in Boston," her husband protested.

"You have a bill of sale?"

"Yes."

"Show me."

"You know damn well I wouldn't have it here," said the man.

"Take them off," Loring ordered, watching carefully as they went into the bag. They came to Walter and Josiah. "Empty out," said Loring.

"Why don't you go to hell, you Tory bastard," said Walter.

A soldier close by raised his musket. Loring smiled. Josiah produced the silver watch Benjamin had given him when he graduated from Harvard. "Contraband," said Loring. He also took the few shillings Walter had in his pocket.

"Take them and be damned," said Walter, tossing them into the bag.

"You never did tell me your name," said Loring.

"Walter Hartford," Walter said defiantly.

"Well, Walter Hartford, maybe we'll meet again someday," said Loring.

"Only if I don't see you first," Walter said.

Loring smiled again. With the sergeant holding the bag of loot, and the soldiers still pointing their muskets, Loring, with Cunningham as always close by, began backing out of the Alehouse. "Everyone better understand," Loring said, "that from now on there is going to be much more obedience to the King's Laws here in Boston, and I am going to make sure that happens. Disobedience is going to be punished severely. Spread the word."

The sergeant was the last one to leave. Holding up the bag, he said, "Thank you, Yankees! England and King George III forever!"

.   .   .

"Do you see now?" said Walter when they were outside the Alehouse. "Do you see why we have to fight? Do you see now why we hate them?"

"I find it difficult to hate," said Josiah," but I've never seen anything so horrible in my life."

"What do you think your friend Hugo would say?"

What would Hugo say? With all his talk of the glory of the Empire and the good that it did, what would he say if he saw what Josiah had seen today?

Then another thought came to him: Would he have to take a side soon, as Walter had said? After what he had seen today, that seemed more and more likely.

"Where are you going now?" said Josiah.

"Never mind, best if you don't know," said Walter.

CHAPTER 9
YANKEE DOODLE

Josiah, walking home from the Alehouse through the dark Boston streets, pulled his coat a little tighter and drew his hat further down on his head. The night was clear and cold, despite the signs of spring popping up everywhere.

The cold did not trouble him nearly as much as what he had just witnessed in the Alehouse. Those British soldiers, and the Americans who commanded them, had behaved like brutes from the Dark Ages. Was this the greatness Hugo spoke of? Was this how the British Empire spread civilization? Could his brother be right, that the British had to be fought with armed force, that there was no reasoning with them?

He was still near the waterfront when his thoughts were interrupted by loud, raucous singing and laughter. He looked up and saw a parade of torches, all of them carried by British soldiers. Drums were pounding, and the soldiers were lustily singing "Yankee Doodle."

"Yankee Doodle went to town
Riding on a pony
Stuck a feather in his cap
And called it macaroni."

"Make way, colonial," said a thickset soldier, who roughly shoved Josiah to one side to let the procession go past. "Make way, and look at what happens to rebel scum."

A small crowd of civilians followed on either side of the soldiers. A young woman with a tear-streaked face, holding a little boy by the hand, was at their head, all of them looking upward at a man who had been tarred and feathered and who was being carried on a rail held up by two of the soldiers. His hands and feet were tied with rope and the white feathers protruded grotesquely from his face and head. Two signs made of wood had been hung from his neck. The one in front had "American Liberty" written on it. The one in back read "Patriot!"

The soldiers stopped singing long enough to jeer, "How do you like your freedom now, rebel? You want your rights? Here are your rights!"

"Elizabeth," the man on the rail called to the woman with the child. "Elizabeth, take the boy away. I don't want him to see me like this!"

"No," the woman cried. "No, I won't leave you. Not while they're doing this to you."

"Please! You can't help me! Go. Please go!"

"Father!" cried the boy.

"Father!" mocked the soldiers. "See what happens to fathers like yours, boy?"

"Please go," the man said again.

Weeping, the woman turned to leave. Now Josiah saw two British officers bringing up the rear of the procession. They weren't singing but in the torchlight Josiah could see they were laughing at what they saw, and with a surge of horror he realized it was Hugo Chamberlain and Banastre Tarleton.

Josiah was about to speak to them when he saw a soldier grab the weeping woman by the arm.

"Don't go yet, Sweet Pie," said the soldier. "Give us a kiss first."

"Let go! Leave me alone!" the woman cried.

"Come on," said the soldier, "just one little kiss, it won't hurt." He grabbed at her more forcefully now, trying to pull her to him. As she cried out once more and the other redcoats laughed, Josiah seized the soldier by the neck threw him to the ground. The woman broke free and ran into the darkness. Another soldier struck at Josiah with the stock of his musket, missed, and as Josiah struggled with another soldier he saw muskets leveled at him, had a vague feeling they might shoot him, and then he heard Hugo's voice.

"Soldiers, stand down!" Hugo ordered. "Josiah, are you mad? You know what could happen to you for interfering with a British soldier?"

"Hugo, make them stop this!" Josiah cried.

"Simmer down, old man, simmer down. They're just having a little fun," said Tarleton.

"Are you out of your mind? Make them stop degrading that poor man. In front of his wife and son, so cruel! Make them stop!"

"Don't meddle in things you don't understand, Josiah," said Hugo, and Josiah now smelled whiskey on his breath, and the sadistic expression on his face made Josiah think of Lord Roger at his worst. "We have to keep order in the city."

"What's he done to merit treatment like that?"

"They say he threw a stone at a soldier," said Tarleton.

"They say! Who says? You saw this yourself?" When neither man answered Josiah went on, "Is this the King's justice you speak of?"

"Can you prove he didn't do it?" said Hugo.

The procession had done an about face and was going past them once more. The shadows bounced around in the torchlight. The soldiers had resumed singing "Yankee Doodle."

"Yankee Doodle keep it up
Yankee Doodle dandy
Mind the music and the step
And with the girls be handy."

As the procession went by again Tarleton and Hugo laughed once more. Tarleton especially seemed pleased at the man's degradation.

"We should've put his whore and his bastard up there with him," he said loudly, and Josiah was gripped with a rage he had never felt before. Never in his life had he felt such an intense desire to drive his fist into another man's face. With an involuntary shout of anger he shoved Hugo aside and backhanded Tarleton with all his might, then pushed him as hard as he could. Tarleton stumbled, fell to the ground, then leaped to his feet.

"I'll kill you if you ever do that again!" Tarleton screamed. He reached, instinctively, for his sword, but in reluctant compliance with General Gage's order that sidearms could not worn while off duty, he came away empty handed. He struggled with Hugo, who was holding him back.

"Ban, Ban, get out of here," Hugo was saying, and Tarleton, after threatening once again to kill Josiah, abruptly turned and walked away, his entire body shaking with fury.

"That was unwise, Josiah," said Hugo when Tarleton was safely out of sight. "You don't do that to a British officer. You want to get yourself into serious trouble? To the point where even I won't be able to help you?" He paused, as if thinking something over, then said, "Let me talk to you, Josiah. Come in here with me," he went on, gesturing toward a tavern on the other side of the street. "Let's have a cup of wine. Come-come-come," he said, pushing Josiah toward the tavern's entrance. A sign, "The Fife and Drum," hung over the door.

The tavern was loud, catering to rowdy British soldiers and sailors. Hugo steered Josiah toward a table in a far corner, out of the way of the drunken men who lurched from place to place, yelling obscene comments at the women who waited on them. "Come, sit, sit," said Hugo, and then with an arrogant gesture he called, "Wine!" to one of the serving women, a redhead who reminded Josiah of Alice.

"Well if it isn't the handsome Lieutenant Chamberlain," she said, brushing back her fiery red hair. "And who is this?" she asked, looking at Josiah. "Where is your usual companion, Lieutenant Light?"

"Do not get any funny ideas, Violet," Hugo said. "This is my good friend Mr. Josiah Hartford. He is a true Boston gentleman."

"Gentleman have one in the same place all the other men do," Violet said, raising her eyebrows knowingly. She put her hands on her hips and looked speculatively at Josiah. "Pleased to meet you, Mr. Hartford."

"Pleased to meet you," Josiah said uncomfortably. This woman, obviously a prostitute, made him uneasy. She stirred feelings he wanted to suppress, the same feelings he felt toward Alice. She seemed to be aware of this, for kept smiling at him as if she knew exactly what he was thinking.

"Stop gawking and get us some wine," Hugo ordered. Josiah watched her as she walked away. Hugo caught the look and smirked.

"You fancy her?" he asked. "Listen, I know you didn't like what you saw. I didn't like it either."

"You're lying," Josiah interjected. "You were enjoying it. So was Tarleton."

"Josiah, you must understand. Someone throws a rock at British soldiers, someone suffers the consequences. Point made."

"Your point. Their suffering."

"You make too much of a small incident," Hugo said, waving his hand dismissively, once again reminding Josiah of Lord Roger. "I admit it wasn't very nice. But the Sons of Violence do that to Loyalists all the time. It's only an eye for an eye. People must know they cannot defy the King. By making an example of that man, we discourage treason."

"Since when do two wrongs make a right?" Josiah retorted.

"Life is cruel, Josiah. Accept it."

Violet brought them a big bottle of red wine and two large cups. "Here we are boys," she said, speaking above the noise of the tavern. "The best we have. I imagine you're used to having the best of everything, aren't you, Mr. Hartford?"

"I told you not to get any ideas about him, Violet," Hugo said. He was already filling his cup with wine. "Now go away, and don't come back until I call you.

"You know," he went on, drinking wine, "if you would help me, we could put an end to all this unpleasantness." He spoke as if this was something he'd been thinking about for some time. To Josiah's puzzled expression he said, "If we knew more about what they're doing, what their plans are, where they've hidden their weapons, we could stop all this."

"What are you saying?"

"You could do it, Josiah. They would welcome you."

"You're drunk, Hugo."

"In no time at all you could become one of their leaders, Josiah. Some of them are even in your employ. Yes, I know about Johnny Bishop and some of the others who work in your shipyard. They trust you. They'll confide in you."

"Are you suggesting I become a spy, an informer?" Josiah said, horrified.

"You've said many times you are against war. Here's your chance to stop a war from happening. Think of how many lives you could save."

"I'd rather cut off my hand than do what you're suggesting," Josiah said. "You must be mad to think I would do anything so loathsome."

If he hadn't been drunk Hugo would not have done what he did next. He drank more wine, then leaned forward and reaching under the table, put his hand on Josiah's leg. "I love you, Josiah," he said, confessing something he had held back for many years. "I always have, since we were boys. All I want is for you to love me too." His hand, which had started on Josiah's knee, now worked its way up toward his groin.

Josiah had not forgotten what the serving girl at The Golden Ball had said Hugo being a "poof." With a small cry of horror he thrust Hugo's hand away and stared at him wordlessly.

"All right," said Hugo, deeply wounded. "I see. You don't want my love. You never have. So be it. Now I'll say something I did not want to say. But you are forcing me. I'm an important man, Josiah. I'm General Gage's adjutant. I see all the dispatches from London, and they are telling him he has to stamp out the rebellion. The day is coming soon when all the traitors are going to hang like dogs. Walter included." Hugo smiled cruelly, the way someone would when they've played their best card.

"What about Walter?"

"Don't play innocent with me, Josiah. We know Walter is one of those little sneaks who work for Paul Revere, scampering all over the city like rats, spying on us. I can have him arrested, Josiah, and put into a cell where he never gets out!"

"I won't listen to any more of this." Josiah picked up his hat. The moment he had been fearing had come: Hugo and he were friends no longer. "Goodbye, Hugo."

He left the tavern, wanting to weep.

•　　•　　•

"What's the matter, ducky, you look like you just lost your best friend," Violet observed. "Where did your pal go? You wouldn't believe the plans I was making for him. Want some more wine? You finished this bottle awfully fast."

"Get lost," he said. "I don't need anything you've got."

"Whoo—hoo! Touchy tonight, are we, Lieutenant? Look what just came through the door. This ought to cheer you up."

Hugo saw Jeremy Light come into the tavern and upon seeing him, came right over to his table.

"I've got my orders to stand by," Jeremy said, the baby face lit up enthusiastically. "We're going any time now. Gage has relieved the flanker companies and confined them to barracks!"

"How can you be going?" Hugo asked, pouring more wine for himself and some for Jeremy as well. "You're neither in the grenadiers or the light infantry."

"Captain Michaelson is ill. I'm taking his place!"

"Promise me you'll be careful," said Hugo. "I don't want to lose you now. You're as handsome as Narcissus, you know that?"

"And you're the best thing about Boston," Jeremy smiled, an expression that made him look even younger than his 19 years. With his fair skin and hair that was almost white, he was almost angelic in appearance. "Action, at last!" he went on. "This time we'll show these rebels something. But no one knows what the target is."

"Except Gage," Hugo said teasingly. "And me."

"Now come on, love, tell me, you promised," Jeremy said, leaning closer to Hugo so that his chin was almost on Hugo's shoulder. "Please."

"Swear you won't let this out?" Hugo said in a low voice. When Jeremy nodded solemnly he said, "Concord."

"I knew it," Jeremy said excitedly.

"It's 22 miles through hostile territory," Hugo cautioned.

"You don't really believe these colonials are going to give us any trouble, do you?"

"No real trouble. But they are capable of shooting from behinds rocks and stone walls. Stay alert. Here." He produced the infinity symbol that Josiah Hartford had given him when he left Boston. "Wear this. It will keep you safe."

"What is it?" Jeremy looked doubtful.

"It's called the lemniscate. The infinity symbol."

"I don't believe in good luck charms," Jeremy declared.

"Do it for me," Hugo urged.

"Oh, all right," Jeremy conceded, draping it around his neck. "For you I'll do it. Come on," he said, tugging at Hugo's hand. "Come on, let's go to your room." He smiled invitingly. "We owe each other that."

"Not tonight," said Hugo. "I enjoy being with you, but tonight isn't the night for it."

"You aren't just using me, are you?"

"Perhaps I am. What difference does it make?"

"I'm so glad we met," Jeremy said.

Hugo smiled in acknowledgement, but his thoughts were on Josiah and the Hartfords. What right did they have to be so happy when he was so miserable? More than once he had had the thought of wanting to hurt them, so they could feel something of what he felt. The sting of Josiah's rejection was still hurting him too. I offer him my love and he throws it back in my face. Who did he think he was?

The Happy Hartfords, he thought again. Damn them. What could I do that would make them suffer?

CHAPTER 10
THE ENGAGEMENT

Benjamin Hartford had built his fortune through ingenuity and hard work. He knew that, and gave himself credit for it. But he also knew he had been much blessed with good luck in the process, and so he had long considered himself among the most fortunate of men.

That feeling of being blessed had taken a new turn when Josiah agreed to follow in his footsteps and take over Hartford Ships. Worry over what would become of the shipyard had plagued him since his heart attack last year. Now Benjamin was certain he could journey into a comfortable old age, reading during the day, watching the heavens at night, and, he hoped, playing with his grandchildren. His weak heart might impose restrictions on what he could do, but he was resolved to get the most from what time he had left in the world.

On this April night he sat in his rocking chair in the big drawing room on the first floor of Hartford Manor, reading from Francis Bacon's *Natural History* and listening to the fire crackling in the fireplace. When Josiah came in and sat down nearby, Benjamin smiled without saying anything. He was always happy to see his children, but he soon sensed that Josiah might be troubled, and he was right.

Josiah had spent the day at the shipyard, intent on burying himself in his work so as not to think about what had taken place with Hugo. He was looking over drawings submitted for a new ship, a sloop, when Charles Waite appeared in the doorway.

He knocked and then came in with a hesitant but determined air. He sat down next to Josiah's desk, removed his hat and held it nervously in his hands. This is one very serious fellow, Josiah thought. A good man, and a good lawyer, but awfully serious. Anne is so lighthearted, and he is so serious—perhaps that's why they fell in love. They do say opposites attract.

"Will you be at Hartford Manor tonight?" Charles asked.

"Of course I will, unless some lust-filled tavern girl distracts me and wants to take me home to her bed," said Josiah, who thought if he made a joke it might lighten his mood. Charles, however, was feeling far too serious to realize that Josiah was being humorous. "A tavern girl?" he asked. "But what about Mercy? I thought you two were all but engaged."

"Never mind, Charles, I was joking. Of course I'll be home tonight. Why do you want to know?"

"I want to speak to your father about Anne," Charles explained.

This cheered Josiah up. "Excellent idea," he said, "and about time too."

"I know I've procrastinated," Charles admitted , "and I should have asked long before this, and I'm sorry, but I just couldn't think of what I would say..." His voice trailed off and he nervously turned his hat round and round in his hands.

"You are too serious, Charlie," said Josiah familiarly. "When will you come by?"

"It will be late, I have some work I have to finish. But if you'll be there would you open the door for me, as it were?"

"You mean, tell my father what you want to speak to him about?"

"No, not that exactly. But if you would just say that I'd like to talk to him, give him a kind of warning, I would feel better."

"Be glad to," said Josiah, "more than glad to," happy to have something to think about other than Hugo.

So he sat down in the drawing room near his father and opened a volume of Plato and turned quickly to the *Symposium*, hoping that the Greeks' ruminations on the nature of love might give him some insights on the subject and drive Hugo further from his mind. He only had read a few pages when Benjamin said, "You look as if you have something on your mind, Josiah. Is everything all right at the shipyard?"

Josiah set the book down and looked at his father, whose white hair, gentle eyes, and triangular shaped face like his own conveyed infinite wisdom and understanding, not just for him but the whole human race. He knew quite well not all fathers were as good as Benjamin Hartford—he only had to think of Lord Roger Chamberlain and how he had treated Hugo to be aware of that. I've been fortunate, he thought.

"Yes, all is going well there, Father. It's amazing how much there is to learn."

"How is that young fellow, Johnny Bishop, doing as the new chief carpenter of his shop?" Benjamin inquired. "When I gave him that job I thought he might not be prepared for it."

"I met him recently. He's doing well," Josiah said. "He showed me how he keeps his corners square by using what he called the 3-4-5 method. I can't wait to tell Patrick about it, for it's really the Pythagorean Theorem put into practical use. He'll love that."

"Is there anything else?" Benjamin asked.

Josiah hesitated. He didn't want to tell his family about Hugo, not yet. He wasn't sure how to put it into words and besides, it would cause them pain.

"No," he said, "unless it's all this talk of war."

"I know," said Benjamin. "It troubles me too. Doesn't it say in the Bible, 'You shall hear of wars and rumors of war'? Maybe that's all it is."

"I never knew you were so religious, Father," Josiah smiled.

"I am, in some ways, especially as I get older. There is much wisdom in the Bible, and great comfort when needed. We all need that sometimes."

"Charles Waite wants to talk to you," Josiah said. "He'll come by later."

"What about?"

"He'll tell you. He's going to work late, then come over here."

"Something having to do with business then. He could just as well bring it up with you. You're in charge now."

From the parlor nearby came the sound of women laughing. "The girls are certainly energetic lately," Benjamin observed. "Your mother, Jessica, Anne, Mercy— going from one room to the next, doing this, doing that, laughing all the time."

"They are certainly happy," Josiah agreed.

"Mercy is especially glad to be here." Benjamin leaned closer to Josiah and said, "When are you going to ask her the question, Josiah?"

"Father, I don't know..."

"Not that I'm trying to push you, you understand, but girls as nice and as charming as Mercy don't come along every day. You couldn't do much better than her."

"I know you and mother would love to have our family and the Willinghams brought together, to form a dynasty," said Josiah. "I'm not sure I'm prepared for marriage yet," not adding that there was the added complication of Alice in this equation. Too bad, he thought, he couldn't talk to his father about Alice. But he felt certain his father would not understand, and would be terribly disappointed in him if he knew what had been going on.

"Do you care for her?" Benjamin asked.

"Yes, I care for her."

"But you aren't sure if you love her?" Benjamin went on. When Josiah nodded he said, "Love is a strange thing. People spend all their lives looking for it. When your mother and I got married I wasn't sure if we what felt for each other was truly love or just strong feelings, but I knew I could spend the rest of my life with her and make her happy."

A knot on an oak log exploded, causing a loud popping sound and a burst of sparks in the fireplace, just as Mercy came prancing into the drawing room. She was followed by Anne and Jessica. "Well, Josiah Hartford, where have you been?" said Mercy. "We haven't seen much of you lately."

"You know I've been busy at the shipyard," Josiah protested.

"You've been busy with other things as well," Jessica said knowingly. She skipped over to the chair Josiah sat in and pulled at his arm. "Stand up," she ordered, "stand up, stand up." When Josiah complied she went on, "Everyone, meet my brother the hero. He knocked down a British soldier the other night, defending a lady's honor." She raised his arm in the air.

Mercy and Anne, Josiah could tell, knew what Jessica was referring to, but Benjamin clearly had no idea. Neither did Martha, who now came in from the kitchen, her oval face drawn up in fear.

"He did what?" she asked. "Do you know how much trouble you could get into, fighting with a British soldier?"

"It wasn't much of a fight," said Josiah. "How did you know about it?" he asked Jessica.

"Boston isn't such a large town," said Jessica. "Word gets around when something like that happens."

"What happened?" asked Benjamin, clearly worried.

Josiah told the story quickly, pointing out that he had not knocked anyone down but had just thrown the British soldier to the ground. He omitted the scuffle with Banastre Tarleton, and was glad to see that Jessica didn't know about it.

"Those soldiers might have shot you," said Martha. "Promise me you won't do anything like that again, Josiah."

"Josiah's our hero," Mercy declared, taking him by the arm and holding on. "I'm sure you would defend me from a rapscallion soldier. But I'm with your mother and father, I don't want you to get shot by a redcoat."

Now Elias appeared. He stood directly below one of the big chandeliers, something he only did when a guest had arrived. The chandelier's light made his dark-green jacket glow like an emerald.

"Mr. Charles Waite is here, Mr. Hartford," he announced in his deep voice.

Martha had already gone back to the kitchen, but now Jessica and Mercy, knowing looks on their faces, began laughing in anticipation, and along with Anne, scurried out of the room too, leaving behind a feeling of expectation.

"Where are they all going?" asked Benjamin, plainly puzzled. He stood and greeted Charles when he came in, then sat back down after shaking hands and inviting Charles to sit as well.

"So, Charles, Josiah tells me things are going well at the yard."

"Yes sir, they are." Charles sat with his hands tightly clutched together. He was a rather awkward man normally, and now, as he sat trying to get up the courage to ask for Anne's hand in marriage his awkwardness multiplied itself. Relax, Josiah thought.

"Glad to hear that." Benjamin lighted his pipe and rocked back and forth a few times. Josiah thought he detected laughter from the next room, and guessed it was Anne, Jessica, and Mercy, trying to overhear what was being said. Benjamin took no notice and clearly had no idea what was afoot. "Well," he went on, "Josiah tells me you needed to see me."

"I wanted to speak to you if I might, yes sir."

This seemed like a good time for Josiah to make his exit, so he said, "I'm going upstairs to bed, it's getting late..."

"No!" Charles cried, holding up one hand restrainingly. "Josiah, stay, please. I'd like you to be here."

"Charles," said Benjamin kindly, "what is it? Is it all the war talk?"

"No, Mr. Hartford, not at all." He abruptly jumped to his feet. "I want to marry her, you see. I love her." At Josiah's signal he sat back down.

"Who do you want to marry?" Benjamin asked.

"Anne."

"Anne! You mean my daughter Anne?"

Josiah saw he was right—his father knew nothing of how Charles and Anne felt about each other.

"I want to ask your permission, Mr. Hartford." Benjamin appeared to be at a loss for words.

"Well, I never," he said after a long pause. "Did you know about this?" he asked Josiah, who smiled, shrugged his shoulders, and said, "Yes, sir, I knew."

"Well, this is a fine how-do-you-do! How does Anne feel about it?"

"She loves me, sir, and that's the God's truth."

Benjamin looked at Josiah for confirmation. "It's true, Father, she does love him."

"Do you have any idea of what you're taking on, when you marry? All the responsibilities that come along with it?"

"Yes sir, I think I have some idea..."

"You can't possibly have any idea, no one does, until they actually start living as man and wife and having a family to take care of," said Benjamin. He reflected a moment, then said, "Before I even consider it, you've got to promise me two things. First, that you'll stay in Boston. I don't want you taking her away to live far from here, like Daniel and Mary-Louise. Second, that you will have lots of children."

"Oh yes, I promise, I don't want to go anywhere except Boston and I've always wanted a lot of children myself."

"Because I want some grandchildren to play with," said Benjamin.

"And I'd like some nieces and nephews," Josiah added.

The laughter from the other room increased and a moment later Anne came in, followed by Martha, Jessica, and Mercy. Anne went over to Charles, who had stood up once more, and took his hand playfully.

"You asked him?" she said, and then, without waiting for an answer, went on. "Father? You said yes, didn't you?"

"Martha, did you know?" asked Benjamin. His wife did not reply but her face gave the answer just as plainly as words could. "Did everyone know about this but me?" he said in an exasperated tone.

"Father, they're in love," said Jessica.

"So I've been told," said Benjamin.

"Father, you must say yes!" said Anne, and when Benjamin said the word everyone in the room burst into happy laughter.

Josiah shook hands with Charles, slapped his shoulder, and said, "Welcome to our family! A more fitting new member we couldn't wish for."

Benjamin put his arm around Martha, and said, "How do you like that, dear? We have a new son, and at our age!"

"That is one of the nicest things anyone has ever said to me," said Charles. He was trying his best to hold back his tears of joy. "You know, I never had a family."

"You have one now," said Josiah.

"Elias, fetch some wine," said Benjamin. "We'll toast this day, April 18, in the year of Our Lord 1775, as an important date in the history of the Hartford family! Our daughter Anne's engagement to Mr. Charles Waite, Esquire."

There was applause as Elias brought out a tray filled with small glasses of wine. "To the engagement of Anne and Charles !" said Benjamin.

As everyone drank their wine Walter came in, just as the big grandfather clock in the corner tolled 11 p.m.

"What is this?" he asked, his face drawn up as if in excitement. "Are we celebrating something?"

"Only the engagement of Charles and Anne," said Jessica.

"Elias, wine for Walter," said Benjamin.

Walter enthusiastically shook hands with Charles , hugged Anne, drank his wine hurriedly, asked for more, looked at Josiah and said, "We have a new brother."

"So we do," said Josiah, "and a fine one too."

"I've been waiting for this," said Walter. "Another sister married off."

"It will be your turn soon," said Jessica.

"Oh no, him first," Walter said, gesturing toward Josiah, who tried not to notice the look Mercy sent his way.

Walter drank more wine, draining his glass, and sent Elias to get another bottle. "Easy there, easy," said Josiah. "Just because these two announced their engagement is no excuse to get blind drunk."

"That's right," said Benjamin. "And just where have you been, out so late?"

"He must have a girl somewhere," said Jessica.

"I have news, important news," said Walter.

"Don't tell me he's getting engaged too," said Mercy. Everyone laughed, but Walter's face was becoming solemn.

"What is it, Walter?" Martha asked, her intuition telling her that something was wrong.

"Please forgive me," he began, "for casting a shadow over this happy occasion." He hesitated, as if unsure of what to say next, then announced, "The British are marching tonight. The soldiers are assembling on the Common right now."

Everyone fell silent.

"So the rumors are true," said Benjamin. "Well, we knew it was coming."

"Father, they are marching to Concord," said Walter plaintively.

Mercy let out a gasp of fright. "Oh no!" she said.

"What about Patrick?" said Jessica. "What will happen to him?"

"Jessica, I'm sure the British won't hurt Patrick," said Martha, but there was a trace of doubt in her voice.

"Everybody needs to remain calm," said Benjamin. "I have no love for the British, God knows, but I can't see them needlessly hurting someone like Patrick."

Josiah could tell that Walter was holding something back. Walter looked at him, as if seeking guidance, and when Josiah briefly nodded Walter continued. "Father," he said gravely, "I don't want to say this, but you don't understand. They are looking for weapons and military supplies, and they are going to search every house, every barn, every stable where they think they might be hidden." These words elicited a cry of horror from Mercy, and she cried out once again when Walter went on. "I'm sorry Mercy. Your house is one of the first on their list." He paused, and then said, "The British are going to burn Concord. They are going to burn it to the ground."

"My house?" asked Mercy. "You're saying they are going to burn my house?"

"I can hardly believe it," said Benjamin.

"And Patrick is right in the line of fire," Josiah declared.

"What will happen to him?" Martha asked. "If the British burn the Willinghams' house, what will he do?"

"He can't take care of himself," said Jessica. "He won't be able to find his way home. He'll just wander off into the woods and die."

"Someone has to ride to Concord tonight and get Patrick out of there," Josiah said firmly. "You say the soldiers haven't left Boston yet?" he asked Walter.

"No, but they'll be leaving any time. It's all but certain they are going across the harbor to Charlestown instead of through the Neck like we thought. If they go by sea, two lanterns will be hung in the tower of the old North Church. Mr. Revere, William Dawes, and some others are standing by right now. As soon as they're sure they are going to ride out to warn the countryside that the British are marching. Mr. Revere will be going out the Lexington Road. Mr. Adams and Mr. Hancock are both in Lexington now, so they have to skedaddle."

"How in the world do you know all this?" asked Benjamin, frowning.

Walter hesitated, then said, "I belong to the Sons of Liberty, Father. I work with Paul Revere and Dr. Warren."

"And how long has this been going on?" Benjamin asked, plainly shocked.

"Two years," Walter confessed. To Josiah he said, "You're right. Someone has to go to Concord and get Patrick. Father, can you have Elias saddle one of the horses for me? I can leave right away and get there before the soldiers do."

"You're not going," Josiah declared. "It's too dangerous for you. Have Elias get Caesar ready for me."

"I'm going too," Walter insisted.

"They can't both go," said Martha. "Benjamin, don't let him."

"I want to go," said Walter.

"No," Josiah said again. "British officers are going to be patrolling the roads tonight, with orders to stop anyone from warning people that the soldiers are marching. It will be a miracle if Revere or any of the others get through. If they catch you outside the city tonight, Walter, they'll shoot you on sight."

"What do you mean?" Walter asked.

"What is this? What are you talking about?" Benjamin wanted to know.

"Yes, how do you know this?" asked Martha.

"They know who Walter is. They have his description and they have his name. They know he's one of Paul Revere's men."

"But those names are all secret!" Walter protested.

"Hugo told me. You think only the Patriots have spies?"

"Is there anything going on in this house that hasn't been kept a secret from me?" said Benjamin, throwing his hands up in exasperation. "And what is this about Hugo?"

"We'll never see Hugo again, Father, not as a friend," Josiah said sadly. "He isn't the person we used to know. He's changed far too much to ever be our friend again. He wanted to recruit me to become an informer for him. He even tried to blackmail me by threatening to have Walter arrested."

"Oh, that's terrible," said Martha, sitting down and covering her face with her hands. "He was like another child to me."

"All right, you must go," said Benjamin to Josiah. "Elias!" he called. "Saddle up Caesar."

"Yes sir," said Elias, hurrying away.

"Will there be fighting?" asked Mercy.

"The plan is that when the British march, the Minutemen and the militias are going to fight," said Walter.

"And that will mean war," said Benjamin. "And nothing good ever came from war."

"Josiah," said Mercy, taking Josiah by the arm, "can you get there before the British do? Will you warn my family?"

"I'll get there before the soldiers," he promised, "and I'll warn them."

"By tomorrow you and Patrick will be back home safe and sound," said Martha comfortingly.

"I can't stand it," said Mercy. "My house, burned down! Oh God, don't let it happen!" She and Jessica sat down on one of the small couches and Josiah saw Jessica trying to comfort her.

"Let me go with you," said Charles. "I can help, and the British aren't looking for me."

"You can be more help staying here and looking after things," Josiah said, then he gestured to Walter to come closer and he spoke to both of them in a low voice. "Just in case anything goes wrong, I'll feel better if you're both here. If I don't make it back, promise me you'll take care of everyone."

"All right," said Charles. "I promise to do that. Just be careful, Josiah."

"I still wish you'd let me come along," said Walter.

"Do you want to kill Mother and Father with worry?" said Josiah sternly. "They need you right now."

"He's right, Walter," said Charles. "Besides, one person has a better chance of getting through than two."

"I need to go to my room, pack up a few things," said Josiah, and he ran upstairs as fast as he could.

He changed clothes quickly, putting on a more comfortable shirt and trousers for riding and also riding boots.

He heard the familiar three quick knocks on his door and Alice entered, closing the door behind her as if demons were chasing her, then flung herself into his arms. In spite of the late hour she was still in her maid's uniform, but she had removed her white bonnet so that her red hair stood out even brighter than usual even in the dim light of Josiah's bedroom. She threw both her arms around him and held on desperately, burying her head in his chest. Then she looked up, the green eyes appealing as a child's and just as frightened.

"Alice, what are you doing here *now*?" Josiah asked.

"What are *you* doing, Josiah?"

"I must get to Concord, tonight, find Patrick and bring him home."

"I know. Is war going to start?"

"I don't know. I hope it all passes over."

"I'm an American now, Josiah. I hate the British. In Ireland I saw what the *Sassenachs* can do. They burned farms, they turned people out of their homes, they hung people who had never done anything. It was because of the British that I was sent over here like a slave. It was because of the British I was raped. But I'm frightened of war, and of what the English might do. I'm terrified that you won't come back. Josiah, do you love me?"

"Alice, you have to go. What if someone comes in?"

"Josiah, I'm going to have a baby!"

Josiah pushed her back, holding her by both shoulders. "No, it can't be."

"It is," said Alice, grabbing both his forearms in a claw-like grip. "I'm sure now."

"I—I don't know what to say."

"Just say you love me! That's all I need right now."

Josiah said the words mechanically, feeling guilty because he knew he didn't mean them, not any longer, and realizing what he had felt for Alice was not love but simply desire.

"I knew it," said Alice happily. "I knew it! I knew you love me and not that girl from Concord. You're an honorable man, from an honorable family, and you'll do what is right, I know you will."

"We must—we'll have to deal with this when I come back," said Josiah. He had nearly finished packing his saddle bags and he was ready to go. "Now go, go."

"All right, my love, I will go," said Alice, smiling. "Just promise me you'll come back safely." She crept to the door, opened it carefully, looked up and down the long hallway, then crept out quietly.

He went downstairs, his saddlebags flung over his shoulder. Everyone had gathered at the back door, the one facing the stables. "Elias says Caesar is saddled," said Benjamin. He handed Josiah a leather purse filled with gold and silver coins. "You might need this," he said.

Martha gave him a cloth bag. "Here's some food," she said. She wiped away a tear. "Please be careful."

"Of course I'll be careful," he said. "No need to worry, Mother. I'll be home tomorrow with Patrick. All this talk of war will soon pass over, it will probably come to nothing."

He said goodbye to everyone—his mother, his father, Walter, Jessica, Anne, Charles. It was nearly 12:00. He placed his left foot into the stirrup and swung himself gracefully into the saddle.

"I'll be home tomorrow," he promised, "with Patrick, all safe and sound."

He spurred Caesar and rode off. What he didn't know was that it would be a year before he came home again.

CHAPTER 11
ESCAPE FROM BOSTON

The only way out of Boston on horseback was through the Neck, that narrow bridge of land that led toward Roxbury and the Lexington Road. As Josiah headed that way mounted on Caesar he passed the Old North Church and saw the two lanterns hanging inside the belfry—the signal Walter had mentioned that indicated the British were coming by sea.

He left home, taking one last look at the lights of Hartford Manor, and rode past the Mill Pond, down the hill along Hillier's Lane, past Hanover Street, heading toward the vicinity of Long Wharf. If the soldiers were assembling on Boston Common he wanted to be on the other side of the city and not encounter them. This roundabout route took longer that it normally would to reach the Neck, but when he got to Rowe's Field he knew Orange Street and the South End were not far off.

Josiah saw nothing unusual at first; if anything out of the ordinary was taking place it didn't show until he got onto Orange Street and neared the Neck itself. There a lot of people were milling about, some on horseback, some on foot, some in carriages or wagons, giving the impression of a crowd of people trying to get through a narrow passageway.

"What's going on?" he asked a man on horseback who was heading in the opposite direction he was and looking as if he wasn't happy about it.

"What do you think?" the man snapped. "The damn British aren't letting anybody leave the city tonight."

Josiah reached out and grabbed the sleeve of the man's jacket. "What do you mean, they won't let anybody leave the city?"

The man angrily pulled his arm free. "I mean they've got a roadblock set up just on the other side of the Neck, that's what! I've got a lady in Roxbury I want to go and see and now I can't! Anything else you want to know?"

The man rode off. Josiah continued riding forward. He passed Byle's Wharf and Gibbon's Ship Yard. He came near the tavern called The Crow's Nest, where he had met with a Hugo a few times, and paused to let a dozen inebriated men and women pass in front of him. He felt a hand on his leg.

"Well, if it isn't Lieutenant Chamberlain's pal, Josiah the Gentleman."

In surprise he saw the redhead he had seen the other night when he was with Hugo.

Violet. Her hair was tied back in a ponytail, and she was smiling at him teasingly. "Does your mother know you're out so late?" Violet went on. "Come on inside."

"I can't," he said. "I have pressing business. Don't you work at The Fife and Drum?"

"I like to move around," she said. "If you're thinking of leaving town you can give that up," she went on. "The bloodybacks aren't having any of it. So come on," she tugged at his trouser leg, "come in and stay a while. I can show you things you never thought of before."

"I can't," Josiah repeated, urging Caesar forward. "What's my name?" Violet called.

"Purple," Josiah called back. "Violet Purple." Violet laughed.

He rode past on past The Crow's Nest. Bawdy, obscene songs were being sung by drunken men accompanied by the squealing laughter of equally drunken women. He felt a stirring inside when he thought of Violet. If I wasn't so busy, he thought, and then put that thought out of his head. No time for anything like that.

Violet was right—there was a roadblock. Two British soldiers stood around a bonfire in the middle of the road, muskets slung over their shoulders. They stopped a carriage as it came near, forcing the driver to turn around, and were waving and gesturing for everyone else who came near to turn back.

Josiah rode closer, and in the light of the bonfire one of the soldiers approached. "No one leaves Boston tonight, sir," he said politely.

"What's going on?"

"Orders, sir, that's all I can tell you. Now turn round, sir, and no trouble."

Josiah nodded meekly and turned Caesar around. He could try to ride past them, but he risked getting shot. Not far away he saw what looked like a blockhouse, and there had to be other soldiers in there.

There were only two soldiers on guard. How to get by them?

He rode back to The Crow's Nest, dismounted, secured Caesar, then began making his way toward the entrance, pushing his way through the crowd. He hadn't even gotten to the door when Violet approached him and threw an arm across his shoulders.

"I told you, didn't I?"

"You were right," Josiah admitted.

"So, change your mind?" Violet asked. "What will it take to get you to be with me?"

"Do you have a friend?" Josiah asked.

"Oh, so I'm not your type?" said Violet indignantly. "Or are you the kind who likes more than one girl at the same time?"

"Neither," said Josiah. He held up some of the silver pieces his father had given him. "I have more like this."

"For that I'll find two friends," said Violet.

"We only need one."

．　　．　　．

The other girl's name was Dahlia. She was a little heavier around the hips than Violet was but equally well-endowed on top and equally eager to show off what she had. In contrast to Violet's red hair, hers was jet black. She followed Josiah and Violet obediently as he led them back toward the Neck.

Josiah handed Dahlia several silver shillings. "Can you do it?" he asked.

Dahlia took this as a challenge to her professional abilities as well as to her womanly charms. "Of course I can," she bristled. "I've never met the man yet I couldn't get to follow me into the bushes."

Smiling, and walking with a suggestive strut, Dahlia approached the two sentries. She spoke to them and they laughed. She carried a bottle of rum in her hand and offered it to the soldiers. They were reluctant at first, although they both obviously wanted some. The one who appeared to be the leader looked about cautiously in every direction, then took a long drink. The other did the same. Dahlia kept offering the bottle to him, all the while getting closer and closer, patting the leader on the shoulder and arm and gesturing toward the bushes nearby.

"Look at her go," said Josiah. "She should be on the stage."

"Hah! That isn't anything," said Violet. "Wait until you see what *I* can do." She looked Josiah over and leered. "Sure you don't want to stay awhile?"

"I just can't."

"Have you ever been with a woman?" she asked invitingly.

"Lots of times," he said.

Violet looked skeptical. "I could make you feel good, Gentleman Josiah. You're rich too, by the look of your clothes and that horse. I like rich boys. I like rich boys because they have lots of money to spend on me. That's my goal, Josiah, to find a rich man to take care of me for the rest of my life."

Dahlia and the soldiers were laughing uproariously now, and she kept tugging on the leader's arm and gesturing toward the bushes on the other side of the road. The soldier's resistance was weakening, and he kept looking around to see if anyone was watching. It was well past midnight now, and there was less traffic in the streets and no other soldiers in sight. The tents near the Neck were nearly deserted, only a few watch- fires going. If what Walter had said was true, more than 700 British soldiers were at this moment being ferried across the Charles River.

The soldier gestured to the other soldier, who nodded and gestured back. Dahlia went off into the trees, and a moment later the soldier followed her.

"Now," said Violet, "now, you just watch me. And when you come back to Boston, you come and see me. Promise?"

"I don't promise anything. But I hope you find the rich man you're looking for," was all Josiah said. Violet smiled and set off.

The soldier still had the bottle of rum Dahlia had brought and he took another drink. It was expensive rum, the best in The Crow's Nest, much better than the cheap stuff the soldiers usually had. Violet approached him with the same come-and-get-me walk Dahlia had used, and to Josiah's inexperienced eyes it seemed she did it quite well. A moment later she and the soldier were talking like old friends. The soldier offered her the bottle and she took a long drink, keeping the bottle so long that the soldier gestured that he wanted it back. He looked at the bottle as if examining what remained, then laughed and Dahlia laughed and they finished the bottle. The soldier threw it toward the ditch at the side of the road as if he never wanted to see it again. A moment later Violet led the soldier toward the side of the road and as soon as they were out of sight Josiah took Caesar by the bridle and stood up.

He was glad he had brought Caesar, who was a quiet and obedient horse. In a moment or two his chance would come, and if he could keep Caesar quiet until they made it into the darkness of the road beyond the Neck he had an excellent chance of getting away.

Now Violet threw her arms around the soldier's neck and kissed him, pulling him so his back was to Josiah. Josiah pulled on Caesar's bridle, and as quickly as he could without running or cause the horse any undue alarm he began moving across the neck, past the fire the soldiers had built. One step, two steps, three—the soldier, still locked in Violet's arms near the ditch, had his back to Josiah and showed no sign of being aware of his presence. But just as Josiah was about to mount, Caesar let out of whinny.

"What was that?" Josiah heard the solider say. "Is somebody there?"

"It's nothing, love, it's nothing," said Violet. She kissed him again, which interested the soldier more than a vague sound in the dark, and after a few more steps Josiah leaped onto Caesar and made his way into the unpromising darkness.

CHAPTER 12
ON LEXINGTON GREEN

The fastest way to Concord was by the Watertown Road. Riding into the darkness, Josiah guided Caesar toward Roxbury, a little more than two miles from Boston. There were no clouds and the moonlight illuminated the wide road making it easy for him to see his way.

While the troops had a head start, Josiah felt certain he could get to Concord long before they did. He would get Patrick, put him on Cleopatra, and be home before the midday meal.

But what to do about Alice, he thought. She said she's going to have a baby! Mine! Better to not dwell on that until this task is over, he told himself, and at the crossroad at Roxbury he saw the signs that read Framingham if he kept going straight and Watertown if he went north. He swung Caesar north.

He saw no one else on the road and as the lights of Watertown shone out of the darkness he kept Caesar at a steady trot rather than a gallop. There was no sense in tiring him, considering how far they had to go.

He rode across the narrow wooden bridge of the Charles River. Watertown lay to his left, and as he crossed the bridge he rode in that direction. The Watertown Road would take him in an arc toward Concord, and he would be riding about five miles from the British column, marching on the Lexington Road. He wouldn't be going through Lexington but past Wright's Tavern near the Concord River.

But as he neared Watertown he saw that this plan was not going to work. A fire on the road ahead, just outside the entrance to the city, and the six or eight British soldiers standing near it, told him so. The British had blocked this road, foiling his plans, and he turned Caesar around before the soldiers took notice of him.

He rode back to the Weston Road. The only choice now was to keep riding north. There were several side roads he could take and still reach his destination. The only trouble was these roads would take longer, he would be closer to the British column, and he would go right past Lexington. According to Walter, there was a good chance there would be fighting there.

He rode back alongside the Charles River, across the Great Bridge, then past the buildings of his beloved Harvard College. Were there any students there now, awake and talking as he and his classmates in the Pandorian Society had, talking excitedly about life and death, wondering whether God really existed and what the future of the world would be. He could see no lights from this distance and felt a twinge of sadness when he remembered that he wouldn't be going back there again but instead was going to remain in Boston and build ships.

As he neared Prospect Hill and was about to take the road toward Menotomy, he heard a shout, followed by the sound of horse's hooves, and he was surrounded by three riders.

They wore cloaks tied at the neck but Josiah could see the scarlet and white uniforms underneath. British officers, he realized, one of the patrols Hugo had mentioned. They were all young men, with the aristocratic look of assumed superiority of British officers. One of them kept his hand inside his cloak, no doubt on the handle of a pistol, and another lit a lantern and looked at Josiah intently.

For a moment no one spoke. Then the one who appeared to be in charge, said, "And what do you think you're doing out so late, boyo?"

"I was just on my way home," said Josiah, trying to sound as innocent and non- threatening as he could.

"And where is that?"

"Medford."

"That doesn't explain what you are doing out at this hour, my lad."

"I was visiting a lady friend," Josiah smiled, then winked.

"And where does this lady friend live?"

"Cambridge."

"Does this lady have a name?"

"I'd tell you, but her husband might object—he's away on business, you know how it is," he said, laughing, and the British officer smiled in a man-to-man way. The others relaxed and the one who'd had his hand under his cloak took the hand out and rested it on his saddle horn.

"Are you a loyal subject of the King?" he asked.

"Long live His Majesty!" Josiah shouted.

The one holding the lantern now held it up for one last look at Josiah's face. "No," he said, "he isn't one of the ones we were told to look for." He lowered the lantern.

"I'm glad you already had your fun," the leader said. He rode a little closer to Josiah until he was within arm's length. "But you see, no one is allowed to ride past here tonight. Some big goings-on about to happen. So you'll have to stay with us until morning, and you can tell us all about your rumpy-pumpy with your married lady friend till dawn do us part—"

With his strong hand Josiah reached out and catching the leader's face, pushed as hard as he could. The man fell from his horse, the horse reared, and Josiah spurred Caesar, who responded by galloping away like a cannonball.

"Hey! Stop him! Come back! We'll shoot!" Josiah heard the shouts behind him, heard the report of a pistol, then the clatter of horse's hooves and knew at least one of the British officers was chasing him. He heard the sharp report as another pistol was fired but he knew it was next to impossible to hit a moving target with a pistol while riding a horse. He looked behind him once and saw one of the officers was about 30 yards back, another considerably behind him. At the sign that said "Menotomy" he saw the fork in the road he was looking for, took it, and found himself on the lesser road, the one he didn't want to take, the one that would take him to Lexington, placing himself on a parallel line with the soldiers.

He continued on the narrow road, urging Caesar over fallen logs and large rocks. This road, not taken care of like the main highway, ran past numerous farms and stone fences, as well as barns and silos and fields where sheep and cattle grazed. Several times he thought he heard what had to be the British column—the sound of many feet, rising and falling at the same time and voices, carrying through the still of the night.

He rode past a farm house with a jack-o-lantern burning brightly on a fence post, something you didn't normally see until autumn at harvest time, and in the dark it looked like a skull with a light coming from within. He then came into open country and emerged onto some flatland. Peering across a wide field of grass he saw, in the moonlight, far ahead of him, the British column on the Lexington Road. The soldiers looked like shadows in the darkness, a long line of black shapes marching in formation, the officers on horseback.

On a far hill he now saw a sudden eruption of flame. It seemed to burst right out of the ground. Someone had lit a fire, a large fire, and it was followed a few minutes later by another on the hill past it, then came another. Josiah rode on, puzzled, the inner road taking him away from the British column now and in an arc around more farms as it swung up toward Lexington. But he could still see the fires, and then in the distance came the sound of church bells ringing.

Of course! He remembered Walter telling him that the militias in the countryside had been anticipating this moment for a year, and they had an elaborate alarm system set up. The watch fires, the church bells—these were warnings that the British were on their way.

It was 5:00 a.m. now and dawn was just starting to break as he neared Lexington and saw the lights of the town. Josiah rode in from the south, and he saw the houses and buildings of the tidy little village, typical of New England: There was the church, and the meeting house where the people came together to shout and argue, the village green in center of town and on the other side of the green, Buckman's Tavern. The tolling of the church bell grew louder and faster, sounding frantic, and as he dismounted and tied Caesar beside a water trough he heard the sound of a drum beating out a rat-tat-tat staccato noise.

The drumming was coming from the village green, and the drummer pounded his drum earnestly. From all directions men came running toward him, all of them carrying muskets and powder-bags. A middle-aged man was directing them to get into two lines as they arrived, pointing and giving orders. He carried a walking stick, and he pointed at the wet dewy grass with long sweeping motions for the men to make two straight lines. They were all ordinary looking men of all ages—farmers, artisans, tradesmen, including one black man who stood in the center of the front row and nodded quickly when the man giving the orders spoke to him.

All along the Concord and Bedford Roads people were gathered, watching, many with their arms folded across their chests or else with their hands held in front of them, as if in prayer. They stood around the church and small school house that was almost directly in front of where Josiah tied up Caesar. Josiah, his curiosity getting the better of him, walked past several of the onlookers and went around to the front of the school house so he could see better. There was a rose garden planted at the back of the school, tended, most likely, by the children, and since he loved flowers Josiah couldn't resist the urge to take one, a lovely pink rose in full bloom, and held it in his hand as he walked closer.

You should push on, he said to himself. You must get to Concord before the soldiers do. But Caesar could use a rest, and he wanted to see what was taking place here. As the church bell kept tolling and the drum kept beating he heard other sounds coming nearer, the sound of more drums accompanied by fifes, and the tune of "The British Grenadiers," being played, and he saw the British column approaching the village.

Officers on horseback led the way, and behind them came row after row of the scarlet-and-white uniformed soldiers. The officers raised their hands for the column to stop as soon as they reached the divide of the Bedford and Concord Roads that ran along both sides of the village green. From where they were they could see the militia forming, and one of the officers rode forward around the meeting house to get a better look. He rode back quickly, the officers held a brief conference, and the one who appeared to be in charge gave an order to the column. The soldiers responded by taking their muskets off their shoulders and then opening a square leather case each man carried on his right hip and removing something from it, then going through a series of practiced motions that involved bringing the object to their mouths and biting off a chunk of it, then transferring the remainder to the opening of their musket barrels and shoving it inside with a ramrod.

My God, Josiah said to himself. They're loading their weapons. They're getting ready to fight.

When the muskets were loaded more orders were given: Each man produced a wicked-looking triangular bayonet and attached it to the end of his musket, then stood at attention once more. A moment later the soldiers resumed their march. The companies in front veered to the right, past

Buckman's Tavern along the Bedford Road, while the rest stayed on the main road, toward Concord.

"Column right!" shouted one of the officers, and from the Concord Road this force turned right, marching onto the green, while on the other side the smaller force made a similar maneuver, but to the left this time, and the two columns met in the center of the green and began forming into lines, about 200 feet from the militiamen.

The militiaman's drum stopped beating, and the church bell went suddenly quiet. The militia commander was speaking to the men in front of him. "Don't fire unless they fire first," he said. "Don't molest them, let them pass."

Josiah estimated there were about 80 men on the green (he later learned the actual number was 77) and they were facing 250 British soldiers who had by now formed into three lines, with the Union Jack flying proudly alongside the regimental colors. Some of the soldiers wore the distinctive bearskin hats he had often seen in Boston. These were the grenadiers—big men, each one tall and strongly built, and he remembered Hugo telling him that the grenadiers were specially chosen for their size and strength. Beside them were the light infantry—smaller, more agile men, trained to move fast through an enemy's line and wreck havoc from the rear. The officers rode about, shouting orders, and then, when they were satisfied the men were lined up properly, the one in charge shouted, "Attention!" and the soldiers all stiffened visibly and then stood like statues in the early morning light.

There was an eerie silence over the green now. Every person seemed to be holding their breath—the militiamen, the soldiers, the spectators who were seeing this from all sides. Many were women, some were children, some were older people, but all of them, Josiah thought, were villagers with husbands or sons standing on the green, facing the British soldiers.

"Present arms!" said the officer in charge, and each soldier raised his musket. "Order arms!" was the next command, and the soldiers leveled their muskets so they were all pointed directly at the militiamen, the ugly bayonets bristling out menacingly.

Now the major rode toward the militiamen. "Disperse, you damn rebels!" he shouted. "Lay down your arms and get off the King's Green!"

"Stay where you are!" the commander of the militia said to his men. "If they mean to have a war, let it begin here."

The major's face took on the expression of a man who has just been challenged to fight. With an obvious effort he kept his temper, and then raised his hand as if to say, "Steady. Not yet," but just as he did so one of the officers in the rear took out his pistol and fired a shot into the air, the yellow flame from the muzzle looking like an arrow in the half-darkness. The report ricocheted around the green. Nearby Josiah saw a woman drop her hands, then raise them again to her face and cover it, as if she knew what would happen next and did not want to see it.

As if on signal, the front rank of the British soldiers began to fire their muskets. They were followed by those behind them, and then the entire British force began to fire into the militiamen. A cry went up from the spectators, and as he saw the bodies toppling over onto the wet ground Josiah dropped the rose he was holding and shouted, "Oh, no!" and then he wished that he could somehow turn back time and prevent this moment from happening.

Men fell, as if pushed by a giant hand. Others simply went down where they stood. Some ran for cover. Some knelt and fired their muskets back at the British, who were by now reloading their weapons and shouting so loudly they couldn't hear their officers, who were calling for them to stop shooting. "Cease fire! Cease fire!" they shouted. But the men either couldn't hear them or weren't obeying, and now some of the soldiers in the front rank gave a ferocious howl and charged forward, soon joined by others, and Josiah's horror increased one hundred-fold as he saw them bayonet wounded and dying men. One man threw up his hands in a gesture of surrender, only to receive a bayonet-thrust into his chest, and Josiah saw a soldier, after stabbing a wounded man, kneel and shoot a man who was running away. Bayoneting seemed to Josiah a more deliberate and personal attack than firing from the ranks, it was more like murder, the soldiers were going out of their way to kill.

The British officers were riding about frantically in the now smoke-covered green, waving their sabers and yelling at the soldiers to cease fire. But they had lost control of their men, and as the surviving militiamen scattered and ran for cover it looked to Josiah as if the soldiers might go after the civilian onlookers next, as some began to move aggressively toward them, threatening with their bayonets. Then a drum began to sound from the rear and the soldiers retreated back toward where they had originally assembled near the center of the green. Not until the lines began to form did it seem that the officers were in charge once more. As silence descended over the green and the soldiers reformed their ranks Josiah saw the commander of the British troops, still sitting on his horse, surveying the bodies lying on the grass, a shocked expression on his face. He lowered his saber and said, "Oh, Christ. Now we've got a war."

The major spurred his horse, rode back to his place in front of his troops, and shouted, "Right face! Forward, march!" and the soldiers marched off to the Bedford Road, wheeling to the right, almost as if the officer wanted to exit the village by the backway, and they went around Lexington to the main road and continued on toward Concord. As they went past the church Josiah heard shouts of "Hurrah!" as if in victory and the drummers and fifers began to play "The British Grenadiers" once again. The main body of the British column came up the road at the same time and the two forces came together, then continued on past Lexington toward Concord.

There were about 20 bodies lying on the green, strewn about like logs, and as the soldiers marched away the people of Lexington ran to their loved ones. Josiah ran toward them as well. He wanted to do something—to help stop their pain, to put all this back together, somehow, although he sensed there might not be any way to repair something this badly broken. He saw, with an anguish he had never imagined, a wounded man crawling on the grass toward the road, and a woman came running toward him, crying, and as she knelt down the man stretched out his arms to her, then died. Other men were calling for help, and there were shrieks and cries as people ran to assist them.

Josiah, standing in the midst of this, looked all about, wanting to help, part of him still not believing what he had just seen and what he was seeing now. Women were kneeling beside their men, wailing, and he saw one woman shaking the body of a man who was obviously dead as if she was trying to wake him from an especially sound sleep. An older man and woman, both on their knees, were crying over the body of young man Josiah assumed was their son. A wounded man tried to get to his feet, failed, then tried again and stood up shakily, then looked around, wondering, even as Josiah was, what to do next.

The man who had been giving the orders to the militia now reappeared, accompanied by another middle-aged man who carried a leather satchel.

"Doctor," said the militia commander, "we need to take care of the wounded. Parson Clarke," he called to a man who wore the clothes of a clergyman, "let's open up the church and get the wounded inside so Dr. Paul can look after them."

"I'll do it right now, Captain," said the Parson. "Doctor, you go with him," said the commander.

"Some of these men are dead, Captain Parker," said the Parson. "What should we do with them?"

"Take them to the church too, until their families can claim them."

"What else can I do?"

"Help the doctor to fix up the wounded. That's his job. You help him and pray. That's your job, and if we ever needed prayer, today is that day." Noticing Josiah standing nearby, he said, "I don't know you. Will you help us?"

"What can I do?" Josiah replied.

"We need to get the wounded men over to the church, and a big strong fellow like you who's still in one piece can do that. Nathaniel," he called to one of the militiamen, a short stocky young fellow who was just now walking back onto the green, clutching his musket, "you and this man start carrying the wounded over to the church. I've got to start reassembling the men. Those damn Brits will be coming back this way and this time it'll be no holds barred."

"I'll help with that, Captain," came another voice, one that sounded strained, as if speaking was an effort, and Josiah saw it was the black man he had seen standing in the front row of the militia.

"You, Estabrook?" said Captain Parker. "You can't even walk. Get over to the church and have Dr. Paul take a look at you."

"I want to help," the man insisted. He was bleeding profusely from the shoulder and saying again he was determined to help with the wounded. Josiah, assisted by the man called Nathaniel, helped him to his feet and with Josiah on one side and Nathaniel on the other they began walking him toward the church.

"Who're you?" the man asked Josiah.

"I'm Josiah Hartford, from Boston. Who might you be?"

"This is Prince Estabrook," said Nathaniel. "Best blacksmith is Massachusetts. One of the first to join the militia, too."

"I only hope I can still wield a hammer," Prince said, looking at his wounded arm.

"There's a lot of dead men back there," said Nathaniel. "What happened to you?"

"One of those soldiers got me with his bayonet," Prince said. "He was aiming for my heart but I moved just in time so he hit me in the arm instead." Looking at Josiah, he said, "Well, Josiah Hartford from Boston, what are you doing here? You come to fight?"

"I was just passing by," said Josiah.

"Funny how that can happen," said Prince. "You think you're just passing by and something happens that changes your whole life."

They reached the front steps of the small church, and the big double doors in front had been thrown open. Dr. Paul stood in the aisle, gesturing with his hand. "Bring him up here," he said. A table had been set up near the altar, with a white cloth thrown over it and some surgical instruments were laid out. "Get him on the table," said the doctor, "and get his jacket off." Josiah helped remove Prince's jacket and shirt, both of which were soaked with blood, and Josiah saw the hole in the man's shoulder.

"You've lost a lot of blood, Prince," said the doctor.

"Will I be able to heft my hammer again?" Prince asked anxiously.

"It'll take more than this to keep you from your work. You two," the doctor said to Josiah and Nathaniel, "go on, there's more men out there."

"What *are* you doing in Lexington, Hartford?" Nathaniel asked Josiah as they went back to the green.

"I'm on my way to Concord. My younger brother is there. I've got to bring him home."

"I wish you luck. God only knows what's going to happen after today," said Nathaniel.

"What's your trade?" Josiah asked.

"No trade, I've got a farm. Nathaniel Monroe's my name. Half the people in these parts are named Monroe, and I'm related to all of them."

Josiah and Nathaniel carried more men into the church. Some of the benches were moved to one side to make room for the wounded, and the men were laid on the wooden floor. Some were bleeding badly and their blood stained the floor in large pools. Some of the men they brought in were dead, and at the doctor's order they moved them to a corner where the

Parson stood reading over them from his Bible. The Parson was a young man, no more than thirty, and he wore the same shocked expression everyone else had as he read, "The Lord is my shepherd, I shall not want..."

"You think the British will come back this way, like Captain Parker said?" asked Nathaniel, as they carried in an unconscious man and laid him gently on the floor.

"You know of any other way to get back to Boston?"

"That's all I want, one more chance at those British bastards," said Nathaniel. "I'm ashamed of myself, after what just happened. When they started shooting I threw myself down on the green and covered my head. Didn't even shoot back. Never fired my musket. Then when they came at us with those bayonets I just ran. I feel like a coward. All my relatives must think so too."

"You'll have to prove them wrong," Josiah observed.

The militiamen were lining up again, and there were more of them now, with more arriving by the minute. Captain Parker was addressing them.

"We've got a lot to get even for," he said. "When they come past Lexington again we'll have our chance to pay them back, to show them what kind of men we are."

An expectant look came onto the faces of the militiamen. "It's a long way back to Boston," Captain Parker said ominously. "A long march back."

At Captain Parker's direction some of the militiamen joined Josiah and Nathaniel in taking the wounded and the dead into the church, and soon the green was cleared.

I've got to get back on the road, Josiah thought. I've got to get to Concord. He was about to go to where Caesar was tied at the water trough when he felt a tug at his sleeve. He turned to see a plain-faced woman looking at him anxiously. "Mr. Hartford?" she asked. "You're wanted inside," and Josiah, hurrying back inside the church, saw Dr. Paul, wearing a white apron stained with blood, standing over a man lying on the table. He was peering intently at the man's midsection, which was covered in blood. The man was groaning in pain, and the doctor's assistant was placing a leather strap in his mouth.

"You, Hartford," said the doctor, "help us hold him down while I get this ball out of his ribs. He fights like a damn lion."

"You haven't got anything to give him for the pain?" asked Josiah, remembering some of what he had seen at the medical college at Harvard.

"Nothing, except whiskey, and he's had all of that he can hold right now. You study medicine?"

"No. I'm a Harvard man, and I knew some people in the medical college."

"Ah!" said the doctor. "I'm a Harvard man too. Parson," he called to the Parson, who was still reading from his Bible over the dead, "We need your help over here." The Parson reluctantly put down his Bible and came over to the operating table and helped Josiah and Nathaniel hold the wounded man down while the doctor, using a long tweezer like steel instrument, dug into the wound on the man's side.

Josiah couldn't look. He held on with both hands, but couldn't bring himself to watch what the doctor was doing.

"Is this your husband?" he asked the woman, who couldn't bear to watch either. "My father," she said. "I told him he was too old for this, but he wouldn't listen. Now look at him! He's going to die."

"Oh, hush, girl," said the doctor, the worst of his work now over. "Look," and he held up the flattened lead ball with the long tweezers. "He'll be all right."

Josiah helped with several more operations, including one in which the man died from loss of blood. "You should think about going into the medical profession, Hartford," said the doctor. "You've got the touch for it."

"I studied philosophy," said Josiah, suddenly tired. "Now I have to get on to Concord, before the British burn the town."

"You'd better be on your way, then," said Dr. Paul, and Josiah hurried outside. The sun was high by now. There were about 150 militiamen gathered on the green, waiting.

"There will be more fighting before this day is over," said Captain Parker. "Why don't you stay and join us? Can you shoot a musket?"

"I've got to get to Concord," Josiah repeated. "My brother is there."

"Well, good luck then," said Parker. "Be careful. God only knows what is going to happen after today."

CHAPTER 13
CONCORD

Concord was six miles away. Josiah rode off on the back road. He felt an awful ache inside, fearing that because he had delayed so long at Lexington he would be late getting to Concord and something terrible would happen to Patrick. If it did, he would never be able to forgive himself.

The Willinghams would take care of Patrick, he thought. Then he remembered what Jessica had said, that if the British burned the town and Patrick was left to his own devices he would just wander off into the forest and die.

Josiah's anxiety increased as he came closer to Concord. He rode through an open field and saw smoke rising into the morning sky. Then he heard shooting, and felt his heart sinking inside.

The village came into sight now, and he rode around through more fields and pastures and toward the back of the Willinghams' house. More smoke was rising, looking like small gray clouds, and he heard more shooting, coming, he now realized, from the north end of the town. He couldn't see any people yet, not any townsfolk or British soldiers. Off to his left were the thick woods he had often played in when the Hartfords visited the Willinghams. He remembered playing hide-and-seek with Mercy when they were both children, with the rolling green hills in the background, and Mercy yelling with delight when Josiah found her.

He spurred Caesar and rode faster, and saw with relief that the Willingham house was not on fire as he had feared. But as he got closer, riding up the dusty road, he saw there had been fighting here.

A dead British soldier lay in the yard beside the vegetable garden, and the fence around the garden was broken in several places. The barn doors were open, and shards of broken glass from the windows at the back of the house lay on the ground. The back doors stood open too, and there were bullet holes in the walls.

Josiah jumped off Caesar, tied the reins to the trunk of a tree, then ran toward the house. The garden had been dug up crudely, the rows of flowers uprooted with bayonets as the soldiers searched for the weapons that were supposedly buried there. Josiah saw another dead soldier near the small barn, then ran through the open back door. "Patrick!" he shouted. "Patrick!"

There was no answer. The house appeared to be deserted. It had also been ransacked. Going into the kitchen Josiah saw broken dishes on the floor, tables turned over, cupboard doors standing open, their contents strewn about.

Josiah ran into the dining room, only to find it in a similar state of disarray. The mahogany table was intact but the chairs were knocked over, more dishes broken, the china hutch opened up. He heard more shooting, and now he smelled smoke. Through the front window he saw several fires burning in the streets nearby.

Upstairs, he thought, could Patrick be hiding upstairs? He ran up the staircase to the second floor, still calling his brother's name, but seeing nobody, and then ran upstairs to the third floor. There were still no signs of life and he went out to the balcony to get a better look at the town.

From here he could see a grand panorama of the village and the surrounding countryside. At the north end, near and around the bridge, he saw a battle taking place, with the redcoats on one side of the river and the militiamen on the other, shooting away at each other. There were more British at the other end of the village, kicking in doors, going into houses and emerging with armloads of bags and sacks and wooden boxes, then throwing them into the streets and setting them on fire.

He saw another dead soldier in the yard, this one only a few feet outside those magnificent gardens the Willinghams were so proud of. Then from the front barn a figure emerged, and with a surge of joy he saw it was Patrick.

"Patrick! Patrick!" he called, waving frantically, and saw his brother look up, smile, then walk toward the dead soldiers. "Stay there! Stay there!"

Josiah shouted, and he bounded down the stairs as fast as he could, then ran out the side door into the garden.

Through the garden fence he saw Patrick, standing over the dead soldier with his usual innocent, quizzical expression, as if trying to understand what this meant. He must have hidden in the barn when the fighting started, Josiah thought, and now he's come out to see what is going on. He held a book in one hand. What's he doing with that, Josiah wondered. He saw Patrick smile, then the smile vanished as he understood, in the depths of his mind, that this wasn't right, but he wasn't certain what exactly was wrong. He bent over the soldier as if wanting to speak to him.

The soldier's musket lay beside him, and Patrick picked it up, regarding it curiously. Josiah saw a flash of scarlet and white, saw a soldier come from the front of the house and into the yard. For an instant Josiah felt himself able to see inside the soldier's mind: The soldier saw his dead comrade, saw the tall stout American boy standing over him, a musket in his hands. Here was his dead comrade; here was his killer. The soldier cried out the same fearsome war cry Josiah had heard when the British charged the militiamen with their bayonets. Then he lunged forward, even as Josiah opened the gate and screamed "No!" with the loudest sound he had ever made, and drove the bayonet into Patrick's chest with the well-drilled motion of the British infantryman. He didn't see Josiah, who exploded through the gate like a demon and seized the musket from the astonished soldier's hands with both his own, then smashed the wooden stock of the Brown Bess into the man's face with all his might. He then turned the musket end- for-end and plunged the bayonet into the soldier's heart, killing him instantly.

Now another soldier came around from the front of the house. Josiah had never fired a musket before but he knew enough to pull the hammer back with his thumb, felt it lock into position, then pulled the trigger. The soldier was less than ten feet away and the musket ball hit him in the middle of his chest. He fell backward, his musket clattering down beside him, and didn't move again.

Josiah dropped the musket and ran to Patrick. Kneeling down, he cradled his brother's head in his arms, all the while weeping and calling his name.

Patrick opened his eyes. "Josiah," he said, trying to smile. "Where were you?"

"Patrick, I wanted to get here faster. I tried, I swear I did."

"My book, where's my book?" For a moment Patrick raised his head, then saw the book lying nearby. It was *La Geometrie* by Descartes, the same book he had brought to Concord to show Scottie Willingham. He lay his head back.

"Older brother, do you see him?"

"Who?"

"Alexander. Josiah, he's here! There he is, can't you see? He's come for me. I knew he would. He's taking me away. Josiah, don't cry. It's beautiful over there. Don't cry for me, Josiah...It's all right..." Patrick's voice trailed off, his eyes closed, and he breathed no more.

Josiah wailed, over and over, calling Patrick's name and feeling the hot tears streaming down his face. Later he would torment himself with the thought that had he only arrived a few minutes sooner he could have saved Patrick, but now all he knew was that Patrick was dead. He died with a smile on his face that froze there, giving him, in death, an angelic, happy expression, as if death was nothing to be dreaded. But to Josiah the grief he felt was the most overwhelming feeling he had ever experienced, and he held his brother's head tightly in his arms and knew nothing else until he heard more shouts and gunfire close by. He looked up, reluctantly, and saw two British soldiers in the yard, and both raised their muskets at the same time, pointed directly at him.

Josiah felt nothing, no fear, no desire to run away or try to defend himself. In a moment I'll be dead like Patrick, he thought, and could think of nothing else. But before the soldiers could fire a blast of shooting erupted from the woods behind him. The two soldiers fell down and were as dead as the ones already lying around the Willingham's house. Josiah heard shouts, then the sound of running feet, and a moment later he was surrounded by at least a dozen men.

He heard them speaking, but their voices were far away and he couldn't understand what they were saying. Then one of the men knelt down beside him, and in a compassionate voice asked, "Say there fella, you hurt?"

Josiah simply shook his head.

"I saw you get these two. Good work."

"What happened here?" said another voice, strong and commanding. "Did you kill all these bloody-backs?"

"Just those two, Captain Jake," said the first voice. "This fella here killed that one and that one single-handed."

"We've got to move. They're coming this way fast."

"We should take this guy along. He's a fighter."

The man called Captain Jake knelt down beside Josiah. "You better come with us," he said.

"This is my brother," Josiah protested, still holding Patrick's head as tightly as he could. "I can't leave him here!"

"You'd best listen to me," said Captain Jake. "There's a hundred grenadiers headed this way. They find you here like this and they'll kill you faster than you can say 'Long live the King.' I'm sorry for your brother but you can't do anything for him."

"No!" Josiah shouted. "Get away from me!"

"Would your brother want you to stay here and be killed?" asked Captain Jake. Josiah's resistance melted and gently, but with a firm hand, he took Josiah by the arm and stood him up. "Get their weapons," he ordered, gesturing to the dead soldiers. There was a crackle of gun fire nearby. "Come on!" he said. "Into the woods, now."

Josiah let out one last cry of anguish for Patrick, took one last look at his brother, lying on his back in the dirt of the Willingham's barnyard, *La Geometrie* on the ground nearby. Then, following the others, he ran into the thick forest, which enveloped them like a blanket. "Crouch down!" said Captain Jake, and he knelt, along with the others, on the prickly pine coated ground and saw one British soldier after another run past, turning into a regular river of scarlet and white.

"You better run, you British bastards," said Captain Jake. "You got a long walk back to Boston ahead of you."

•   •   •

Two hours later Josiah was standing on a hillside, holding a musket and looking down at the British column on the road below him.

These hours were a blur in his mind. The shock of Patrick's death, his killing of the British soldiers, the fact that he was now running with one of the colonial militias—it was all so hard to process, but he felt his senses sharpening and he was coming back to himself now, watching as the British force marched along in the bright mid-day sun.

There were 30 men in the group he had fallen in with. They seemed to be primarily farmers, dressed in the rough clothing of the militias, carrying the muskets and powder bags they had brought from home. Their ages ranged from boys still in their teens all the way to several who appeared to be past 50.

Their commander was called "Captain Jake," and he introduced himself to Josiah as Jake Entwhistle, a cartwright by trade, from Bedford. He was a tall slim man of 40, and carried himself and gave orders with the air of a natural leader.

The youngest of the group was known as "Little Tommy," and he looked to Josiah as if he were no more than 12, although he later learned he was 14, simply small for his age. He moved, quietly and stealthily and was employed, as Josiah was to learn, as a scout, able to get close to the enemy without being seen or heard.

After the shooting at the Willingham's house they had made their way through the forest that ran parallel to the road to Lexington, trying to always keep the British column in sight. From a hilltop they had watched the British assemble near the South Bridge, then begin their march back toward Boston, the commander, whom Captain Jake identified as Colonel Francis Smith, in a horse-drawn chaise at the head of the column, trailed closely behind by the wagons of wounded men. Without any fanfare the British left Concord, with the fires still burning, and began their journey back the same way they had come, the men marching in formation, the officers on horseback.

From a nearby hill a group of militiamen had gathered, and as the British marched out of Concord a hail of fire rained down on them. Josiah saw several redcoats fall, saw an officer on a horse get shot and tumble down to the dirt road, saw a company of soldiers rush the hill and saw the militiamen fire several shots and then retreat. Once the British had cleared the hill they returned to the main column, which was moving slowly, with more shooting coming at it all the time.

The road toward Lexington ran through a valley surrounded by small round hills and forests. There were farmhouses, barns, clumps of trees, boulders, and the kind of stone walls so common to the New England countryside. On the hills on the other side of the valley Josiah saw more and more militia men gathering, following the British column just as his group was. With each passing moment the number of rebels grew, and when Josiah's company came into a particularly dense strip of forest that took them away from the main road they could hear shooting and more shooting and they all realized the rebels were attacking the British column in force, getting bolder with each foot of hostile territory the British crossed, and while he could no longer see what was happening Josiah guessed that a real battle was taking place.

Several times Josiah's company (they were, he was to learn, called the Bedford Militia Company), came out of the woods and went toward the British column, intending to join in the fight. But each time they were stopped by a force of British soldiers, who had been dispatched from the main column to intercept any militia companies coming out of the forest that wanted to attack the main column. Each time there was shooting as both sides fired away at each other, but no real damage was done as each time the Bedford men retreated back into the woods and kept moving.

"Flankers," Captain Jake said. "Smith," (he meant the British commander) "I didn't think you were that smart. I know you from the war against the French, and you weren't too bright then. He's sending out flanker groups to protect the column from these hit-and-run attacks. That won't always work, Smith. Sooner or later we're going to get close to you."

The Bedford men kept moving through the woods, and the sound of the battle on the Lexington road never died down. They came upon the bodies of militiamen and redcoats, and then to a farmhouse a distance off the main road. Both the barn and the house had been set on fire and as the company ran toward it they saw, ahead of them, ten or twelve British soldiers running away.

"Damn them!" the man next to Josiah said, and cursing, he shook his big fist at the soldiers as they disappeared from sight.

"We'll take a rest here," said Captain Jake, and as the men gathered around the well to get water they found the bodies of a soldier and a militiaman lying side by side.

"They killed each other," the man beside Josiah declared. "Tarnation! How do you like that? They killed each other."

He was, Josiah realized, the same man who had first knelt beside him right after Patrick died. He was an outsized man, tall and broad shouldered, wearing a large round hat like the frontiersmen wore, but his had a big white feather stuck in the crown, giving him a jaunty appearance, and carried a hatchet in his belt along with a big knife.

"Have a drink?" he invited, taking a flask from his shoulder bag. As he pulled out the stopper Josiah took in the smell of rum, then took a drink of the fiery liquid. He managed not to cough as it went down, thanked the man, then handed it back.

"What's your name?" he asked. "I'm Adam."

"Josiah Hartford, Boston."

"What were you doing back there where we found you?"

"I came to get my brother, to take him home," said Josiah. "Now he's—"

"Dead, I know, I saw that too. British bastards." He took a drink for himself, then put the flask back in his shoulder bag. "We'll save the rest for later, I've got a feeling we'll need it. You're lucky we found you. We heard the British were marching to Concord so we assembled our boys and high-tailed it over there. There was some shooting around North Bridge. We got a few Brits, they got some of our boys, and we went in a loop around the town and come into the woods there just as your brother got it and you dispatched them two soldiers. When the other soldiers ran up we opened fire. We saved your life."

"Yes, I know," Josiah said tonelessly.

"Captain Jake there is a good man to have as a leader. He fought in the last war, so he knows his business. Never gets excited, always keeps his head."

They kept moving along through the forest, passing more looted and burning farm houses, the sound of the battle on the Lexington Road never out of earshot. When they were about a mile from Lexington and five miles out of Concord they went through a clearing and up a hill, through more trees, and came out of the trees into another clearing and looked down at the British column.

From the hillside Josiah could see the rebels moving alongside the British with their muskets, and from a stone wall or beside a barn or a clump of trees they would fire at the British and then disappear.

Captain Jake now turned around. "Where's Little Tommy?" As if by magic the boy popped up, seemingly out of the ground beside him, and

Captain Jake said, "Tommy, you scout ahead, get as close to them as you can, then meet up with us by the wall down there."

"Yes sir," said the boy, and he scampered off toward the column of red coats.

At Captain Jake's signal the men began moving down the hill toward a stone wall about sixty yards from the road, crouching down, getting closer and closer to the British column until Josiah could see them clearly.

It was the same road they had marched after the shooting in Lexington but by now a very different looking force of men. There were no drummers pounding their drums, no fifers playing. There was no élan in their step, and the tight, closed formations had vanished. The most distinguishing feature was the look of torment on their faces, a torment mixed with fear and bordering on hysteria.

The road was littered with the corpses of British soldiers. Many of those still marching had their heads wrapped in bandages with blood soaking through. Others marched with difficulty, tiredly, and others could only move by being helped by one of their comrades. The officers no longer rode their horses but walked along with the common soldiers, for officers on horseback were easy targets for the colonial militiamen, who were shooting at the British column from all directions. Even if they missed their mark, the shots caused the British to duck and jump in fear, and the terror caused by being shot at was taking its toll. Added to this was the frustration the soldiers felt at being such easy targets and unable to do anything about it except keep moving.

On the other side of the road Josiah saw a stone wall similar to the one he was now crouched behind. Several men popped up from behind that wall and pointed their muskets at the British. They fired, then ran for the woods, and another British soldier fell dead. Several of the soldiers fired back, but their bullets harmlessly whizzed into the air and did no damage.

Little Tommy now reappeared and knelt down beside Captain Jake. "I got so close to 'em I heard their officers sayin' they was ready to surrender," he reported. "Only they don't know who to surrender to. They're out of water, and almost out of ammunition. He said their only chance is to get to Lexington and wait for a relief column."

"Then the time to hit them is now," said Captain Jake. "Men, make ready!" Take aim!" he ordered. "Fire!" and thirty muskets went off at once, creating a deafening roar, and more British soldiers fell.

"Back to the woods!" Captain Jake ordered, and the whole group made for the woods.

They kept moving along through the trees, always keeping the road and the British column in sight. The rattle of musket fire from the road never ceased, but grew in intensity, and several times Josiah could see more militiamen descending on the British column from the hills.

As they neared a clearing, closer to the column than before, Josiah felt a bullet whiz past his ear, and was startled when it struck the tree beside him, the "whumping" sound and the bark flying off making him jump involuntarily. Ahead in the clearing was a squad of British soldiers, shooting determinedly at the Bedford men.

"Get down! Shoot!" ordered Captain Jake, and as the two sides began to exchange fire there was a war-whoop and from the trees poured a crowd of men, all of them dressed in leather leggings, deerskin shirts and fox-skin hats. Howling like madmen, they fell on the British with tomahawks and long knives. In less than a minute it was over. The Bedford men, standing up now and watching this, stood with their mouths open, all except Captain Jake, who smiled with understanding as the scene unfolded.

"Well, look who's here," he said when the last British soldier had been dispatched. "Thomas Rowley. Last time I saw you was when we were being chased by the Hurons. What are you doing here? I thought you stayed in Vermont."

"It's Major Rowley now," the man said, coming over to shake hands with Captain Jake. "We heard that a war might start here any day and we decided we couldn't let you Massachusetts men have all the fun."

"What've we got here, Captain Jake?" asked Adam, coming forward and surveying the men behind Major Rowley, uncertain what to make of them.

"Fellas, these are the famous Green Mountain Boys," said Captain Jake. "Come all the way here to help us fight the British."

"You're damn right," said one of the Vermont men. He stood next to Major Rowley, giving the impression of being his second in command (it turned out he was) and he held a weapon unlike anything Josiah had ever seen. It was similar to a musket, only the barrel was longer and thinner and the bore was much smaller than that of a musket. Adam noticed it too."

"What the hell kind of a musket you got there, fella?"

"That's no musket," said Captain Jake.

"Is that a Kentucky long rifle?" asked Adam.

"You're damn right," the Vermont man said again. He was nearly as big a man as Adam, and the two of them stood looking at each other, eye-for-eye, sizing one another up.

"He can probably pick off one of those bloody-backs from here with that," said Captain Jake.

"You're damn right," said the man.

"Are those the only three words you know?" asked Adam. "There's no chance in hell you could hit them from here. They must be close to 300 yards away."

"Wanna bet?" said the man. He took a chunk of chewing tobacco out of his pocket, bit off a hunk, and began chewing it determinedly.

"Anytime," Adam said, but something of the self-assured expression on the man's face caused him to change his mind. "No," he amended, "just show me," and the man, who sported an ill trimmed beard and what to Josiah seemed a disagreeable face, like that of a pirate, took aim with his long but (Josiah had to admit) beautifully crafted weapon, closed one eye, then pulled the trigger. A British soldier at the rear of the column fell, wounded.

"Damn!" said Adam. "I wouldn't believe it if I hadn't seen it."

Some return shots came from the column below, but they fell far short of the men on the hill. The British were more disorganized than ever, their column clearly in danger of falling completely apart as they approached the last hill before they reached Lexington. "Are you the poet?" Josiah asked, for he had read some poetry by a man named Thomas Rowley at Harvard. "Yes," Rowley said.

"Written anything lately?" asked Captain Jake.

"None I'd want you to read."

"What say we join forces?" Captain Jake asked.

"You all know the terrain better," Rowley agreed. "So tell us, what's the best way to get after them again?"

"Lexington is just over that hill," said Captain Jake. "My scout here," he patted Little Tommy on the head, "tells me they're hoping to meet up with a relief column there."

"There's a little village called Lincoln just a stone's throw from Lexington," said Adam. "I've got a feeling we could meet up with some other militias there, get a bigger force together, and get after them again when they set out for Boston."

"Count me in," the piratical-looking man agreed.

"What is it, you can't speak in sentences more than three words?" Adam asked.

"Not very often," the man replied.

"Have a drink?" Adam invited, getting out his flask. "Massachusetts rum."

"Naw, try mine," said the man. "Vermont whiskey," and each drank some of the other's liquor as they set off through the woods toward Lincoln township, Captain Jake and Major Rowley leading the way.

CHAPTER 14
THE RETREAT

"What in God's name has happened?" asked Hugo, staring in disbelief as he saw cartload after cartload of battered and bloody soldiers going by, their faces vacant with exhaustion and shock. Many had suffered head wounds, so they had blood-stained bandages wrapped around their foreheads, and others had their arms in slings and they too, showed where the blood had soaked through. Some were dead, having succumbed from loss of blood as they were transported back toward Boston from the fighting taking place outside the city.

Hugo and Tarleton had been sent by General Gage to Charlestown Neck to find out what was going on as the first cartloads of dead and wounded soldiers neared Boston. It was late in the afternoon, the sun was getting ready to set, and in the distance they could hear musket fire and then the boom of Lord Percy's cannon, for the relief column, unlike Colonel Smith's force, had taken artillery with it, and the thunder of the cannons carried many miles.

The reports had been coming in all day: scattered, frantic, sometimes contradictory accounts of what was happening in the countryside. The first reports seemed to indicate all was going well. But when the official word came from Colonel Smith requesting Lord Percy's relief column be mobilized and sent at once, Hugo, as well as Gage and the rest of the staff, began to fear that something had gone terribly wrong. Then more reports came in: Fighting at Lexington. Rebels dead. Resistance at Concord. Fighting at North Bridge. Column under attack. By the time Lord Percy had marched his force out of Boston it was mid-day and the reports were taking on a desperate tone: Send relief column to Lexington as fast as possible. Casualties heavy. Rebels attacking from all directions. Request assistance at once. Rebels all around.

Lord Percy had ordered the wounded sent back first, and they were arriving now, wagonload after wagonload. The wagons made their way over the narrow Charlestown Neck, toward the wharf at Charlestown where ship's boats were waiting to take them to hospitals in Boston. Many of the wounded men, Hugo realized, would never get the help they needed, for they were dead already or else soon would be, for while he had never seen dead people before Hugo could tell that some of these men, while they were still breathing, had not long to live and there was nothing anyone could do to save them. Most horrible of all were those who were bleeding to death. Their faces were so pale as to have taken on an unnatural and ugly white color, rather like wax, and their eyes were vacant, as if they were already part way out of this world but not quite into the next.

"What happened?" Hugo repeated his question to a soldier with a wounded arm.

"Rebels, sir, thousands of rebels."

"Thousands, you say?" asked Tarleton.

"Yes sir, they were coming at us from every direction. The hills were swarming with them."

"They was shooting at us from the trees, from the houses, from behind rocks and fences," said another private. "They won't come out and fight in the open like men. They shoot at you and then run."

"Cowards," said Tarleton through gritted teach. "Goddamn cowards." Then, in a gentler voice, he asked the soldier whose arm was in a sling, "Where you from?"

"London, sir," he replied. "I wish I was there now, walking with me girl alongside the Thames."

"It's always nice to think about home and girls," said Tarleton.

"Johnny here is from the Midlands, ain't you Johnny?" said the soldier, poking at the man next to him, who appeared to be asleep. But the man didn't move, and when the soldier nudged him he toppled over onto the soldier's lap. "Johnny? Johnny?" The soldier shook him repeatedly, then let out a howl of terror. "He's dead! Oh God! Get him off me! Get him off me!" The soldier continued to yell until Tarleton slapped his face.

"Stop that, soldier," he said sternly. "Don't ever do that in front of anybody."

The soldier subsided, and looked on gratefully as Tarleton ordered some able- bodied men to remove the body of the dead man from the cart.

"Thank you, sir," said the soldier.

"A British soldier has to behave better than that," said Tarleton sternly. "Now go on, get yourself fixed up so you can go fight the rebels again."

"Yes sir. I can't wait for another crack at them."

"That's the spirit," said Tarleton.

They moved on to the next wagon. "What did you see out there, soldiers?" Tarleton asked us.

"It's awful, sir," said a private. "They was in front of us, behind us, even on top of Tarleton looked keenly at the soldier, the harshness on the falcon face fading for the moment. "You're from Liverpool," he declared.

"That's right sir," the soldier said. "I was born right 'longside the Mersey River. Me father was a waterman."

"I thought so," said Tarleton. "I'm from Liverpool too. What's your name?"

"Jones, sir. Tommy Jones." He and Tarleton exchanged smiles, and the soldier, a small black-haired man, said, "You know what's terrible, sir? They're scalping our boys."

"Scalping?" Tarleton gasped. "Scalping?"

"Yes sir."

"No," said Tarleton.

"Yes sir, I seen it myself," said Private Jones, and several of the other men in the cart nodded in agreement. "I seen their bloody heads, sir. The rebels took their scalps just like Indian savages, and they hack at our boys with their tomahawks, even when they're down and can't defend themselves."

"Scalped!" Tarleton said again. "You're telling me these rebels scalped British soldiers? Oh, these bloody cowards are going to pay for that! I'm going after them right now!" He turned and went to his horse, preparing to mount.

"Ban! Stop it!" said Hugo.

"Get off me!" said Tarleton, pushing him away, and as he had before, Hugo noted the man's unusual strength. "I'm going out there and get a piece of those rebels myself."

"Ban, don't be a fool. You haven't gotten any orders to engage the enemy. You go out there and General Gage will have you court-martialed and sent back to England in irons. Come on Ban, use your head!"

Tarleton already had a hold on his saddle horn and he stopped, reluctantly, and returned with Hugo to the road toward Charlestown.

Hugo now thought of Jeremy, and asked a soldier in the next wagon, "Have you seen Lieutenant Light? He was with Colonel Smith."

"No sir, haven't seen him."

Hugo and Tarleton remounted their horses and continued along the road. They could hear more cannons booming, and as the sun went down, could see the flashes from the cannons' muzzles. Talking to more men, they were able to piece together what had happened:

Colonel Smith's force, battered and bruised, had made its way over the last hill on the Lexington Road and there beheld the most wonderful sight any of them had ever seen: Lord Percy's relief column, spread out in all its glory across the Lexington Green and beyond. Colonel Smith's men, exhausted, maddened from lack of water and from the rebels' constant harassment, had lost all semblance of discipline and broke and ran for the safety of the green. As the rebels came into sight they were greeted with artillery fire, which quickly dissuaded them from taking any concerted action on the British in Lexington. Then, when Colonel Smith's men had rested and the wounded were placed in wagons, the British force, now numbering around 1,300 men, had begun making its way back toward Boston, with the rebels still attacking them every step of the way, their numbers growing by the minute, continuing to shoot from behind stone fences, from farmhouses, from barns, from clumps of trees.

The narrow road was becoming clogged with wagons and soldiers. As Hugo and Tarleton continued their ride they saw more and more of Colonel Smith's men, interspersed with the wagonloads of wounded, and once again, Hugo was shocked at what he saw.

"My God, look at them," said Hugo. Some of the men marched as if they were asleep. They were dirty, their uniforms and their faces covered with dust and grime from the road. They slogged along, some carrying their muskets on their shoulders by the barrel, some with no muskets at all. The more badly walking wounded held onto horses to give them a little more stability and to make walking easier. One of the horses looked familiar to Hugo and slowing down, he said to a soldier, "Is that Lieutenant Light's horse?"

"Yes sir," said the soldier. "Lieutenant Light was good enough to let us use it, sir."

"Where is Lieutenant Light?" Hugo asked anxiously. "Is he all right?" The men exchanged glances, and one of them said, "He got wounded, sir."

"Wounded! How bad?" asked Hugo.

"When the fighting first started, back at the North Bridge, in Concord, I think," said the soldier. "I can't remember exactly."

"You better remember, soldier," said Hugo. "Or I'll see you get a damn good hiding! Now what happened to Lieutenant Light?"

"Sir, I'm trying to remember," said the soldier defensively.

"The man's exhausted, he's wounded, and he's been shot at all day," said Tarleton, giving Hugo a quizzical look. "Give him a chance to think."

"He can think later! I want to know what happened to Jeremy," Hugo said sharply.

Then he looked at the soldier again. "Tell me, soldier."

"We crossed the North Bridge, sir, looking for rebel supplies, and them rebels attacked us, hundreds of them, so we had to retreat," said the soldier. "There was so many rebels shooting at us it might have been a real rout, but Lieutenant Light come up, and he stopped the retreat. He says, 'Reform, and stand your ground men,' and we did. We held that bridge, thanks to him, long enough to get the rest of our company across. By then there was rebels everywhere so we had to retreat through the town. Lieutenant Light done a great job, sir. He's a real man. Then as we was retreating, he was holding the rear with some other boys, and that's when he got it in the arm."

"He got shot in the arm?" Hugo gasped.

"I don't think it was too bad, sir. They bounded it up tight to stop the bleeding. I think he's all right, sir."

"He better be all right, or you will pay," said Hugo, and he and Tarleton kept riding alongside the road.

"What is all this?" asked Tarleton, and when Hugo didn't answer he went on, "Jeremy Light, a bloody hero. Who would have thought? The youngest and least experienced officer in Boston. I only wish I'd been there." Then his expression turned ugly, as more wagonloads of wounded went by and some of the men in them called for water, for at the same time he saw several American boys sitting on a nearby well, watching the procession. Leaping from his horse, he drew his sword in one hand and his pistol in the other. "You!" he shouted. "Fill that bucket with water and take it to the soldiers in the wagons! Now! Move or I'll kill you, goddamn little rebel bastards!"

"We're ain't rebels, sir," a freckle-faced boy protested. "We're Tories."

"That's a damn lie," Tarleton declared, and he made the boys draw buckets of water from the well and take it to the soldiers in the wagons.

Tarleton watched, relentlessly, as the boys took water to the men in the wagon, all the while cursing them and threatening to kill them if they didn't do as he said.

The fighting was getting closer and closer as the last of the wagonloads of wounded and dead men went by. Seeing the wagonloads of dead men bothered Hugo more than anything else, although Tarleton seemed unfazed by it. The dead men were stacked up on top of one another, many of them with bloody heads and blood-stained uniforms, and they looked unnatural, out of place.

"I hope they bury them all quickly," said Hugo. "I don't like seeing them like this."

"There's a lot more left behind, I'll wager," said Tarleton. "Look at that one! He's been scalped, I'll take my oath."

These wagons were followed by more of the exhausted men of Colonel Smith's command. Hugo and Tarleton continued riding along the road, closer and closer to the fighting, and in the distance Hugo saw large fires burning. When Captain James Gore came riding up to them, Hugo asked him what those fires were.

Gore's face was covered with dust from the road. "Those?" he said. "I'll tell you. General Percy, he knows how to deal with these rebels. Those are barns and farmhouses. The rebels were shooting at us from inside the houses and from on top of the barns. So Lord Percy ordered all the farms along the road burned down. That'll teach them rebels to hide amongst civilians."

"Good for Lord Percy," said Tarleton. "I hope some of those rebels were inside when the houses burned."

"Gore, have you seen Jeremy Light?" Hugo asked.

"Haven't seen him," said Gore. "You two are ordered to come with me. Lord Percy wants you."

"Gage ordered us to reconnoiter, then report back to him," said Hugo.

"That's your problem. Lord Percy wants you to report to him right now. Follow me. Those are orders."

Hugo and Tarleton exchanged glances, then followed Captain Gore on their horses.

"At least tell us what's going on, why Percy wants us so badly," said Tarleton. "Are we going to fight?"

"See up there?" said Gore, pointing to the north. "Rebel positions."

Hugo now got his first look at the rebels—a small force gathering near Mystic River. They moved about busily, digging in, preparing to fight. Hugo heard more shooting, then felt something he had never felt before but would never forget: the whoosh of air as a musket ball flew past his head. It was followed by another, and Hugo realized he was being shot at. They're trying to kill me, he thought.

"Keep your heads down," said Gore. "Some of these colonials have Kentucky long rifles. They can hit you from 300 yards with those."

They followed the road in an arc, away from the Mystic River and toward Cambridge and Watson's Corner. They were still passing Colonel Smith's men and up ahead, Hugo saw the flash of artillery fire, followed by the roar of the cannon. There was a circle of wagons and a large conglomeration of soldiers there, and as they got closer Hugo saw a knot of officers, in the center of which was the tall, ungainly form of General Lord Percy.

"Dismount, and come with me," said Gore.

Lord Percy spoke in his usual way, getting right to the point. There was never any nonsense with this man, and Hugo, looking him in the eye, saw with grudging admiration the resoluteness and firmness of character that made a good leader.

"I'm running low on officers," he said curtly. "The rebels deliberately target them. What is that up there?"

"Why, that's Prospect Hill, sir," said Hugo.

"Correct. The rebels have seized it," said Percy. "We have to drive them off."

Hugo, looking at the small hill, small, but larger than the others that dotted the roads of the Boston countryside, saw the rebels at the summit, crouching down as the shots from the artillery came down on them. "They appear to be concentrating their forces up there," Percy continued. "If they come down off that hill in sufficient numbers they can cut the column in half."

A cannon roared nearby. Hugo heard the distinctive sound of the cannonball flying toward the rebels on the hill, followed by the crash as the cannonball hit. He stole a quick glance at the crew of the artillery piece—a six pounder, he saw, and watched as they swabbed out the barrel and prepared to reload.

"Are we going to attack the hill, sir?" asked Tarleton eagerly. "I want a chance at these cowards."

"Cowards?" Percy said sharply. "Who do you think has been killing British soldiers all day, Lieutenant? The bloody Coldstream Guards? The rebels know what they're doing. They aren't stupid enough to fight us our way. So they're fighting their way and they are making it work. That shows a lot more intelligence than you are showing right now. Wise up, Lieutenant. *Know your enemy.* You'll be a better officer that way."

"Yes sir," Tarleton said sullenly.

"Tarleton, you will go with Gore and attack from the right. Chamberlain, you go with Vickers here and attack from the left. We'll focus the artillery in the center. The rebels don't stand up to artillery fire."

"I think your plan will work, sir," said Hugo.

"It has to," said Percy. "We're almost out of shot and shell. If we don't drive the rebels off that hill the column is done for. I've only got four flanker companies left. You'll take two each. Go and get ready."

At long last, Hugo thought, at long last I'm going into battle. I'm a soldier and I'm going into battle. He felt a thrill, followed by fear. What if I get killed? But he put that thought out of his mind. Him, killed? No, it was impossible. Then, inexplicably, he thought of Josiah Hartford.

He wondered where Josiah was right now, and what he would think of all this. Josiah had said so many times that he was against war, and wouldn't fight in one. Fool, Hugo thought. Too bad Josiah isn't here to feel what I'm feeling now, a sense of excitement and elation beyond anything either of us ever thought of. This was war, it was all around him, and when he heard

Major Vickers' voice for the troops to make ready to charge the hill, he felt a thrill run through him, energizing him from top to bottom with a feeling that he could jump over mountains. "My first action," he thought. He drew his sword and stood beside Major Vickers, in the proper manner of a British officer, and when General Percy gave the order he waved his sword and shouted along with all the other men and they began running up the hill toward the rebel positions, and he felt once again the whoosh of a musket ball as it went past him. In the darkness he could see the muzzle flashes as the rebels fired, and he wondered what it felt like to kill a man in combat and found himself hoping he could do that in the next few minutes. He was, however, to be disappointed.

•   •   •

Hugo Chamberlain had no idea that his one-time best friend, Josiah Hartford, was less than half a mile away from him. He was at the crest of Prospect Hill with the men of the Bedford Militia Company and the Vermont Green Mountain Boys. They had been ordered by General William Heath, who had come from his home in Roxbury to take command of the militias in their ongoing battle with the retreating British, to occupy the hill. Heath had seen the importance of Prospect Hill and understood that if the rebels could attack the British column from here they could cut it in two and possibly capture a good-sized chunk of it. So he had ordered these units to seize the hill and wait for reinforcements.

Josiah, kneeling near Captain Jake, Adam, Major Rowley, and the man he had nicknamed "The Pirate," did not know that Hugo was one of the many British soldiers he could see on the road at the bottom of the hill. He crouched, holding his musket, which he thought he must have fired at least 30 times since they had left the hill outside Lexington and set off for Lincoln, as Adam had suggested. There they had joined up with some militias from Cambridge and Charlestown, and had been harrying the British column every chance it had, as the British made their way slowly back toward Boston.

They had gone past Russell House and Cooper's Tavern, always shooting, always retreating into whatever cover they could find, only to emerge and shoot again. Josiah had no idea of how many soldiers he may have killed or wounded. He fired, reloaded, fired again, sometimes aiming carefully, sometimes not, but always the thick smoke from the muskets clouded his view and so he really for the most part wasn't certain if his shots found their mark or not.

There had been fierce fighting at Menotomy, but it was at the Alewife Brook that runs off the Mystic River that he had felt real terror for the first time, for that was the first time he was exposed to artillery fire.

The rebels were aware that Lord Percy was now in command of the British force, and according to Captain Jake, he was a much more capable man than Colonel Smith. "He's one of the best they've got," he said. "He's brought cannons with him."

"Cannons?" Adam asked anxiously.

"Those are six pounders. Small ones. Don't worry about them," he said, but when Josiah and the others heard the screeching, rocket-like sound of the cannonballs as they tore through the air they were frightened as never before. A musket ball fired your way was bad enough, but the cannons brought terror to a new level. On the other side of Alewife Brook a British flanker unit of light infantry had made a stand, and backed up by the cannons, they had prevented the rebels from cutting off the road to Boston.

"Holy Jesus!" Adam burst out, the first time a cannonball landed nearby. "If that's a small one I hate to think what the big ones must be like." More cannonballs fell, and several men were literally torn apart. Others wet themselves and ran for their lives, only to come back when the cannons stopped firing, shame-faced. As the British flankers advanced the colonists pulled back, then made a wide circling march behind the British column and across the road, then ran to Prospect Hill, and waited and watched as the British continued passing by. But then the column stopped, and it became obvious the British were planning something.

"What do you think they're up to down there, Captain Jake?" asked Adam.

"If I was them I'd attack this hill," said Captain Jake. "You think so, Rowley?"

"We need more men up here, right now," said Rowley, "or we'll never hold this."

"You're damn right," said The Pirate.

Captain Jake summoned Little Tommy. He hastily scrawled some words on a piece of paper and gave it to the boy. "You high-tail it over to General Heath and give this to him. Tell him we need more men up here, as many as he can spare." At that moment an artillery barrage began, and the rocketing sound of the cannonballs flying filled the air. "Tell him there's no time to lose."

Tommy dashed off, running as fast he could down the hill. The men hunkered down, covering their heads as the cannonballs began to hit and throw big columns of dirt into the air. Another burst overhead, raining flakes of hot steel down on them.

"Jesus!" said Adam. "What the hell was that?"

"That was shot," said Captain Jake. "Explodes in the air. I didn't think they would bring any out here."

"You were wrong about that!" Adam retorted.

It was nearly dark by now and the flashes from the cannons' muzzles flared brightly each time one was fired. The bursting shot overhead lit up the sky and reflected on the ground. Then suddenly the cannonade stopped. As the sound died away and the light from the bursting shot faded, there was a roar of men shouting and from both sides the British soldiers came running up the hill, their bayonets fixed and yelling at the top of their voices. The militiamen rose from the ground and all began shooting and when Josiah fired he saw a British soldier fall, 50 yards away from him.

"There's way too many, we better clear out fast," said Major Rowley to Captain Jake, who hesitated at first, then agreed.

"Fall back, fall back," he shouted, and the rebels retreated off the hill, running down the same way Little Tommy had. Josiah, so weary he sometimes wondered if he could move another step, ran as well, and when they had reached the bottom of the hill they turned and looked, even as they heard, and saw British soldiers on top of Prospect Hill, cheering and waving their muskets.

They went past Winter Hill, and encountered other groups of militiamen. Captain Jake went off to see if he could find out what the overall situation was, and they soon found themselves alongside Mystic River, where they sat down amongst the trees and watched as the river, now bathed in moonlight, rolled by toward the bay.

"Looks like the fighting's over for today," Captain Jake reported. The Bedford men and the Green Mountain Boys were all sitting around campfires next to the river. "The British are holed up in Charlestown, and making their way into Boston by boat. The new militias coming in are being ordered to dig in all around the city. I think we're going to have a siege. Men are coming from all over New England now. Take a look." Josiah and the others all stood up and looking out, saw hundreds, perhaps thousands of campfires, lighting up the ever increasing darkness. "We'll bed down here tonight," Captain Jake went on, "and see what tomorrow brings."

Night had fallen completely now, ending the longest day of Josiah Hartford's life. The big fellow, Adam, sat on his right, offering him the last of the rum he carried in his flask. The other men sat around the campfire, stoking it with wood when needed, and as Josiah stared at the flames he saw the face of his dead brother, speaking and smiling at him, and the faces of the two British soldiers he had killed in the Willingham's yard. He had killed other men today too, but he hadn't been close enough to them to see their faces, but they mingled with the bodies of the dead he had seen strewn along the Lexington- Concord Road, one after another, some in the British scarlet-and-white and some in the rough clothes of the militiamen. He also saw the burned and looted houses and the shocked faces of the people who had been driven out of their homes.

The men all seemed as tired as Josiah, except for the boisterous Adam, who said, "That was some lickin' we give 'em today. What's next?"

No one seemed to know. A jug of cheap whiskey was being passed around, and Josiah drank it before he fell into the deepest sleep of his life, lying on a rough blanket next to a fire and surrounded by strangers.

•   •   •

When he awoke he didn't know where he was. All around him men were talking, stretching, throwing wood on the fire which had nearly gone out during the night. Surprised and frightened, he leaped to his feet, and then the events of the day before all came back to him. Picking up the few belongings he had left, he found Captain Jake talking to Major Rowley, Adam, and the Pirate.

"Captain Jake," he said earnestly, "I've got to get back to Boston now. Do you know if there's a horse or a wagon I can use? I can pay for it. I'll walk all the way if I have to, but a ride would be good if I can get one."

Captain Jake and the others looked at him incredulously. "You can't go to Boston, Hartford," said the Captain.

"But I need to go home. My family will be worried about me. They don't know where I am—or, that my brother is dead. I have to go."

"You can't," Captain Jake said gently. "The city's cut off. We have lines around it, and so do the British. No one is going in or out. It looks like we're going to have a siege."

"But I have to—I must—my mother—my father—"

Josiah moved as if to go around Captain Jake, but the Captain stepped in front of him. "You're a soldier now, Hartford. A soldier in this army." When Josiah tried to get past him Captain Jake took him by the shoulders and shook him, not hard but with enough force to get his attention. "You can't go, Hartford. You're here. Get used to it!"

Josiah looked at the other men, and saw from their faces that the Captain was right. He walked away, sat down on the blanket he had used the night before, covered his face with his hands, and silently wept until he had no tears left.

CHAPTER 15
SIEGE

"Hugo tells me you are recovering fast," said Tarleton. "How's the arm?"

"I will be ecstatically happy to get out of here," said Jeremy Light. He sat upright in bed, clad in a dirty white hospital-issue nightshirt. His hair, however, was neatly combed and he was clean shaven as always. The baby face, which made him look even younger than his nineteen years, shone with happiness at the sight of Hugo and Tarleton. Jeremy's blue eyes, which to Hugo were his most attractive feature, never seemed to lose their sparkle. In the month since the fighting at Lexington and Concord, while he convalesced in the hospital, Jeremy had never lost his cheerful attitude or optimistic outlook. "The arm?" he said. "Mending quite well. Look, they've taken the bandages off, all I have left now are some scars." He peeled back the oversized sleeve to show some red scars on his arm and shoulder.

"You were fortunate," said Tarleton. "When do you leave?"

"Tomorrow, thank the Lord," said Jeremy. "Back on duty! Back to my room on Barton's Point! Ban, how come you haven't come to see me before? Hugo comes every chance he gets."

"I don't like hospitals," said Tarleton. "Too many people die in them."

"I shouldn't think death would bother you," said Jeremy.

"Sometimes it does," admitted Tarleton. "I don't want Death getting any ideas about me before my time comes."

"But when your time does come, what then?" Jeremy pressed.

"Then there isn't much you can do," said Tarleton. "But there's no sense in inviting it or hurrying it along."

"What makes it even worse is that this place is located right next to a cemetery," said Hugo.

They were in the British Army Hospital near School Street and Long Acre. It had once been a workhouse but the Army had converted it into a hospital to accommodate all the wounded and dying men after the fighting on April 19. It sat close to one of Boston's oldest burying grounds and rumor had it that it had been selected for just that reason— when men died they wouldn't have to be taken far to be buried. Already there were a number of fresh graves and crosses, mingling with the old ones, and Hugo wondered how many more boys from London or Manchester would end up there, buried so far from home. But that was the price of Empire.

Hugo surveyed the rows of beds filled with wounded and sick men. Many were asleep, others simply lying listlessly and staring at nothing. The stench of medicine, of human waste, and of sick and unwashed human beings revolted him. It will be nice, he thought, when Jeremy leaves this place.

Jeremy had been one of the last of the column to get back to Boston on April 19. He had lost a great deal of blood and was so exhausted he appeared to be walking in his sleep. Hugo had brought him to the hospital himself and worried night and day that the boy wasn't going to live, or that he might lose the wounded arm. Amputation was the surgeons' favorite method of dealing with wounds to the limbs, just hacking them off like the branches of a tree. Jeremy had indeed been fortunate. The rebel ball had missed the bone. Another had grazed him, leaving a wound in his side requiring stitches but causing no lasting damage.

"Jeremy Light, a hero," said Tarleton, as if he couldn't believe it.

"Gage mentioned you in the dispatches," said Hugo. "You'll be getting a decoration."

"You're not joking with me, are you?" said Jeremy seriously.

"I saw the dispatches myself."

"What's the latest?" Jeremy asked. "Anything new going on?"

"Every day more rebels join those already out there," said Hugo. "There must be close to 20,000 of them now."

"Scrubs and scallies, the lot of them," Tarleton declared. His hatred for the rebels had only intensified after April 19. The rumor that British soldiers had been scalped spread through the garrison and while there was no proof that this had actually happened, everyone believed it. This fanned the fires of rancor among the troops and it would be hard to find a single soldier in Boston who was not dying for a chance to get even with the rebels.

"How's your social life, Ban?" asked Jeremy, who as always loved to gossip. "Tell us about your latest conquest."

"I've been too busy soldiering to have time for women," said Tarleton.

"That can't be true!" Jeremy scoffed.

"It is," said Tarleton. He got up and put on his hat. "In fact, I have to go and do some soldiering right now."

"Where to?" asked Jeremy.

"My new job," Tarleton said eagerly. "Leading raiding parties on the other side of the Charles. Hit and run. Setting barns on fire, scouting rebel positions,"

"Honestly?" said Jeremy.

"And getting damn good at it too," said Hugo. "Ban is becoming the best scout in the colonies."

"Off I go," said Tarleton. "Down the rebels!"

"Up the Empire!" Hugo and Jeremy said at the same time. "Tarleton a scout," said Jeremy.

"It's the perfect task for him," said Hugo. "He's made for it." On foot or mounted, Tarleton could lead a small detachment of men and move stealthily along the river, carefully noting where the rebels were weakest and strongest and bringing the information back to Province House. After the incident with the Dinwiddies Gage had no use for Tarleton and had only given him this assignment because he was short of officers after the fighting on April 19 and badly needed intelligence about the rebel positions outside Boston. Tarleton had performed it so well that Gage had then allowed him to launch some probing attacks along the rebel lines, using the fast-moving light infantry.

The rumors had it that Gage was planning an attack of his own, but no one, not even Hugo, knew what was actually in Gage's mind right now. After the disasters of April 19 Gage had taken to his bed for a week, claiming to be so ill as to see no one. Only Hugo and Lord Percy knew he was actually in shock at what had happened and so depressed that he could barely function. He had confessed to Hugo that in the days immediately following the fiasco of Concord he had considered blowing his brains out. All his careful planning and preparation for the strike on Concord had blown up in his face. He had failed, and he knew it, and even worse, he knew he would be blamed for it.

"I have to leave too," said Hugo. "I just got word there is some sort of flap at Headquarters. No doubt there will be plenty for you to do when you report for duty tomorrow."

"I can't wait," said Jeremy. "I can't bear to be stuck in this bed anymore. Wait. I've been meaning to give this back to you." He produced the infinity symbol medallion Hugo had given him before he left for Concord. "You know what? You were right. I think this saved me."

"I told you," said Hugo with a great deal of self-satisfaction and placing it around his neck once again. "Next time you'll listen to me."

"I always listen to you," said Jeremy. He looked around quickly to see if anyone could be watching, and satisfied no one was, took Hugo's hand and squeezed. "I've missed you," he said softly.

"And I you," Hugo replied, withdrawing his hand and standing up. Jeremy was a bit careless at times. "I have to go. See you tomorrow."

Hugo set off for Province House, going along Bishop's Alley, past the shops selling their trinkets and candies, then turned left on Milk Street and across Marlborough to Province House. A private had brought him a note that his presence was needed at headquarters immediately, so he hurried along and when he got to the third floor he found the big double doors to Gage's office shut, something that only happened when a momentous event was about to take place. When he was shown in he found General Gage and Lord Percy sitting close to one another at the big conference table. Gage was holding an official dispatch from London in his hands, staring as if it was his death warrant.

"When will he be arriving?" Lord Percy was asking as Hugo entered.

"May 25, on the *Cerebus*," said Gage. "This can only mean one thing," he went on, glumly. "I wonder how Margaret is going to take it?"

"Thomas, it doesn't necessarily mean that," said Percy, in an uncharacteristically gentle voice and using Gage's first name, something he rarely did with anyone, let alone Gage, with whom he was not on the friendliest of terms.

"I wish I knew what it was about," said Hugo.

"See for yourself," said Gage, handing the dispatch to him. It bore, Hugo saw immediately, the seal of the Secretary of the Colonies, meaning it came directly from Lord Dartmouth in London. It informed General Thomas Gage, Commander in Chief of the North American Colonies, that Major General William Howe would arrive in Boston on May 25, aboard the ship *Cerebus*, to assist Gage in "restoring order in Boston and putting down the rebellion in Massachusetts."

"There's no gainsaying this," said Gage. "It's all over for me."

London was sending the most senior officer in the British Army to Boston. The implications were crystal clear: Gage had failed to put down the rebellion. Howe was being sent to clean up the mess he had made. Gage held his head in his hands and appeared ready to weep.

Boston was a city under siege. Gun emplacements were everywhere, more trenches were being dug, and preparations continued to repulse a rebel attack. Daily the rebel army got bigger, and at night their campfires dotted the hills and the countryside, reminding the people of Boston and the British garrison of how many there were.

But in spite of the rebels' numerical superiority most of the officers were of the opinion the rebels could be defeated, that if the British were to mount a determined attack they could break the rebel lines. The fighting on April 19 had only deepened the contempt the officers held for the Americans, who had to shoot from behind rocks and stone walls and didn't have the courage to face the British in the field and fight the way soldiers were supposed to fight.

Only Lord Percy disagreed. His opinion of the rebels had changed drastically on April 19. He maintained that the rebels were a much more formidable force than anyone gave them credit for. Cowards couldn't have shot up Colonel Smith's column, and cowards couldn't be holding the garrison in the city at bay. Percy, who had once despised the rebels, was now outspoken in his views that the Americans knew perfectly well what they were about and that it was going to be a long and costly war—perhaps too costly for the British people to bear.

"We haven't finished paying for the last war," Percy said to Hugo one day. "And now these fools in London want to start another! Wars are expensive, Chamberlain. All these politicians think of is the 'glory' of war, they never think of the liability. And the King is thinking of bringing Germans over here! What folly! That is going to cost a lot and will almost certainly mean we'll lose."

"I don't follow that line of thinking, sir," Hugo said.

"Bringing in foreign mercenaries will turn the Americans against us like nothing else," Percy declared. "Most Americans are loyal to the King. If we bring Germans over here and turn them loose that will tip the balance, for no one likes to have foreigners rampaging about their land, and no one rampages like Germans."

"Do you think the Prussian king would really lend out his army that way, sir?"

"Not Prussians, Chamberlain. Hessians."

"Hessians?" Hugo repeated.

"Yes, Chamberlain, Hessians." He allowed the word "Hessians" to hang in the air for a moment, then said, "I'd like to go home if His Majesty will allow it. This is going to be a long war and it may end badly for us."

The news that General Howe would soon be arriving sent Gage into another paroxysm of depression. His wife put up a much braver front. Hugo sensed that Margaret Gage didn't mind the prospect of leaving Boston and all of its stresses behind and looked forward to a pleasant and peaceful life in England at Firle Castle in Sussex, home of the Gage family since the 1400s. Quite soon she was busy planning a party to honor the arrival of General Howe, a party which all the senior officers and the leading Tories of Boston would be invited.

Joshua Loring was often seen at headquarters, accompanied by the brutish Cunningham. He had, shortly after the events of April 19, gotten the shocked and distracted Gage to enable him to take charge of the rebel prisoners who had been taken that day. Despite their small numbers there seemed to be an endless of amount of paperwork that had to be done regarding them, and it seemed to Hugo that every day Loring was there with a new document to be signed. It had nothing to do with Hugo's work, but his distaste for Loring caused him to believe that whatever it was, the man was up to no good.

As the last days of May approached Gage started to appear at headquarters once again.

"I'll be going home in a few months, Chamberlain," he said sadly.

"You don't know that, sir."

"No need to spare my feelings. They'll spell failure with my name now. Thomas Gage, the man who couldn't quash the rebellion in the American colonies." Gage sighed and was silent for a moment, thinking this over. "I'd be obliged if you'd stay on as my adjutant, Hugo. Help me with the transfer of power, settle all my affairs here."

"Of course I will, sir. You know you can count on me."

"Thank you," Gage said gratefully, offering his hand. "Informers have been my undoing, Chamberlain. If Revere hadn't alerted the rebel militias we might have pulled off our mission on April 19. If that had succeeded I might not be in this fix. How did they know we were marching that night?"

Hugo had no idea, so he simply shook his head. Gage hadn't expected an answer. Still looking disheartened, he continued: "The next operation has to be kept secret. I can't stand to have another security breach on my shoulders."

Hugo had wondered who had tipped off the rebels on April 18. Some of the officers thought it might be Mrs. Gage. Gossip had long held that she and Dr. Joseph Warren were lovers. Dark-haired and regal, Margaret Kemble Gage had never expressed any support for the rebel cause, but she was an American and had never expressed her opposition to it either, so her loyalties were suspect. She enjoyed the company of the handsome young officers of the Boston garrison but there was no proof she ever let it go beyond that.

Whatever else she might have been, Mrs. Gage was a wonderful hostess. She loved giving parties and since this could be one of the last she would host in Boston she appeared especially radiant at the one she gave at Province House in honor of General Howe.

Howe was an impressive sight. Forty-five years old, dark-haired and handsome, with a square jaw and chiseled features, he seemed the epitome of an English nobleman in his prime. Six feet tall and solidly built, he was said to be directly related to the royal family. Stories of his exploits in the war against the French, how he had led the charge in the first assault up the steep path to the Plains of Abraham during the capture of Quebec in 1759, were told and retold. He had also fought in the War of the Spanish Succession. If any man could bring the rebels to heel, William Howe was the man.

He stood smiling easily at the people surrounding him. These included Joshua Loring and his wife Elizabeth. Loring, like a terrier eager to get at his prey, had elbowed his way in and introduced himself to Howe and enthusiastically shaken his hand. Howe at first regarded this pushy American with some reserve, but when Loring brought his wife forward Howe's attitude changed instantly. The specter of what Banastre Tarleton had called "the most ravishing blond God ever made" stopped Howe in his tracks. He smiled grandly, bowed, and kissed her proffered hand. Mrs. Loring responded with the most obvious "I'm yours if you want me" expression Hugo had ever seen. Joshua Loring, watching with the expression of a man whose plan is playing out perfectly, saw Hugo standing nearby.

"Lieutenant Chamberlain, you know my wife, Elizabeth, I believe," said Loring. "It is always nice to see the handsome Lieutenant Chamberlain," Elizabeth purred. "Hugo, I was about to tell General Howe of all the treason afoot in Boston," Loring went on. "Wouldn't you agree?"

"In what way, Mr. Loring?" Hugo replied, deliberately using "Mr." rather than "Joshua." He resented Loring's familiarity and wanted Howe to know that.

"The rebels knew we were marching on April 18," said Loring. "The question is, how did they know?"

"Security, compromised?" asked Howe seriously. Hugo didn't know how to respond.

"I'm not certain that's what happened," he said evasively.

"Hugo, no need to be modest," said Loring expansively. "He always pretends to know less than he does, General Howe. You have to admit, Lieutenant, that if surprise had been achieved things would have gone much differently."

"Warren, Adams, and Hancock do have a network of spies in Boston," Hugo admitted.

"Do we know who they are?" asked Howe.

"Some of them," Hugo said.

"Then why haven't they been arrested?"

"That's just the thing, General," said Elizabeth. "They should be, every single one of them. And the man to do it is right here," she went on, smiling at her husband. "The Sheriff of Boston," she said proudly.

Howe looked puzzled, and then Loring said, "Of course I don't mean any disrespect to General Gage. He's trying to maintain good relations with the people of Boston. But sometimes harsher measures are called for. Don't you think so, Lieutenant?"

Hugo was forced to agree; many of these men should have been locked up long ago, and he had said as much to Gage himself. But he saw what Loring was up to: As Sheriff of Boston, he wanted the authority to arrest whomever he pleased. Gage had not given it to him, and he was hoping that with a new regime his luck might change.

"Are Hancock and Adams still at large in the city?" asked Howe.

"No, they are both hiding in the countryside," said Loring.

"What about this Warren?"

"Warren is still about, isn't he Chamberlain?" asked Loring.

"We aren't sure. He hasn't been seen in Boston recently."

"Why wasn't he detained?" asked Howe.

Loring said nothing, just looked silently in General Gage's direction. "I see," said Howe. "Well, this is a subject for another time."

"I quite agree, General," said Loring fawningly. "Once you get settled in I hope we can have another conversation."

"I share my husband's wish," said Elizabeth. "I hope we can see you again sometime soon."

"That will be my pleasure," said Howe. "In fact, I will be looking forward to it."

●　　●　　●

But in spite of the parties and receptions given in his honor—everyone wanted to meet the "new" general, as he was being called—Howe quickly settled down to work on a plan to break the siege. He was at Province House every day, reading and re-reading reports on the events of April 19 and the information gathered by scouts like Tarleton. He was especially interested in the geography of the surrounding area, and Hugo was pleased to learn that the reconnaissance work he had done in the weeks prior to April 19 seemed to carry a lot of weight.

By day Howe was all business, totally focused on his work. He was careful, methodical, a detailed planner with an excellent memory. But when the day's work was over he shed the perfect officer persona and became another man completely, one who laughed and enjoyed life, told jokes, and had a penchant for cards, wine, and the company of women. Before long he was a fixture at the Plymouth Club, appearing there night after night, usually accompanied by Mrs. Loring, who sat next to him at the faro tables while her husband looked on.

New troops were arriving, regiments from England and Ireland filled with men eager to fight the rebels. Boston Common was a forest of tents, and more and more Loyalist families were boarding officers in their homes. Morale, which had slipped after the battles of April 19, was on the rise. Howe said that once he had 6,000 battle-ready soldiers he could attack the rebel lines and break out of Boston. The Continental Army would then fall apart and the rebellion would come to an end. The Americans would see they couldn't win, and their silly insurrection would melt away like snow in the spring.

By early June the plan had been finalized. It would be a three-pronged attack, one from the north, focusing on Dorchester Heights, one from the south, with the objective of capturing Roxbury, and main thrust through the center, going over Breed's Hill and Bunker Hill on the Charlestown Peninsula and capturing Cambridge, headquarters of the rebel army.

Howe was certain of success as long as the rebels were caught by surprise. "If we can keep this quiet," he said, "then the rebels are not going to know what hit them."

CHAPTER 16
THE ARMY CAMP

"Attention!" shouted Captain Jake. "Right shoulder arms! Left shoulder arms! Right face! Forward march!"

Drill was becoming routine. They marched about the camp, paused, marched again, presented arms, marched some more.

By now Josiah could do the manual-of-arms perfectly. He could march just as well as any of the men in his company. But his heart knew no peace. While he was adjusting to life in the colonial army encamped outside Boston, he found it impossible to stop thinking of his family, just a few miles away. But he was unable to contact them and tell them he was alive and that Patrick was dead. The agony his father, his mother, Jessica, Walter, and Anne must be going through troubled him day and night.

Six weeks had passed since the battles of Lexington and Concord. Josiah was a soldier now, a private in what was becoming known as the Continental Army, since it was widely rumored that the Continental Congress in Philadelphia was going to officially make the force outside Boston its own and appoint someone—probably John Hancock— as its commander-in-chief. But Josiah had no uniform and did not feel any more like a soldier now than he did when he rode out of Boston at midnight on April 19. He wore the rough brown clothes that constituted the unofficial uniform of the army: a long shirt (called a rifle shirt) that came almost to his knees, tied around his waist, knee breeches and walking shoes.

There had been much reorganization of the militias since the siege of Boston began. Josiah and the rest of Bedford Company was placed in a regiment commanded by Colonel William Prescott. They were bivouacked in Cambridge, right in front of his beloved Harvard College. That was a small consolation, being so close to the place where he had spent so many happy years.

Josiah had known nothing about military life; now, he was forced to learn. The Continental Army was commanded by General Artemus Ward. The army was then divided into two divisions, each commanded by its own general. Bedford Company was in the division commanded by Israel Putnam, known as "Old Put" to the men. Each division was further broken down into regiments, and then into companies.

Much of Josiah's knowledge came from Sergeant Jake Entwhistle, a lean and leathery man known to all as "Captain Jake," since that was the rank he had held in the war against the French and the Indians. Josiah was beginning to admire him the same way he had admired some of his professors at Harvard.

"We're fortunate," Captain Jake explained to him one day, "to have Old Put as our general and Colonel Prescott as our regimental commander. Two better fighters you couldn't ask for."

"So I assume they both fought in the last war?"

"You assume right, Hartford. Old Put, he was with Roger's Rangers, fought at Quebec and Ticonderoga. He learned to fight Indian-style, using a knife and a tomahawk, sneak up on your enemy when he isn't expecting you, then cut his throat or split his head open. He got so good at it the Indians and Frenchies knew who he was and were afraid of him."

"And Colonel Prescott?"

"Colonel Prescott fought so well the Brits offered him a commission," said Captain Jake, "a rare honor for a 'colonial.' You wait and see. When we fight again he'll be right in the thick of it."

He had seen the generals and the other officers around the camp, and since headquarters at Hastings House was not far from where his company was bivouacked he often saw them coming and going. He had seen General Putnam, a stout, jovial looking man in his late fifties often talking with Colonel Prescott, an impressively tall man with a leader's bearing and a look of grim determination on his face.

Josiah lived in a tent with 11 other men and when a break was called from drill they all sat down in a circle, the men from each tent tending to stay together, and as usual he sat beside Adam Bigelow, who had become his closest friend in camp.

"You feel like a soldier now?" asked Adam after Captain Jake shouted, "At ease."

"I don't know what a soldier should feel like," said Josiah.

"Me neither. Hell, when I was a stevedore in Boston I didn't know what a stevedore was supposed to feel like, and when I worked in that sugar warehouse in New York I didn't know what I was supposed to feel like then either. I guess you just feel the way you feel, wherever you are and whatever you're doing—soldiering, unloading ships, wrestling, or being with a woman, ha-ha! It's all the same."

He was known through the camp as "Big Adam," not only because of his name but also because of his great size: At six feet four inches tall he towered over nearly all the other men. He also boasted that he was the strongest man in the army and so far no one had ever been able to disprove that, for the men often engaged in contests involving feats of strength which Adam invariably won. He could bend horseshoes with his bare hands and lift ordinary-sized men above his head without much effort. When two men sat down at a table and joined hands in what the men called the "test of strength" Adam always forced the other man's hand down, again usually without showing any noticeable effort.

Adam was also the camp's champion wrestler. While working as a stevedore years ago in New York he had learned some arcane grips and throws from Greek and Italian sailors and so when grappling with another man he would suddenly turn and throw his opponent over his shoulder and the astonished fellow would end up on the ground, looking up and wondering how he got there. The only one who was able to come close to matching Adam in strength or wrestling was the big Vermonter that Josiah thought of as "The Pirate." His name was actually Sidney Rourke and he had given Adam a good tussle a few times in the wrestling matches that took place every night when drill was over, but in the end he gave up and admitted that Adam was the best wrestler he had ever seen.

At 28, Adam was older than most of the other men. Although the ages varied from youngsters like Little Tommy to men in their fifties, most were in their early twenties. Adam was a farmer from Bedford, a big happy boisterous fellow who seemed always ready to play or to fight, it was all the same to him. He had a wife and two children who he had left behind on his farm.

Some of the men in his company and in camp Josiah found more interesting than others, just as he had found some of the men at Harvard more interesting than others. Besides Little Tommy Hoover, there was old Joe Cyrus, who was past 50 but determined, as he said, to fight for liberty. Like many of the older men he had fought in the war against the Indians and the French. There was a black man in their company, Peter Salem, who made it a point to tell everyone he was a free man and not a runaway slave. He was one of the few black soldiers in the camp; another was Prince Estabrook, whom Josiah remembered from the first day at Lexington, now recovered from his wound and was in camp with Nathaniel Monroe and the other Lexington men.

Then there was Sam Chapin, known simply as "Reverend Sam." He went about giving sermons from the Bible and preaching abstinence and temperance, lecturing all and sundry about the evils of "demon rum" and relations with loose women. This didn't amount to much in a place where cheap whiskey and rum were plentiful and there was no end of opportunities to consort with the prostitutes who were often lurking outside camp, but Reverend Sam was undaunted. He referred to each man as "Brother" and conducted Sunday services to which many of the worst drunkards and prostitute- chasers went, only to start their sinning again the next day. The Reverend was of some indeterminate age—no one knew exactly how old he was, but like Captain Jake and Joe Cyrus he had fought in the last war.

Josiah got on well with the men in his company, just as he had gotten along with the men at Harvard—all except one: A tall melancholy fellow named Zacharias Brown, whose raven-black hair reflected the darkness inside him, for he struck Josiah as an unhappy person who carried some secret grief he preferred to keep to himself. He seemed to dislike Josiah on sight and went out of his way to be unfriendly toward him.

Josiah was puzzled. In spite of his melancholy air Brown didn't seem a bad sort. He went about the camp playing the violin, whipping out lively versions of "Yankee Doodle" and "Nobody's Jig," playing with a zest that belied his unhappy countenance. It reminded Josiah of how Elias played, and he thought of the night Hugo and Banastre Tarleton had come to Hartford Manor and they had all danced to the Lillibulero.

"You're like a troubadour," Josiah said to him one day, in an effort to make friends.

"A what?" Brown asked, scowling.

"A troubadour," Josiah explained. "From the Middle Ages. They went about singing and playing their instruments, making people happy."

"And you're sayin' that's what I do?"

"Our butler, Elias, plays the violin too," Josiah went on. "I'd love to see you play together someday."

To Josiah's surprise, his words made Brown angry. "I don't give a damn about your fuckin' butler, Hartford," he snarled. "When did I ever see a goddamn butler?"

"I only meant that I like how you play," Josiah said. "I think it's nice, how you go about, playing for the fellas."

"I don't care what you think, Hartford," Brown shot back. "Middle ages. I hope one day someone busts you over the head with your butler and your middle ages."

"Hold on there, Sourpuss," Adam said warningly. "We all got to get along here."

"Hah," Brown snorted. "Get along. One day I'll show you how to get along, Hartford." He slouched away, his violin in one hand and the bow in the other.

"I don't like that guy," Adam said. "I never saw such a gloomy fella in all my life. Just being around him makes me feel bad. You better watch out. He's just waitin' for a chance to take a swing at you and he isn't the type to give any warning."

Josiah was perplexed. "I don't know why. I never did anything to him."

"Sometimes it don't take any reason, a guy will take a swing at you only 'cause he feels like it. Hell, maybe he just wants to make friends and don't know how."

"That's a crazy way to try and make friends," Josiah said.

This was a new experience for Josiah. He had never dealt with someone who disliked him so intensely for no reason.

Brown sometimes went off by himself and sat with his back against a tree and played the most mournful tunes Josiah had ever heard, songs that were so sad and lonely they sounded like the cries of someone in great pain.

He definitely has some big hurt, deep inside, Josiah thought, and with this in mind he decided to try and cultivate Brown once again.

"How long have you been playing the violin, Brown?"

"All my life," Brown replied sullenly.

"Who taught you?"

"Nobody never taught me."

"Where did you get your violin, then?"

"It was my grandfather's," Brown said reluctantly. Then he added, "It was passed on to me."

"So it's a natural gift," Josiah declared. "You just picked it up and taught yourself to play."

"So what?" said Brown. "And I call it a fiddle, not a violin. A violin is for high- class folks like you. A fiddle is what us common people have."

"A fiddle, a violin, it's all the same," Josiah said.

He spoke admiringly, not realizing that Brown felt Josiah was mocking him. The sullen look that was nearly always on Brown's face deepened, and his body tensed like that of a man getting ready to fight or to run.

"What the hell is any of that to you, Hartford? Get away from me before I knock all your teeth out."

Brown rose angrily, for they had been seated near a campfire, and stalked away, his arms bent at the elbows and his fists clenched.

"I can't figure it," Josiah said to Adam. "Why does he hate me?"

"I got a feeling you'll find out soon," Adam predicted. "He can't hold back much longer."

This turned out to be true, for only a few days later when Josiah was telling some of new arrivals what he'd seen at Lexington the morning it all began, he heard Zack Brown's voice ring out.

"If you saw them standing there, Hartford, why didn't you get a gun and join them?"

Josiah looked at him, surprised and unsure of how to respond. "What was it," Brown went on, "you afraid of getting your little rich-boy's hands dirty? Or maybe you're just yellow."

It was obvious Brown had come looking for a fight, and the men who had been listening to Josiah moved out of the way. Brown came closer, looking Josiah over. They were the same size and build.

"Well? Answer me," Brown demanded. "Are you yellow?" Coming close now, he pushed Josiah with both hands.

Josiah pushed back, instinctively, all the while wondering why Brown wanted to fight him. After two more back-and-forth shoves, he said, "What the hell's wrong with you, Brown? What's your quarrel with me?"

Brown paused a moment, looking Josiah in the eye. "Don't remember me, do you?"

"I never saw you before in my life."

"You probably didn't, up there in your fancy-ass office all high and mighty, you wouldn't take any notice of someone like me."

"You don't make any sense, Brown. What the hell are you talking about?"

"Guess," Brown sneered.

"I don't like guessing games. Tell me, or shut your trap."

Brown swung wildly, missed Josiah's head, then lunged forward, seizing Josiah about the shoulders. The two men grappled, neither able to gain an advantage over the other. Then Brown, realizing Josiah was his equal in strength, abruptly let go.

"At that shipyard of yours," he said, panting. "I saw you there, all dressed up in your fine clothes that cost more money than my family ever saw in their whole life. I worked hard, too, but you gave me the sack."

"I never sacked anybody," Josiah protested.

"You lie! The notice I got has your name on it!" Brown cried, yelling for the first time and drawing a folded paper from his pocket and waving it in Josiah's face. "See! There's your name, right there, right where it says 'Your services—no longer needed.'"

Now Josiah remembered. Johnny Bishop, the chief carpenter, had recommended a new man be let go for showing up late for work. Josiah had simply taken Johnny's word, and had approved it.

"Johnny Bishop said you came to work late," Josiah said.

"Only once! The bastard had it in for me. My family needed the money. I got there quick as I could! It was a long way and my mother was sick. Now she's dead."

"I'm sorry your mother is dead, Brown," said Josiah.

"It wasn't all your doing," Brown admitted, the rage seeming to flow out of him. "She'd been sick for a long time. My old man died years ago, and the rest of my family's either dead or gone out west. There was just me to take care of her, and then she died. It ain't right to blame you for it. I—I'm"—Brown seemed on the verge of saying "I'm sorry," but unable to manage that, said instead, "I'd like to shake hands and forget it. You want to do that?"

"Sure," said Josiah, offering his hand. "When this is over, I'll give you another chance, Brown."

"Oh, take that job and shove it up your ass," said Brown. "I didn't like it anyway."

• • •

Each day the American camp got bigger, as men came from all over New England and beyond, all wanting to join in the fight against the British. There were men from Rhode Island, led by a man named Nathaniel Greene, and a group from Connecticut, led by a fellow named Benedict Arnold, who was soon promoted to Colonel and spread the word that he would be leaving soon on a secret mission. More Vermont Green Mountain Boys arrived, led by their famous commander, Ethan Allen, who, like Benedict Arnold, also let it be known that he would be going on a secret mission soon. Men from New York, New Jersey, and Pennsylvania were arriving. There were at least 20,000 men in the camp now, and at night the glow of the campfires lit up the sky and the countryside as far as anyone could see. Josiah, looking out at all the campfires, wondered what the people of Boston thought when they saw so many fires burning just outside their city and as always, thought of his family and wondered what they thought of it too.

Life in camp was for the most part boring. Besides marching and drilling there was little to do. In their idle hours the men ran races, played cards, boxed, wrestled, and drank.

There was no lack of cheap rum and whiskey to be had, and the men drank prodigious amounts of it, the New Englanders preferring rum, the frontiersmen and the men from the other states liking whiskey. The drunkenness made the men quarrelsome, especially when they were gambling. Fist fights were common, and in some cases fists were followed by knives, and some men were seriously hurt after being stabbed. Josiah had tasted both rum and whiskey and liked neither, and so at night when the men gathered around their campfires and jugs or bottles of liquor were passed around he usually declined. From what he knew of liquor it occurred to him that drinking might help relieve the torment that never left his heart but he knew enough to realize that was no solution.

There were a few consolations to camp life. The weather was warm, as spring was now in full bloom, and if the snoring of the men in his tent became too noisy he would take his blankets and go sleep in the open, under the stars. There was plenty of food— beef, pork, corn, beans, and bread. He enjoyed the campfire comradery with the other men, some of whom, like Adam, he was becoming close friends with. But he could never escape the loneliness he felt, nor the torment in his heart about his family and Patrick's death.

But camp life had its drawbacks. Josiah was used to cleanliness and privacy, and there was little of either in camp. Men simply relieved themselves wherever they happened to be, and the stench that resulted was unbearable at times, especially as the weather warmed. Many of the men swam naked in the Charles River, not caring that Boston ladies might be able to see them from the other side; in fact, some of the men seemed to revel in that, something Josiah found especially revolting.

At night, sitting around the campfires, the men sang songs and told stories. Little Tommy Hoover, who had a cherubic face and welkin eyes that made Josiah think of Patrick, had a true gift for singing, carrying a tune without being accompanied by an instrument of any kind. One night, as he sat on a hill looking out at all the fires and the lights from Boston, with Adam sitting beside him, he heard, from nearby, Tommy begin singing "The White Cockade."

"One day as I was walking
Out on yon fields of moss
I had no thought of enlisting till
Some soldiers did me cross..."

"My sister used to sing that song," said Josiah. "Before all this started, back at home. Seems so long ago now, but it hasn't been two months, even."

"You miss your family?" asked Adam.

"Every moment," said Josiah. "I imagine you miss your wife and children."

"All the time," said Adam. "My wife's a good woman."

"What's her name?"

"Emmaline. Everyone calls her Emma. I wish you could meet her. Say, if we ever get the chance, you could come to my house. Emma will cook us a meal you won't believe."

"Sure, I'd like that. And if we ever get into Boston, I'll take you to Hartford Manor, you can meet my family."

"If we get into Boston," said Adam. "With so many men here, I don't know why we don't attack the city."

"So he took out his handkerchief," sang Little Tommy. "To wipe my flowing eye..."

"My gosh, how that boy can sing. You have anyone at home, waiting for you?" asked Adam.

Josiah thought of Alice, then of Mercy Willingham. "There's two girls, actually."

"Two!" said Adam. "Tarnation! Aren't you the ladies' man! And you can't decide which one you really want?"

"I can't figure any of this out," said Josiah. "All I wanted to do was read my books, write my ideas down on paper, travel to the great universities of Europe. Then my father told me I had to build ships like he does, and I had thought that's what I'd be doing. Now I'm here."

One day Josiah went over to Harvard and walked around, disappointed to find the buildings were now empty and there were no people to be seen. But just being on the campus made him feel better, and he discovered old Mr. Singletary, the Harvard Librarian, coming out of Massachusetts Hall. As always his spectacles were pushed up onto his prominent forehead and he appeared to be not fully on earth but somewhere else, contemplating a complicated math problem or a question of philosophy, such as what happens when an irresistible force meets an immoveable object. But when he heard Josiah calling his name he came down to earth, at least partially, and smiled in surprise.

"Well I never—Josiah Hartford! How do you come to be here?"

Josiah gave him a brief account of what had happened to him. "And by a strange twist of fate my company is camped out not far from here. But tell me, what's going on here at Harvard? Where is everybody?"

"The college is closed," said Mr. Singletary sadly. "Since May 1. The Committee of Public Safety is taking it over, to help with the war effort. The

Halls are going to be turned into barracks for you soldiers to stay in. All the books in the library are going to be packed up and sent to Concord in the fall—that's when classes will start again"

"Is the library still open?" asked Josiah.

"No, it's closed too."

"Could I borrow some books? There's no books in the camp and I've had nothing to read since this war started."

"I probably shouldn't," said Mr. Singletary, "but since I know you so well I'm sure it's all right. But only one or two."

•   •   •

With great excitement Josiah went into the Harvard Library with Mr. Singletary. Seeing the volumes on the wooden shelves gave him a feeling of reconnecting with his old life, the one he had known and loved so much before that day, April 19, when the world he knew got turned upside down.

Josiah quickly found volumes of Plutarch, Plato, and Aristotle. "This should do for a while," he said.

He returned to camp, eager to begin reading, but before he could start Captain Jake appeared, followed by Adam. "Come on, Hartford," he said. "You're on sentry duty tonight. You, me, and this big lug."

"We never had sentry duty before," Adam protested in his good-natured way. "Something new," said Captain Jake. "Orders from Colonel Prescott. The Brits have been sending raiding parties across the river, and we need to keep an eye out for them."

The three marched off toward the river, muskets on their shoulders. "Don't look so disappointed, Hartford," said Captain Jake. "You can read your books tomorrow. Sentry duty isn't so bad. Who knows, we might even encounter some women."

"Women?" exclaimed Adam. "What kind of women?"

"The kind of women Reverend Sam warns you about," said Captain Jake. "But don't get all worked up, Bigelow. You're a married man."

"My wife is a good woman and she's far away," said Adam. "What she don't know won't hurt her."

"Hah!" Captain Jake scoffed. "What do you know about women?"

"I know enough about women. I've been married five years, and before that I knew plenty of women, specially when I worked on the docks in Boston and New York."

"Then you oughta know that a woman always knows what her man is up to," said Captain Jake, "even when he's far away. What about you, Hartford? You married?"

"No," said Josiah. He almost added, "But I'm going to be a father soon," but felt it best to keep that to himself.

"He's got two girls at home waiting for him," said Adam.

"Two girls, no less. A regular Romeo, this guy."

"What's a Romeo?" asked Adam.

"He's a character from Shakespeare," Josiah explained.

"What's Shakespeare?"

"Never mind," said Captain Jake.

They marched to the far end of the colonial army camp, Captain Jake setting a fast pace, for like Josiah, he was a wiry man, able to move quickly and for a long distance. As the tent line receded they came closer to the Charles River, and Josiah could see the reflections of the watch fires on the water. On the other side of the river he saw more fires, and men in scarlet and white uniforms moving about.

"They've been on the move lately," said Captain Jake. "Sending men over to our side to take a few pot shots at us, set buildings on fire, then skedaddling back to their own side fast as they can."

"We ought to be doing the same to them," Adam declared.

"Tell that to the bigwigs," said Captain Jake. "Our orders are to patrol this sector, keep an eye out for anybody trying to get across the river, and go for help if they do."

"Do we shoot if they come across the river?" asked Josiah.

"We're at war, Hartford. What do you think?"

They took their positions on some rocks that offered a plain view of the river and the surrounding area. On the other side of the river some British soldiers were doing the same. They built a fire as night fell, as did Captain Jake, Josiah, and Adam.

"They're just out of musket range," Captain Jake observed. "We can't shoot at them and they don't shoot at us."

But they weren't out of shouting distance, and not long after it got dark Josiah heard a voice calling in a heavy British accent: "Hello, you Yankees over there. Got any rum or whiskey?"

"We'll sell you some rum," Captain Jake called back.

"Are you crazy, Captain?" said Adam.

"Orders," said Captain Jake. "We don't mind if they get drunk on guard duty."

"How much for one bottle?" the British voice called back. "A shilling?"

"Two shillings."

"All right, two shillings, you Yankee robbers."

"Hartford and Bigelow, take this," said Captain Jake, handing them a glass bottle with a cork plugged firmly into its opening. "Use that little boat there. Meet them halfway."

Keeping their muskets close, Josiah and Adam made their way down to the riverbank. They found a small dingy moored there, and Josiah rowed them toward a similar vessel coming from the other side of the river.

"I've got a feeling this is a regular practice," Adam observed.

Two British soldiers were in the boat opposite them. "Here you go, mate," said one, handing over two silver coins. "Let's have the bottle, then."

Adam tossed him the bottle. The soldier pulled the cork and quickly took a drink. "Good," he said. "We can't get any over there where we are."

"Hey, let me have some," said the other soldier.

"There's more where that came from," said Adam.

"You Yankees are lucky. Got plenty of everything. Wish I could join your army."

"Don't talk like that," said the other soldier.

"What harm is there in telling the truth, then?" said the first soldier.

"I'll tell you what 'arm. They'll have the hide off your back for talkin' that way, that's what 'arm."

"Bloody hell. If I had my way, we'd all just go home. This war would be over. Do they flog you, over there where you are?"

"No," said Adam.

"My name's Colin, and I'm from London," said the first, more talkative soldier. "If it was up to us soldiers we'd all just go home and live 'appily ever after. You boys got any women where you are?"

"There's women," said Adam.

"One thing we got plenty of is women," said Colin. "Tavern girls. You ever need a woman, let me know, I can fix it up, see?"

From the other side of the river a voice called. "Come on Colin, we need to get back," said the other soldier.

"All right, Yankees," said Colin, and he began rowing back toward shore. "See you about."

"If this ain't the damnedest thing," said Adam. "Talking to them. Selling them liquor. Tomorrow we might have to kill them. War is a strange business."

He agreed with Adam—he found this a strange contradiction. They could talk to the enemy soldiers pleasantly on a nice moonlit night.But tomorrow Colin and his companion would no doubt shoot him and Adam without hesitation. It was hard to make sense of.

"How did it go?' asked Captain Jake when they returned. He listened carefully to everything as Josiah and Adam described it. "We keep getting reports that their morale is slipping," he said. "They're starting to desert, coming over to our side. We want to encourage them."

The more Josiah saw of Captain Jake the better he liked him. He was a born leader, with a phenomenal memory, able to recall pieces of information from weeks ago when it became relevant. He knew where everything was and how it could be used, and because of this he became the man people went to when they needed something, anything from a keg of nails to building a fence or where a cache of rum or whiskey could be had. He was also, as the men said, "in the know," for he always seemed to know what was going on in camp. Like Benjamin Hartford, he was self-educated, something else Josiah admired.

Josiah began volunteering for sentry duty. It made him feel closer to his family. It also broke the monotony of camp life. He was astonished at the fraternization that went on between the rebel soldiers and the British—that day on the river was no anomaly. The British and American sentries spoke often, even if it meant shouting from a good distance away. Some of the conversations were interesting in an odd way. He was able to get an idea of what the ordinary British soldiers were thinking. While most hated the war and wanted to go home, they were also adamant about who was at fault for starting it.

"You think I wanted to come here?" one of them called to Josiah one day in May. "I'd rather be home in Bristol. But no, you damn rebels gotta make all this trouble, rising up against your king."

"He isn't my king," Josiah called back. "I didn't elect him."

"Elect? Nobody elects a king. God makes kings. God puts the king on earth to rule over the likes of you and me."

"How do you know God made the king?" Josiah called back. "Who made God?"

"Nobody made God, you crazy Yankee."

"Did God make himself?"

"You ask too many questions," the Britisher replied. "It's not good for a man to ask so many questions."

"Not too bright, these British soldiers," said Captain Jake.

Whenever he could Josiah would sit with his back against a tree near Harvard Yard and read. One day as he sat in the sunlight reading Plutarch's account of the life of Alcibiades, he became aware of someone nearby. It was Peter Salem, who moved so quietly Josiah hadn't noticed him.

"I don't mean to disturb you," he said.

"It's all right," said Josiah. From what he had seen, he had the impression Peter would be worth getting to know.

"What are you reading?"

"Plutarch."

"Who was he?"

"He was a Greek historian."

"They tell me you went to school there," said Peter, indicating the Harvard buildings.

"Yes."

"They told me you're a professor, that you know everything."

"That isn't true. I'm no professor and I certainly don't know everything. In fact, every day I realize how little I really know."

"But you're what they call an educated man?"

"I suppose," said Josiah, "although I'm getting a different kind of education now."

"You know much about mathematics?" asked Peter.

"I know about math," said Josiah.

"I can both read and write," Peter said proudly. "I ain't no runaway. I'm a free man. So was my daddy. I can add and subtract too, but I want to learn more. You know about fractions?"

"I could tell you about fractions."

"Would you teach me? I really want to learn about fractions, quarters and halves and eighths and such."

With help from Captain Jake, who found some slate boards and chalk, Josiah began teaching Peter Salem some basic mathematics. He soon discovered that Peter had a quick and nimble mind, eager to learn, but while he could add and subtract he couldn't multiply or divide, and Josiah insisted he learn that before he taught him anything else.

"But I want to learn about fractions."

"You have to know how to multiply and divide first," said Josiah, and before long Peter had mastered the multiplication tables and learned how to do long division. He learned so well and so fast that Josiah got permission from Mr. Singletary to use of the empty classrooms in Massachusetts Hall and work with Peter there. When he began to learn about fractions he was delighted, especially when it came to multiplying and dividing them.

"This makes my head spin," he kept saying. "You multiply a regular number and you get more. But you multiply fractions and you get less. And when you divide a number you get less of the number, but when you divide up a fraction it gets bigger."

Inevitably some of the other men noticed what Peter and Josiah were doing, and began asking questions.

"Are you telling me that if you break up a number and divide it, that number gets bigger?" Old Joe Cyrus said.

"That's right," said Peter. "But that only happens with fractions."

"That can't be. He's teasin' you."

"It's true. Come over to the classroom sometime and I'll prove it."

"I'm way too old to go back to school," said Joe. "I never went much even when I was a youngster."

"Hell, we're in school now, learning about the army, learning about this war," said Adam. "I'll go."

So a few days later Joe, Adam, Tommy Hoover, Captain Jake, Reverend Sam, and a few others came over to the classroom in Massachusetts Hall where Josiah had been instructing Peter. Peter, nervous but determined, got in front of the slate board with a piece of chalk and wrote, "1/8 ÷ 1/4" then went through the steps and showed them how it equaled two. "But if you multiply these two numbers, you something much smaller—one thirty-second."

Josiah sat watching this display proudly, the way a teacher feels when they see their prize pupil perform.

"Well, I'll be jiggered," said Adam. "Let me try that," and he went to the slate board and worked a problem himself, with Peter's help.

"Let me show you something else Josiah taught me," said Peter. "It's geometry." He drew a right triangle. "If this side is three inches, and this bottom line is four inches, then what is this line here?"

"Six inches," said Adam.

"Yes, six inches, Brother Adam is right," said Reverend Sam.

Only Captain Jake came up with the right answer. "Five inches," he said. "I've studied geometry. That top line is called the hypotenuse."

"The what?" said Adam.

"The hypotenuse. It's from—what is it, Hartford?"

"The Pythagorean Theorem," said Josiah.

"It's true no matter what numbers you use in a triangle like this," said Peter, remembering what Josiah had told him.

"Brother Josiah has got some passel of knowledge in his head, that's for sure," said the Reverend. "Too bad he doesn't spend more time reading the Bible."

"What use is any of this?" asked Old Joe. "Besides giving a man a headache?"

"It could be of a lot of use in this war," said Captain Jake. "Wait and see. You better believe the Brits have got men who know this, engineers who know how to lay out a fort or build earthworks by using geometry."

Late in May people began leaving Boston. It began as a small trickle. A few people on foot, some on wagons pulled by horses, some on carts pulled by oxen, some riding horses. Some had their belongings with them, others only the clothes on their backs. Josiah, seeing the exodus, began asking people about his family.

"Do you know the Hartfords of Beacon Hill?" he would ask. "The Hartfords, have you seen them?"

But no one knew anything. Josiah kept watching the passers-by eagerly. Perhaps someone from his family would leave the city too. But he saw no one he knew until the third day when he spotted a tall auburn haired girl with a striking face, wearing a green dress and looking somewhat haggard, walking alone.

"Mercy!" he shouted. "Mercy Willingham! Over here!"

Mercy paused, turned, and seeing Josiah her face broke into a smile of pure surprised joy. She ran toward him, her arms outstretched, crying out joyously, but just before she reached him at the side of the road she stopped short, her countenance hardening, and she slapped him ringingly across the face.

"That's for you, Josiah Hartford! Damn you anyway!"

This brought howls of laughter from Josiah's tent mates. They had seen this young woman run toward Josiah as if overjoyed at seeing him, then slapping him and using the kind of language they would not expect from a well-brought up young lady. Josiah, through the reddening of his face which came both from the embarrassment he felt and the slap Mercy had given him, heard the men laughing and Adam's booming voice, "Doesn't he have a way with women!"

"Damn you!" Mercy said again. "We all thought you were dead!"

"Is that why you hit me? Because you're glad I'm not dead?"

"No, it's because..." She leaned forward, putting her hands on his shoulders and spoke into his ear: "That girl is pregnant!"

"You mean Alice?"

"Of course I mean Alice! Why, are there others?"

"Does anybody else know?" asked Josiah.

"Everyone knows! And they know who's responsible for it, too!"

"Are they all right? My Mother, Father—"

"Yes, they're all right, but worried to death about you and Patrick. Where is Patrick?"

"Patrick is in heaven," said Josiah stoically. "A British soldier killed him in your yard."

"Oh God," said Mercy. "Oh—so sad." Tears ran down her cheeks, which she quickly wiped away. "How we'll miss him. And your mother and father don't even know."

"Where are you going?" Josiah asked.

"Home, of course. General Gage is letting people leave if they want. Did you see any of my family? Did the British burn my house?"

"No, your house was all right. I didn't see anybody from your family but I'm sure nothing happened to them."

"Can you come to Concord?" she asked.

"I will, when I can," he promised. "I'll write you from camp."

"So you're a soldier now?" She looked at him skeptically. "I'm not much of a soldier."

"Have you been in many battles?"

"Only on that first day."

"Have you killed any British?"

"Yes," he admitted. He didn't like talking about the men he had killed.

Mercy turned, looked at the line of people going past. "I want to go," she said. "I want to go home. Mother and Father must be as worried about me as yours were about you. I'm glad I saw you, Josiah. Promise you'll come to Concord?"

"I promise. As soon as I can get leave, I'll come."

As if on impulse Mercy kissed him, much as she had that night in Concord. This brought more laughter from the men watching, and she turned and skipped back to the line of people on the highway. She turned and waved several times to Josiah.

"First a slap, then a kiss," said Adam. "Well, that's how women are. They smack you, then they want to roll in the hay with you. She one of your sweethearts?"

"Her family and mine go way back. I've known her since she we were both little."

"She's bigger now," said Adam, "and in all the right places too! Got spirit all right. That's important in a woman, I can tell you. You ever been with a woman?"

"Sure I have."

"How many times?"

"Enough times," Josiah said, thinking of Alice.

The camp, as always, was full of rumors, and one that kept going around and troubled Josiah the most was that the British were going to abandon Boston, but would burn it to the ground first. That was dispelled by another rumor: The British were going to try to break out of Boston. General Gage was going to attack.

By the second week of June the men in the colonial army camp became aware of a great flurry of activity at the highest levels, a sure sign that action was coming. General Ward had called a meeting of the Committee of Public Safety, and then another with General Thomas, General Heath, General Putnam and Colonel Prescott. Spies were reporting that the British were about to come across the bay, just as they had on April 18, and attack the colonial lines near Roxbury.

Josiah, hearing all this, paid it little heed until Captain Jake told them to get ready, action was coming soon.

"Oh boy," said Adam eagerly. "Just what I've been hoping for. What's it going to be, Sarge?"

"The word is the British are going to come through Charlestown," said Captain Jake.

"But we know they're coming," said Adam.

"We know they're coming, and we'll be waiting."

"An ambush!" said Adam.

"When is all this going to happen?" asked Josiah.

"Day or two. So be ready."

The rumors became more pronounced the next day, which was Friday, June 16.

Late in the afternoon Captain Jake reported they were moving out.

"Where?" a dozen men asked, but there was no answer. But from all over the camp came the sound of men shouting excitedly, and as the drums began to pound Josiah and the others formed into two lines. Ahead of him Josiah saw more men, long lines of men, getting ready to march. The word was given and the march began, the drums still beating, and Josiah saw Colonel Prescott on his horse, leading the way. It seemed to him they were heading toward Cambridge Commons, right next to Harvard.

"Come on Sarge," said Adam. "Where are we going?"

"First over to Cambridge, in front of the Hastings House, and parade in front of the bigwigs," said Captain Jake, adding, "This is going to be a big one."

"Where?" Josiah pressed.

"Bunker Hill."

CHAPTER 17
ON BREED'S HILL

The colonial army marched out of camp and as Josiah had surmised, they marched past Harvard and over to Cambridge. As the sun went down they stopped and formed ranks in front of Hastings House. To Josiah's great delight the Reverend Samuel Langdon, the President of Harvard College, now appeared. Standing on an open wooden platform, he addressed the more than 1,000 men who stood at attention in front of him.

"We beseech thee, O Lord," he said, "to watch over our brave and gallant men in the battle to come. Guide them, Lord, inspire them, give them courage to defeat our enemies. Smite them, O Lord, as You once did help David to smite Goliath in the days of old. This we pray in the name of our Lord Jesus Christ, amen."

The order was given to march and the long columns moved out once again, with the drummers and fifers playing "The Turkish March." Josiah and the others noticed that several wagons of picks and shovels were accompanying them. "I've got a feeling we're going to get plenty dirty tonight," said Peter Salem.

"With all the digging we've done, you'd think one of us would have struck gold by now," said Adam.

"Look at that!" said Tommy Hoover. "Artillery!" He gestured toward some field pieces that were trailing behind the wagons, drawn by horses. "This must be one big battle they're planning."

There were more wagons in the train, these filled with barrels and bundles of wood, and alongside them rode a colonel Josiah had seen often around camp but who's name was unknown to him.

"That's Colonel Richard Gridley," Captain Jake explained. "The engineering officer. We'll be building some kind of fortification tonight, that's for sure."

The men marched out of Cambridge and toward the Neck, three miles away. Darkness fell. Josiah saw the Mystic River on his left and the Mill Pond on his right. Over there, amidst the flickering lights of the city, was his home and his family, but he couldn't see them or let them know he was alive.

They marched from the Neck right onto the trail that took them up Bunker Hill. Here they paused, and from this 110 foot high crest Josiah, Adam, Captain Jake and the others gazed down at the magnificent view of the harbor and the city. There was no moon, but no clouds either, so the stars reflected in the water quite merrily.

"I played here on this hill when I was a boy," he said.

"Now you're going to fight a battle on it," said Adam. "Bet you never thought of that."

"When do we start digging, Sarge?" Peter Salem wondered as the minutes passed. "I'll go see what I can find out," said Captain Jake.

The men sat down to wait as Captain Jake went off toward a group of officers that were gathered nearby. Old Joe Cyrus took a bottle of rum from his haversack and took a quick drink before Reverend Sam could notice. In the darkness Josiah could dimly see Captain Jake standing outside the group of officers, which included Colonel Gridley, Colonel Prescott, and General Putnam. These three were in a heated conversation, with much arm-waving and pointing in one direction, and then in another. Colonel Prescott kept pointing and gesturing toward the city. He stamped his feet for added emphasis, and after a while it seemed he had convinced the other two of whatever point it was he was trying to make.

When Captain Jake returned he said, "Change in plans. We're moving on."

"Where to?" the men all wanted to know.

"I thought we were digging in here," said Adam.

"New orders. We're going to dig in on Breed's Hill instead."

The men moved out, marching down Bunker Hill toward the empty city of Charlestown, then up the smaller Breed's Hill, all in the dark, each man with his musket on his shoulder and making his way carefully.

"What in the hell are we doing, Sarge?" asked Adam.

"We're going to build a fort on Breed's Hill."

"Breed's Hill?" said Josiah dubiously.

"Something wrong with Breed's Hill, Hartford?" asked Captain Jake.

"Breed's Hill is much closer to the harbor," said Josiah. "We could be in range of the guns on Copp's Hill and the ships."

"Don't ask me what the bigwigs are thinking," said Captain Jake.

When they had reached the top of Breed's Hill Colonel Prescott appeared. "I'm putting you men right here," he said. "This is where our redoubt has to be strongest. This is where they're going to attack, so I'm counting on you. Put down your muskets, get your tools, and start digging. Tonight we dig, tomorrow we fight."

The wagons with the entrenching tools stood nearby. Josiah got hold of a pick, just as Colonel Gridley appeared and standing next to Colonel Prescott, he began gesturing with a long walking stick. "Dig along here," he said.

Now the men began digging in the dark. They were divided into four gangs, each one digging a separate wall of the redoubt. The picks and shovels rose and fell. Dirt flew and was piled into an ever-growing wall. Colonel Gridley was everywhere, up and down the lines of men, watching everything, giving orders here, giving instructions there, measuring the trench and the progress the walls were making, and fretting over how little time remained until sunrise. He was followed by Colonel Prescott, who kept saying, "Faster, men, dig faster, when the sun comes up I want those Brits to be in for the biggest surprise of their lives."

They were only five hundred yards from the water's edge. It seemed impossible to Josiah that on this quiet night with no wind the sailors on board the ships couldn't hear the digging even if they weren't able to see it. The horses made sounds too. No one was talking much, but the sound of the shovels and picks hitting the rocky soil had to carry some distance. He tried not to think about it, but instead focused on the job at hand: Digging, digging, and more digging.

"Dig, dig, dig," said Old Joe Cyrus. "That's all I've done since I joined this army."

"Oh, keep quiet, you old coot," said Adam playfully. "Last week you said all you ever did was drill, drill, drill."

"That's it. Dig and drill, dig and drill, that's all we do in this war."

"If you want action, I've got a feeling you'll see plenty before this day is over," said Captain Jake.

As the night passed and the digging went on the men could begin to see, in spite of the dark, that what they were doing was taking a definite shape. More wagons arrived, filled with bundles of wood called fascines, along with empty wooden barrels and gabions—cages filled with rocks. At Colonel Gridley's direction these were packed into the ever-deepening walls of the redoubt, making the earthworks even stronger.

"I saw earthworks like these in the last war," said Captain Jake. "You'll be amazed at how strong they are."

"Will they stand up to cannon fire, Sarge?" asked Peter Salem.

"Damn right they will."

"Hey, there's the Colonel," said Adam, as he spied Colonel Prescott's tall form coming toward them. "Whaddya say, Colonel?"

Prescott smiled grimly, and appeared to be about to reply when he took notice of something taking place several yards further down the line. Josiah heard a shout, and he saw some men from Connecticut being hectored by their corporal as they attempted to lift an especially large stone and place it in the redoubt's wall.

"Come on you men," the corporal shouted. "Put your backs into it! Heave! Heave I say."

Prescott walked over. "Corporal," he said, "if you'll lend them a hand you'll be able to get that rock into place a lot faster."

"I am the corporal, whoever you are, can't you see that?" the corporal replied. Then he understood who he was speaking to. His face turned red and he saluted.

"Oh, a corporal, well, I ask your pardon, sir," said Prescott, who took off his coat and joined the men in lifting the stone into place. All around there was laughter. The corporal looked as if he wished he could find a hole to hide in.

Josiah's admiration Prescott increased even more upon seeing this, he made bold to say, "Colonel, how is it those sailors on board the ships in the harbor can't hear us?"

"What's your name?" asked Prescott.

"Private Hartford, sir."

"Of the shipbuilding family?" When Josiah nodded Prescott said, "Well Private Hartford, you think you can find your way down to the meeting house in Charlestown and then hotfoot it back up here?"

"Yes sir, definitely."

"I sent a fellow by name of Farnsworth there for just that purpose, to keep an eye and an ear out for what those tars might be doing. He hasn't reported back yet."

"Can I go along with him, Colonel?" asked Adam.

"Aren't you the one they call Big Adam, who claims to be the strongest fellow in this man's army?" asked Prescott.

"Yes sir, that's me," Adam said, proudly flexing his biceps.

"Then you stay here. When somebody needs another big rock lifted I'll send for you." There was a ripple of laughter all around and Adam grinned good-naturedly. "You, Hartford," Colonel Prescott pointed at Josiah, "get on down there at the double."

Josiah was happy to get away from the monotonous digging for a while. Taking his musket, he made his way down the trail in the dark toward Charlestown. As he approached the meeting house he heard a voice in the darkness say, "Who goes there?"

"Private Hartford, Bedford Company, by order of Colonel Prescott."

Two men now appeared. One he recognized as the short, broad shouldered Nathaniel Monroe from Lexington. Monroe recognized him at the same instant and came forward quickly to shake hands. "Well, I never," he said. "Good to see you again."

"Keep your voices down," said the other man.

"What brings you here?" asked Monroe, whispering.

"I need to find a guy named Farnsworth. Colonel Prescott wants a report from him."

"He's inside. How's it going up there?"

"We're digging like crazy men."

"Did you ever make it to Concord, Hartford? Did you find your brother?"

"I found him," Josiah fumbled the words, "but he was killed by the Brits."

"Sorry. Forgive me for asking. May your brother rest in peace."

Inside the meeting house were a group of men, gathered at the windows but keeping their heads down. They were led by another Lexington man, Amos Farnsworth. When he learned of Josiah's mission he said, "There's two ships out there, the Falcon and the Lively. Listen!" A few minutes later they heard a voice carrying over the water: "All's well!"

"That was the Lively," said Farnsworth. "We'll hear the Falcon now." A moment later they heard the watch on the Falcon call out. "You can tell Colonel Prescott those British sailors don't suspect a damn thing."

Next to him sat another man Josiah recognized from Lexington. "If it isn't the best blacksmith in Massachusetts," he said, and shook hands with Prince Estabrook.

"He's recovered from the stick in the arm that Brit gave him," said Nathaniel Monroe.

"Now I'm here and I'm out to get even," said Estabrook.

Josiah, as fast as he could, made his way back to the redoubt, going back up the hill the same way he had come, and he saw the beginnings of daylight starting to appear. In these few hours they had accomplished an amazing feat of engineering. They had constructed a formidable redoubt on Breed's Hill overlooking Boston Harbor. Each side was over 100 feet long and had a trench in front of it. When the sun came up the British were going to see the Americans had built a fort that would cost a lot of British lives to capture. Despite the fatigue he felt from going without sleep and the hours of backbreaking work, Josiah, after reporting to Colonel Prescott, redoubled his efforts.

"How are things in Charlestown?" Adam asked, just as the sun was rising.

"You can hear the sailors on the ships calling out," said Josiah. "What I can't figure is how they haven't seen us yet."

An explosion suddenly ripped through the morning's half-light. The men on the hill saw the burst of orange-red flames from the side of one of the ships in the harbor.

"That answers that question," Adam said dryly.

"Jeez, what makes you think so?" said Captain Jake.

Josiah heard the hissing sound of the cannonball cutting through the air. There was a loud thud as it hit the ground and buried itself in the dirt.

More blasts came from the harbor as the other ship began firing at the men in the redoubt. As the cannonade continued Colonel Prescott jumped onto the parapet so that his tall figure was silhouetted against the light, and waving his tri-cornered hat he faced the harbor. "Shoot all you want, you British bastards!" he shouted. "Hit me if you can!" His coat swirled about him like a long, colorful cape, making him an even more inspiring figure to the men. He then turned to the men watching him, turning his back on the danger the ships in the harbor presented, and he said, "Cannons make a lot of noise, men, but from that far away they can't do much damage. Don't let them scare you. Be brave and carry on!"

"Hooray for Colonel Prescott!" shouted Adam, and all rest of the men joined in, from one end of the trench to the other. They cheered Colonel Prescott, who modestly held up his hand for them to stop, and then renewed their work with a vengeance. Colonel Prescott continued walking back and forth on the parapet, fearlessly exposing himself to the British cannon fire, disdainful of any cannonballs that might come his way.

The cannonballs continued to land in various places along the trench line. Some of the cannonballs landed in front of the earthworks, some flew overhead and landed behind the line, inside the redoubt. None seemed to be doing any real damage or hitting anyone. But as Colonel Prescott walked in front of Josiah's section a young lieutenant approached. He looked shaken, and he said, "Sir, we have a dead man from one of the cannonballs. What should we do with him?"

"Bury him!" Prescott snapped.

"Colonel, I'll go say a prayer over his poor body as his soul makes its way to heaven," said Reverend Sam.

"No, Reverend, you stay right there," Prescott ordered.

Reverend Sam looked surprised and a little indignant but kept on digging. The lieutenant scurried away. As if responding to the first casualty of the day, the bells in the Old North Church began to ring. By now all of Boston knew something was happening, and from where he was at the crest of the hill Josiah could see people coming into the streets and clambering onto rooftops, onto the steeples of churches, all wanting to get a look at Breed's Hill.

What's my family thinking now? Josiah wondered. I'm about to fight a battle here and they have no idea. How strange is war.

•   •   •

Hugo Chamberlain woke up early, not because he wanted to but because Jeremy was in his bed, and he needed to get him back to his own room before anyone found them together. But before he woke Jeremy, who was sleeping peacefully after the delights of the night they had spent together, Hugo decided to go look out his window at what appeared to be a glorious sunrise. He had always loved the sunrise in Boston. He imagined it illuminating the entire vast continent to the west in a kind of rolling fashion, all the way from here to the Pacific Ocean.

· · ·

Hugo's room was on the 3rd floor of a mansion on Barton Point where a lot of other British officers were boarded. As he stood in his nightshirt stretching and contemplating the pleasures he and Jeremy had shared he saw people scurrying about on Breed's Hill. Dirt was flying in the air and there were hundreds of men working like beavers building a dam. Since he wasn't yet fully awake it took him a moment to process what he was seeing and to fully grasp what it meant. When he did, he let out a gasp of indignation, then went to the bed and began shaking Jeremy.

"Jeremy, wake up. You need to get to your room."

Jeremy's eyes popped open and he sat up as if pulled by a rope. "Oh, good morning, love."

"You won't think it's so good when you see this," said Hugo, leading Jeremy to the window.

"What in bloody hell is going on out there?" said Jeremy. "How did they know?"

"Now be a good boy and get back to your room," said Hugo. "I've got to go tell the old man."

"He's likely to have apoplexy when he sees that," Jeremy agreed.

Jeremy departed quickly and quietly.Hugo dressed as fast as he could, then hurried toward Province House.

· · ·

Hugo was not the only one to notice what was taking place on Breed's Hill. As he reached Province House and was admitted by the sentries the sound of cannon fire from the harbor split the morning quiet, rattling windows and waking people rudely from their slumber. The firing awakened Gage too, who, still clad in his nightclothes, opened the big double doors of his bedroom just as Hugo approached. Behind Gage Hugo could see the slender figure of Mrs. Gage, stirring about in bed.

"What in God's name is going on, Chamberlain?" Gage demanded. "Who's firing, and what for?"

"Sir, the colonials are fortifying Breed's Hill," Hugo reported.

"The hell you say!"

"See for yourself, General," said Hugo, and he accompanied Gage as he ran to the balcony, a spyglass in hand, and peered out.

Gage was thunderstruck. His jaw dropped as he peered through the spyglass. "How in God's name did they find out?" he said.

Gage still harbored some hope that if he won a decisive victory over the rebels he might redeem his reputation in London. But once again the colonials had been one step ahead of him, and he saw his chance for redemption vanishing.

"I want all the staff downstairs as soon as they can get here," Gage ordered.

The senior staff was soon assembled, none of them looking pleased at being roused so early in the morning and to the sound of cannon fire to boot. Gage had also sent for Abijah Willard, one of the leaders of Boston's Loyalists.

Willard was a banker, a man of no small influence. He and Gage were personal friends. After the initial greetings Gage requested Willard look through the spyglass at what was happening on Breed's Hill.

"I sent for you, Abijah, because I thought you might know some of the men out there," said Gage.

"He probably knows every one of them," said Banastre Tarleton under his breath.

"Better go easy on that kind of talk, Ban," cautioned Hugo.

Gage had been paying special attention to the tall, commanding figure of Colonel Prescott, who was walking defiantly back and forth on the parapet, waving his hat and daring the British cannonballs to hit him. Now Willard, looking intently through the spyglass, exclaimed, "That's my brother-in-law, William Prescott."

"Is he going to fight?" asked Gage.

"He will fight you all the way to the gates of hell," Willard declared solemnly.

"You should know," said Tarleton, just loud enough.

"Can I look, sir?" asked Hugo.

Gage nodded and Willard handed Hugo the spyglass. He looked at the earthworks the colonials had dug in such a short space of time. It was a simple structure, but those earthen walls presented a formidable challenge to any force sent to assault it. He saw Prescott, who walked about giving orders and speaking to his men, his entire bearing a challenge to the British. Then he saw another figure, clad in the same rough clothes as all the others and wearing a tri-cornered hat, come out of the digging behind the wall, jump athletically onto the top and say something to Prescott. Prescott nodded, and as the figure turned Hugo could see his face plainly.

"What in the name of God are you doing, Josiah?" he exclaimed.

"Someone you know?" asked Gage.

"He said he would never go to war," Hugo said, still shocked.

"Hartford is out there?" asked Tarleton, taking the spyglass from Hugo and seeing for himself.

"Can you believe it?" asked Hugo.

"I knew he was a traitor," Tarleton declared. He hadn't forgotten how Josiah had backhanded him that night outside the Fife and Drum. "Him and his entire family. I knew it all the time."

"How the devil did they know of our plans to march today?" wondered General Howe.

This elicited a snort of disgust from Banastre Tarleton, who now said belligerently, "Knew? Of course they bloody knew." He looked indignantly at Willard. "How many sides are you on, anyway?"

"Now, just a minute, sir," said Willard in a shaky voice, for he knew full well he was speaking to the dreaded Banastre Tarleton. "I protest that I am as loyal a subject of the King as any man in these colonies."

"His brother-in-law!" said Tarleton. "His fucking brother-in-law is the leader of the rebels, and the man says he is loyal!"

Willard made no reply, but now Gage intervened. "Watch your language, Lieutenant. Mr. Willard knew nothing of our plans. And he's as loyal as any man here."

"That's what he wants you to think!"

"Silence, Lieutenant!"

Tarleton knew better than to say anything more. He subsided, but he saw several of the other officers nodding approvingly, as he was saying what many of them thought. Americans couldn't be trusted, no matter how many times they professed their loyalty.

Howe had been studying a map of Charlestown and the surrounding area and discussing how best to dislodge the rebels from Breed's Hill. They could attack them from the rear by going through Charleston Neck and capturing Bunker Hill. That would trap the Americans between the British forces and the waters of Boston Harbor. But that would leave the British vulnerable to an attack from the main American force camped near Cambridge. That meant there was only one course open to them: A direct assault on Breed's Hill.

"Those are some formidable earthworks," said Howe. "A frontal attack is going to cost a lot of lives."

"Can you think of another way of taking that hill?" asked Gage.

"General Gage, it's your decision," said Howe.

Gage was silent for a moment, and then he said, "We assault Breed's Hill."

"I will lead the attack myself," said Howe. "May God be with us."

"Sir, I'd like to go along," said Hugo eagerly.

"So would I, sir," said Tarleton.

"Out of the question," said Gage. "I'll need you both as observers."

As the meeting broke up and the generals began the preparations for the attack Hugo kept thinking of Josiah Hartford on Breed's Hill. Josiah, once his friend, once his brother, Josiah who had said he would never fight in a war, had joined the rebel army. It was hard to digest.

"We might still get a chance to fight," said Tarleton. "When a battle begins you never know what can happen."

•　　•　　•

When the first cannonballs began to land Josiah felt the same terror he had felt at Alewife Creek, only magnified, because whereas the artillery the British had there was the relatively small six pound field piece, these were much larger ship's cannons. The whistling sound the cannonballs made was louder and more frightening, the crash they made when they hit the ground harder and heavier.

But as the cannonade went on his fear elapsed. Most of the cannonballs came arcing down and hit the ground harmlessly, burying themselves in the dirt and hurting no one. A few, coming in at a different angle, hit the ground and then bounced along like a flat stone thrown across a pond before coming to a stop. The earthen walls of the redoubt were able to absorb the impact of the cannonballs with great effectiveness, and Josiah once again complimented the skill of Colonel Gridley in the construction of it.

Now there was a louder boom than any before and in spite of himself, Josiah was startled. The big guns on Copp's Hill, on the other side of the harbor, had now joined in the attack, and these fired cannonballs that weighed twenty-five pounds. These literally shook the ground when they hit, and even at a distance Josiah and the others could feel the ground move when the cannonball slammed into it. But the earthen walls still held.

•　　•　　•

Shortly after 1:00 the British troops began assembling on Boston Common. In the harbor, at Long Wharf and North Battery, boats were being made ready to ferry the troops across the Charles River to Morton's Point, where they would re-assemble and prepare for the attack.

To the dirty, exhausted men on Breed's Hills it was obvious the British assault was coming at any moment. From his rucksack Joe Cyrus removed his bottle of rum, and, as he had been doing since they arrived on Breed's Hill, took a quick drink. He tried to put the bottle back before Reverend Sam saw him, but it was too late, and the Reverend turned his fervent eyes on him.

"Joe Cyrus, I saw that," said the Reverend. "I'm surprised at you, a man of your years setting such a bad example. Throw away that witches' potion!"

"Reverend, we might all be dead in a little while," said Joe. Since he had been caught he knew there was no use in trying to hide the jug any longer, so he took it out and defiantly had another shot of rum. "There's no harm."

"Better to die with a clean soul than live with one drenched in demon rum," said the Reverend unforgivingly. Then he noticed the expression on the faces of some of the other men, who obviously wanted a drink too, and he stopped to reconsider. "I think the Lord will forgive one drink at a moment like this. But you be sure we are going to pray after!"

This was agreeable to everyone and the bottle was passed around. Even Little Tommy Hoover had a sip. Josiah, never fond of either rum or whiskey, took a drink too, and Adam had a long swig with obvious relish.

At the Reverend's beckoning, they all gathered around into a prayer circle. The Reverend produced a Bible, which he did not open but simply held in a tight grip. "Hear us, O Lord, Your obedient children, on this day of our ordeal. Give us the courage we need to face our enemy on this battlefield. Have mercy on us all, and give us victory. We fight in Your Name and if need be we'll die in Your Name. Bless us, one and all, O Lord. Amen."

Everyone said "Amen," and Adam, his voice uncharacteristically serious, said, "I just want to say, that if this is my day to die, I can't think of a better way to go, or better company for a man to die with."

There was another chorus of "Amens" and then every man took up his position on the parapet, his musket in hand, and looked down over the grass toward the beach where the British were. Am I going to die today? Josiah thought. Looking down the hill to where the British were forming ranks, he wondered if Hugo might be there and what a terrible irony it would be if Hugo came marching up the hill and Josiah had to shoot him. There were still more British troops being ferried across the water in those ugly barges, their scarlet uniforms a sharp contrast to the blueness of the bay. The sun was high and the day was hot and a voice in his head kept asking, "What am I doing here? How did I get here?" He looked down the line at the men on either side of him in the redoubt. Did any of them feel the same way? Adam was on his right, Captain Jake on his left, Peter Salem, Old Joe, Little Tommy further down the line. How did we all get here, he wondered.

Now he heard a voice saying, "Can I get in here?" Turning, he saw Zack Brown getting between them. "How are you doing, Hartford?" he said, his tone friendly.

"What are you doing, Brown?" Josiah asked.

"I don't know...I just wanted to be near you when the fighting starts."

Brown took no notice of Josiah's puzzled expression, but looked steadily at the British soldiers who were now assembling on the beach below. Josiah turned to Adam, who was standing on his left, and gave him a quizzical look, tilting his head toward Brown. "He can't decide if he loves you or hates you," Adam, who had never liked Brown, said in a whisper. "Strange guy."

A great quiet fell over the men in the redoubt. As more British troops arrived sergeants and officers were scurrying about, shouting orders, pointing, pushing men into neatly formed lines. I wonder what those men down there are thinking? Josiah thought. Are they as frightened as I am? Do any of them wish they could run away? He was aware of Colonel Prescott behind him, pacing up and down the line, his face intense, focused on the battle to come, and he could see, now, why men in war had to have confidence in their leaders.

The British were now drawn up into three lines, similar to the ones Josiah had seen at Lexington, only on a much bigger scale, and each line was split into sections, with the sergeants and officers to the sides, ready to give the orders to advance.

"How many do you reckon are down there now?" Adam asked.

"At least 2,000," said Captain Jake. "Maybe more."

Now the men heard a new sound—musket fire. It was coming from Charlestown, off to their right. The men Colonel Prescott had sent there last night had climbed onto the roofs of the buildings there and were sniping at the British troops on the beach.

The first shots of the battle, Josiah thought. How many more are going to be fired before this day is over? His mouth was dry again and he looked about for the boy who had taking water around the redoubt, but there was no sign of him. He looked back toward the beach where the British were still preparing to attack and then he heard the men cheering from the back of the redoubt, cheers that spread quickly to the other three sides.

He turned to see what the applause was about and saw, to his great surprise, Dr. Joseph Warren entering the redoubt. He was dressed in his usual fine clothes, a light cloth coat with silver buttons and a silk-fringed vest, almost as if he was on his way to a dinner party. The walking stick he carried completed the impression of a dandy out for a stroll, but the determined look behind his usual smile belied that. He walked purposefully toward Colonel Prescott and saluted.

Colonel Prescott returned the salute and the two men shook hands. "So glad to see you here, General," said Colonel Prescott, for the Committee of

Safety had recently made the doctor a Major General. "I turn over my command to you."

"Nonsense, Colonel," said Dr. Warren. "You have been in command and you will remain in command. I am here as a private soldier, ready to fight those British scoundrels! Just give me a musket and tell me where I should take up my position."

There was more applause at this and Colonel Prescott pointed to the front of the redoubt. When Dr. Warren saw Josiah his face took on an expression of wonder.

"Josiah, is that really you?" he said. "We all thought you dead!"

"How is my family?" Josiah asked. "Are they all right?"

"They would be so much happier if they knew you were alive," said Dr. Warren. "How did you get here?"

Josiah told him the story quickly, explaining how Patrick had been killed and how he had gotten hooked up with the men from Bedford.

"I'm proud of you, son," said the doctor. "Out here fighting for your country this way. I'm sure your father would be proud of you too."

"The fighting is about to start," said Colonel Prescott. "Get ready, men. Here they come."

· · ·

In all his life, Hugo Chamberlain had never beheld a more glorious sight: 2,400 men, drawn into their regimental formations on the battlefield, getting ready to march toward the enemy on the hill and give them the thrashing they so richly deserved. Like all the other British officers in Boston, he had been waiting for this moment since that day two months ago when the rebels had attacked Colonel Smith's column. Those impudent colonial bumpkins had dared to crow that this was a great victory over the vaunted British Army, when it was nothing but a lot of farmers shooting at retreating soldiers from behind stone walls, not having the courage to come out and fight in the open.

He and Tarleton had been sent by Gage to observe the attack on Breed's Hill and to act as aides to Howe as the battle progressed. Being so close to the fighting gave both of them hope that they would yet get a chance to take part in it. Tarleton was positioned on the left side of the formation, Hugo on the right, closest to where Howe and his officers were watching as the final preparations were made for the attack.

"All right, we are ready," said Howe, and Hugo felt another thrill run through him. But just as Howe was about to march to the front of the troops and give the order to advance, Tarleton appeared.

"Sir, we're taking fire from Charlestown," he reported.

"Charlestown?" said Howe, and a moment later they heard the crackle of musket fire from the town. Hugo saw a puff of smoke coming from one of the church steeples. It was followed by more and more shots that didn't hit anyone but made some of the marines on the left flank duck. If the troops marched up toward the hill now they would have to go past Charlestown and be exposed to the snipers there.

"We'll have to eliminate that before we attack," said Howe.

Hugo saw Admiral Graves, commander of the British naval forces, approaching. "You see what's going on?" he asked Howe. "Give the word and I'll burn them down."

"The word is given," said Howe. "Burn them."

A few moments later Charlestown was bursting into flame as the guns of the Lively and the Falcon poured round after round of burning shot into it. The houses, the churches, every building in fact was catching fire. The flames and the smoke reached high into the afternoon sky. The church steeple was becoming a great pyramid of fire. A few figures came out of the town and ran toward the redoubt on the hill.

"Coordinated naval and military operations, Chamberlain," said Howe. "That's the way wars are going to be fought in the future."

"Brilliant, sir," said Hugo.

"I've been watching you, Chamberlain, and I think you have a lot of potential," said Howe. "I'd like you to consider becoming my aide."

Hugo felt a thrill run through him. "You mean when you assume command here, sir?" he asked.

"No, I mean now, as soon as it can be arranged."

Howe finished his tea, then handed the cup and saucer to the orderly as Hugo sought for a reply. If he accepted, it could be a big boost to his career. But it would also be a betrayal and an insult to General Gage, who had been good to him. What if today's action was a success and Gage redeemed himself and was not sent back to London? He would be giving up a coveted position and making an enemy of the commander in chief of the colonies. But if he turned Howe down, and Howe, as everyone predicted, took Gage's place, he would be placing himself on Howe's bad side and missing out on a huge opportunity.

"Can I think it over, sir, and tell you tomorrow?"

"A British officer has to be decisive, Chamberlain. He has to know his own mind." It's now or never, Hugo thought.

"I accept, sir," he said, "and thank you for having so much confidence in me."

Howe offered his hand. "Good," he said. "Now, let's do what we came here to do." Saber drawn, every inch the English Lord, Howe marched to the front of his troops.

Speaking in a loud ringing voice that every man could hear, he said:

"Men of England! Soldiers of His Majesty, King George III! You are the finest troops in the greatest army in the world. It is my honor to lead you into battle today. Do your country proud! Soldiers of Great Britain— Forward March!"

Now the drummers began pounding out "The British Grenadiers," and were soon joined by the fifers. As General Howe began to march the officers and sergeants signaled with their sabers also, and the rest of the regiments began to move, their colors flying, the men marching at the half-step, up the slopes toward the rebel positions on Breed's Hill. Each man held his musket in front of him, bayonet gleaming in the sun. "Oh dear God, what a sight!" thought Hugo, "How I wish I was going with them. To be part of that! How glorious!" His eyes filled with tears. He had never felt prouder of being a British soldier. He looked at the rebel positions again, thought of Josiah Hartford who was up there behind those walls. Now it's our turn, he thought.

•　　•　　•

In the redoubt on Breed's Hill, Josiah and the others saw Charlestown burning, saw the signals given for the attack to begin, saw the scarlet-and-white uniforms begin to move, and heard the drums begin to pound.

Josiah looked at Adam, who looked back at him with the same worried expression, his hand thoughtfully on his chin. This wasn't like April 19, when they had been chasing the British and shooting at them from the trees. This was the armed might of the British Empire, coming directly at them, and the musket he held in his hands seemed a small defense against what he saw coming his way. The earthworks which he stood behind, however, gave him heart.

"Irresistible force versus immoveable object," he murmured.

"What?" Adam asked.

"In my philosophy classes at Harvard we used to ask what would happen if an irresistible force met an immoveable object," said Josiah.

"You educated guys are always bragging."

Further along the redoubt Josiah heard a gray-haired man from Connecticut saying, "I thank thee, O Lord, for sparing me to fight this day. Blessed be the name of the Lord."

The pounding of the drums grew louder as the British force got closer. The sound of the drums added to the tension and Josiah felt he might burst if there wasn't some relief soon, and he could tell the men close to him were feeling the same way. Even Doctor Warren looked grim. After marching here, digging all night and into the morning they were all dirty, tired, and hungry, for they hadn't eaten since yesterday and no one, it appeared, had thought to make arrangements for food to be provided for the men on Breed's Hill. Josiah felt the fatigue falling away as he contemplated what was about to happen. But the pounding of the British drums was taking its toll.

It was, to everyone's surprise, Little Tommy Hoover who saved the day. Looking down one side of the line and then the other, he drew in a breath, then began to sing "The Girl I Left Behind Me."

> "I'm lonesome since I crossed the hill
> And over the moorland valley
> Such heavy thoughts my heart do fill
> Since parting from my Sally."

Josiah began to sing too. So did Doctor Warren, Adam, then Captain Jake, Reverend Sam, Zack Brown and Peter Salem.

> "I seek no more the fair and gay
> For each just does remind me

How sweet the hours I passed away
With the girl I left behind me."

From behind them now came the powerful voice of Colonel Prescott. "Sing!" he shouted. "Sing! Sing loud as you can! Sing, I say!"

"O ne'er shall I forget that night
The stars were bright above me
The moon it lent its silvery light
When first she vowed to love me.
But now I'm bound to Brighton camp
Kind heaven then pray guide me,
And send me safely back again
To the girl I left behind me."

Every man was singing, louder and louder. Next to him Adam waved his musket about encouragingly, singing at the top of his strong voice, as the song reached its final stanza:

"Her golden hair in ringlets fair
Her eyes like diamonds shining,
Her slender waist, her heavenly face
That leaves my heart still pining.
Ye gods above oh hear my prayer
To my beauteous fair to find me
And send me safely back again
To the girl I left behind me."

The song was over and the men were all laughing—at what, no one knew. Josiah laughed too, and a great relief swept over him even though, as he looked out and saw the lines of scarlet-and-white getting closer, nothing had changed.

"Now hear me, all of you!" shouted Colonel Prescott. "We aren't going to fire until they get close. Aim low. Aim for their legs. Shoot the officers first. We aren't going to fire until they get so close we can smell their foul British stench! You all hear that?"

"Yes sir!" They all shouted back in unison.

"I will personally cut the heart out of any man who shoots before I tell him to!" shouted Colonel Prescott. "You hear me? Bigelow, do you hear?"

"Yes sir!"

"Salem, you hear what I said?"

"Yes sir. Don't fire until you say so."

"Hartford?"

"Yes sir."

"No one shoots until I tell him to. Don't fire until they get close. *Don't fire until you can see the whites of their eyes!*"

The British were now so close that it seemed to Josiah that in a moment he *would* be able to see the whites of their eyes. The sound of the drums and the fifes was deafening. The sunlight was glinting off the bayonets, and Josiah and the other men in the redoubt could see the expression on the faces of the British soldiers, which was grim and businesslike. They were coming up the hill to do the job they were trained to do—kill— and every man there knew British soldiers were very good at that.

"Christ, I could throw a rock and hit them," Adam muttered.

"Come on, come on, let us shoot!" Brown hissed.

At last the order came. "All right, men. Make ready!"

"Make ready!"

"Take aim!"

"Take aim!"

Several more seconds passed. The British were now less than fifty feet from the redoubt.

"Fire!"

Three hundred muskets went off at once, and a terrible moan came from the British lines. Josiah saw men falling, saw them wincing in pain as the musket balls hit them. Some threw their arms back, others simply fell over, some clutched themselves where they had been hit. The heavy weight of their packs dragged them down the hill after they fell. Josiah reloaded, raised his musket again, waited until he heard the command from Colonel Prescott, fired again in unison with the others, saw more redcoats falling. As the process was repeated over and over the field in front of him was so covered in smoke he could see little, but what he could see were hundreds of British soldiers lying in the grass, and the rest fleeing back down the hill in a tangle of red-and-white. As the smoke cleared a great shout of triumph went up from the men in the redoubt, and they all saw the British running away and heard Colonel Prescott shouting, "Cease fire! Cease fire!"

Every man in the redoubt took off his hat and waved it about his head, yelling in relief and joy. "Come on back and get more of that, you British bastards!" Adam kept yelling. "Come on back and get more!"

"They won't be back," Dr. Warren declared. "Not after taking those losses."

At long last the bucket boys arrived with water, and the buckets were taken along the line. Water had never tasted so good, Josiah thought, and he saw each man drinking gratefully.

"How do you feel now?" Adam asked. "You feel like a soldier yet?"

"I wonder how they feel?" asked Josiah, looking down the hill at the British on the beach. The soldiers were milling about, some sitting down, worn from their exertions.

"I think they heard you, Bigelow," said Captain Jake, and now they all saw the officers and sergeants gesturing to the soldiers, who were by now reforming into lines.

"It can't be," thought Josiah. They couldn't be planning to attack again.

CHAPTER 18
THE REDOUBT

Standing on the beach, Hugo Chamberlain stood watching the battle and the retreat down the slope of Breed's Hill with the same feeling of disbelief he had when he watched the wounded come into Boston on April 19. This cannot be happening, he thought. But there was no denying what his eyes told him: The rebels on Breed's Hill had beaten back an assault by the British Army, inflicting severe casualties while suffering few of their own. The hill was spotted with red-and-white bodies, some wounded, many dead, and from behind the walls of their little fortress the rebels were cheering and waving their hats, taunting the retreating British soldiers.

"Do you hear that?" said Tarleton, coming over from the other side of the beach. "Damn rebel bastards!" He shook his fist at the rebel stronghold. "You'll pay! I swear by God Almighty, you're going to pay!"

General Howe was one of the last to come down from the hill. His white gaiters were splotched with blood and his dark, handsome face wore the same expression of shock that Hugo and Tarleton had.

"Reform your ranks!" he was shouting. All around him officers and sergeants were getting their men back into their lines.

"We're attacking again, sir?" asked Tarleton.

"We are going to take that hill," declared Howe, once more surveying the carnage.

"Can we go along this time, sir?" asked Hugo.

"Gage forbade it," Howe snapped.

Within 15 minutes, the lines were reformed. Hugo couldn't help but notice how much thinner the lines were this time. The wounded who had made it back down the hill were being gathered along the shoreline, others were being brought back by stretcher bearers. Some— pitiful creatures— were lying close to the American redoubt, and Hugo could see some of them moving. For a moment he was seized with a desire to run up there and try to help them. But there was nothing he could do, and in his mind he cursed the men who had done this.

This time General Howe made no speech. He stood in front of his troops and simply gave the command, "Forward march!" and the scarlet and white lines began moving up the hill and toward the redoubt once again.

.   .   .

Josiah, Adam, Dr. Warren, Captain Jake and the others had watched the British retreat, saw, as the smoke lifted, the many casualties they had brought upon on the enemy and heard the groaning of the wounded. Some of them were crying out for their mothers. The June sun was getting hotter as the afternoon went on and Josiah, fighting his own feelings of thirst, wondered how the British, lying out there in their heavy wool uniforms, could stand it. The men in the redoubt had precious little water but at least they had that. Those poor wretches lying out there had none, and soon the groans of pain were accompanied by piteous cries of "Water! Water!"

Now the British were coming again, General Howe leading them as before. Colonel Prescott, marching up and down the redoubt, said, "Same as last time, men, same as last time. Don't fire until I tell you. Aim low. Aim for their legs. Shoot the officers first. Don't fire till they get close."

"Who's that little fellow over there?" asked Dr. Warren, nodding toward Tommy Hoover. "How did he get here? Firing a musket that's almost as long as he is."

"We call him Little Tommy. He's been with us since the first day at Concord," Captain Jake explained.

"Too bad a boy like him has to be in midst of something like this," said Dr. Warren.

"He wanted to fight, just like all of us," said Adam. "How you doing over there, Tommy?" he called.

Tommy turned and smiled. "These bloody-backs aren't so scary," he said.

"One thing's sure, he'll have plenty to tell his grandchildren," said Adam.

"If he doesn't get killed," said Zack Brown.

"You're always so cheerful," Adam said.

"Make ready!" shouted Colonel Prescott.

"Make ready!"

"Take aim!"

"Take aim!"

"Fire!"

Load and fire, load and fire, Josiah thought, as once again the British received a withering blast of musket balls, and once again huge holes were torn in their lines. Men screamed when they were hit. Some paused to shoot back, making them easy targets for the rebel sharpshooters. They got no closer to the parapet than before, and when one rank after another had been cut to pieces Josiah, his face and hands filthy from dirt, powder and smoke, heard the drums sounding retreat and the British were once again running pell-mell down the hill, leaving hundreds of their comrades to lie dead and dying in the tall grass. But to Josiah's right a small unit of British soldiers was holding out, hunkered down in the grass behind some old brick kilns, refusing to retreat and firing their muskets. Dr. Warren said suddenly, "Hey, that's Smithson!" and pointed at the officer who was in charge of this small band of die-hards.

"Who's he?"

"A British colonel who says Americans are cowards."

Spontaneously, without being told, Josiah, Dr. Warren, Adam, Captain Jake and at least five other men pointed their muskets at the British soldiers who were gathered near the kilns and fired at the same time. Colonel Smithson winced as he was hit over and over, cried out and then fell.

"Still think we're cowards?" called Adam as the British retreated, carrying the body of their colonel with them.

Half-way down the hill Josiah could see the figure of General Howe, standing alone except for an orderly. He stood forlornly, looking at the hundreds of bodies all around him.

"'A horse! A horse! My kingdom for a horse!'" quoted Dr. Warren.

"A horse?" asked Adam.

"What Richard III said when he lost the Battle of Bosworth Field," said Josiah.

"Sounds like more of that Shakespeare guy. You educated fellas get on my nerves," said Adam. "How many bodies you reckon are out there?"

"Five hundred, six hundred, maybe more," said Dr. Warren. "Counting the ones they've carried away, we must have given them close to eight hundred dead and wounded." He looked about. "We've lost hardly any."

"But will they come again?" asked Adam.

Josiah looked at his ammunition pouch. He had three paper cartridges left. He showed this to Adam, who checked his own and discovered the same: He was almost out too.

"Sergeant, can you ask Colonel Prescott to get us more ammunition?" Dr. Warren suggested. "We're depleted here."

Jake set off to find Colonel Prescott. "Look!" said Adam, pointing toward the beach.

"Reinforcements," said Dr. Warren. "I guess that answers our question."

Josiah saw barges with soldiers coming past North Battery, each one filled with fresh troops. The first landed on the beach on the right hand side of Charlestown and the soldiers got out, muskets on their shoulders, and began forming up.

Josiah saw Captain Jake on the far side of the redoubt, talking to Colonel Prescott. The Colonel was shaking his head. Captain Jake pointed in the direction of the front wall, stamped his foot, then came walking back to where his men were waiting.

"When will we get the powder and ball we need, Sarge?" asked Adam.

Captain Jake took his musket barrel in both hands and swung it about his head. "Any of you boys ever kill a man with a club?" he asked.

•   •   •

Hugo saw stretcher bearers coming down the hill, and saw General Howe walk quickly over to one of them, saw his face take on a look of pain as he saw the unconscious form of Colonel Smithson.

More barges were arriving and disgorging their cargoes of fresh troops from Boston. Many of them were Royal Marines, and Hugo saw Major Pitcairn leading them. Pitcairn walked over to General Howe and the two began talking quickly, General Howe pointing this way and that as he outlined his plan for the third attack on Breed's Hill.

Once the barges were empty of soldiers the sailors and the stretcher bearers began loading the wounded onto them. Some of the wounded were unconscious but most were wide-awake and in great pain. Many of the uniforms were soaked with blood. For a moment General Howe stood looking on, shaking his head. "These are the ugliest wounds I've ever seen," he said. Turning to Hugo and Tarleton, he went on: "Smithson was my last senior officer. I've got almost no officers left. I'm seconding you both to my staff and I'll have it out with Gage later. You'll go with the next assault. Major," he turned to Pitcairn, "put your men on the left. This time we'll advance in columns, and we won't spread out into attack formations until we get within fifty feet of the rebels. The men can leave their packs behind and tell them not to stop to fire until we get into the redoubt."

When the men were ready, Howe again addressed the troops.

"My brave boys," he shouted, "times like this echo in history. Times like this tell the true measure of a man.

"When a moment like this arrives, British soldiers have two choices: 'Conquer or die!' We are going to capture that hill, or we are going to die in the trying! Who's with me?"

There was a great roar of assent. "Conquer or die! Conquer or die!"

"Then follow me! British soldiers, forward march!"

The men began their third march up Breed's Hill, shouting, "Conquer or die!"

●　　●　　●

"I wish I could say I was dreaming," said Dr. Warren.

The British were coming toward the redoubt again, this time in single file, stepping over the bodies of their fallen comrades as they came.

"What are they doing, Captain Jake?" asked Adam.

"Howe's changing tactics," Jake replied. "Fewer targets for us to shoot at. Am I right, Colonel?" he asked Prescott, who was standing close by.

"They'll get to around fifty feet of us and then they'll spread out," said Prescott.

As the British came closer the rebels in the redoubt could hear them chanting: "Conquer or die! Conquer or die!"

As the British lines got within range American sharpshooters began picking off the first man in each column. Josiah marveled as he saw one man fall and the one behind him step right over his dead or wounded body and keep on coming, knowing full well he was going to be the next to fall.

Like a great door swinging on its hinges, the British columns opened up, and once again they were coming straight on, row after row, bayonets lowered, and they came toward the redoubt from three sides, still chanting "Conquer or die!" At a command from their officers they increased their speed as once again they were hit with one blast of musket balls after another. Josiah fired his last round and looking along the redoubt saw the other men doing the same. The final American volley sputtered out like a dying candle.

The first British soldier to get over the wall came from the right side. He vaulted to his feet and stood for a moment, and Josiah recognized him as the major who had been in command that April morning at Lexington. The man waved his sword, urging his men onward, and a moment later more soldiers came over the wall and jumped into the redoubt, shouting "Conquer or die!" and "Follow Major Pitcairn."

Josiah was about to run over to that side and fight whatever way he could, but before he could move he heard Adam shout, "Look out!" and he saw the face of a British soldier coming over the wall right in front of him, wearing a murderous expression as he fired his musket. Josiah felt the whoosh of the air as the ball whizzed past him, missing him by inches, and before he could process this the soldier thrust his bayonet at him. Josiah dodged, and as the soldier drew back for another try Adam hit him a tremendous blow to the forehead with the stock of his musket, knocking him unconscious.

Now the soldiers were pouring into the redoubt, coming over the walls in waves. The Americans were being forced back toward the rear, and many were running toward the sally-port even before Colonel Prescott began ordering retreat.

"Come on boy, we better get out of here," cried Adam, pulling at Josiah's arm. Captain Jake agreed, and began calling to his men to follow him out of redoubt. They fell into a line behind him, led by Tommy Hoover, followed by

Joe Cyrus and Reverend Sam, pushing their way through the tangle of humanity all around them.

The men were being pushed back by the weight of the British assault. On all sides Josiah saw men fighting savagely, struggling hand-to-hand with the British soldiers, who appeared to be determined to kill them all. The British were using their bayonets; the Americans fought back with knives and the stocks of their muskets. Colonel Prescott had drawn his sword, slashed one soldier with it, stabbed another, and then knocked the musket out of the hands of another with a quick downward motion that cut the man's hand to the bone. As the musket fell to the ground Peter Salem picked it up, stabbed inexpertly at a soldier with the bayonet, missed him, then began to retreat with the others. Dr. Warren also drew his sword and he quickly felled a British officer. The officer's sword dropped out of his hand. Josiah scooped it up, felt the weight of it, then before he knew it he had thrust it into the chest of the soldier closest to him. As the man fell dead an officer came toward Josiah, thrusting his sword with a confident air, certain he could polish off this bumpkin easily. Josiah engaged him, wounding his arm with the first thrust, smiled at the man's shocked expression as he realized he was up against an opponent far better than he was. Josiah feinted right. The officer went for the feint, leaving his front completely exposed, a moment later he fell as dead as the other.

"Tarnation!" Adam shouted. "Look at that boy go!"

Two more officers now approached, swords drawn, looking at Josiah cautiously. Josiah, remembering what Lord Roger had taught him about facing two opponents, quickly engaged one, killing him, and then turned to the other so quickly the man literally jumped backwards with a frightened expression and began shouting, "Tarleton! Tarleton! Help me!" and a moment later Josiah stood facing Banastre Tarleton. His sword was stained with blood and his face wore a murderous look. Josiah parried the first thrust and replied with one of his own, causing Tarleton to retreat, his sword still out in front of him, waving back and forth like a snake. He moves fast, Josiah thought.

"I'm going to enjoy this," said Tarleton. "I've wanted to kill you for a long time. Your friend Chamberlain sends his regards. "But he won't weep over your body after you're dead."

"Who'll weep for you, Tarleton?" said Josiah, and he used his best move, feinting to his left and then going left, and against anyone else it would have succeeded. But Tarleton was too quick. He saw it coming, met Josiah's blade with his own, then slashed at him. Josiah parried, faked to his right and was able to drive the point of his sword into Tarleton's left shoulder. Tarleton cried out as a spot of blood appeared, and then they fought, stroke after stroke, until a knot of men, British and Americans alike, came between them. Josiah felt a strong hand on his shoulder, saw Colonel Prescott, heard him saying, "Retreat, Hartford, retreat," and as the hand pulled him back he saw Dr. Warren, still in the middle of the battle, stab at a soldier, missed, then had his sword knocked from his hand by a soldier who struck at him from the side with his musket. Seeing he was surrounded, Dr. Warren threw up his hands in a gesture of surrender.

"This is the most traitorous, treasonous swine," said Tarleton. "I can put an end to you," and stabbed Dr. Warren through the heart.

"Did you see that?" Adam shouted.

"He killed Dr. Warren!" Captain Jake cried. "He killed a helpless man who was trying to surrender! Coward! Cowardly dog!"

As the Americans retreated there were shouts of "Coward!" and "Murderer!" directed toward Tarleton, and cries of grief for Dr. Warren. But there was nothing anyone could do. They were being forced back toward the rear of the redoubt as if pushed by a giant wave.

The rebels retreated toward the sally port. Josiah turned about, fended off more soldiers' bayonets with his sword, saw coming toward him the husky form of Major Pitcairn, who was carefully aiming his pistol at Colonel Prescott. Before he could pull the trigger Peter Salem, on Josiah's right side, cocked the British musket and fired. Major Pitcairn fell, coughing and choking, and a moment later Josiah was through the sally port and running with the others toward Bunker Hill.

•   •   •

Hugo had not seen the duel between Josiah and Tarleton. He had seen Josiah for a blurred moment, as the rebel retreat began, and he had seen Tarleton kill Dr. Warren. He had been standing on the parapet, having gotten up the hill behind the first wave of soldiers to break the barricade, and he was filled with the same blood lust all the others felt. He knew nothing except a desire to make the rebels pay for all the pain they had inflicted on his comrades that day.

By now the rebels were in full retreat. The redoubt was covered in smoke, and it was hard to see what was close by. Sword in hand, he leaped into the fray, hoping to encounter Josiah. He slashed about, sometimes hitting rebels, sometimes missing them, and as the rebel retreat continued more soldiers neared the sally port and the back wall of the redoubt. The remaining rebels, realizing their escape was cut off, surrendered. The soldiers began forcing them toward the side wall, gesturing to them to keep their hands up. Hugo saw that Tarleton wasn't having any of it. He began killing the prisoners with his sword, cutting them down methodically, one at a time.

Hugo's first feeling was one of elation. His hatred of the rebels, his desire to see them suffer, had been so intense he would have been happy to see them all roasted alive. But as the killing continued he was revolted. He ran over just as Tarleton was about to kill a boy of no more than sixteen, who stood with his hands protectively out in front of him in a gesture that was half surrender and half prayer, and before Tarleton could plunge the sharp point of his sword into the boy's chest Hugo grabbed his arm.

"For God's sake Ban, they're surrendering!"

Tarleton turned on him with a snarl, a wild, mad look in his eyes and Hugo realized Tarleton would not hesitate to kill him too. Tarleton jerked his arm free and stood looking menacingly, first at Hugo, then at the remaining prisoners. As the last shots of the battle died away Tarleton reluctantly lowered his sword, and the fiendish look on his face faded. The battle was over. The British had triumphed, but at a terrible cost. General Howe would never forget the slaughter of his men on Breed's Hill. That memory would disturb his sleep for the rest of his life. Never again would he send his men on a direct attack against entrenched American positions.

And on this day two legends were born: One of a battle named after a hill that was not the one upon which men fought and died, and of Banastre Tarleton, "Bloody Ban," the most brutal killer in the British Army, the man who took no prisoners and to whom mercy was a word he never heard of. In the years to come he would be the most feared and hated of all British officers, and his name would reek from Massachusetts to South Carolina.

CHAPTER 19
GENERAL WASHINGTON

July 3, 1775

Three thousand five hundred men were drawn up in Cambridge Common that morning. It was a Monday and they stood in regimental formations. Most of them, like Josiah, were veterans of the fighting on April 19 and Breed's Hill. There were regiments from Massachusetts, New Hampshire, Connecticut, and Rhode Island. The colonels from each regiment, and their staffs, sat on their horses in front of their men, waiting.

Opposite the formations of soldiers, on a slight elevation, a reviewing stand had been set up at the base of a huge elm tree. General Artemus Ward sat on his horse, facing the men, along with the other generals: Putnam, Greene, Thomas, Sullivan, Heath, and Spencer. Behind them were several hundred spectators, all finely dressed, including some members of the Provincial Congress. They had come out to see General Ward be demoted to second in command and his place taken by the man from Virginia that the Continental Congress had decided would be the new commander-in-chief of what would from now on be known as the Continental Army. This had been decided on June 18, the day after the fighting at Breed's Hill, but word had not gotten to the men encamped outside Boston until a week later, and since then there had been much talk about this transfer of power.

"So, who is this who's coming to be our new general-in-chief?" Captain Jake asked.

"Some fella from Virginia, I hear," said Adam. "Name of Washington."

"Never heard of him."

"I've read about him," said Josiah. "He made a name for himself in the last war."

"He's rich, too, I hear," said Adam. "One of the richest men in the country. Owns hundreds of slaves and has a huge plantation, and he lives in a house big as a castle that he calls Mount Vernon. He's serving without pay."

"So, do we call him General George or King George?" asked Captain Jake. "Why are they sending a Virginia man? Who's been doing the fighting in this war? New England men, that's who."

"I don't know why they want to replace old Ward," said Joe Cyrus. "He was doing a good job. A real slap in the face for him, being made second in command this way."

This resentment was shared by many of the other men in the camp, and for different reasons. Some did not want to be under the command of a southerner. Others preferred John Hancock as the new commander, for the rumor had been that he would be the one chosen by Congress, not this man from Virginia, and as they waited in the morning sun for the new man to arrive Josiah wondered what Washington would do differently than General Ward. In camp there was a feeling that they should attack Boston and drive the British out, and the talk was that Washington would be the man to do that, for his reputation from the French and Indian War was that he was an aggressive officer, willing to take more initiative in battle than the cautious Ward.

The Battle on Breed's Hill, while strictly speaking a defeat for the Americans, was instead regarded as a resounding victory. The British had suffered appallingly high casualties, while American losses had been slight and coming mostly at the end of the battle, when they ran out of ammunition. Reports from Boston indicated the British had endured over 1,000 killed and wounded. Hospitals were overflowing with wounded and dying men. "I wish we could sell them a dozen hills at that price," Colonel Prescott had said. The British couldn't afford to keep losing that many men.

None of the men from Josiah's company had been killed in the battle, except, of course, Dr. Warren. The story of his being slain by Banastre Tarleton while trying to surrender had spread all over the army, as had word of how Tarleton had murdered other helpless prisoners.

The battle had given the men much confidence. They had stood up to the best troops the British had, commanded by their best general, and had only been forced to retreat when their supply of gunpowder ran out. They were certain they were going to win this war.

At exactly 10:00 am the men heard the sound of drums beating and fifers playing. The pounding of the drums got louder as the fifers and drummers got closer, playing "The Turkish March" as they came into the Common. They marched all the way to the end of the line of regiments, then turned and marched back to the center and stood to the right of the reviewing stand.

Now three men in bright blue uniforms rode slowly into the Common on oversized horses. Trailing closely behind them was a black man on a horse. "Who's he?" asked Peter Salem. "What's he doing there?" They were followed by a squadron of cavalry, also in blue uniforms, with drawn sabers. They rode in front of Ward and his officers, came to a halt, and exchanged salutes.

"Which one is Washington? Who are the other two?" Adam whispered excitedly. "Washington is the one in the middle," said Josiah. "That's General Charles Lee on his left and General Horatio Gates on his right."

"He does look like a king, doesn't he?" said Adam, watching, as they all were, as he shook hands with the man he was relieving.

If General Ward resented his demotion, he showed no signs of it. He seemed as much in awe of the new commander as everyone else. Washington had the same air about him that had characterized Lord Roger Chamberlain—a lofty appearance, as if his title and rank had been conferred on him by a higher power that ordinary human beings had no business challenging. Washington's face was grave but purposeful, and Josiah realized he was seeing a man who had come with a definite sense of mission.

Washington was a tall, powerfully built man, which amplified his regal bearing. His uniform was dark blue, with golden epaulets on his shoulders. He wore a black three-cornered hat and a golden sword. His white breeches fairly glowed, contrasting sharply with his black boots.

For a few moments Washington seemed content to let the tension build as he sat on his big white stallion. He looked fixedly at the men before him. "He has a sense of drama, that's for sure," Josiah whispered.

Now Washington eased his big horse forward. In a clear voice , he read:

"By order of the Continental Congress, and by the unanimous voice of the colonies, I assume command of the Continental Army. May God grant that I be worthy of this honor and that I prove capable of such a momentous task. I can answer for but three things: a firm belief in the justice of our cause, a close attention to the prosecution of it, and the strictest integrity in its pursuit. May God grant us victory!"

He then handed his orders to the black man who had ridden into the Commons behind him, and with a swift, graceful move, Washington drew his saber. Placing it on his right shoulder, he nodded to General Gates on his right, who called out, "Pass and review."

The fifes and drums began playing again, this time in a marching tempo. "Right face!" was called out, and each regiment turned right and, marched straight ahead, then turned left, then left again, and marched in review before the new commander, Colonel Prescott and the other veterans of Breed's Hill leading the procession. "Eyes right!" ordered Prescott, and as every head turned to look at the reviewing stand General Washington brought his sword downward so that it lay parallel with his leg in its stirrup.

The men marched well, Josiah thought, even though few had uniforms they were still an impressive sight. With the martial music playing, the drums sounding, Josiah, in spite of himself, felt a pride he had never felt before.

"Well, what happens now?" Adam asked when they were back in camp.

"Now we wait and see what our new commander-in-chief is like," said Captain Jake.

·   ·   ·

They did not have to wait long. The new commander didn't waste any time making his presence felt. Washington, usually accompanied by General Gates and General Lee, rode from one end of the camp to the other, looking at this, taking note of that, telling his subordinates to write something down. He inspected each regiment, walking imperiously past the men who were lined up in rows, looking each man in the eye. His manner was stern and distant. It was hard to gauge what he was thinking, but Josiah guessed that the disorderliness and lack of discipline in the camp was not to the man's liking.

In this he was right, for within days of taking command Washington began issuing one new order after another: Men had to relieve themselves in designated latrines. Men swimming in the Charles River had to be decently clothed. Soldiers were to stand and salute when an officer passed by. Superiors were to be addressed as "sir" at all times. There would be no more fist fights or knife fights. Because of the number of weapons that had been accidentally discharged, all firearms were to be kept unloaded.

"Dear Mercy," Josiah wrote (he had begun writing to Mercy the day after encountering her on the road out of Boston, and was delighted at how quickly she responded with letters of her own) "we all thought our new commander, General Washington, would want to liberate Boston right away, but instead he seems determined to reorganize the army in his own image. We get new orders every day: Any man who is caught drunk on duty will be given 39 lashes on his bare back. Any soldier found guilty of insubordination to a superior officer will be given 39 lashes. There is to be no more fraternizing with the enemy while on guard duty.

"At first the men haven't been taking these new orders too seriously. But it turns out General Washington means what he says. Yesterday we were drawn up in ranks to witness punishment. A man from Connecticut was whipped for hitting his captain.

"Seeing a man whipped is an awful sight. As in the British Army, the biggest and strongest man from the offender's unit is ordered to wield the lash, which means Adam would have to be the one to do it if anybody from my company is ever punished like that. He hates the idea and says he would rather cut off his arm than whip anybody. Captain Jake says it would serve him right, because he is always bragging about being the strongest man in the army.

"General Washington lives in grand style. He's moved into Vassall House on Tory Row in Cambridge, which you remember is the biggest house in Massachusetts, even bigger than Hartford Manor. (The Tories who own it have long since fled to Boston). They say he's the richest man in the colonies so I suppose he's used to high living, but it rubs some of the men the wrong way. They call him 'the new King George' and 'His Lordship the General' and other unflattering names, and many say they are going home as soon as their enlistments are up.

"He certainly does act like a king, for he has a haughty and superior manner. He starts out each day with a horseback ride, accompanied by his Negro servant, Billy. He's an amazingly good rider, in fact he sits on his horse like a centaur. The story is that he's the best rider in the colonies, and Billy is second best.

"Billy really gets on Peter's nerves. He is as snooty as the General. Peter says that since there are so few Negroes in camp they should at least be nice to each other. Several times Peter has tried to get Billy to notice him by saying hello or waving to him, but Billy just ignores him.

"I've applied for leave so I can come to Concord to visit you and your family. Colonel Prescott approved it, so don't be surprised if I show up at the Willingham House one day soon.

"My love to you and all the Willinghams, Josiah."

He waited anxiously for his leave to be approved and also for a return letter from Mercy. He wanted to see Mercy again, for he had decided, during the long months in the army camp, that he wanted to marry her.

"Dear Josiah," Mercy wrote, "the whole family is thrilled that you will be coming to see us soon. How long will you be able to stay? Please write as often as you can. Everyone enjoys your letters. Whenever a new one arrives I read it first and then read it out loud to everyone else.

"Life here in Concord is almost like normal. If it wasn't for the regiments of soldiers going past sometimes you wouldn't know there was a war going on. Scotty has been saying he would like to enlist but he is too young and Mother and Father won't hear of it. He has taken Patrick's death very hard and at times acts as if he still doesn't accept it. We keep telling him that Patrick has gone to a better place but I don't think he understands that. What is death anyway, where do we go when we die? If we are truly the spirit made flesh then perhaps only our bodies die but our spirit lives on in some other way. I wish I knew, but that would be cheating, wouldn't it? Cora's husband Isaiah is thinking of enlisting also, but only if they promise to make him an officer. If that doesn't happen he is going to run for the Continental Congress, which I think would suit him better, since he loves to make speeches.

"We are all is so sorry that dear Dr. Warren was killed. That officer who killed him, Tarleton, must be a true monster.

"You asked me in an earlier letter what happened that day poor Patrick went to his Maker. I finally got Father to tell me about it.

"It seems that a rider came from Lexington, telling them all that fighting had started there and that the British were on their way. Then Mr. Adams and Mr. Hancock arrived in a wagon, and told Father that our house was one of the first the soldiers were going to raid, just like Walter said. Both Mr. Adams and Mr. Hancock advised Father that it would be a good idea to leave, in case the British burned the house down.

"So, Father gathered the family together, including Patrick of course, and they all began walking toward the north end of town. They all thought it would be safer there.

"They had just started when the soldiers arrived and there was the sound of shooting coming from several directions, frightening them all to death. Then Patrick told Scotty that he had to go back to the house and get his algebra book, *La Géométrie* by Rene Descartes, the one he had brought with him when he first came to visit.

"Scotty tried to stop him but Patrick got away too fast. Father tried to go after him but he ran into a group of soldiers. They were shooting at some militia men, and the militia men were shooting back, and Father just couldn't get past them, so he had to go back to where the rest of the family was. They went on toward North Bridge, and saw the fighting that had started there too. So, they went to the Johnson's barn, and hid there until some of the militiamen came by and told them the British had left.

"They went on home and found Patrick in the yard beside the house, and all the dead British soldiers too.

"Patrick is buried in the old Concord Cemetery. We found his book next to him. Scotty wants to know if he can keep it to remember Patrick by."

"Please come as soon as you can, Josiah. Everyone sends their love. Mercy."

He found that writing to Mercy gave him a much-needed outlet, a way to connect with his past life and to express his feelings. He also enjoyed telling Mercy and the Willinghams about life in camp.

"Men are still coming in from all over the colonies, some from as far away as Georgia," he wrote. "Others are arriving from New York, Pennsylvania and New Jersey. But one regiment that stands out is a group of about 100 men from Virginia.

"This company was specially raised by the Continental Congress for the sole purpose of harassing the British sentries and forward outposts, for they are all frontiersmen and supposed to be deadly shots. They came swaggering into camp as if the war is over because they're here, wearing their buckskin and leather clothes and carrying those famous Kentucky long rifles.

"They bivouacked in Harvard Yard, not far from us and close to the Marblehead regiment. The Marbleheaders are mostly sailors and fishermen and the Virginians seem to have gotten on their nerves right away. The Marbleheaders have never seen anything like the Virginians, and the Virginians had never seen sailors and fishermen before. I suppose a clash is inevitable when you put men so different from one another close together.

"The bad blood started when one of the Marbleheaders said something unflattering about the frontiersmen's attire—I heard he called them a lot of backwoods bumpkins wearing animal skins, and the Virginian said the Marbleheaders still smelled like the fish they used to catch. There was a fight which got broken up quickly, but the bad feelings remained.

"Yesterday afternoon I was sitting and talking with Peter, Adam, Captain Jake, Tommy Hoover, and this strange fellow Zack that I told you about, when we heard yelling and cursing from Harvard Yard, near the library. We went to see what was going on and we saw about thirty Marbleheaders and the same number of Virginians standing opposite each other. They were yelling insults and even throwing rocks back and forth. It reminded me of what used to happen in Boston when a group of Tories and a group of Liberty Boys like Walter would face off before a riot began.

"The leader of the Virginians is a rangy fellow named Johnny Elliot. The leader of the Marbleheaders is a sailor named Abraham Cosser.

"They were standing there cursing each other and both men took out their knives. 'We should try to stop this before someone gets killed,' said Captain Jake. Just about that time Elliot took a swipe at Cosser with his knife, missed him, and Cosser stabbed at Elliot but he missed also.

"Then there was a clatter of horse's hooves and General Washington came riding into the midst of this. He came riding in so fast nobody saw him until he pulled up his horse and jumped off, rather gracefully for such a heavy man, and before anyone knew what to do he had grabbed both men by the neck and shook them the way you would shake a rag doll.

"'Drop those knives!'" he said. "Drop them I say!'"

"The General must be an amazingly strong man, for both men dropped their knives like they were trying to throw them away, and their faces got red as the General continued to squeeze their necks. He gave them another good shaking, then let them go. But he wasn't finished with them yet.

'You want to fight?" he said. "Out for blood, are you? You'll get plenty of fighting. This war has just started. Wait till you're in an open field and you see a regiment of redcoats coming at you and you've got no place to run, and a cannonball blows the head off the man next to you, then you can tell me how you want to fight.

"I could have you both flogged," he went on, "and the rest of you as well, for just standing there and watching while these two nincompoops kill each other. But I won't this time if you shake hands and promise to stop this nonsense."

"So Cosser and Elliot shook hands like the General said. Then one of the Marbleheaders went over to the Virginians and started shaking hands with them, and a moment later the Virginians did the same, and next thing you know they were all shaking hands and smiling at one other.

"The General got on his horse. 'That's better,' he said from way up there. "From now on you men remember you're on the same side in this war! The enemy is over there," he gestured toward Boston, "and that's who we're going to fight! When the time comes, I will summon you to battle. Will you be ready?"

"We all sang out, 'Yes!' as loud as he could.

"'Good,'" said the General. "'You're brave men, all of you. We're all here for the same purpose, to fight for our freedom! Wait for that day. Live for that day! Live for the day when we are all free men!'

"We cheered like crazy men and he rode off. "Did we just see another Alexander or Caesar?" said Captain Jake. "I think that's what they would have done." We all felt the same way. There's more to General Washington than we thought.

"Some wonderful news, Mercy: My leave has been approved! Who knows, I might even get to Concord before this letter arrives. Captain Jake is arranging a horse for me to ride. Look for me in a few days. My love to all, Josiah."

He sealed the letter and addressed it, then noticed that Peter Salem was sitting nearby.

"You sure do write fast," said Peter.

"Comes from a lot of practice, Peter."

"You 'spose I'll ever be able to write like that?"

"Sure, just keep on it."

"Who you writin' to?"

"Friends of my family, in Concord."

"I'll wager one member of that family is a tall brown haired girl with lots of spirit and isn't afraid to show her feelings by smacking a man in the face," said Adam, who was sitting nearby.

"Could be," said Josiah.

"Somebody's gonna have himself a real good time," Adam declared.

"It isn't like that," Josiah protested, but he could see none of the men believed him, for they all smiled knowingly.

"Look out, attention everybody," said Peter, jumping to his feet. "Here comes the General and that stuck-up servant of his."

Washington, accompanied by his servant Billy, now rode past on his oversized white stallion. Billy, as always, was close behind. The men all got to their feet and saluted.

Washington took no notice, but simply rode on. Peter smiled and waved at Billy, who took no more notice than Washington had.

"Stuck up bastard," said Peter. "Who does he think he is?"

• • •

Josiah stood staring at the newly-hewn marble tablet: "Patrick Joseph Hartford," it read. "Born Feb. 18, 1759. Died April 19, 1775, age 16 years and 2 months. Gone But Not Forgotten."

He did not shed any tears. When he learned from the Willinghams that Patrick's headstone had just been completed and set in place, he had feared that when he saw his brother's final resting place he would break down completely. But he had kept his composure, except for a few tears that came involuntarily and that he quickly wiped away. Only Mercy, standing beside him, was aware of them.

When he had arrived in Concord on the horse Captain Jake had procured for him he went directly to the spot in the Willingham's yard where he had left Patrick's body. He had formed that picture in his mind so many times that he expected Patrick to still be lying there, along with the bodies of the British soldiers. But they were gone, and he dismounted from the horse and stood staring at this spot, and he remained there until Mercy, who had been waiting for him to arrive, saw him and came outside.

"Josiah, how long have you been here?"

"This is where it happened, Mercy," he said. "This is where Patrick died."

"And the British soldiers too," said Mercy. "Did you kill them?"

"Some of them."

"Come inside," she said.

She did not, he noticed, take him by the hand as she normally did, and in the week he spent with the Willinghams he felt as if an invisible barrier had come up between them. There was nothing he could point to, but she was strangely stand-offish. Something was troubling her, he could tell, but whatever it was, she was keeping it to herself.

That did not prevent them from spending most of their time together during his stay. They visited Patrick's grave several more times, walked through town, walked in the woods and stood on the hills around Concord, looking out at the long valleys and the farm houses and the forests beyond. He told her, and the rest of the Willinghams, about life in camp, and the Battle of Breed's Hill, and how Dr. Warren had been killed. But through it all there was no denying that part of Mercy's mind was somewhere else.

The day before he was to leave and go back to camp, he told Mercy that he loved her and wanted to marry her. "I wasn't sure before," he said. "But now I am. I want to marry you. I want us to spend our lives together."

"I've waited so long for you to say that," said Mercy. "I've longed for you to say those words to me. I've dreamed of it, and I thought that when you did I would happier than I've ever been before. I can't marry you, Josiah."

"Why can't you?"

"You should marry *her*! She's going to have your baby, remember?"

"I don't want to marry Alice," he protested. "I never did."

"You have to," Mercy insisted. "That's the honorable thing to do."

"I couldn't marry someone I don't love, Mercy. I couldn't marry her when it's you I love."

"Do you really love me, Josiah?"

"Yes, I do," he declared solemnly.

"Then marry Alice!"

"I can't. How could I?"

"How could you do what you did?" Mercy cried with a flash of anger that was half anguish. "How could you bed her, if you don't love her? How could you, if you love me?"

"It was just—" Josiah struggled for the words "—it was weakness, a moment of weakness," he confessed. "Mercy, you don't know how badly I wish it hadn't happened."

"How do I know that if we were to get married, you won't have that weakness again? I want to be with you so badly, Josiah, I feel it in every corner of my body," she cried, "but I can't stand the thought of you in another woman's arms. If you aren't going to marry her, what are you going to do?"

"I'm going to marry you," he declared. "That's what I'm going to do." When she shook her head, Josiah grabbed her by the shoulders. "Don't tell me you don't love me, Mercy."

"I do love you, Josiah. I would marry you tomorrow, if it wasn't for this. But now I can't, I wouldn't marry you for all the world."

"You don't mean that," Josiah declared. "I can't believe you really mean it."

Mercy looked at the setting sun, far away to the west, turning now a blood red as it prepared to vanish.

"It's getting dark," she said Mercy. "We better go back to the house."

"Mercy—" Josiah began.

"Let it go, Josiah," she said. "Let it be." Suddenly she burst into tears. "I've loved you for so long, and I've always thought we'd get married someday. But now that's gone, gone forever! Can't you see that? We can never be together now!"

She turned away from him, sobbing, covering her face with her hands. "I don't believe it," said Josiah. "There has to be a way, there has to be."

"There isn't," Mercy insisted. "You can't put something back together again when it's broken so badly there's no pieces left to pick up. I don't know who I'll marry now but it won't be you."

"You might marry someone else someday but it's my face you'll see when you're with him, not his," Josiah declared.

"Did you see my face when you were with her?" she snapped back. "I don't think so. I've thought about this, day and night, since Alice announced she was pregnant and that you were the father, and I knew right then there never could be anything more between you and me. So let it go, Josiah, go back to the army camp and forget about me. I'm going to try my best to forget about you." She choked back a sob. "I shouldn't have encouraged you to come here. Seeing you hurts too much. I'm glad you're going back tomorrow, some of this pain will go away then."

"I can't bear the idea of it ending like this," said Josiah. "Promise me this isn't the end."

"Neither of us needs any more pain," Mercy said. "It's better this way." She kissed him on the cheek. "I love you, Josiah Hartford."

• • •

"How did it go?" Adam asked when Josiah returned to camp the next day.

"It was good to get away for a little while. I can't believe it, but it feels good to be back."

"How did things go with your girl?"

"I asked her to marry me."

"Tarnation! What did she say?"

"She said no. She loves me, she says, but she won't marry me."

"That's a woman for you, always full of contradictions. Why didn't she say yes?"

"It's—" Josiah hesitated, unsure if he wanted to tell Adam the real reason. Then it occurred to him that it might feel good to confess to the man who had become his best friend. "Back in Boston, our maid, this girl from Ireland, Alice is her name—she used to come upstairs to my bedroom, late at night. One thing led to another, and the night I left for Concord, she told me was *enceinte*."

"She was what?" asked Adam.

"With child."

"Oh. Why you old devil you," said Adam, giving him a playful push on the shoulder. "And your girl in Concord knows about it?"

"Damn right she does."

"She'll come around," Adam predicted. "Just give her some time to get used to it."

"Anything exciting happen while I was gone?" he asked, not wanting to continue the subject of Mercy any longer.

"Just the same old stuff, digging and drilling. Old George is waiting for something, but whatever it is, nobody knows. Jake says he's sent Colonel Knox on a secret mission somewhere up north to get more artillery for us. There's also a big shortage of gunpowder, and he's trying to find more."

"I wonder how much longer we'll have to wait till we attack Boston?" asked Josiah.

"It can't be too long," Adam declared. "Maybe your girl will change her mind by then."

"I'm not counting on it. But when we finally do get into Boston, at least I'll be able to see my family again."

I wonder what they'll say when they see me, he thought.

CHAPTER 20
HOMECOMING

March, 1776

"Mother! Father!"

He knew he was too far away for anyone to hear him, but he was so excited to be getting close to home that he couldn't contain himself. In front of him sat Hartford Manor, as solid and everlasting as a cathedral. For almost a year he had been picturing this moment, when he could come home and see his family again. How happy and surprised they would all be to see him, and how sad they would be when they heard about Patrick.

As he got closer he saw a vegetable garden alongside the house where none had ever been before. A small wire fence surrounded it and in the center stood a scarecrow wearing a battered straw hat. Beside the scarecrow was Jessica, kneeling down and digging amidst the neat rows of dark moist earth with a small trowel. She stood up, brushing off her apron, and when she heard Josiah cry out "Jessica!" and saw him coming toward her she dropped the trowel and brought both hands to her face.

"No!" she gasped. "No! I'm dreaming. It can't be you!"

She was much thinner than he remembered and she looked older, with deep lines of worry etched into her face. She was pale, and as he came closer to throw his arms around her he saw dark circles under her eyes. "No, you aren't dreaming Jessi. It's me, I've come home. You didn't give up on me, did you?"

She held onto him like she never wanted to let him go. Then she pulled away. "Let me see you," she said, looking at him intensely. "We thought you dead. When you didn't come back we thought we'd never see you again."

"Where is everyone?" Josiah asked. "I've got to see them! Mother!" he shouted toward the house. "Father! Walter! Anne!" He started for the door, one arm around Jessica, who unexpectedly held him back.

"No, don't," she said, "not yet. Where have you been? What are these clothes you have on? Why do you have this gun?" She wiped her eyes, for she had not stopped crying since stepping out of the garden.

"I'm a soldier," he explained, for he had his musket in his hand and his powder bag thrown over his shoulder. He wore his rifle shirt and brown knee breeches. "In the Continental Army. We just marched into the city."

"I knew about that," she said, "and about the cursed British leaving. But I never dreamed of you being a soldier. Where's Patrick?"

"Patrick won't be coming home," Josiah said gravely.

This brought more tears from Jessica. "Oh God," she said. "Father knew. He knew. He always said you would come back someday. But he never said that about Patrick."

"Why do you say 'Father knew'? He isn't—"

"We don't know where Father is."

They went inside the house, Jessica leading the way and cautioning him not to be in too much of a hurry or to talk too loud. As he set his musket and powder bag down and went into the drawing room he noticed that the house was quiet, too quiet, there seemed to be no one around. Then the silence was broken by the sound of a baby crying. "That's your son, Josiah," said Jessica. "He's five months old. You didn't know you had a son, did you?"

"Alice told me. The night I left she told me she was expecting. Where is she?"

"Alice is dead, Josiah," Jessica said in a flat tone. "She died bringing Little Josiah into the world."

Alice dead. His father gone. It was a great deal to process so suddenly.

"Where is Mother? I want to see her, and my son too." He started for the stairs, but Jessica seized his arm with a bony hand.

"No Josiah, wait, please, you have to let me tell her first. Mother isn't well. She might not be able to stand the shock of seeing you."

"What is wrong with her? And what happened to Father?"

"The soldiers came. They took Father away. Walter too."

"Where did they take them?"

"No one knows. Hugo wouldn't tell us."

"What did Hugo have to do with it?"

"Hugo was the one who denounced us. He was in charge of the soldiers who came. He had a warrant signed by General Howe and Joshua Loring."

Hugo, he thought. How could he do that? "What about Mother?" he asked.

"It was too much for her. You and Patrick gone, Alice's death, a new baby, Father and Walter taken away—and by Hugo! She broke when that happened. She kept saying, 'Hugo, what are you doing to us?' But he was a stranger, Josiah. He kept saying, 'The Happy Hartfords! A lot of spies and traitors! You defy the King!' You know how much Mother loved him. It broke her heart. Now she just stays on her bed all day, staring at nothing. She won't eat, she sleeps most of the time. Bell looks after her, and Little Josiah."

"Bell?"

"She's the nurse we hired for the baby. She takes care of Mother too."

They went up the stairs to the second floor and stood outside their parent's bedroom. "Wait here," said Jessica. "Wait here while I prepare her."

Josiah leaned against one of the smooth-polished bannisters. The moment he had waited for was finally here, but it was not anything like he had imagined.

He could hear his mother's voice from inside the bedroom, and Jessica's as well. A moment later she appeared.

"Josiah, you can come in now," she said softly.

Josiah carefully entered the oversized bedroom and saw Martha half sitting, half lying on the bed, propped up against a mass of pillows, her face strangely vacant of expression. Her once dark hair now showed a great deal of gray, and like Jessica she had lost weight. On the other side of the room, near the fireplace (which was not lit despite the cold of the March day) a woman he had never seen before sat next to a big wooden cradle, gently rocking it back and forth.

Josiah took off his hat and went over to Martha, Jessica in front of him. "You see, Mother," she said. "I was telling the truth. Josiah is here."

Martha looked at him with sad dark eyes and continued looking at him for so long he began to fear she didn't recognize him. As if it was a great effort to do so, she managed a smile and put out her hand. "Yes, it is Josiah," she said. "My son, Josiah. You've come back."

"Mother," he said, taking hold of the limp cold hand she had extended and sitting near her. "Mother, are you all right?"

"Where have you been, Josiah? We've been waiting for you to come home for so long."

"I'm sorry. I couldn't get back until now."

This was not the woman he remembered. Martha had always been such a strong person, full of life and the enjoyment of it, with so much love to give out there was no way to contain it all. She was like the sun, radiating the light of joy. This frail woman was exhausted, defeated, spiritless.

"Mother—" Josiah began.

"Where is Patrick?" Martha asked. "Didn't you bring him back?"

"No, Mother, Patrick won't be coming home."

"Why not? Where is he? You said you would bring him back, you promised."

"He's—he's—" Josiah faltered for the words. How could he tell her? What could he say?

"Patrick's in heaven, Mother," said Jessica. "He's in heaven with the angels."

"I'm sorry, Mother," Josiah said. "I failed you."

"I thought you were dead. I was sure. You never came back. You were gone. Patrick is gone. Your father and Walter are gone too." She began sobbing wrackingly. "Alice is dead, we couldn't save her. Everyone is gone. I wish I was dead too."

"Mother, you shouldn't talk that way."

"She's been saying that since Father and Walter were taken away," Jessica said.

"Mother, please, I don't want to hear you talk like that," said Josiah. Martha didn't respond but kept on crying and repeating her wish to be dead. Jessica put her hand on his shoulder.

"Best to let her alone when she gets like this, Josiah," she said. "She'll cry for a while and then go to sleep. Come and see your son."

Josiah looked at the tiny creature, now sleeping peacefully in the cradle. My own, he thought, my flesh and blood. What do I say, what do I do now?

The nurse, Bell, a middle-aged black woman with merry eyes and a serious face, smiled at him without speaking. She looked uncertainly at Jessica when Josiah reached for the baby.

"Let him sleep," said Jessica. "You can hold him later."

"Where is Anne?" Josiah asked as he and Jessica went back downstairs.

"She and Charles got married in June. They have a house near Long Wharf."

"Why are you all so thin?" asked Josiah. "And why are Mother and my son in that cold room with no fire?"

"We've been cold and hungry all winter, Josiah. We are almost out of food, and there's no wood for a fire."

That explains the garden, Josiah thought. "Is Elias still here? And Maureen?"

"Yes. I sent them both out to try and find some food for us."

"Can you let Anne and Charles know I'm home? Bring them over for dinner tonight."

"And eat what, Josiah? All we have are a few vegetables and some corn meal."

"There's plenty of food in camp. I'll go over there now and bring back all the food you can eat."

"Oh thank God," said Jessica, throwing her arms around him again. "It's been so hard. I'm so glad you're back. You can help me try to get things back to normal."

"I'm not staying," he said, saddened to see the way her face fell when he told her this. "The army will be marching south soon."

"And you have to go?" Jessica asked.

"I'm a soldier, I have to go."

"But we need you here! We, us, your family! Tell me what happened, Josiah. How come you never came back? What happened to Patrick? How did you become a soldier?"

"There's a lot to tell, Jessi," he said. "It will have to wait until I get back."

"Then hurry," she said, pushing him toward the door. "Hurry up so I know this isn't all a dream."

•   •   •

They were waiting for him when he returned—Jessica, Anne, Charles, Elias and Maureen—gathered in front of Hartford Manor with an expectant air, and they let out a collective cry of joy as he came riding in, Adam and three army horses in his train. The horses carried flour, beans, corn meal, baskets of dried fruit, beef and bacon in burlap bags, as well as bundles of firewood.

As he and Adam came near Adam burst forth with a loud whoop, followed by a long, low whistle.

"Will you look at that?" he said, more than a touch of awe in his voice. "I thought you might be stretching the truth when you told me about your house. Only it's not a house, it's a palace."

"One of the biggest in New England," Josiah told him, unable to resist boasting a little. "I can't wait to show you the inside."

"Who are all these folks in front?"

"My sister Jessica, my sister Anne, her husband Charles, Elias our butler and Maureen, our cook. Wait till you taste her cooking. Beats army chow by a country mile."

"I wouldn't mind tasting her some myself," said Adam. "She's a good-looking woman. A little on the thin side, maybe, but it's been a long season without rain."

"There will be none of that," Josiah said. "Things are complicated enough without you making a play for the cook. Besides, she way too small for a big guy like you."

"Large or small, they all got it in the same place," Adam declared.

They reined in their horses and dismounted, only to have Charles, Anne, and Jessica swarm over Josiah with tears, hugs and kisses, Maureen and Elias holding back but unable to restrain their smiles and gestures of delight. Charles wrung Josiah's hand while Anne kissed his cheek over and over. "This is a wonderful day," Jessica kept saying. "I still can't believe it's real." Her attention now turned to Adam, who stood next to his horse, his big round hat in his hands, as if uncertain of what he should do next and continuing to gaze in wonder at Hartford Manor. "Who is this?" she asked.

"This is Adam Bigelow. He's my best friend in the army, and I promised him a long time ago that he could see Hartford Manor."

"I hope you all don't mind my bustin' in this way," Adam said.

"How could we?" said Jessica brightly. "Any friend of Josiah's, especially one who is fighting the God-cursed English, is welcome here."

"Oh, look Elias, just look at all this," Maureen squealed, looking over the food Josiah and Adam has brought. "Butter! Sugar! Oh, thank the Lord. I can bake us a cake. I can make biscuits. There's even some coffee!"

"I'm thanking the Lord that Young Master Josiah has come back," said Elias. He and Josiah embraced. "I never thought I'd see you again, Young Master." He wiped tears away from his eyes.

"It's good to see you, Elias," said Josiah, nearly crying himself. "So damn good."

"Let's get all this into the kitchen," Jessica said in an authoritative tone, and Josiah realized that Jessica had taken over as mistress of the house. "Elias, get us some wine to drink while Maureen makes dinner. Come on inside, Mr. Bigelow," she said to Adam, "and please regard Hartford Manor as your home."

"I don't see how I could ever do that," Adam replied, throwing a bag of corn meal over his shoulder. "But I sure do appreciate the invitation."

Elias went to fetch the wine while everyone else carried to the bags of food into the kitchen. "You eat well in the army," Charles observed. "Perhaps I'll enlist."

"You will do no such thing," Anne said firmly. "I won't have my new husband going off and getting himself killed."

"Are you married, Mr. Bigelow?" Jessica asked, pouring herself a glass of the wine Elias had just arrived with. She drank half of it, then refilled her glass and drank more.

"Yes, ma'am, I sure am. Got a wife, Emmy, and two young ones."

"Why is it every handsome man I meet is married already?" Jessica said. "Come on, let's all go into the drawing room while Maureen makes dinner. We have a great deal of catching up to do."

"Yes, you've got to tell us, Josiah," said Anne. Like the others else she had lost weight, and her face showed the effect of stress and worry. She seated herself on the sofa, Charles beside her. He too looked older, and his face, which Josiah had always thought was too serious, was now grim. This winter must have been terrible for them, he thought.

As he sat down he saw Adam standing hesitantly close by, still holding his hat in his hands and staring upward at the high ceiling and the crystal chandeliers. "Come and sit down, Adam," Josiah said. "Sit over here, by me."

"Let's toast Josiah's return," Jessica said, raising her glass, and when the toast was over she filled it once again. "Now," she said to Josiah, "you have to tell us what happened."

"Yes, please," Charles implored. "For an entire year we've wondered what happened after you left that night."

"Yes, that night, that night that changed my life, that changed all our lives," Josiah said slowly, determined to tell it all and not leave anything out.

He told them everything: How he had ridden out of Boston through the Neck, how he had been challenged by the British officers and how he'd gotten away from them. He told them how he paused his journey at Lexington and had seen the first shots fired there, then stayed to help with the wounded and the dying.

"The British said the 'damned rebel militia' fired first," said Charles. "You're saying that isn't what happened?"

"I saw it myself," Josiah told them. "A British officer pulled his pistol and fired into the air. All hell broke loose after that."

"God-curse the British," Jessica said bitterly. "They will say anything and do anything, as long as it's against us."

"Patrick might still be alive today," Josiah said, admitting out loud something that up to now he had always kept to himself, "if I hadn't lingered in Lexington to help with the wounded. But when they asked me, I didn't see how I could do anything else, those men were suffering. But still..." His voice trailed off; for a moment he couldn't find any more words.

"Of course you couldn't," said Anne, and he was glad to see all the others nodding in agreement. "They needed your help, and after seeing what you had just seen, how could you have said no?"

Josiah felt better, happy to have gotten that off his chest, and continued his tale.

He told them how he had gotten to Concord after the fighting started, how he had searched for Patrick in the Willingham house, how he had seen him from the third floor and called to him, and then how he had been killed by the British soldier. When he got to what happened next, Adam spoke for the first time.

"I saw it—Josiah killed those two Brits, it was a real sight to see. Then we saw him crying over your poor brother."

Josiah, with help from Adam, described what happened after: The retreat of the British column back toward Concord, how the men of Bedford Company and later the Vermont Green Mountain Boys harried them every step of the way, all the way to Boston.

"Were you in that battle on Breed's Hill?" Charles asked. "We watched it from the loft upstairs."

"Yes, we were there," said Josiah. "From the start to the finish."

"Did you kill many British?" Jessica asked.

"A lot of people died that day."

"What about you, Mr. Bigelow?" Jessica asked Adam. "Have you killed many English?"

"Yes ma'am, I guess I've killed my share."

"Good," Jessica said, with a venom in her voice that made Josiah uncomfortable. "I hope you kill a lot more."

"This isn't like you, Jessi," he said.

"When it come to the damn British, the more killing the better," Jessica said defiantly. "I'll hate them until the day I die."

Her malevolence toward the British was reflected in the faces of Anne and Charles, who obviously shared her feelings. "You don't know what it's been like here since the siege began," said Charles. "These past few months have been hell for us. The British steal our food so they can eat while we starve. They take all the wood so they can keep warm while we freeze. They arrest people and take them to Castle Island and hold them for ransom. We think that's where Benjamin and Walter are. I've made inquiries day after day, but they won't tell me anything."

"We'll go to Castle Island tomorrow," Josiah declared. "We'll see if Father and Walter are there."

When they all sat down to dinner at the big dining table Josiah finally felt the sense of being home that he had hoped for. The absence of Martha, as well as Benjamin, Walter and Patrick, lessened that feeling, but the smell of the cooked food and the sight of Maureen and Elias coming in and out with tray after tray was good to see.

"You told me the food would be good," said Adam, "and you sure weren't lying. This is some meal."

"Does your wife cook like this, Mr. Bigelow?" asked Jessica, finished yet another glass of wine.

"My Emmy's a good cook, yes ma'am she is," said Adam proudly. "A good cook and a good woman too."

"When did you see her last? Has it been a long time?"

"Oh, just a few months ago, I reckon. There wasn't much doing in camp right then, in the midst of the winter and all, so Colonel Prescott said they could do without me for a couple weeks. I was going to take this guy along, but he'd already have some leave and he didn't want us both gone at the same time."

"You had leave, Josiah?" Anne asked. "Where did you go?"

"I went to Concord," Josiah said hesitantly.

"Concord?" Anne pressed. "Why?"

"I went to see Mercy. I asked her to marry me." He paused, then decided it would be best to get this out and be done with it. "She said no. Because of Alice."

A silence fell over the table at the mention of Alice, a silence that wasn't broken until Charles asked, "What finally persuaded the British to leave Boston?"

"Yes, we wondered about that," Jessica said.

"Did it have anything to do with that awful bombardment a few weeks ago?" asked Anne. "I don't think anyone in Boston slept that night. That was the most noise anyone ever heard."

"We saw the muzzle flashes from the cannons," said Charles. "They lit up the sky like lightning bolts."

"The way we heard it," Josiah said as they went back into the drawing room, as dinner had come to an end, "was that Colonel Knox told General Washington that if he was given enough men he could fetch the artillery that was captured at Fort Ticonderoga. Washington agreed to let him try, and one day in the dead of winter there he was, coming into camp with more cannons than you could count."

"At first we were all dancin' with joy when he got to camp with all that artillery," said Adam, "but then we had to start digging emplacements to put those cannons in, and we had to pull on ropes, hundreds of us at a time, to pull them into position. That was somethin', wasn't it Josiah?"

"We had to dig in the frozen ground with picks and shovels, then wheel those metal monsters into position," Josiah said. "Then Colonel Knox would show up and say he wanted them put somewhere else, so we had to start all over again."

But by March 4, all the guns were in place. That night the bombardment began, a cannonade bigger than anyone had ever seen before. Guns at Roxbury, Lechmere Point, and Cobble Hill all started firing. Josiah learned later that the thunder of the guns could be heard in Braintree, thirteen miles away. The fiery trails of the shells could be seen streaking across the night sky like a meteor, arcing into the air and crashing to the ground. The bombardment went on into the night.

"The next day we captured Dorchester Heights," Josiah went on. "Now every British soldier in Boston was under the gun with no place to hide." A few days later a British delegation appeared, carrying a white flag, and asked to see General Washington. Howe offered to abandon Boston by March 17 if there were no further attacks by the Americans. Washington agreed, and at the appointed hour the Continental Army had marched into the city, even as the last of the British ships were sailing out of the harbor. The people of Boston had turned out to cheer the soldiers as they arrived, but all Josiah could think about was getting home. They knew the rest.

By now the fire that Elias had built with the wood Josiah had brought was crackling away merrily. Everyone drew their chairs in closer to the fireplace as the evening temperature began to drop. Then came the sound of Little Josiah crying upstairs.

"You have such a strong, lovely son," said Anne. "Have you noticed how much he looks like you?"

"I think he looks more like his mother."

Silence fell over them again. They are all thinking the same thing, Josiah thought, and so he said, "Won't someone tell me what happened with her?" No one answered. Jessica was looking uncertainly at Adam, and Josiah said, "You can speak in front of Adam. He knows all about it."

Anne and Charles looked at Jessica, who, with a slight roll of her eyes, said, "I suppose it has to fall on me. You truly want to know this, Josiah?"

"Of course I do!" he burst out. "Now tell me, please, before I go mad with wonder."

"I think I was the first to notice," Jessica began. "She was trying to hide her pregnancy. But she just kept getting bigger and bigger. Soon we all knew.

"But Alice was stubborn, and proud too. She wouldn't tell who the father was."

"But Jessica guessed the truth," Anne said.

"I had a suspicion," Jessica admitted. "I'd seen how she looked at you. Mercy had noticed it too, and then she told me how she had seen Alice sneaking around the house late at night, coming down the stairs from your room. So we confronted her one day.

"'That's Josiah's baby, isn't it?'" Mercy asked.

"We could tell by how she reacted that we were right. Then she admitted it. 'Yes,' she said, 'it's Josiah's, and he promised to marry me, and when he comes back he will.'"

"Did you promised to marry her, Josiah?" Anne asked sharply.

"No," Josiah said, embarrassed, glad for the darkness that prevented them all from seeing how red his face was getting. "No, I didn't promise her that."

"When you take a woman to bed you are making a promise, said or unsaid," Anne told him in a scolding tone. "But flesh can be weak, and we live in strange times, when everything seems to be changing and nothing is the way it used to be."

"That doesn't make what Josiah did all right," said Jessica, drinking more wine. "You hurt Mercy badly."

"I know I hurt Mercy," said Josiah. "I told her how sorry I am."

"Mercy tried to act as if it didn't matter to her," said Jessica, "but I heard her crying in her room. She loves you, Josiah, and since she and Alice had become friends she felt betrayed by both of you. But before she left she had a long talk with Alice. Alice told me later that Mercy forgave her."

That night Josiah slept in his own bed. He slept badly, for after sleeping in the tent with the rest of his messmates for so long he wasn't used to sleeping in a bed and being by himself. He lay awake a long time, thinking about everything that had happened, about his mother and father and Little Josiah as well as Alice and Hugo. He thought of Mercy, too, and how he would like to hold her in his arms as he had once held Alice.

The next day Adam went back to camp, returning the two horses and the mule, and Josiah went with Charles to Joshua Loring's office near Province House, but there was no one there; the office was deserted.

"We'd best hire a boat and go to Castle Island," said Charles . "That's where the prisoners were being held."

But save a few wretched men who greeted them joyously as they came ashore, Castle Island was empty.

"Did you bring us food?" one of the pitiful creatures asked. He held out his hands supplicatingly. Josiah recognized him as Prince Estabrook, the blacksmith from Lexington. Like the people of Boston, these men were half-starved, dirty and dressed in rags. "Give us food," Estabrook pleaded. "They said you would bring us food."

"Who told you that?"

"The Brits, before they left," said another man, whom Josiah remembered as the corporal on Breed's Hill who hadn't wanted to help his men lift the stone into place. Josiah recalled hearing that he had been captured in the redoubt. "We begged them to leave us some food, but they took it all and said someone from Boston would come and bring food to us."

"I think you've been lied to," said Charles.

"What happened to the rest of the prisoners?" Josiah asked.

"They took them all," said Estabrook. "They left us because there wasn't any room."

"Did you see anything of a tall, white haired man and his son?"

"I saw them, yes, they were here," said Estabrook.

"Did the British take them too?

"At first they were going to leave them behind," said the Connecticut corporal. "I heard Loring say, 'Leave those two, they're of no use,' but then a young British captain came over. He says to Loring, 'Bring them, I want them brought along.' It appeared they knew each other, because the white-haired man kept saying 'Hugo, what has come over you?' and the younger one kept shouting and cussing this Hugo fellow."

Hugo, thought Josiah, that cursed Hugo. Not content with what he had done already, now he had to make sure that his father and brother were taken to God-knows- where, under the tender mercies of Joshua Loring. What could have caused Hugo to turn on his family this way?

From the prisoners Josiah and Charles learned that Loring and his flunky William Cunningham had arrested numerous people in Boston, then let them go if they paid a bribe. He received a sum of money for the upkeep of each prisoner from the British every day, but kept most of it for himself and saw to it that the prisoners received barely enough food to keep them alive. Cunningham was in charge of the prisoners and he frequently beat them with a billhook.

"He didn't beat my father and brother, did he?" asked Josiah. "Not your father," said the Connecticut corporal.

"But my brother?"

"He got his share of whacks. He kept cursing and defying them. Your father kept trying to restrain him, but he wasn't successful."

That sounds like Walter, Josiah thought.

Disappointed, Josiah and Charles returned to Boston. Charles went to arrange for a boat to be sent to Castle Island to rescue the men left behind there. Josiah went home.

• • •

"Haven't you done enough?" Jessica asked. "You've fought in two big battles. You've killed lots of the enemy. You've been in the army a whole year. Can't they let you go? Can't someone else take your place? We need you here. Your family needs you. I need you. Your son needs you."

"It isn't like I have a choice," Josiah protested. "You want me to get shot for desertion?"

"Can't you tell them what is happening to us?"

"It doesn't work that way. You don't know what it's like in the army."

"When you came back, Josiah, when I saw you coming toward me, I thought, 'God has answered my prayers. Josiah is here, he can help me carry this load God has put on me.' Now I find out you're leaving, making me take on the entire burden once again. Why, Josiah, why?"

As the weather grew warmer and the winter snow disappeared, the day when the army would march south to New York drew ever nearer. When Jessica understood this she began imploring Josiah to find a way to get out of the army and stay at home. He protested that it was impossible, that General Washington had ordered that deserters be shot, and besides that, he would be leaving the men he had served with and grown so close to.

"So your friends in the army mean more to you than your family?" Jessica asked bitterly.

"I didn't say that," Josiah snapped.

"That is what it sounds like," Jessica maintained. "This is not the life I wanted, Josiah. I want a home of my own, a husband, children. Now I wonder if I'll ever have them. I'm past twenty, Josiah. What man is going to want me in a few more years? I'm losing all my hope, and when that's gone what is there left?"

Jessica's words were sobering, and while he continued to tell everyone that he couldn't leave the army and stay behind in Hartford Manor, inwardly he was beginning to think about it. Every time he held Little Josiah he enjoyed it more and more. Soon he'll be taking his first step and saying his first word, and I won't be here, he thought.

Then there was his mother. Day after day she sat on her bed, staring at nothing, hardly aware of anyone else being around her. Then she would call for Benjamin. "Benjamin!" she would cry. "Where are you? Where have you gone? Where is he?" Saddest of all was when she cried about Hugo and what he had done.

"Hugo! Hugo! What are you doing? Hugo, make them stop! You can't take Benjamin, he's not well. You can't take Walter! Somebody stop them!"

After one of these outbursts she would sob wrackingly, covering her face with her arms and eventually fall asleep.

But it wasn't until he thought of Mercy that he made up his mind.

He had tried not to think of her ever since she turned down his proposal last year. The harder he tried the less he succeeded, and there were times when he was so overcome with thoughts about her he feared he might go mad. But when it occurred to him that with the way things had changed since the last time he saw her she would accept his proposal and become his wife. In fact, the more he thought about it the more certain he became. The next day he went to see Colonel Prescott.

"You're asking a lot, Hartford," Prescott said when he heard Josiah's request. "You think you're the only man who wants to go home? We need men like you who've been in battle. The word is the British are assembling a huge force in Nova Scotia, preparing to sail to New York and attack us there. The real fighting of this war hasn't started yet."

"I know that, sir," Josiah said.

"On the other hand, you have done your share, as you say. With your father and brother taken—damn these Brits—your other brother dead, your family has certainly sacrificed more for our cause than most." Prescott was silent for a moment as he thought this over. "Come back tomorrow, Hartford. I'll go see General Greene."

"There's one condition, Hartford," Colonel Prescott said the following day. "General Greene agrees that you have done enough in our fight for liberty. But if this war goes on too long we may need a navy. You could help build one. So you have to promise to reopen your father's shipyard."

"Yes, of course, Colonel, in fact I had been thinking about already." The yard had closed soon after the siege began. Many other businesses had closed their doors as well, bringing widespread unemployment in Boston, further adding to the city's miseries.

"All right, then, Hartford, here are your discharge papers," said Prescott." Congratulations, you are a civilian again."

"Thank you, sir, thank you," said Josiah, shaking Prescott's proffered hand. "I hope you don't think less of me for this."

"How could I? You'll have your hands full, getting the shipbuilding business going again. You have any other plans?"

"I'm thinking of getting married."

"To the Willingham girl? Lucky fellow!" Prescott extended his hand once again. "On your way Hartford. Go get married, have lots of children and build ships for our country."

There was much celebration in Hartford Manor that night. Jessica was beside herself with joy. She consumed a great deal of wine and kept repeating that her prayers had been answered. Anne and Charles were equally happy. Maureen fixed a special dinner and even made a cake. When dinner was over Anne, Charles and Josiah stood around the piano while Jessica played the "Lillibulero" and *Aupres de ma Blonde*." Elias played his fiddle.

"Almost like old times," Charles said.

"I'm counting on you to help me open the yard," Josiah said to him.

"Of course! Of course! Anything I can do." Like Josiah, Charles wasn't much of a drinker, but even he was getting a little tipsy tonight. "My law practice has dwindled to almost nothing, so I have plenty of time on my hands these days."

"How are you enjoying married life?" Josiah asked.

"Very much, very much." He gave Josiah a man-to-man wink. "I'm so fortunate to be married to Anne, and into such a wonderful family."

"No kids yet, I notice," Josiah observed.

"We're trying," Charles said rakishly. "We're trying very hard."

I intend to join you in marital bliss very soon, Josiah thought. But he didn't say it out loud, fearing it might bring some bad luck on what he intended to do tomorrow, which was to ride to Concord, find Mercy and ask her to marry him.

CHAPTER 21
THE WHITE COCKADE

Josiah's unexpected arrival made everyone at the Willingham house uncomfortable. All conversation in the drawing room came to an end. Mercy, who had been talking with Dolly Hancock, looked dismayed, and John Hancock, standing near the fireplace speaking with Mercy's father Jessup, abruptly stopped and looked at Josiah curiously. Josiah suddenly realized they all knew that Mercy had turned him down when he proposed last year, so his unanticipated appearance was a surprise.

Hancock came to the rescue. In the grandiose way he did everything he approached Josiah with his hand extended.

"I am always happy to greet one of our brave heroes fighting for our freedom," he said, shaking Josiah's hand enthusiastically. "I understand you were at that battle on Bunker Hill."

"The fighting actually took place on Breed's Hill, Mr. Hancock."

"What a glorious day for our country," Hancock went on. "It will be a long time before the Brits forget that licking we gave them."

"But we lost the battle, John," the lawyer Isaiah Donaldson protested.

"Not so, sir, not so," Hancock maintained. "It was a Pyrrhic victory for the English. A few more such victories and there will be nothing left of the British Army. Am I right, Hartford?"

Josiah recalled the dead and dying British soldiers lying on the grass in front of the redoubt, moaning in pain and calling for water. "It was a bad day for all the men there, sir," he said. "British and American both."

"Of course, of course," said Hancock patronizingly. "How are the people in Boston?" he asked.

"It was a hard winter for them," said Josiah.

"And your family, how are they?" Jessup Willingham inquired. "Did they make it through the siege all right, as I imagine they would?"

"Not so well, Mr. Willingham. You see, the British arrested my father and my brother Walter and took them away. We don't know where they are."

This news brought about a gasp of outrage from all the people in the room, followed by a general damning of the English.

"Army life agrees with you, Josiah," said Donaldson, never one to be left out of a conversation. "You're looking very fit and healthy."

"Don't tell me you're thinking of joining the army, Isaiah," said Dolly Quincy in a sweet tone from her place next to Mercy.

"Well, um, no, not at the moment," said Donaldson uncomfortably. "I have far too much to do right here."

Josiah suppressed a smile. Donaldson was a frail looking man, bespectacled, tall and reedy in build. The rigors of army life would be hard on him.

Josiah noticed that Mercy was stealing glances at him. When he looked in her direction she averted her head, determined not to make eye contact.

"What brings you all the way from Philadelphia, Mr. Hancock?" he asked.

"When I learned the British had left Boston I came as quickly as I could," Hancock replied. "I must confer with General Washington about the progress of the war."

Dolly Hancock had been taking note of the looks that passed between Mercy and Josiah. She surmised why Josiah had come. Looking at her husband, she said, "We need to be leaving, John."

"Yes, and so should we," said Cora Donaldson, who also had a notion of what Josiah was doing there.

Amidst all the goodbyes and farewells that were soon being said Josiah saw Dolly lean over and say something to Mercy. A few moments later Josiah and Mercy were alone in the big drawing room.

"Damn you, Josiah," Mercy said. "I was finally starting to get over all the hurt you caused me. Now here you are, and I can feel that hurt starting again. Why have you come here?"

"There is something you must know," Josiah began, but Mercy cut him off. "How is Alice?" she asked. "Are you married now?"

"Alice is dead. She died in childbirth."

"Oh-oh!" Mercy rocked her body back and forth on the sofa. "That poor girl. What a terrible time she had in her life. That she had to die that way, how sad. Did the baby survive? Was it a boy or girl?"

"They named him Little Josiah. He's strong and healthy."

"I'm glad of that," Mercy said. "I'm so glad of that."

"He's going to need a mother, Mercy. Someone to take care of him as he grows up."

"Why did you come here, Josiah?" Mercy asked again.

"I want you to marry me," Josiah said. "Marry me, raise Little Josiah with me, and have children of our own."

"Why should I marry you now, Josiah? Just because Alice is out of the way? Why would I want to marry you and see you go off to the war and not come back? I don't want to get married just to become a widow."

"I'm not going anywhere," Josiah said. "When the army leaves, I'm staying behind."

"Are you allowed to do that?"

"Colonel Prescott arranged for me to get an early discharge. I'm staying in Boston to reopen the shipyard. Mercy, I want you to be there with me." Mercy's face was still saying no. "I know you love me, Mercy."

"Dolly told me to forgive you your trespasses. She said, 'Men are weak creatures. They can't resist the temptations of the flesh.'"

"You told her?"

"Yes, I told her. You and Alice, Alice's pregnancy, all of it. She's the only one I could confide in when they wanted to know why I turned you down. What could I tell them? I couldn't tell them the truth, that you had been having it on with the maid and that she was going to have your baby. Dolly was the only one I could tell. If she were here I'm sure she would advise me to say yes. But I can't bear the thought of being hurt that way again. My loving you only makes worse. Whenever I saw Little Josiah I would see Alice. When we were together as man and wife I would feel Alice there, and when I was in your arms I would wonder if it was me you were making love to or her."

Josiah began to protest, but Mercy had made up her mind. "Go away from here, Josiah! Go away and don't come back! I can't bear it." She was weeping now, with tears running over her cheekbones and leaving small trails behind. "I don't want to see you. It hurts too much. Go away, Josiah, please, go away." She ran from the room, still crying, leaving Josiah by himself.

•   •   •

Mercy's cry of "Go away! Go away!" tormented him all the way back to Boston. He had been so certain Mercy would say yes. Now that she had said no, so forcefully that there was no chance of her ever changing her mind, he wondered what he should do now. All his plans of reopening the shipyard and staying in Boston were now up in smoke. He felt as if he had been put in a boat and then cut adrift. What was he to do?

His way home took him past The Alehouse, and when he heard the raucous laughter and music from inside he paused. I feel like getting good and drunk, he thought. Isn't that what men do when the woman they love does what Mercy just did? He tied Augustus to a post and went inside.

He sat at a table by himself and ordered whiskey, telling Mr. Phillip to bring a bottle of the best he had. He poured some into the shot glass, drank half of it, then had to do his best to keep from coughing as the fiery liquid made its way down his throat. Better take it more slowly, he thought. "Just sip it, boy," Adam would say.

He was going to miss Adam. Adam, Captain Jake, Little Tommy, Pastor Sam, Old Joe, Peter Salem, even Zack Brown—he hadn't realized how fond he had grown of them until it struck home that he wouldn't see them anymore. I feel lonely, he thought. They probably will think I let them down. They will all be marching south toward New York and I'll be staying behind.

He had finished his first shot of whiskey and had poured himself another when a voice said, "Am I seeing things, or is that Gentleman Josiah sitting there all alone?"

Josiah saw the shock of flaming red hair and gleaming green eyes. "What's my name?" she demanded.

"Purple. Violet Purple," he said, feeling a surge of happiness at the sight of her that he hadn't expected and couldn't have explained. She was pretty in a way that reminded him of Alice, and she had a smile that was both friendly and mysterious.

"Aren't you going to ask me to sit down?"

"Yes, yes, sit, please join me," Josiah said awkwardly. "Have a drink?"

"Why thank you, Mr. Gentleman Josiah. I don't mind if I do," Violet said. "Oh," she said when she tasted the whiskey. "Nothing but the best for you I see. What are you doing here?"

"I was going to ask you the same thing. The last time I saw you—"

"Was at The Crow's Nest. And before that at the Fife and Drum. You see, I have a good memory." She sipped her whiskey, smiled and winked at Josiah. "I'm more curious about you. For a man like you to sit drinking by himself he must have troubles of some kind. What kind of trouble do you have, Mr. Gentleman Josiah? Is it money trouble? I don't think so. So if it isn't money trouble it must be woman trouble. Is that it, Mr. Josiah? You're not answering but your handsome face gives you away. Want to tell me about it? I'm a good listener. You can tell me all about her, cry on my shoulder all night if you want to."

Josiah smiled, surprising himself. He hadn't expected to find anything like happiness tonight. There was something winning about this red-headed young woman, and he felt an enormous attraction for her, just as he had felt last year when he enlisted her aid in getting past the British soldiers. It was the same desire he'd felt for Alice, a physical one, but he had no intention of acting on it.

> "Drink to me only with thine eyes
> And I will pledge with mine
> Or leave a kiss within the cup
> And I'll not ask for wine."

It was the same players that he had heard last year, once again singing "Drink To Me Only With Thine Eyes." Violet closed her eyes and hummed along with the music.

> "The thirst that from the soul doth rise
> Doth ask a drink divine
> But might I of Jove's nectar sup

I would not change for thine."

"Could there be love like that?" Violet asked. "True love, deep and pure. Eternal love. Does it exist?"

"I take it you haven't found the rich man you were searching for?" Josiah asked.

"Not yet," she said, looking at him intently.

A shadow fell across the table. Josiah looked up to see old Gordon the Grouch, the gray bearded, bad-tempered shipwright, and his two journeymen, Ruben and Willie.

"Sorry to bother you, sir," said Gordon respectfully, holding his hat in his hands. "But we heard tell you're reopenin' the shipyard. Now that you're back, I mean."

"We know about the damn Brits takin' Mr. Hartford," said Ruben. "He was one of the finest gentlemen that ever walked these streets."

"Amen to that," said Gordon reverently.

"The yard will reopen," Josiah said.

"When will that be?" Gordon asked. "Sorry to be pushy, sir. We been out of work a long time. I'm anxious to get back to it, have my tools in my hands again."

"It's what the old sod lives for," the other journeyman, Willie, said. "Same with us."

"There is much that has to be done first," said Josiah.

"Bless you, sir, bless you," said Gordon. This is a switch, Josiah thought.

"Bein' unemployed knocked the starch out of him," Ruben explained. "Didn't it, Gordy, you old porcupine you."

"I reckon you can say that," Gordon agreed. "It was a long winter, that's for sure.

"Goodbye sir," he said, and the three of them went on their way.

"So you own a shipyard," Violet declared. "How about that." She looked at Josiah reflectively. "You're lonely, aren't you? I can tell when a man feels lonely. There's a certain look they get in their eyes. They may have family and businesses to run but they don't have anyone they can truly talk to. Don't you think so, Mr. Josiah, Shipyard Owner?"

"I think you're lonely too," Josiah said.

"I am, but in a different way," Violet admitted. "I have people I can tell my troubles to, but there's no one special in my life. Maybe someday there will be. I can ease your loneliness, Josiah. Come upstairs with me."

"That isn't why I came here," Josiah said.

"I can make you feel good," Violet coaxed. "I'm real good at that."

"I'm sure you are."

Violet reached under the table and ran her hand along his leg. "I can feel you," she said knowingly. "Come on. I know you want to."

Josiah felt his resistance melting. "Just to talk," he said. "We'll just talk."

"If that's what you want," Violet said, as if she knew better. "If that's all you want to do, we'll only talk."

Josiah knew as soon as he left the table and headed toward the stairs that he would do more than just converse with Violet once they were alone. But he kept up the pretense as long as he could, thinking of Mercy and Alice too, remembering how much unhappiness his yielding to temptation with Alice had caused not only him but so many other people as well. And when he joined Violet in her bed it proved to be a greater pleasure and delight than he had known before, and he knew he had pleased Violet as well. When he woke in the morning he felt less lonely than he had the night before, and as he went about his daily business he told himself that feeling less lonely was enough, at least for right now.

· · ·

Josiah threw himself into getting the shipyard ready to open. He spent all day at the yard and sometimes well into the night, but more often he brought the work home with him and continued with it there. He set up an office in an unused room on the first floor, and working by lamplight, he poured over bills that hadn't been paid, letters from creditors that hadn't been answered, plans and ideas for ships that had yet to be built. He wrote to the Continental Congress, informing them that Hartford Ships would soon be open for business once more. He went into the warehouse below the office, taking note of all the supplies, materials and tools that were stored there: Rope, nails, long sheets of copper to be attached to the bottom of a ship, forms that were used to bend wood after it had been heated with steam, yards and yards of canvas to be used for sails, buckets of oakum, that mixture of hemp and tar that was used to make the ship watertight. There were saws, axes, anvils, calipers, mallets, chisels, lathes, jack planes—some hung from the walls, others neatly stacked in rows.

Josiah knew perfectly well what he was doing: He was burying himself in his work so he wouldn't have time to think about Mercy. But before long two more errant thoughts were plaguing him: Violet and Bedford Company.

Violet's had been a sweet embrace, such delights and pleasures he hadn't known since Alice, and the desire to experience them again soon took hold of him. He resisted it, and he avoided going anywhere near the Alehouse, knowing that if he saw Violet he would be unable to stop those feelings that he knew would come over him.

The men of Bedford Company troubled his mind as well. He felt he should go and see them. They were still camped outside Boston and no doubt by now they knew he wasn't coming back. He had spent a year with these men, and it wasn't until he had been away from them that he realized how strong a bond had been formed. He feared they would think he had deserted them, and that thought bothered him just as the thoughts of Mercy and Violet did.

But getting the yard going again came before everything else. He told himself nothing else mattered, this was what he had to do.

It seemed a monumental task, and he wondered, privately, if he hadn't taken on something beyond him. There was so much to do and learn, and he had no place to turn for the kind of help and guidance that his father would have provided. Charles knew the business end, but nothing about the practical side, the part about actually putting the ships together. Charles, always somewhat inclined toward seeing a glass as half-empty rather than half-full, wore a melancholy expression the first day they went to the yard, unlocked the gate and then the door of what had been Benjamin's office above the warehouse. The same bust of Hadrian greeted them, but it was covered with a fine film of dust, as was the desk and the windowsills. Charles traced a line on the desk with his forefinger, then gave Josiah an unhappy look that clearly said, "What do we do now?" He took his spectacles off and began cleaning them with a handkerchief. Then he looked out the window and down at the shipyard, once so busy with men working at their various crafts, now as quiet as a ghost town. Three unfinished ships, one much larger than the others, sat forlornly in their frames. Josiah forced himself to be optimistic.

"We can do this, Charles," he said brightly. "We can get it all going again. Let's start by finding out who ordered those three ships. We can make a list of what supplies we need and what we have on hand. We need to find out how much longer it will take to finish those ships, and how many men we'll need to do it."

"What if the buyers don't want them anymore?" Charles asked, still looking mournful.

"We'll finish them anyway," Josiah decided, "and sell them on the open market."

"Yes," said Charles, brightening a bit, "yes, we can do that. There was always a demand for our ships. We could sell them easily, I'll wager."

There was a credenza on the other side of the room, the top covered in tightly rolled up ship's plans. Josiah began looking through them, and when he found one titled "New Amsterdam. East Indiaman," he paused and looked at it closely, fixing on all the lines and arrows and the notes at the bottom, much of which was as alien to him as if it were written in Chinese. "These are the plans for the big one sitting out there," he said finally. "It's an East India Merchantman. 1200 tons. 175 feet long end to end. 43 feet wide. 17 feet draft. 144 foot keel. 3 masts."

He was resuming the education he had begun last year when he originally agreed to take over the shipyard, and as he had with his studies at Harvard, he gave it all he had. Once more he marveled at all there was to learn.

Then there were all the various kinds of ships: Sloops, schooners, barks and brigantines. According to his father's notes, each ton of a ship's weight required one and one half tons of wood, and the largest ships each consumed as many as 2,000 trees. One three-master required half a ton of copper and iron nails, ten to twelve miles of hemp rope, and two acres of canvas sail. For every 100 tons of ship one ton of iron was needed.

Each ship was built to order, and the buyer knew precisely what he wanted, down to the finest detail. This was especially true of various kinds of wood that was used. Wood had always been wood as far as Josiah was concerned, but now he learned the differences between oak, pine, elm, locust, maple, beech, birch, hickory, ash and cedar—all of which could be found in abundance in the forests of New England. White oak was used for the hulls, due to its hardness and the fact that it held up so well against water and decay. Dowels made of locust wood called "tree nails" but pronounced "trunnels" held the hull in place and were used instead of iron to attach the hull to the frame, since iron would rust and rot out the wood surrounding it. But iron was used to hold the frame to the keel, which was made of oak or elm.

"Don't you ever sleep?" Jessica asked one night. He was sitting at his desk and looked up to see Jessica standing in the doorway, swaying slightly and trying to smile, something she had done so little of over the past year.

"Don't you sleep, Brother?" she repeated, seating herself in one of the chairs. "Night after night you're in here, working until the wee hours. Or else you don't come home until 11 or 12 o'clock. Don't forget, 'all work and no play makes Jack a dull boy.' If I didn't know better I would think you had a woman tucked away somewhere."

"It appears we are both afflicted with insomnia," Josiah observed, looking up from a book titled *Principles of Shipbuilding*. "I have a reason—I've got to learn all this." He pointed toward the books and plans and paperwork on his desk. "What's yours, Jessi?"

"I haven't slept for months," Jessica confessed. "Not since they took Father and Walter away. I keep wondering where they are, if they are alive or not. I lie awake, worrying about them, about Mother, and thinking about the future. The only way I can sleep is if I drink a lot of wine. I get sozzled every night now, Josiah, have you noticed? Lately I've been moving on to drinking whiskey, taking a shot or two on top of the wine or else during the day when no one is looking. You've seen it, haven't you, Josiah? You've seen what's happening to me. I drink like a fish. I've become a regular guzzler— 'making too free with the glass,' as they say. I'm sure you've seen it. You're just too much of a gentleman to say anything."

"Why are you doing this to yourself?" he asked. He felt a throb of pity for his sister. Aside from Walter, he felt closer to her than to any of his other siblings. Her hair was dark like Martha's, and her eyes, until recently, were bright and lively. Nowadays they were sad, as Josiah assumed his were as well, and he kept asking himself if there was any way to bring back the joy that had once been there.

"I just feel—lost," Jessica said. "I feel as if I've been cast adrift on a strange ocean and I don't know where to go."

"I often feel the same way," Josiah said. "But all this drinking—you're wasting your life, Jessi."

"That's the hell of it, Josiah," Jessica said, her voice almost a wail. "I know it. You're fortunate, you have a purpose, you have something meaningful to do."

"You kept our family together during the terrible time we just went through," said Josiah. "What you did was wonderful. But I'm here now, you can rest."

"That means—so much to me," she said gratefully. "What are those?"

"Ships' plans."

"You mean, how to put a ship together?" she asked, idly unrolling one, a design for a two-masted schooner. Her face took on an interested look. "What's the difference between a schooner and a sloop?" she asked. "When we were growing up we always heard Father talk about sloops and schooners and all those other kinds of ships, and sometimes he would take us to the wharf and we'd watch one of them be launched. May I take this?" she asked.

"What could you possibly want with it?" Josiah had no objection to Jessica taking it, but he couldn't imagine why she would want to.

"I'm not sure—it looks interesting," she said.

"Go right ahead," said Josiah. "One thing about this—" he swept his arm over the books and papers on his desk—"is that it is a great cure for insomnia. Better than whiskey."

•   •   •

Little Tommy Hoover saw him first. "Hey!" he cried. "It's Josiah!" A moment later a dozen heads were turned in his direction as he came riding in, then dismounted and tied Augustus off to a nearby tree.

Adam was the first to greet him, coming over with long strides, his round hat thrown back at a jaunty angle, his face set in a huge smile. He and Josiah shook hands enthusiastically, neither of them able to hide their smiles of delight at seeing each other again. He was followed by the men from Bedford Company, all of them wanting to shake Josiah's hand and say hello. But they also looked at him curiously, surprised at his fine clothes and the big horse he was riding, one that would rival the horses General Washington rode.

"Tarnation!" Adam whooped. "Will you just look at this? This boy dresses better than King George himself!"

Josiah was taken aback. It hadn't occurred to him, when he rode Augustus out of Boston and over to where the Army was camped, that what were to him his everyday clothes would make a marked contrast to the rifle shirt, brown breeches and tan boots he had worn while in the army. Now he was once again the wealthy young Boston gentleman, wearing a blue jacket, a vest and silver buckled shoes. The difference was startling, and the men all noticed it.

"So this is the real you, Josiah," Captain Jake said thoughtfully.

"I guess this explains why you won't be going with us when we march," Peter Salem said, sounding disappointed. "You've gone back to being what you used to be."

A good job I didn't ride over in the carriage, Josiah thought.

Word had reached Boston that the Continental Army would be marching soon, heading south to New York. When Josiah heard this he left the shipyard, not bothering to change into riding clothes, and ridden Augustus across the Neck and over to where the army was camped. He couldn't let these men go without saying goodbye.

There was much excitement in camp, the kind that precedes a march or a battle. Josiah recalled that feeling, that sense of personal liberation, that anything was possible. All around he saw men loading wagons, pulling artillery pieces into place and readying them for the horses they would be hitched to. Men smiled, waved, and sang. Josiah felt a stab in his heart. He was going to miss being part of this.

He shook hands with Reverend Sam, Old Joe, and Little Tommy. He noticed Zack Brown coming nearer, hands in his pockets, the usual half-sneering, sly look on his face. "What brings you over here, Hartford?" he asked, looking at Josiah disdainfully, as if his fine clothes were a personal insult. "I thought we were done with you. One last look at how the other half lives?"

"Hell, give him a break, Brown," said Adam. "He's got bigger and better things to do."

"Like what?" Brown sneered.

"He's going to build ships," said Captain Jake. "Ships for our navy."

"Navy? What navy? We don't have a navy. He never used a hammer or sawed a piece of wood in his life, he's always had servants to do that for him."

"He owns a shipyard, dummy," said Adam.

Brown's only reply was a contemptuous "Humpf!" sound, as if to say none of this meant anything to him. Then he said, "I knew that," and turned away. He pointed and called out, "Look! It's General Washington."

A great cheer went up now as Washington, flanked by Generals Greene and Gates, and trailed by the ever-present Billy Lee, rode past. Washington looked as imperious as ever, not deigning to notice how the men were cheering for him. Greene and Gates, however, could not keep the smiles of satisfaction off their faces, and they nodded and waved to the men in appreciation.

They rode close enough that Peter Salem was able to approach Billy Lee. "Hi Billy!" he said, waving and smiling. But Billy, just as stand-offish as his master, did not take any notice. "You stuck up bastard!" Peter shouted. "Who do you think you are?"

At this Billy turned about in his saddle. He didn't smile, but he looked amused, and said, "I'm just like you. But I get to ride, and you have to walk. I'll see you in New York, soldier."

"Damn right you will!" Peter shouted back.

"Well, he's happy," Adam observed. Turning to Josiah, he said, "Things all right at home? How's that girl of yours?"

"I proposed again, she turned me down again," Josiah said stoically.

"Tarnation! Still angry about the maid, I'll wager? Don't give up, she might come around. How's your son?"

"He's well. He seems to get bigger all the time. Adam, the men don't think I'm a deserter, do they?"

"Oh, hell no," Adam assured him.

"I'd like to be going with you when you march. You know that, don't you?"

"'Course I do."

Josiah stayed a few minutes longer, saying goodbye, wishing them well and shaking hands with them all —all except Brown, who, he could tell, was deliberately snubbing him.

"Goodbye Josiah," said Little Tommy, who had grown since Josiah first saw him last year, but was still small for his age. His welkin eyes reminded Josiah of Patrick. "Are you sure you can't come with us? I'm going to miss you something awful."

"I am going to miss you too," Josiah said.

Adam had to be the last he said goodbye to. "I don't know if we'll ever see each other again. If you ever get out Bedford way, look me up," he said.

"I will," Josiah promised. "Tommy, look after this guy, will you? Don't let him do anything crazy. And thrash those Brits good for me."

They shook hands one last time and Josiah began walking back to where Augustus was tied. As he started to mount he heard a voice calling, "Hey, Hartford, hold it a second."

Josiah turned to see Zack Brown coming toward him. "So long, Hartford," he said, offering his hand. "Too bad you can't come with us. You're gonna miss out on a whole lotta fun."

"I know," said Josiah.

"Bigelow says there are a lot of good-looking women in New York," Brown went on. "There's a place called Holy Ground, where there's more women than you can shake a stick at."

"I know," Josiah repeated. "If you find a willing woman there, give her a poke for me."

"I'll give her two," Zack promised. "Well, I guess there ain't nothin' more to say except goodbye, so, goodbye." He offered his hand again and Josiah shook it. "Goodbye," Josiah said. "Be safe." He mounted Augustus and rode back toward Boston, his heart heavy in his chest.

•   •   •

"It isn't done," Josiah said, wishing he could come up with something better than that to say in response to Jessica's idea. Just saying something isn't done did not seem like a good reason not to do it. It had no logic to it. On the other side of the room stood Charles, nervously cleaning his spectacles and looking as nonplused as Josiah, who said again, "It just isn't done."

"Why not?" Jessica demanded. "Can you give me at least one good reason, Brother, other than simply repeating that it's never been done before?"

They were in the shipyard office. From outside came the sound of men working— sawing, hammering, calling out to one another as they labored on the ships in the yard. Looking from the window Josiah could see the carpenter Johnny Bishop, a hammer in one hand and a chisel in the other, walking toward the New Amsterdam. A number of other men stood on the frame that surrounded her, kneeling as they worked. Some men were fitting a piece of the hull together, the oak having been heated so it could be curved just enough to fit perfectly over the one below it.

Everything connected with the shipyard was going well, so well, in fact, that while Josiah was not a believer in luck he did acknowledge that fortune seemed to be smiling on him in his efforts to get the yard open. The first workers had been brought back, tasked with finishing the merchantman, and by a lovely coincidence a representative from the Dutch firm that had ordered the ship arrived from Rotterdam, a Mr. Anton Devries, and he had not only made the final payment on the New Amsterdam and he also ordered another ship, this one a two-masted brigantine.

"Hey, it's Mr. Hartford," came a voice from the yard below. It was Ruben, the shipwright who worked with old Gordon the Grouch. Seeing Josiah standing in the window, he let out a cheer. "Hoo-ray for Mr. Hartford! Bless you, bless you!" he called.

The other workers joined in, cheering and waving their tools in the air. Josiah smiled and waved back.

"That must feel good," Jessica observed, coming over to the window to stand beside him. "To be cheered that way. If you get any more popular you can run for office. Come on, Brother, give me a real reason why a woman can't design a ship."

"You are exasperating, Jessica Hartford," Josiah declared. "Isn't she, Charles?"

"That she is," Charles agreed, still vigorously rubbing his glasses. "These Hartford women are born that way, it seems. All the more so because she might be right. I can't think of a single reason that makes any sense to prove her wrong."

Neither can I, Josiah thought. But I never expected this.

It had started the night Jessica had come into his study and asked if she could look over one of the ship's plans. She was fascinated, and asked to see one design after another. She sat in his study, quiet and not disturbing him while he worked, comparing one plan after another, digesting them one at a time. Josiah could almost see her mind working as she took this information in. Soon she was reading the books on shipbuilding that Josiah had brought home, eagerly devouring one page and then going on to the next.

Josiah was delighted to see Jessica occupied this way and not focusing so much on what troubled her. Soon she was drinking less. Her eyes became brighter, and when she asked to come to the yard and see for herself how ships were put together Josiah was happy to oblige. She would be the first woman to set foot there.

She had watched, entranced, as the work toward finishing the New Amsterdam progressed. Josiah forbade her from walking about the yard to get a closer look—it would distract the men, he said—but from the office she could see all that went on. She watched as the long oak sections were heated with steam and then bent to just the right shape on a form and placed on the hull, then fasted to the frames. She saw the caulkers pounding the oakum in between each section to make the ship watertight.

But when she said she wanted to draw up the plans for the new brigantine ordered by the Dutch firm, Josiah was flummoxed. This was not something women did. Jessica was smart, no doubt, but this was unheard of—a woman designing a ship. According to sailor's lore, women were bad luck on ships. What would they say about a ship a woman designed?

"The Dutch are particular," he said, "and hard to please. I heard Father say so many times. They want it done exactly as they specify."

"I've got it all right here," she said, holding up a handful of papers. "Just as Mr. De Vriess presented them. Length 110 feet. Beam 43 feet. Draft 18 feet. Total tons 105. Need I go on? They want the captain's quarters to be made from maple and cherry wood. The keel they want made of elm. They insist that—"

"Enough," Josiah said. "Charles? What do you think?"

"Times are changing. You've said it yourself, Josiah. New times call for new ways of doing things."

"That they do," Josiah agreed, his opposition fading away. "We'll make history. When we get home tonight we'll drink to the first-ever brigantine designed by a female of the species, and it will be done right here."

"Oh, thank you!" Jessica cried, flinging her arms around Josiah. "I'll draw up the best ship's plans you or anybody else ever saw. This will be the best-designed brigantine to ever sail the seas. Father would be so proud!"

•   •   •

The next few weeks passed quickly and good fortune continued to smile on Josiah and Hartford Ships. More men were hired back. The sloop was finished and sold for a tidy profit. Work began on the schooner. The yard was just as busy as it had been before the war. As he rode Augustus to work in the morning people waved and thanked him for reopening the yard and putting men back to work.

Boston was coming back to life. The war that had started here a year ago now seemed far away. The markets around the waterfront were open again. Food was coming in from the countryside. The taverns, which had never closed even during the darkest days of the siege, were doing a thriving business once more. There were few Tories left. More than 1,000 of them had left when the British did, after pleading desperately with General Howe not to leave them behind and expose them to the Patriots' vengeance. Those that remained were staying out of sight.

They were in the midst of dinner when Anne looked at Charles, who replied to her unspoken question with a nod.

"I have an announcement to make," Anne said, as she and Charles smiled happily. "Is this what I hope it is?" asked Jessica.

"Little Josiah is going to have a cousin to play with," Anne said.

"It took you a while," Jessica observed. "How long have you been married?"

"Just long enough," said Anne.

Josiah couldn't help but notice that Jessica, in spite of her outward show of genuine gladness for her sister and Charles, had a hint of melancholy in her demeanor as she and Josiah congratulated them and drank a toast to the upcoming new member of the family. Later that evening, after Charles and Anne had gone home, he asked her if what he had noticed was real.

"I am glad for them," she said. "I'm happier for them than I can say. But I'm envious of Anne. Please don't tell her I said this. I know envy is a bad thing. Didn't Mother always say so? But Anne is younger than I am and she already has a husband, and soon she'll have a child too. I have a lot to offer someone. Will I ever be able to give it to him? The years are passing, Josiah, and I feel they are leaving me behind."

Jessica came to the yard every day. She watched as work began on "her" ship, the 105 ton brigantine. She saw the frame built by the carpenters, and looked on as the keel, made of elm as the Dutch had requested, was laid on the wooden blocks, then saw how the frames were fitted into place and saw how they were fastened with iron plates. "One ton of iron for every 100 tons of ship, that's the rule of thumb, isn't it?" she asked rhetorically. "It won't be long," she went on, "until I see my ship launched into the water. And then we'll have a celebration like no one ever had before!"

Jessica did more than watch. As if by osmosis, she took in the day to day running of the yard, as did Charles, so some of that burden was lifted from Josiah's shoulder. This proved a mixed blessing, however. With less work to do and more time to think, Josiah began to brood. His heart was no more at peace now than it had been during the siege. He thought of Mercy, and wished over and over she had said yes when he proposed. He thought of Alice and the great wrong he had done her and how he couldn't undo it. He thought of Little Josiah and how he would soon begin crawling around Hartford Manor. He thought of Violet, and the stirring he felt inside when he did started to become overwhelming, and several times he was on verge of mounting Augustus and riding over to the Alehouse to see her. And he thought of the men in the army, especially those of Bedford Company, and when he could no longer keep these thoughts out of his mind his misery increased ten-fold.

•   •   •

Word had come to Boston that the army had reached New York and was camped outside the city. In spite of its reputation as a haven for Loyalists, the story was that the New Yorkers had given the Continental Army a welcome no one who was there would ever forget. Led by General Washington, the army had marched down Broadway as the band played "The Liberty Song," then "Yankee Doodle," "Over the Hills and Far Away," and "The Turkish March." The people cheered and waved white handkerchiefs. Josiah, reading about this in the *Boston Gazette*, felt a surge of envy, followed by an equally strong surge of guilt. His friends were there, preparing for the battle that was sure to come, and here he was, safe and comfortable.

It was enough, he thought, to drive a man to drink, and that was precisely what happened. Just as Jessica's drinking lessened, Josiah began to drink heavily. A glass of wine after dinner was followed by another, then a third and a fourth. The wine helped him go to sleep, but he awoke unhappy with himself and feeling worse than before.

A new and disturbing thought entered his mind: What if I went back? It made him grimace. That's insane, he thought. You must be out of your mind to even think such a thing.

But the idea wouldn't leave him, and that night instead of drinking wine he drank whiskey, which blotted the thought from his mind for a short while but in the morning it was there again, stronger than ever. The idea became a torment, like the harpies of Greek mythology tormenting King Phineus, and whiskey became his only defense against it. Before he left for work he filled a flask with it and when no one was looking he opened it and took a quick drink, then put the stopper back in and hid the flask before anyone saw him.

Supplies were being ordered, new orders were coming in. Hartford Ships was back, so to speak, and he noted how well Charles and Jessica were learning to run the yard. Already the yard had enough work to keep it busy for a year at least.

It's impossible, he told himself. You can't do it. Look at what you would be leaving behind. Your family, your home, your son—you can't do it, and that's final.

He did wish he had someone to tell this to.

•　　•　　•

"I knew you would come back," Violet said. "I've been waiting for you."

"You couldn't have known. I didn't know myself until a short while ago."

"I feel things. I knew from the way you held me when you were here before that you'd come to see me again. You need me. You have something on your mind."

"How can you know that?"

"I feel a connection with you," she said. "A closeness. I can't explain it, but it's there."

Josiah wondered if Violet said that to the other men that came to her, decided it was better not to know. It was enough just to lie beside her for now.

"I hear things," she went on. "You'd be amazed at what people tell me. I keep hearing about you. People think highly of you. The men who work for you love you. You're well known in the community, you and your family. 'The Happy Hartfords,' that's what people call you, isn't it?"

"Not so happy anymore," Josiah said. "My youngest brother is dead, my father and my other brother taken away by the British."

"So what is on your mind?" Violet asked. "Is it Mercy again?"

"I'm done with Mercy," he said, and from where he lay he was unable to see the reaction this elicited from Violet. "I'm thinking of going away," he went on. "To New York. To rejoin the army."

Violet was silent for so long Josiah wondered if she had fallen asleep, for she was lying on her side, turned away from him.

"Are you mad?" she asked finally.

"My family is going to think so."

"Why would you want to do that?" Violet asked. "Aren't you afraid of getting killed?"

"I'll only be gone for a year," he said. "That's my plan, to re-enlist for a year."

"But why?" she persisted. "Why would you want to go back to the war?"

"I realized I'll never be at peace with myself if I don't go," he said. "I'll be sorry the rest of my life."

"I still think you're mad," Violet said, turning over to lie face to face with him. "Absolutely mad. But everyone is going to miss you."

"Will you miss me?"

"More than you know. And I want to have you one more time before you leave."

He left Violet's feeling somewhat better, just as he had the last time, but the feeling soon faded. He drank a great deal of whiskey that night and in the morning he felt terrible. He saw his face in the looking-glass, haggard and bleary-eyed, and he realized he was going down a road he didn't want to travel. I should get away from here before this gets out of control, he thought.

•　　•　　•

Later Josiah would wish he didn't have to spoil so many appetites when he dropped his bombshell, but he couldn't think of a more opportune time to make his announcement. As he had feared, the general consensus was that he had lost his mind.

"Have you taken leave of your senses, Josiah?" Anne asked. "You can't just up and go away now."

"And Jessica and I can't run the yard without you," Charles protested. "You're the one in charge." He took off his spectacles and began cleaning them with a cloth.

"On that score, I have no qualms," Josiah said. "I'm certain you and Jessica can take care of things there perfectly well. When I come back in a year I'm sure business will be booming."

"Don't you mean 'if you come back?'" Jessica said bitterly. "What if you get killed, what then?"

"Jessica, don't say something like that," said Anne, horrified. "Say a prayer, quickly, to take that thought away."

"Oh, the hell with that," Jessica shot back. "We're talking about Josiah's life. What about Little Josiah? He's already lost his mother. Now you want him to grow up without a father too?"

"And Mother, what about Mother?" Anne asked. "Are you going to leave her too?" Their faces took on a sad look, as they all thought of the once happy and vigorous woman who now sat upstairs on her bed, day after day, staring at nothing, silent save for an occasional outburst when she would call for her husband or one of her children, but otherwise oblivious to the world around her. Jessica had hoped Josiah's return might help her come out of it, but she hadn't changed at all.

Josiah was silent. How could he explain something he didn't completely understand himself? That he missed Adam, who had become the best friend he'd had since Hugo Chamberlain, that he missed Captain Jake's cool leadership, Peter Salem's curiosity, Little Tommy Hoover's innocence? He missed the comradery, the long evenings around the campfires singing songs and telling tall tales. He missed the feats of strength and the wrestling matches. Most what of drove him, though, was the feeling that he had deserted his friends and that he should be with them when the fighting started again.

Anne was looking at him with a piercing gaze, as if trying to get inside his mind. She had always been in awe of her older brother, gifted and superior as he was in so many ways, and she had spent a fair amount of time trying to understand and emulate him. Now she had a sudden flash of insight, and she said, "This is because of Mercy, isn't it?" she declared. "So you're going back to the war because you have a broken heart. That's so original, Josiah. Like something out of bad play or a corny song."

Josiah decided he might as well admit it. "Yes," he confessed, "that is part of it."

In spite of all their entreaties, Josiah wouldn't budge. At last Jessica rose and threw her napkin on the table. "Thank you spoiling my appetite," she said, and then left the room as she began to cry.

"Happy now?" asked Anne. Then she too stopped eating and left to go and comfort Jessica, leaving Charles and Josiah alone at the table.

"When do you intend to leave, Josiah?" Charles asked after being silent for a few minutes.

"In a few days. There are still some loose ends at the yard I want to tie up before I go."

"I still don't understand why you are doing this," Charles declared.

"I know I am making a lot of people that I care about unhappy," Josiah said. "But I also know I will never be able to live with myself if I don't do this."

"So your conscience is clear?"

"My conscience will never be clear, Charles. I did Mercy wrong, I did Alice wrong, I did Patrick wrong because I didn't get to Concord in time to save him. No, my conscience will never be clear. But out of a lot of bad choices this is the one I have to make."

•   •   •

Martha did not truly understand what was taking place, and that make saying goodbye even harder for Josiah to bear.

"Away? You can go away, Josiah. Your father isn't well. He wants you to take over the business. You can't be going away."

"I have to, Mother," he said gently. "But I'll be back, I promise."

Martha stared at him with vacant eyes. Her hair was getting grayer every day. Her mouth was downturned into a permanently mournful expression, and with each passing day she seemed more feeble. The thought struck Josiah that she might not be here when he came back.

"You're a good boy, Josiah, you always were. So is Walter, but I don't know where he is. And Patrick, he's so helpless, why didn't he come home? I want to see him again. Where is he?" She began sobbing, covering her face with her hands, and Josiah could see there was nothing more her could say to her now.

He held Little Josiah one last time. He was nearly six months old and was already showing signs of crawling. "He'll be walking and talking before you know it," said Bell, the nurse. "He's wide eyed, getting ready to face the world.

"I have to go away," Josiah said, gently rocking his son back and forth. "But I'll come back to you, I swear. Cross my heart and hope to die." For the first time he wiped away tears while holding his son, then gave him back to Bell. He left the room quickly, and went upstairs, where he changed into his rifle shirt, boots and brown breeches, noting how comfortable they were and how good it felt to have them on again. He got his musket and powder bag, and then saw his sword hanging on the wall. I'll take it, he thought it, it could come in handy.

All was ready, except for his hat, which was gone. He had hung it on a peg near his sword and that peg was empty. Strange, he thought, where could it be?

He descended the stairs, intending to say goodbye to Jessica, and as he feared, she was nowhere in sight. She had barely spoken to him since his announcement that he was leaving and had avoided him as much as possible. "I will not say goodbye to you, Josiah," she had said. "I will not." That was two days ago, and he had hardly seen her since then. That's a shame, he thought, a shame to not be able to say goodbye to her.

Elias was waiting in front of the house for him. He had gotten Augustus ready for the journey, including some saddlebags filled with food that Maureen had prepared.

"I feel like we already did this once, Master Josiah," Elias said, thinking back to that night in April last year when Josiah had left for Concord. "And here we are, doing it again."

"It does indeed feel that way," said Josiah. "Promise me you'll watch over everyone until I come back."

"I will, Master Josiah, with all my heart and soul," Elias vowed. He sighed. "I was just getting used to you being home. Now you're leaving again." He held out his hands, as if offering to give Josiah a boost onto Augustus, although he knew Josiah would have no trouble getting on the horse by himself. It was a gesture of love and friendship, but before Josiah could accept or deny it Elias lowered his hands and almost smiled in surprise.

"Well, I declare," he said as he saw Jessica approaching. "Will you just look at this."

"Here," she said, walking up quickly and handing him his missing hat. "If you must go, you might as well do it right." Josiah now saw what she meant: She had sewn a white cockade onto his hat.

Josiah, smiling, put his hat on. "It'll give me a kind of jaunty look, don't you think?" he said. "And it's the nicest white cockade anyone could ask for."

"I'm hoping it will keep you safe," said Jessica. "I've prayed and prayed that it will protect you. Soldiers fighting the English during the Jacobite Rebellion wore these. I want you to come back, Josiah. You have to come back. You swear?"

"I could lie and say I promise," Josiah said, "but since you are all that is left to hold our family together you have to bear the truth. I can't make that promise. After all the death and killing I've seen I can't promise that."

"What is there left to hope for anymore?" Jessica said bitterly. "What is there to believe in? Will things ever be like they were before? Can we ever be happy again? Josiah, is it too much to want to be happy?"

"It's not what we thought our lives would be like, is it?" Josiah said. "We thought we would have such different futures." A sudden impulse came over him, and he handed his sword to Jessica. "In case I don't come back, give this to my son. Tell him I love him and that I'm sorry this is all I have to give him. Let him grow up here, in Hartford Manor, with you and all the rest of our family. Please, Jessi, swear you'll do that."

"Must I?" Jessica said. "I guess, I guess it's the only thing to do. All right, I promise." She held the sword close to her. "But I will hope and pray every night that I won't have to keep that promise. Now go, go, before both our hearts break."

"Mine is broken already, but nothing can ever break yours, Jessi. I know that. Farewell."

He spurred Augustus and rode away, quickly, and did not look back. He rode to the Neck and then onto the Lexington Road and headed south. Despite his sadness, he felt a sense of release, of leaving the old behind and of journeying into something new and unexplored.

It was, he knew, 220 miles from Boston to New York City. It was going to take him about a week to ride that far. He had money, and so the trip would not be uncomfortable, for there were plenty of inns he could stay at and more than enough places to eat and rest Augustus. And what, he wondered, would the men say when they saw him? He kept on riding south.

• • •

It was one of the most welcome sounds he had ever heard—someone playing "Yankee Doodle" in an especially spirited way, many hands clapping in time to the music, and another person singing the words with a high tenor voice:

"Father and I went down to camp
Along with Captain Gooding
There we saw the men and boys
As thick as hasty pudding
Yankee Doodle keep it up
Yankee Doodle dandy
Mind the music and the step
And with the girls be handy."

That has to be Zack, Josiah thought, nobody else plays Yankee Doodle like that, and the singer could only be Little Tommy Hoover. As he got closer he saw people dancing in the gathering darkness and the firelight, twirling and spinning. Then he saw Adam's big frame—there was no mistaking him—dancing with one of at least 20 women come from goodness-knows-where, all of them dancing with an exuberance that could be felt. It was contagious, and Josiah wanted to dance too.

I'm back, he thought.

The song came to an end and Josiah, still mounted on Augustus, rode a bit closer and surveyed the scene. Besides Adam, Zack, and Little Tommy, he made out the figures of Captain Jake, Joe Cyrus and Peter Salem.

Now Adam spotted him, and he let out one of his loud whoops. "Hoo-whee!" he shouted. "Didn't I say so? Didn't I say he'd come back?"

"Just like a bad penny," Josiah said, dismounting and shaking hands as the men swarmed around him. "I just couldn't let you guys have all the fun."

"Are you back to stay this time, Hartford?" asked Captain Jake. "Did you re-up?"

"For a year," Josiah told him.

"That's if the war lasts that long," Adam said. "I got a feeling it's all gonna be over by Christmas."

"Damn, it's good to see you again," said Peter Salem. "This is the fella that taught me the algebra," he said to the woman he'd been dancing with, a small, shy-looking dark-skinned girl.

"Pleased to meet you," she said.

"Where's the Reverend?" Josiah asked, for he did not see Reverend Sam anywhere. "He's off sulking somewhere. He don't approve of dancing, and he 'specially don't approve of dancing with women like these," Adam said. "But he's around, ornery as ever, callin' New York the new Sodom and Gomorrah and preaching to everybody that will listen about the evils of drinkin' whiskey and consorting with low women. I expect you'll run into him before too long."

"So you just couldn't stay away?" asked Zack, coming closer, his fiddle still in his hand, the bow in the other. "What are you, Hartford? Crazy? If I had a big house like you and owned a shipyard, you wouldn't catch me coming back to the army and taking a chance on getting my ass shot off."

"So I take it you're happy to see me, eh Brown?" Josiah said.

"Hell, I ain't seen anything yet that makes this boy happy, exceptin' when he plays his fiddle. Trying to make him happy is about as useless as putting a plug in the billy goat's ass. Come on, Sourpuss, give us another song," Adam said.

"Not yet," said Zack, walking away.

"Where did you find all these women?" Josiah asked, for he was certain it was Adam who had brought them to camp.

"New York s full of 'em," Adam declared. "You wait, boy. Now that you're back, we can pay a visit to Holy Ground. Wait till you get a load of the women there. Speaking of women, is there anything new on that girl of yours?"

"I'm done with that," Josiah said. "I don't think about her anymore."

"I got a feelin' that's a lie," Adam said good-naturedly, "but it's all the more reason to go to Holy Ground. No better way to forget about one woman is to have it on with another."

"Can I come?" Tommy Hoover asked eagerly.

"You are too young," Adam said.

"I am not!" Tommy protested. "Why, every morning when I wake up my thing is so—"

"Spare us the details, Tommy," said Josiah. "We know how that is."

"But I'm just saying I'm ready to do it," Tommy went on. "You told me yourself, Adam, that when it was time, I'd know."

"What do you think you know? You can go tell old Sourpuss there that it's time for him to play another song, that's what you can do."

"You want another song?" asked Zack. "Here's a song for you. I bet even you have never heard this one, Hartford." Lifting his fiddle to his chin, he played the beginning of *"Aupres de ma Blonde"* with a smile that vanished when Josiah said, "Sorry to disappoint you, Zack. It's *Aupres de ma Blonde*, a French song."

"Damn you," Zack said. "You know the words too, I suppose?"

"Yes," Josiah admitted.

"Hartford, you are hard to like," Zack said.

The woman Adam had been dancing with, tall, with jet-black hair and a ready smile that did not extend to her eyes, came toward them with her hand outstretched. "I love this song," she said. "Let's dance."

"All right, you talked me into it," said Adam, moving toward her, but she shooed him away.

"I don't mean you," she said. "I mean you." She grabbed Josiah's wrist in a strong grip. "Come on, handsome. Dance with me."

To Adam's indignant protest she simply laughed coquettishly, and led Josiah over to where the others were dancing. As Zack played his violin, she sang along:

"Dans les jardins de mon père
Les lilas sont fleuris
Dans les jardins de mon père,"

287

"You speak French?" Josiah asked.

"Only when I need to." Josiah, remembering the words, sang along with her.

"*Auprès de ma blonde,*
Qu'il fait bon, fait bon, fait bon."

"I like how you sing," she said. "Don't stop, keep singing with me."

She danced gracefully, just as Josiah did, and when the song was over she told him that her name was Tess and how she hated the British and enjoyed coming to camp from her home in the city to dance with the boys who were fighting them.

"I'm not a whore, mind," she said. "Some of these other women are, but that's not what I am. That's just so you don't get any funny ideas, Josiah Hartford."

"How do you know my name?" Josiah asked, surprised.

"I've heard the men talk of you. I knew who you were the moment I saw you ride up on your horse." She looked at him appraisingly. "They say you're rich, that you own a shipyard, and that you killed three Brits with a sword once. Is it true?"

"Most of it," Josiah said. He didn't mind being a little mysterious.

"And you're building ships to fight the British," Tess went on. "Is that true too?"

"It might be. If we can get Zack to play another tune, I'd like to dance with you again."

"I hope your ships send every last Brit to the bottom of the sea," she said fiercely. "I'll dance with you again, but then I have to leave. But will he play another song? He seems awfully sullen tonight."

"He's always that way," said Josiah. "Hey Zack," he called. "Play 'Nobody's Jig.'"

"Why that?" Zack called back.

"Why not?" Josiah said.

"Do *you* want to hear that?" Zack asked Tess.

"It's another song I love," she replied.

"All right. For you I'll play it. I'm not playing it for you, Hartford. I'm playing it for her."

They began to dance, and as they danced Tess reached into the pocket of her dress and pulled out a piece of paper and gave it to Josiah.

"This is my address in the city, if you ever want to come to see me." She gave his hand a squeeze. "Please. Come see me if you can. Soon. We can sing together again."

The song ended and she turned without another word and a moment later disappeared into the darkness. Strange woman, Josiah thought. What is she up to? He said as much to Adam later in the evening, when they unrolled their sleeping bundles on a hill overlooking the lights of New York City.

"I've had that thought too," Adam agreed. "Something not quite right about her. She keeps asking me when the fighting is going to start and what we'll do when it does. I've tried to get with her a few times, but never got all the way. She doesn't say yes, but she doesn't say no either. When it comes to women, who can say? Maybe she's a spy? What matters is that you're back with us. Am I right, fellas?"

The rest of the men of Bedford Company, spread out around them, all echoed Adam's sentiments, even Zack, who had positioned himself not far from Josiah. "Glad you're back, Hartford," he said. "I still think you're crazy, though."

That all felt good to Josiah, and as he lay back and looked up at the stars, for it was a clear, warm night, he was more certain than ever that coming back was the right thing to do. This is where I should be, he thought. He listened as Tommy Hoover sang:

"One day as I was walking,
O'er yon fields of moss
I had no thoughts of enlisting till
Some soldiers did me cross."

Hearing Tommy sing made him feel even more at home. He might not have felt so happy had he known what had transpired at Hartford Manor, that same day.

•   •   •

It was Sunday afternoon, and as she always did on Sunday, Jessica Hartford was working in her garden.

She did not have as much time for her garden as she had back in March, when she had first planted it, nor was it needed as badly as it had been then. With the siege over and the hated British gone, food was no longer scarce in Boston and the garden seemed superfluous. But working in it was soothing to Jessica. She enjoyed watching the vegetables as they began to grow and ripen, and she was looking forward to the day when she would be able to present some of them to Maureen and say, "Prepare these for dinner tonight. They are fresh from my garden."

She had little time to spare these days. The shipyard required almost all of her attention; Josiah's departure had settled that. And while Jessica resented Josiah for leaving she was discovering that running the yard gave her a sense of purpose and fulfillment that had been lacking in her life. She felt happier now than she had in a long time. The awful winter was over, it was springtime and summer wasn't far off. Yesterday, as she was discussing the plans for the new brigantine with Johnny Bishop, the chief carpenter, she'd had a flash of insight: Josiah had been right, she and Charles could manage the shipyard until he came back. She was delighted to find that Bishop, a roughly- made man with large calloused hands and a face that was handsome in a rugged way, listened to her just as respectfully as he would to her father or to Josiah, and if there were any bad feelings among the men at having a woman as one of their bosses, it had yet to make itself known.

She was thinking about the shipyard and about Johnny Bishop when she heard the clatter of horses' hooves and saw, to her great surprise, the Willinghams' carriage approaching. Before the carriage had completely come to a stop Mercy fairly burst out the door, and pulling up her long blue dress so it didn't trail on the ground, she came running toward Jessica.

"Surprise! Surprise!" she said exuberantly. "Jessica, where's Josiah?"

Jessica stood up beside the scarecrow and wiped her hands on her apron. "Josiah? Why he's—"

"Where is he? I must see him!" Mercy cried.

"Why? What's so damn urgent?" Jessica asked as she stepped over the fence that surrounded the garden.

"I've been such a fool," Mercy said. "I've got to tell him so." To Jessica's questioning glance she said, "I've changed my mind. I want to marry him after all."

Inexplicably, Jessica began to laugh, a dry bitter laugh that had no mirth in it. She threw both her arms around Mercy, her strange laughter on the verge of turning into tears.

"O Lord," she said, "what have our lives come to? How did it ever end up like this? Is it something we did? I love you as if you were my own sister, Mercy. Come inside, and we can cry together."

Mercy was perplexed, and her face plainly showed it, but Jessica said nothing more. As they walked into the house they heard the sound of a baby crying upstairs.

"Is that—" Mercy began.

"Yes, that's Little Josiah. Would you like to see him?"

"You'll never know how much I want to see him," Mercy replied.

"Maureen," Jessica called toward the kitchen, "bring some wine, and then have Bell bring the baby down here. Let's have some wine, Mercy. It helps to ease the pain."

They sat down near the fireplace as Maureen brought a bottle of wine and two glasses. Jessica poured the wine, then raised her glass in a mock toast. "Here's to—I don't know what. What should we drink to, Mercy?"

"I didn't come here to get drunk, Jessica," Mercy said impatiently. "What is going on? Where is Josiah? Has something happened to him? I'm going to burst wide open if you won't tell me. What is all this?"

"Josiah is gone," Jessica said tonelessly.

"Gone?" Mercy gasped. "Well, where did he go? When will he come back?"

"He went to New York. To rejoin the army. He left the rest of us here, high and dry."

Mercy's face lost all expression, making Jessica think of a basin with all the water running out of it when the plug is pulled. She drank the entire glass of wine Maureen had brought, asked for another and drank half of that. Then she too let out a bitter laugh.

"It's too funny," she said. "It's so—so—ironic, isn't it? When Josiah asked me to marry him I said no because I was still angry about Alice. Now I come here, so certain I was going to set everything right, and he's gone. If only I could laugh." She drank more wine and said, "You're right, Jessica, the wine does help to ease the pain."

Jessica drank her wine, then poured herself a little more. "I have to be careful not to consume too much of this," she said. "Once I get started it's hard for me to stop. Look, here comes Bell with Little Josiah."

"Oh my gosh, just look at him," said Mercy reverently. "He's so beautiful. Let me hold him."

Bell obediently handed him over to Mercy. Little Josiah opened his eyes, cooed a bit, and took hold of Mercy's little finger.

"Josiah's baby," Mercy said, rocking him back and forth.

"Josiah and Alice's baby," Jessica reminded. "Don't forget that."

"He likes you," Bell observed, taking the baby back. "It's time for me to feed him," she explained. Mercy reluctantly gave him up.

"You wish he was yours, don't you?" asked Jessica.

"I would like to have Josiah's child," Mercy admitted.

"You still want to marry Josiah, in spite of what he did with Alice?" Jessica asked. "I don't know if I could be so forgiving."

"I've thought about it and thought about it," said Mercy. "When I realized Josiah is the only man I'll ever love I knew I had to come here and tell him. I don't know if I will ever be able to forgive him, not completely, and I don't know if I won't see Alice's ghost coming between us in the night."

"And you are prepared for that?" Jessica asked thoughtfully.

"Yes I am, Jessica," Mercy vowed. "But what do I do now? He's gone. What can I do?"

"You want to cry, don't you?" said Jessica. "Sometimes it's the only thing to do."

"Do you cry?"

"Often."

This isn't the way our lives were supposed to turn out, Jessica thought. It was an idea she couldn't stop thinking about. The lives of the Hartfords and the Willinghams and so many others in Boston were supposed to be so well planned out, their futures so rosy and bright, now blotted with uncertainty, all their dreams and plans and hopes exploded as if a bomb had gone off and blown them all the cinders. The British, she thought, the British were to blame, and she felt once again the great hatred she had for the English people.

"Jessica, what do I do now?" Mercy asked again.

Jessica had no answer. She watched Mercy weeping and wished she had something to say that would make her feel better. But there was nothing. Jessica cried too.

Two hundred miles away, Josiah knew none of this. When he fell asleep that night he only knew he had done the right thing by coming back and waiting for the war to begin again. *When I go home next time it will be for good. I'll live in Hartford Manor, I'll build ships, I'll find a wife to help me raise Little Josiah and have more children too. I'll do all the things Mother and Father expected me to do. But I must do this first, I know it deep down inside. Is it my destiny? Normally I don't believe in such things, but now I wonder. I know I'm supposed to be here, and I'll stay until I know it is time to leave.*

Tommy was still singing "The White Cockade."

"My true love he is listed
He wears a white cockade..."

About the Author

Mark James Miller is a novelist, columnist, and teacher. He grew up in Southern California and graduated from the University of California at Irvine. He teaches English at Allan Hancock College in Santa Maria, California, where he was Instructor of the Year in 2015. His columns appear in four newspapers. He lives in Arroyo Grande, California, with his wife Carol. Always a history aficionado, *The White Cockade* is his second novel, with more to come.

Note from the Author

Word-of-mouth is crucial for any author to succeed. If you enjoyed *The White Cockade*, please leave a review online—anywhere you are able. Even if it's just a sentence or two. It would make all the difference and would be very much appreciated.

Thanks!
Mark James Miller

Thank you so much for reading one of Mark James Miller's novels. If you enjoyed the experience, please check out our recommended title for your next great read!

Red Tide

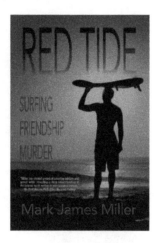

"Miller has created a work of amazing subtlety and power while revealing a deep understanding of the human heart roiling in psychological turmoil."
–Dr. Fred Manzo, PhD, Allan Hancock College

CPSIA information can be obtained
at www.ICGtesting.com
Printed in the USA
BVHW071022210921
617187BV00002B/60